ROLLER BABES

ROLLER BABES

1950s Women of Roller Derby

Tim Patten

iUniverse

ROLLER BABES
1950S WOMEN OF ROLLER DERBY

Copyright © 2015 Tim Patten.
Cover art: Rebecca Renier

All rights reserved. No part of this book may be used or reproduced by any means, graphic, electronic, or mechanical, including photocopying, recording, taping or by any information storage retrieval system without the written permission of the author except in the case of brief quotations embodied in critical articles and reviews.

iUniverse books may be ordered through booksellers or by contacting:

iUniverse
1663 Liberty Drive
Bloomington, IN 47403
www.iuniverse.com
1-800-Authors (1-800-288-4677)

Because of the dynamic nature of the Internet, any web addresses or links contained in this book may have changed since publication and may no longer be valid. The views expressed in this work are solely those of the author and do not necessarily reflect the views of the publisher, and the publisher hereby disclaims any responsibility for them.

Any people depicted in stock imagery provided by Thinkstock are models, and such images are being used for illustrative purposes only. Certain stock imagery © Thinkstock.

ISBN: 978-1-4917-8329-0 (sc)
ISBN: 978-1-4917-8328-3 (e)

Library of Congress Control Number: 2015919130

Print information available on the last page.

iUniverse rev. date: 11/12/2015

**Dedicated to
Elsie Mae and Harold**

ACKNOWLEDGEMENTS

I originally published *Roller Babes* under the pen name D. M. Bordner, my literary feminine side. I raced this story through the publishing process because I was in hospice care and was expected to pass away. As you see, I am still here. I wanted to revise and correct some of the problems that were left over from the rushed first printing. For this second edition, I've injected fresh emotion and new life into these historic characters.

This sport has been good to me, and has faithfully served the growing world of women in sports since its inception in 1935. I'm grateful to the skating fans, skaters, roller girls and baby-boomer television viewers who remember the origins of this popular television sport. The fans built the derby, from its humble beginnings to an internationally-recognized phenomenon, and they continue to push all women's sports further into the mainstream.

Today, roller derby continues to rage on waves of new-school enthusiasm; with over 2,000 active roller derby teams and many groups and leagues around the world. I want to thank my family of close friends who have kept my fires burning during the completion of this second edition of my novel.

ABOUT THE CHARACTERS

All of the characters portrayed in this novel are fictitious though they do exist in realistic settings from the 1930s through the 1950s. Lottie Zimmerman was partially inspired by legendary skater and personal friend: Loretta Behrens (Little Iodine). The plot and characters are roughly based upon the vaudeville-styled lives and experiences of many of America's greatest roller derby athletes. Some are still skating or alive to this day. Any likeness between these fictionalized composite characters and any one person's real life is unintentional.

INTRODUCTION

R*oller Babes* honors the women of 1950s professional roller derby: indomitable athletes who inspired millions of others to find independence and personal freedom in the world of sports. Their soaring aspirations, hard-won accomplishments and wrenching mêlées have all been documented in the annals of history ... *but now I'd like to invite you in for a closer look.*

Come live alongside these legendary women, besieged with physical desperation but set apart by their exceptional grit and the adoration of their fans.

Welcome to a secret world from the past. It's a family of sisters, a clan of sports innovators and a team of dedicated survivalists.

Decades before the birth control pill, Gloria Steinem, or the National Organization for Women; these early paradigm-shifters of roller derby struggled for liberation from traditional societal roles. Some found success; others encountered the most heart-wrenching defeat. These early athletes had no women's studies to encourage them, yet they developed remarkable drive. Their iron-willed spirit hurtled them across countless social obstacles on the path to their goals and dreams. Dedication to their sport rewarded these incredible professionals with adulation in the hearts and minds of Americans and enthusiasts around the world.

CHAPTER 1

HEY, TOMBOY – YOU'RE UGLY

Lottie Zimmerman's 15-year-old fingers clenched the end of the sawed-off broomstick, knuckles whitening as her grip tightened. She planted skinny legs into a batter's stance and the neighborhood boys curled their lips, pinched their eyebrows and sneered. Lottie squared the stick-bat as the sun set, etching dusky shadows over the skyline of row houses in her Bronx neighborhood.

"She'll never hit it!" Timothy Olsen yelled from centerfield. Crewcut red hair poked out from the sides of a beat-up Yankees cap.

Lottie's chest tightened as she concentrated on the centerfielder. She bit her lip and watched Olsen's eyes connect with his ragtag teammates positioned around the street that served as their impromptu stickball field. She regained focus, gazed past the red haired Olsen kid, and found her target. It was left of the Chinese cleaners and right of the Irish pub's darkened windows. The store squeezed between them was her objective: the cramped butcher's market.

"C'mon, already!" the boy playing right field scratched his crotch. "Get the louse out! She's a pipsqueak nothing!"

Lottie's breath quickened. She suddenly became aware of her heartbeat. Her opponents' assaults cut deep, knifing her to the core.

"You can do it, Lottie!" Joseph Rodriguez cheered as he stood with the rest of her team along the sidelines. "Pull it out, just like last year's Yankees!" For a second, the Yankees' 1951 World Series flashed in Lottie's mind, and she eased her grip. "You can win this for us, Lottie!" Rodriguez hollered. "It's up to you! We're down to our last out!"

"Ha!" Olsen spat at the ground. "You'll never win with that pill! Lottie's bad news!"

"Yeah, she belongs in a nuthouse!" another voice heckled. "She's a sideshow freak!"

Lottie's blood chilled as she wove together a mass of emotions: embarrassment, determination and terror. All eyes seared into her as she hunched over the dented garbage can lid that served as home plate. She had heard these mean remarks many times before, but that didn't make them any easier to endure. The boys seemed to thrill in telling her how they hated her skinny face, and how her Bob Hope nose resembled the end of an eyedropper. They tugged her dirty blonde, cowlick-filled hair. She wore most of it spit-patted into place, but a few strands always escaped to stand at attention.

"Easy out!" The shortstop jammed a thumbs up.

Lottie's spine straightened and her eyes narrowed as she glared at the target. Her heartbeat seemed to slow.

The boys wanted Lottie out of their games for good. She felt her pulse in her throat. As the only girl, she had never fit in. Even among other girls, Lottie stood out from the crowd, and not in a good way: gawky, rough-and-tumble, forever uncomfortable among the little ladies in their pretty dresses and beautifully curled hair. Lottie's hair was choppy. She was an oddball.

"I'll show you, fellas!" She raised an arm. "I can run just as fast and hit the ball just as far as any of you!"

"C'mon, already!" the shortstop whined. "It's almost suppertime. Strike the chicken liver out!"

"She's an easy out." The pitcher held the ball behind his back, fingers adjusting the spin he would put on the throw. Lottie took a few practice swings, slicing the stick through the air like a sword. She strained to keep her hands from shaking ... and waited.

"Let 'em have it, Lottie!" Maurio Santini jogged a dangerous lead off first base. He squeezed a cigarette pack under his shirtsleeve. "I'm ready to scram to second. Clobber the ball, Lottie! Make it fly!"

"This is our last chance!" Rodriguez shifted back and forth. "Knock it all the way past the fourth sewer!"

Lottie focused. The famous 'fourth sewer' was the stickball version of the green wall at Yankee Stadium. Clearing it meant the batter slugged a 450-foot homerun. With razor-sharp eyes, Lottie counted the sewers and focused on the spot between the Chinese laundry and the Irish pub. She stuck out her chest like a flat washboard, feeling determined to win the game for her team.

"Go, Lottie, go!" her friend Elsie Mae Kealy cheered from the sidelines. Elsie tossed her head back; silky hair moving in slow motion like a movie star.

"Throw her a curve!" the shortstop gritted his teeth. "The goon'll never hit that."

The pitcher spat out a wad of gum and went into his windup. He brought his knee high into his chest, a move he copped from the major-leaguers. Lottie's vision flashed. When the ball left the pitcher's hand, the entire street fell silent. Lottie clenched her teeth and narrowed her eyes as it whizzed toward her. Then she widened them and held her breath. In a flash, her skinny arms mustered up a powerful swing and the sound of the wooden stick making perfect contact with the rubber ball echoed, *CRACK*, over the rooftops. The ball took wing toward the famed sewer! The world went into slow motion as it sailed through the air. Lottie's heart skipped a beat. She wished she could fly away with the ball.

"Lay a patch, Lottie!" Maurio yelled as he rounded second base. "Make tracks, tomboy!"

Lottie's heart soared. She flung the stick aside and dashed toward the tin can top that served as first base, running for her life. Maurio headed toward third, both arms pumping like pistons.

"Put it to the floor and *run!*" Elsie Mae twitched her pink dress watching it furl around her ankles like a gown a princess might wear.

Lottie glanced back just long enough to see red haired Rebecca Peterson jump up, arms high, and cheer before she wrapped both arms around her chest. Then Lottie saw her lower her head, look aside, and melt back into the group of bystanders. Invisible again.

Lottie blinked. The rubber ball slammed onto the pavement just short of the butcher's market, smack-dab in the center of the street. She heaved a breath as Olsen charged after the ball.

"Hurry, Olsen!" the leftfielder screamed. "We can cut her down at third!"

"Get the lead out, Lottie!" Elsie Mae rooted.

Lottie felt the blood race through her body so fast that her fingers burned. Cheers of encouragement bounced off the walls of the shops and buildings while the screams from the opposing team grew louder.

"Get the wet smack!" The rightfielder raised a fist across his chest. "Kill the tiny string bean!"

"Ugly hag!" Olsen shouted. "She's asking for it."

"Make tracks, Lottie!" Rodriguez coached, rocking clenched hands to and from his armpits. Excitement almost killing him.

Lottie's tattered dress fluttered around gangly legs while clodhopper shoes clunked against the blacktop as she rounded the homemade baseball diamond. Ignoring everyone, focused only on her sprinting legs, she was manic. Her chest thrummed as a clattering sound echoed through the air. Maurio stomped on the dented home plate. Cheers echoed.

"One more run!" Rodriguez screamed with a finger pointed in the air. "That's all we need!"

"Run, Lottie!" another voice shouted. "Go all the way!"

Olsen arched backwards and hurled the ball toward the third baseman. It cut through the air like a missile. "We got her!" he jumped up and down. "The creep will never make it! We'll pound her if she does!"

Lottie ducked under the flying ball and rounded third, blood gushing through her veins. She felt the heat of everyone's eyes focused directly upon her.

"Hold up at third!" Rodriguez ordered.

Lottie glanced over her shoulder, tracking the flight of the ball and gauging the distance to home plate. In a split-second decision, she ran beyond third base and put on the steam toward home.

"No!" Elsie Mae's hands cupped her mouth muting a real scream she couldn't control.

"Go back, Lottie!" Rodriguez begged. "They're gonna take you out!"

"We got her!" the shortstop pumped his fist into the air. "I knew she'd be too dumb to hold up!"

The third baseman caught the ball and sailed it toward the catcher. "Hurry, get her!"

Voices muffled into white noise in Lottie's head. She tuned everything out. Lungs burning. Nothing would come between her and home plate—not even the catcher.

"Get out of my way!" she warned, yelling at the top of her lungs.

The catcher was not about to let a girl tell him what to do—or let her cross the plate without a fight. He launched his body upward, stretched out a long arm, and snatched the ball out of the air. Lottie dove down beneath him, scrape-sliding her body across the dusty pavement. The catcher immediately swung his arm down, missing the base runner. She skidded between his legs and slammed her hand into the garbage can lid. The lid flew into the air with a violent rattle which assaulted everyone's ears.

"Safe!" Rodriguez roared. "She made it! Way to go, Lottie!"

Her teammates celebrated, tossing their mitts skyward. Her opponents scowled.

"You're a skunk!" the catcher snarled.

"You stink!" Olsen wrinkled his nose.

"Just a dumb jackass," the catcher growled.

Lottie lay sprawled, breathless on the street; skinned palms and knees encrusted with pebbles and dirt.

"Oh, God!" Elsie Mae gasped. "Lottie, are you all right?"

Lottie pulled herself up off the ground and dusted a further tattered dress off. Her spirits were soaring. She pulled her shoulders back, straightening as tall as she possibly could. Some skinned knees and a scratch on her face couldn't keep her down at this moment of victory. Her teammates patted her on the back and ruffled up her dirty hair.

"You did it, Lottie," Maurio said. "You're one tough player. You brought it home!"

Lottie smiled amidst the camaraderie, but deep down, she felt a sense of longing. She wished the boys would treat her equally all the time, not just when she drove in the winning run.

"No-good rotten egg." Olsen pounded his fist into his glove.

"You got lucky, cockroach," the opposing shortstop grunted. "Don't go thinking otherwise."

Rodriguez gave Lottie a playful punch in the arm. "Pretty rugged, slugger."

Lottie smiled. Being part of the team meant everything. Her pulse spiked. She lived for moments like these and she wanted to see to it that they happened more often.

"I gotta go home," Rodriguez said. "Tomorrow, we play kick the can—and we'll murder these bums all over again." With that, he turned and trotted off toward a red brick house.

"Yeah, I gotta cut out, too," Maurio added. "My pop will be home soon. Hey, guys, come to my place later. Bring your marbles so we can trade. Then we'll watch *Roller Derby* on television."

"Yeah!" another boy cheered. "I'll be there!"

The opposing team members trudged down the street.

"Let's blow this place," Olsen grumbled with a scowl.

The stickball game officially broke up. Lottie's teammates turned their attention elsewhere and once again, the girl who never felt like she fit in found herself alone, a cavity hollowed out inside her chest. She watched the players disappear in different directions. Moments later, the street sounds lulled as if the game and Lottie's shining homerun had never taken place.

Lottie imagined the army of neighborhood fathers returning home from work and all the families gathering around the supper table, settling in for an evening meal. Later, they would sit together as they listened to their Philco radios or watched their favorite shows on television before turning in for the night. The pleasant visions made Lottie's eyes well up with tears. The thought of going home killed her inner fire.

Before facing her unavoidable fate, Lottie was graced with one last moment of victory.

"Wow! That sure was amazing, Lottie!" Elsie Mae hopped up and down on her toes. She and Rebecca surrounded Lottie as they headed down the sidewalk.

"Thanks!" Lottie replied, flashing a trace of a smile. "I really like your new skirt and bobby socks." Lottie rolled her hands down her sides in an attempt to smooth out the wrinkles of her own rumpled graying dress.

"Thanks," Elsie Mae responded. "It's the latest—a poodle skirt. You'd look pretty in one."

Lottie fidgeted, then her vision dropped down to her beat-up shoes as she scuffed the concrete. "I could never afford clothes like that."

Rebecca quickly changed the mood. "That hit was so boss, Lottie! The way you ran past third, even when everyone told you to stop. What spunk!" She smiled as she waved strands of bright red hair out of her eyes and pushed plastic glasses up her nose. "Watching that was more fun than knitting."

"I don't knit." Lottie smiled.

Rebecca and Elsie Mae turned to each other. "We *know*," they said in unison. They each let out a girlish giggle.

"You may have flunked Home Ec," Elsie Mae said, "but tonight, you hit the winning run!"

Though Lottie tried to appear unmoved on the outside, on the inside she was basking in one of her few moments of glory. This small homerun made her feel like she was alright. "No sweat. I'm glad you guys liked it."

Elsie Mae leaned closer to the two other girls, as if to share a startling secret. "Boys," she swooned in a whisper. The girls giggled and began shuffling down the sidewalk, glancing over their shoulders to catch glimpses of the boys.

"Hey, Lottie." Rebecca stopped. "Want to hang out on my roof tomorrow? We can play games and stuff."

"Sure," Lottie answered. "That sounds like fun—and I can get outta the house for a while."

Elsie Mae winked at one of the boys who had lingered after the game ended. In return, he rolled his eyes as if to blow her off.

Lottie noticed Rebecca picking some invisible lint off of her sweater. She always took on the look of a hurt, neglected puppy whenever Elsie Mae flirted with boys.

"How about you, Elsie Mae?" Lottie asked, redirecting the girl's attention. "Are you up for another ladies' social on Rebecca's roof?"

Elsie Mae smiled and popped her gum. "You shred it, wheat!"

"That settles it," Rebecca announced. "We've got a date. See you on the roof." She trotted off, clutching schoolbooks to her chest.

"I'll be heading on home, too," Elsie Mae said. She tossed shiny, perfect hair over a tiny shoulder. "See you later, alligator."

Lottie waved as her two friends skipped off in opposite directions. She drew in a deep breath.

Half a block from her building, Lottie noticed an injured pigeon fluttering its wing in the street gutter. Her heartbeat slowed, matching a nauseating surge each time the pigeon struggled and a crooked wing twitched.

"You poor little thing," she cried. She knelt down next to the bird, expecting it to panic and hobble away. This pigeon, though, was special. It was white, like a dove. She was surprised when it remained still. "What's the matter, little guy?" she asked and carefully reached over to stroke a finger across the bird's head. The pigeon blinked, drew closer, and made a cooing sound. Its ruffled feathers all askew reminded Lottie of her own skinny arms and flyaway hair. She choked up and propped the little bird's body upright. "Don't worry," she said softly. "You'll be just fine."

"Hey, stink bomb!"

The harsh, squeaky voice startled Lottie. She spun her head around to see her ten-year-old neighbor pointing in her direction. Two of his friends laughed.

"Why you so skinny?" he sneered.

"Halloween's over!" another boy cackled. "You can take off the mask!"

"You got cooties!" the third boy mocked.

The first boy hurled a rock in Lottie's direction. His aim was terrible and the rock skidded across the sidewalk well wide of its mark. That didn't make Lottie feel any safer, however. She hung her neck and spine forward. "Leave me alone!" She jumped to her feet and walked toward her house, leaving the fluttering pigeon alone in the gutter.

Chapter 2

HOME

Still hanging her head, Lottie clambered up the rickety steps to her front door, kicking paint chips aside and being careful not to catch a foot on any of the loose nails coming out of the rotting wood. She remembered the sight of the rubber ball flying off her bat and the cheers ringing through the air as she crossed home plate to score the winning run. No one could steal that moment from her. She wouldn't let them.

As Lottie pushed open the front door, a harsh voice from the other room startled her.

"I told you, I don't want to eat now, woman!"

Her father, Murray, was home. His bellowing, along with the nauseating smell of high-proof liquor, wafted through the air. Lottie's eyes darted past the dilapidated sofa and frayed living room rug over to the kitchen. On the back wall, her father's shadow towered over her mother's. As he moved into the light, the image magnified in her mind emphasizing his wiry hair, the deep lines etched between his eyebrows and his terminally-clenched jaw. Lottie's hands began to shake.

"I've been waiting all day for you," her mother, Esther, said to Murray. "I was hoping we could eat together and have a chance to sit and talk."

There was an uncomfortable pause. Lottie slipped through the living room, scrambled up the stairs and headed straight down the hall to the room shared with her little sisters. There, she found Rhoda and Betty shivering together on the full-sized bed.

"I already fed the kids," Lottie heard her mother say from downstairs, "but I haven't eaten yet."

"Geez, Esther," her father growled in response. "Are you ditzy?"

The sound of a saucepan clattering in the sink followed the racket of a plate skidding across the floor.

"Murray, don't!"

"Damn it, Esther!"

Lottie jumped at the sound and struggled to appear unconcerned for the sake of her little sisters.

"Murray, please! Not so loud. The kids will hear."

"So, let 'em hear! I don't give a damn!"

Rhoda sobbed quietly. Lottie wrapped a blanket around her shoulders and pulled her close. She muffled her own desire to cry. This familiar scene between her parents played out almost weekly. Lottie had stopped bringing Elsie Mae and Rebecca over long ago.

"Can't I get a break on a Friday night?" Murray complained. "I work all week long to bring home a check. I don't want to be bothered taking care of people when I come home. All I want to do is rest."

His tirade was punctuated by the sound of breaking glass. The last remaining images of that magnificent game-winning homerun faded from Lottie's memory.

"Lottie," Rhoda asked, almost in a whisper, "are we poor?"

Lottie threw her arms around both of her sisters' shoulders and gave them a big squeeze. "Daddy's just tired. He has to work really hard. We're not rich. Not yet, anyway," she said. "But someday, we'll have everything we need."

Rhoda and Betty heard Lottie talk about 'someday' all the time. Lottie spoke with confidence, but she was more often than not unsure if 'someday' would come at all.

"I've got an idea," Lottie said, intent on changing the mood. "Let's play rock, paper, scissors."

The two smaller girls nodded, faint smiles taking over their faces.

"I work, too!" The sound of Esther's voice traveled up the stairs. "I spend all day cleaning, cooking and looking after the children. What I do isn't easy, you know!"

Lottie caught herself nodding at the statement. Her mother *did* work hard. Lottie could see it in her hands. Esther never had nice smooth hands or manicured fingernails. In fact, her nails were worn down to the nubs and her fingers had wrinkles from an endless cycle of manual household labor.

While Lottie contemplated this, her sisters waited for the game to begin. Their fists were tightly closed, as if to hide their strategies. Lottie placed her attention back onto the game.

"One, two, three!"

The sisters all opened their hands.

"You spent more of my money today, didn't you?" Murray's voice accused.

The girls all knew money was a problem.

"I went to the store for a few things," Esther said.

"You can't be doing that, Esther!" Murray whined. "I keep telling you that, and you never listen. You can't go around buying things we don't need. We sold off the last of our war bonds, remember?"

Lottie gazed down at her sisters' hands. "That's two paper and one scissors. You win, Betty."

Betty smiled with pride. "Let's play again."

Lottie glanced around the room and then at her rumpled dress. "I wish I could get a job," she said with a sigh.

"A job?" Rhoda asked. "Why do you want to have a job?"

"If I could make some money, I could help buy some of the things we need," she explained.

"Do girls work?" Rhoda eyed her big sister closely. "You're not gonna leave us, are you?"

Lottie smiled and held out her hand. "Let's play again."

"I didn't spend all that much," Esther argued. "The kids need to eat, Murray."

"Damn kids."

Lottie's heart sank. Those biting words made her feel unwanted. She prayed nightly that her parents would get along better. At that moment, her sisters looked up at her, waiting for her lead.

Roller Babes

"Okay, next game."

"Maybe we should spend more time together," Esther suggested.

Lottie strained to hear the words as they traveled up the stairs, but she pretended to focus on the game.

Murray let out an exhausted sigh. "And do what?" he groaned. "I've got people constantly badgering me all day at work. I have to work hard, long hours. Is it so bad for me to want to be left alone in the evening? In my own damn house?"

Lottie's ears were assaulted by the coarse sound of a chair scraping against the hardwood floor.

"It's just that I don't get to see you all day," Esther said.

"You see me enough," Murray grunted. "I spend ten hours each day trying to please all those damn customers. None of them know what they want. At night, I just want to come home and have some peace and quiet."

There was a long pause. Lottie tried to picture what was happening on the floor below. With a sudden urgency, Lottie huddled her sisters together. "Okay, next game. Ready?"

The girls held their closed hands in a circle.

"For crying out loud, Esther!" Murray suddenly roared. "What's all this stuff here?"

"I had to get some things at the store," Esther explained. "I needed some Kotex and a few things for the kids."

"These things damn well better be important!" Murray growled. "I can hardly afford to pay the GI mortgage for the house this month!"

"One, two, *three*."

The girls all opened their hands, revealing their symbols.

"Rock breaks scissors. Rhoda wins!"

Rhoda smiled in victory, but the gleeful moment was short-lived.

"You don't really need all this stuff!" Murray ranted. "You don't know how to manage money."

"I do the best I can with what we've got, to make sure the kids have what they need," Esther insisted.

Betty looked down at the floor. "I wish they would stop."

Lottie's insides ached. "Yeah, me too."

Murray's muffled voice bounced up the stairs, but Lottie couldn't make out the words this time.

The girls continued to listen as heavy footsteps paced across the downstairs floor.

"I'm going out for a drink," they heard Murray announce.

A moment later, the front door slammed—a familiar sound that still managed to startle Murray's young daughters. When Lottie's breath returned, she could make out the sounds of her mother's sobs from the kitchen. She tossed a blanket over Rhoda's head, trying to appear silly and playful, while at the same time covering her younger sister's ears to keep her from hearing Esther's cries. As Rhoda happily played around in the blanket, Lottie smiled; but in the back of her mind, she hoped that when she grew up her life would be much different than her mom's.

Lottie spent the next few minutes playfully flipping the blanket over each of her sister's heads. Their laughter, even when it was tired and subdued, gave her a great sense of satisfaction. Making them smile was Lottie's way of taking care of them. She flung the blanket out as wide as it would go and caught a pocket of air.

"Everybody under!" she said.

The two younger girls huddled close to their older sister as the blanket drifted downward, enclosing them all in the safety of the fortress.

"Kids?"

Lottie flipped the blanket off of their heads when she heard their mother's voice call out. "Yes, Mom?" she answered.

"It's television time. Do you want to watch with me?" Esther's invitation accompanied the delicious aroma of popping corn wafting up the stairs.

"On the way down!" Betty bounced off the bed and bounded down the staircase.

Rhoda flashed a happy grin and quickly followed. Lottie folded the blanket neatly on the bed and went down to join them. By the time she reached the living room, her kid sisters had already planted themselves in their usual places on the frazzled rug. Lottie sat in her unofficially designated spot on the couch. Their mother came in carrying a large bowl of buttered popcorn and a few smaller empty bowls under her arm. The girls couldn't wait for their own bowls to be filled. Instead, they all dug out a handful of popcorn from the large bowl and started munching—it was their special television-time tradition.

"Where's Daddy?" Rhoda asked.

Lottie frowned.

"Out for a while," their mom replied flatly.

No one pressed for further details.

"Is *The Lone Ranger* on?" Betty asked.

"How about *The Ed Sullivan Show*?" Rhoda wondered.

Esther divvied up the popcorn into smaller bowls and passed them around. "There's a different show on tonight," she said. "I thought we'd watch it to see what it's like."

The television screen flickered, taking its usual minute or two to warm up. Lottie walked over and fiddled with the rabbit ears. She squinted at the fuzzy display of snow until a blurry image appeared, eventually burning into focus. The screen revealed a large racetrack inside a cavernous arena. The building was jammed to the rafters with screaming spectators.

"Look!" Lottie's heart skipped a beat.

The girls leaned in closer while tossing handfuls of popcorn into their mouths. They saw a wooden track with uniformed athletes whizzing around the giant circle on roller skates. A perky ditty that sounded like the Andrews Sisters piped out of the television's tiny speaker. The cheerful tune created a sense of brightness within Lottie's living room, and the parental conflict from earlier was immediately forgotten. "*And they went around and around and around in the roller derby ...*" went the tune.

Lottie hopped backwards onto the couch, absorbed in the lyrics. "*When the wheels start to spin, then you know that you're in for a chill ... oh, what a thrill ... at the roller derby.*"

"What is this?" Lottie wondered aloud, her insides fluttering.

"It's called the roller derby," Esther explained. "Twelve years ago, they used to do it down at the pier." She rolled back on the couch at the sight of a skater falling into a breathless heap. "Oh my!"

"I heard someone talk about this today after our stickball game." Lottie tilted her head from side to side.

"It's been on television for a few weeks now," her mom replied. "Because it's a sport, I thought you might enjoy it."

Lottie's pulse increased. Leaning forward, she felt her spirits lift in a way never felt before. She handed her bowl of popcorn to her kid sisters. "Here, Sweet Pea," she offered, not wanting to let the munching and crunching get in the way of her concentration on the television set. "Women skaters," she said quietly to herself. "Wow!"

"Lottie Zimmerman!" Her mother's voice snapped her out of her trance.

"You've scratched up your face! How many times have I told you to be careful? You know we can't afford to run off to the doctor all the time!"

Lottie let out a laugh. "It's no big deal Mom," she insisted. "It's just a little scratch. Besides, I hit the game-winning homerun, so it was worth it." She returned her attention to the television.

Esther gave her daughter a playful swat on the arm. "Oh, you!"

Lottie watched closely and held her breath as ten female skaters zoomed around the track at breakneck speed. Most of the girls were teenagers, just about her age. "This is amazing," she said. "The only skater I've ever seen on television before is Sonja Henie."

Lottie had seen the beautiful Henie on television many times. A famous and elegant figure skater, Henie became the first woman to make the jump from competitive skating to television and movie appearances. Dressed in exquisite ballerina costumes, Henie moved like a delicate flower petal gracefully dancing on a gentle breeze. The roller derby skaters were something altogether different. They slammed into each other like football players. They jabbed one another with elbows; rugged determination on their faces as they rounded every turn. Lottie felt a kinship with them.

"Are they all girls?" Betty asked. "Some of them look like men."

"Naw, they're all girls." Lottie crossed her arms. "They're Amazon women, and they're swell!"

"I don't get it, Mom," Rhoda said. "How do they score?"

"Honey, you just missed the announcer," Esther said. "He said there are five skaters on each team, and they skate close together to form a pack."

Lottie watched the players leave the guardrail and infield. Ten of them rolled alongside one another, forming two lines skating close, side by side.

"Like that?" Rhoda pointed to the tiny screen.

"Yes," Mom said. "Someone will eventually try to sprint away from the pack. She will skate as fast as she can, and go all the way around. She gets two minutes to pass as many opposing skaters as she can."

On the screen a referee raised his hand and dropped it. The whistle blared; the ten skaters zigzagged, blocking and bouncing off one another like balls in a pinball machine. One skater soon sprinted away from the tightly-knit pack.

"Bobbie Beal is alone in this play!" the announcer exclaimed. "She's out on the jam!"

The camera zoomed in on the skater as she crouched and pumped her legs, breaking away from the gyrating host of competitors.

"So fast!" Lottie lightly fingered the base of her neck, deciding that a jam must be the amount of time a fast skater had to race around and score.

"So, it's like a race?" Betty asked. "But with hitting?"

"Yes," her mom replied. "The jammer is out now. For every skater she passes, her team gets one point. The team with the most points at the end of the night wins."

"I wonder what it's like to compete on a team with just girls," Lottie thought aloud.

Esther scooped up a handful of popcorn, her eyes still glued to the screen. "When I was young, girls didn't play sports, especially something dangerous like this. It wasn't considered ladylike."

"I bet it's really fun," Lottie said as if she hadn't heard, but she had. "Look how they work together. They are really cooking!"

"But it is dangerous."

Lottie thought about how long she had waited for the neighborhood boys to invite her to finally play in their stickball games. Now she was watching a fast, rugged sport played entirely by girls. She had never seen anything so amazing.

"Bobbie Beal nears the rear of the pack, ready to score. Look at her go!" the announcer cheered. "The jam is over!"

Lottie drew even closer to the screen, completely fascinated.

"Lottie, don't sit too close to the television," her mother urged. "You'll ruin your eyes. We can't afford an eye doctor." Suddenly, Esther's own attention was pulled back to the action. "Oh no! Look out!"

Lottie's mouth dropped open as she watched Bobbie Beal get body-checked so hard that she flew over the railing. Something inside Lottie shifted. Her tummy tickled with an unfamiliar sensation. Excitement zinged from her toes to her head. She realized she was not alone. There were other girls out there who didn't knit or pass Home Ec. There were other girls who liked to be a part of rugged action and compete at the highest level. Lottie wanted this thrill for herself. The thought inhabited her imagination from the moment the television clicked off for the night until she started to nod off in bed.

In a dream that very night, the injured pigeon appeared again. Its ruffled white feathers were smoothed and repaired. The bird stood tall and strong. Lottie began to feel the same way.

Chapter 3

DON'T TELL ANYONE

Lottie dashed up four flights of stairs, vaulting two steps at a time. She finally reached the rooftop, breathing hard. She rammed her body into the heavy metal door, shoved it open and slipped out into the daylight. The blast of midday sun made her squint until her eyes adjusted to the brightness.

"C'mon, baby!" Elsie Mae chanted. "I need some twosies!"

Multi-colored jacks bounced off the tar-covered rooftop, eventually coming to rest amid some gravel and several discarded Bazooka bubblegum wrappers.

"Hi, Elsie Mae. I'm ready to play before I become a woman. Where's Rebecca?"

"Never too old for play." Elsie Mae focused sharply on the jacks. Carefully plotting her strategy for capturing them, she cocked her head toward the other end of the roof. "Rebecca's over there."

Lottie glided past Elsie Mae and her jacks, standing beside Rebecca. She was gazing out at the skyline, book clutched to a budding chest.

"Hey, Rebecca. Whatcha doin'?" As Lottie spoke, the taste of the icky tar-smelling air rose up from the rooftop and slipped onto her tongue.

"Hey, Lottie." Tar bubbles crunched and popped beneath the soles of Rebecca's shoes as she turned around. "See that?" she asked as she pointed west toward the Third Avenue El. "The noon train is on its way to the station."

The Orient Express, the lone elevated train, resembled a shiny silver caterpillar as it crawled into its Bronx stop.

"And look over there," Rebecca nudged her head in another direction. "There's Patio's Paradise Theatre. You can even see the brass doors next to the Federal Savings and Loan clock tower."

Lottie sharpened her gaze into the distance. She inhaled slowly, and let a memory take over. "Those doors don't look like they're made of brass."

"They're grummy and tarnished," Rebecca said. "The weather beats them down. Someone should give them a shine."

Lottie detected a sense of longing in Rebecca's voice. She listened to the sounds from the apartments below ... mothers and daughters preparing lunch. The clanging of pots and pans accompanied the sweet aroma of fresh-baked bread and garlic-spiced cabbage. A small gust of wind slapped the rows of television antennae wires against their metal poles along the skyline, sending a rattle through the air. The hint of Frankie Laine's song *Jezebel* floated in and out of direct hearing; prickling the hairs on the back of Lottie's neck.

"I love it up here," Rebecca said through a deep sigh. "It's like a totally different world. It feels so far away from the trouble at home."

A thickness came to Lottie's throat. "I know what you mean. It's nice and quiet up on the roof. We're sitting way above all that rotten stuff down below. It's like our private getaway, our secret hideout."

Rebecca pinched her lips together, then let out a frustrated huff. "It makes me so angry."

Lottie's heart dropped and her throat closed up. "What are you so mad about?"

Rebecca bit her lip and picked a piece of lint off her shoulder. "Do you *really* want to know?"

Lottie shrugged. "Sure. Why wouldn't I?"

Rebecca suppressed a nervous laugh. Lottie wondered if that meant Rebecca was afraid to say what was on her mind for fear it might sound silly.

"I guess I just feel safe up here." Rebecca opened her hand and let a small piece of lint catch the breeze. The girls' eyes followed it for a moment until it disappeared into the New York sky. "There's nobody up here throwing stuff at us," Rebecca went on, "and nobody's calling us awful names."

Lottie's heart ached. "The creeps can't get us up here." She straightened. "Ha! To hell with them!"

Rebecca didn't respond. Instead, she continued to look longingly out over the city's vast horizon.

Lottie dropped her bravado. "Rebecca, are you all right?" she asked softly. "You look hurt."

"I've got a problem," Rebecca's chin dropped.

Lottie's arm hair bristled. "What kind of problem? It's nothing we can't handle, right?"

"I don't know," Rebecca answered quietly. She brushed back a few strands of coppery hair that had blown into her face. "I'm just glad that no one else is up here right now."

"It's just us today," Lottie agreed. "You, me and Elsie Mae."

"And no one can touch us up here," Rebecca's voice drifted off.

Lottie sensed a pain in the back of her throat. Her gut was yelling that something was really, REALLY wrong; something bad was happening. "You mean no one can pick on us or give us a hard time ... right?"

Rebecca's eyes wandered over toward Elsie Mae, still happily enthralled with her jacks. "Do you think she can hear what we're saying?"

Lottie looked back, rubbing her neck. "Doubt it."

Rebecca closed her eyes and heaved a sigh. "I've gotta do something, Lottie," she said. "I'm almost out of school."

Lottie noticed the dark circles under Rebecca's eyes, something her normally carefree demeanor had always managed to disguise.

"This is our last year," Lottie said. "We all have to find something."

The distraught puppy expression once again took over Rebecca's face. "Lottie, can you keep a secret?" Rebecca's lips trembled and her fingers twitched nervously as she spoke.

"Definitely," Lottie said as a compassionate ache rose deep inside her chest. "You can tell me anything."

"You *promise*?"

"Yes, I *promise*."

"Pinky promise?"

Lottie lifted her crooked little finger. Rebecca wrapped her pinkie around it. They tugged and Lottie said, "Yes, pinky promise."

"Well ... he warned me not to tell ... you won't sing?"

A frightening chill ran down Lottie's spine. "Who's *he*?"

Rebecca sucked in a deep breath and exhaled slowly. She looked about to speak, to purge herself of a painful truth, but then quickly pulled back; body tensing.

Without waiting for an explanation, Lottie swished some saliva around inside her mouth. She spat a gob onto the rooftop and stomped the spittle with her right foot as if she were crushing out a still-burning cigarette. Rebecca watched in silence. Lottie stood at attention, held up her left hand and placed her right hand over her heart. "Honest, Rebecca," Lottie proclaimed. "Whatever it is, you can trust me to keep your secret."

Rebecca turned away. There was a long, quiet pause between them. Lottie didn't pressure her friend.

"This is so embarrassing. You know ... bad news," Rebecca finally gasped. "I swear, Lottie, I've got to get out of here." She swallowed hard. Her eyes appeared darker than Lottie had ever seen them before.

Lottie's stamina faded. "I'm not sure if I can take this," she quietly confessed, "but I'm your friend, Rebecca—now and forever. No matter what it is, I'll always be your friend."

As Rebecca turned back toward Lottie, a trace of redness appeared in her eyes. With a determined expression, she drew in another deep breath. "Sometimes," she began, "my dad touches me."

Lottie's chest collapsed and her mouth dropped open. "He *touches* you?" she whispered.

"Yeah," Rebecca answered, "on the leg, and then sometimes ..." her voice trailed off as if she were afraid she had unleashed an evil thought that should never have been spoken.

Lottie's mind latched onto the ghastly image and a sober sensation flooded her gut. Her body felt cold. So many times her mother had warned her about boys, and how they might tell her that they loved her when they were really only after one thing. Esther had never said anything to Lottie or her sisters about grown men touching young girls, least of all a girl's father. Lottie found her father's drinking to be terrible enough. She couldn't imagine Rebecca's father—or anyone else's for that matter—doing something so despicable. "I ... ah ... I ..." she stammered, "... don't know ... what to say."

"I know."

Lottie placed her hand gently on Rebecca's shoulder in an effort to comfort her friend, but Rebecca took a step backward, dropping Lottie's hand.

"I can't stand the sight of the louse anymore." Rebecca's eyes narrowed into tiny slits.

"Did you tell him to stop it?" Lottie heart raced.

"I want to," Rebecca replied. "I've *always* wanted to, but I couldn't. I know I should have told him a long time ago. This has been going on since I was nine. I don't know how I can possibly make him stop now. Sometimes, he just comes into my room at night. I hate going to sleep. I have nightmares. Some nights, I try to stay awake until the sun comes up so I won't have any bad dreams."

"Oh, Rebecca." Lottie's arms slumped at her sides. Another shiver zagged down her spine. "Is there anything I can do?"

"Just don't tell anyone," Rebecca begged. "I'm so ashamed."

Lottie's gut squeezed like a wrung-out dishrag. "*He's* the one who should be ashamed," she countered. Anger starting to grow. "This is *not* your fault."

Rebecca's eyes dropped to the ground.

"Don't worry, Rebecca." Lottie lifted her chin upwards. "I promised I wouldn't tell anyone—and I won't. But can't you find someone who will make him stop? What about your mom?"

Rebecca winced. "I'm afraid to tell her," she confessed. "I don't know what would happen. I mean, what if she doesn't believe me?"

"It's not like you have a good reason to make something like this up," Lottie said.

"Yeah, but even if she did believe me, what could she do about it?" Rebecca wondered. "What would happen if she said something to him?"

"He'd probably blast you," Lottie whispered. "I see what you mean. It scares me just thinking about it."

Rebecca let out a quivering huff. "I wish I had done something to make him stop back in the beginning." Her eyes watered as she rubbed a red runny nose on the cuff of her sweater. "It's too late now. After all this time, he thinks he has a right to do it. I just need to get out of here. I need to escape."

The Third Avenue El eased its way out of the station. It squirmed through the neighborhood, off to a new and mysterious destination. Lottie wanted to be alone for a moment. Sparks from the screeching metal wheels scraping against the tracks bathed the cars in blue light from below.

"Me too," Lottie said. "I wish I could get both of us away from all this terrible stuff."

Together, the two gazed out at the skyline, silently imagining what their lives would be like if they traveled to another place and time.

"Hey, you guys!" Elsie Mae's voice startled them from their trance. "You came to play jacks, didn't you?"

Lottie reached over and took Rebecca's hand. She gave it a reassuring squeeze. She turned toward Elsie Mae. "We sure did! And you better be ready, 'cause here we come!"

"What were you two gabbing about over there?" Elsie Mae asked as her friends approached. She had been stooped over and her concentration had never veered from the jacks. A frown wrinkled her pretty face as she tossed the ball and scooped up the tiny metal objects.

Rebecca let out a nervous laugh. "We were just talking about how we plan to take over the world someday. Picture it: Empresses Rebecca and Lottie!" She tossed her book aside, flung her arms out as if to engulf the cityscape, and beamed a forced smile.

Lottie liked the idea of being idolized as an empress. She couldn't help but get lost in the mere thought of it. She cupped her hands around her mouth. "Beloved subjects!" she announced. "All must bow down to the Empress Rebecca!" She grabbed Rebecca's hand and raised it up into the air.

Rebecca straightened tall and stepped forward, waving her hands as if she were anointing invisible minions. "Charmed," she exclaimed in an imitation British accent. She sashayed across the rooftop for a few steps, then bowed down in an elegant curtsy. "And now, also for the world to adore, I present the glorious Empress Lottie!"

Lottie staggered and took a grand step forward to address the imaginary throng of admirers; but her big shoe caught one of the pipes jutting out from the roof. She teetered backward. Before she could regain her balance, she fell back on her ass. Rebecca and Elsie Mae instantly burst into fits of uncontrollable laughter.

"That's not funny!" Lottie scowled; pushing out her lower lip. She always hated it when people laughed at her. Then again, as she glanced up at her friends, she realized how ridiculous that must have looked, and was finally able to join in their laughter. "Someday, I'm gonna buy a decent pair of shoes."

"How about a pair of glasses to go with them?" Rebecca giggled.

Elsie Mae motioned them over to her area of the roof. "C'mon, you guys," she said with a laugh. "Get over here and play jacks!"

As soon as Lottie scrambled to her feet, she leaned over and whispered in Rebecca's ear. "Don't worry. I won't tell a soul."

The girls crouched in a small circle, counted, tossed; taking turns as the play settled into a fun rhythm. Rebecca reached back and snatched up her book during a lull between turns.

"Rebecca, you're such an Abercrombie," Elsie Mae commented. "What are you reading now?"

"I just finished the new *Nancy Drew* mystery," Rebecca said. "She's the best."

Elsie Mae smiled and shook her head. "Straight-A student and teacher's pet. I wish that was me."

"I don't like reading much." Lottie bounced the ball and scooped up a handful of jacks. "The kids at school don't like me much, either."

"Who do you think *we* are?" Elsie Mae gasped as she gave Lottie a playful smack on the shoulder. "We're kids from your school."

"Lottie, you shouldn't be such a scrub," Rebecca gave an understanding nod. "You're very smart. You could do better in school if you really wanted to."

"You're the one with all the brains, Rebecca." Lottie lowered her head. "All the smart kids hang around you. I don't fit in."

"Lottie, you're good at the things you like to do," Elsie Mae said. "You never liked school. Me neither, except for all those hip boys I meet there."

Rebecca rolled her eyes. "Oh, brother," she gasped. "What in the world will we do when we're out of school?"

Elsie Mae bounced the ball, scooped up three jacks and raised her brows. "I'm going to Hollywood."

"Watch out for all those communists," Lottie cracked.

"My family can't afford to send me to college," Rebecca said through a soft sigh. "Hey, maybe I could write a book like this one I'm reading."

When her turn was finished, Elsie Mae handed Rebecca the ball and picked up the book. "Nancy Drew *is* the neatest," she said. "I would love to play her in a movie." She placed her palms on her cheeks and cocked her head in a glamorous movie star pose.

"Elsie Mae, that's boss. You'd be so good!" Rebecca cheered. "You'd make a great Nancy Drew."

"You're so smooth." Lottie's heart slugged. She hoped her friends would find their dreams. "I bet you could be a big star. You'll meet a famous man and he'll help you."

"I know ... but ... I need to get out of the Bronx," Elsie Mae said quietly. "I'm nothing here. Someday, I'm going to be rich. Then I'll show them all."

"When you become rich, send for me and Empress Lottie," Rebecca urged. "We'll come to Hollywood and clean your mansion."

"Then you can go out on dates with all those handsome California boys," Lottie said with a laugh, as her tummy flipped just thinking about really living in Hollywood. One of her hands gripped the opposite elbow and her demeanor quickly changed. She drew both knees to her chest. "I wish I was pretty," she continued sadly. "I think my dad wants me to get married."

"Well, what else is there?" Elsie Mae replied. "You don't want to be an old maid, now, do you?" She rolled the ball over to Lottie. "That's why we have all these curves, to attract the male of the species."

"*You've* got the curves," Lottie's bottom lip trembled. "I'm nobody's filly."

"I wish I didn't have curves," Rebecca blurted. Her shoulders and fingers shivered. "I can't stand it when guys try to touch me."

Lottie felt the need to quickly change the subject. "My mom and dad argue a lot," she told them. "I don't want to live like that. I guess that means I'm not the marrying kind." She bounced the ball and skillfully scooped up some jacks.

"Me, neither," Rebecca muttered. "I'm never getting married."

Elsie Mae brushed back her hair. "I don't even know what my mom and dad do most of the time," she said. "I almost never see them. My mom never pays attention to me now that my new dad is here."

Lottie listened closely, scooped up more jacks, and counted them under her breath. "You never talk much about your first dad," she said. "Why not?"

"I don't know." Elsie Mae slowly rubbed an ear. "I guess it just isn't all that easy to talk about. When I was a little girl, Daddy always told me how pretty I looked." She closed her eyes and sighed, overcome with the memory. "Six years ago, he went off to fight in the war in Europe. He was one of the infantrymen that landed on Omaha Beach with the First Division." She paused for a moment, Lottie and Rebecca noticed the trace of tears welling up in her eyes. "The stinkin' Germans shot him four times. Lousy war."

"Oh my gosh!" Rebecca gasped.

"That's terrible!" Lottie patted Elsie Mae's leg and scooched over, letting her knee touch Elsie Mae's.

"The army raced him to a French hospital." Elsie Mae swallowed hard. "He died there."

For a tense moment the girls sat in a circle, almost afraid to speak. Lottie's eyelids were gummy. She rolled the ball around in her palm and gave it a tight squeeze, as if to confine all this sadness about the world into the tiny rubber object.

"I really miss my daddy," Elsie Mae whispered and sunk her chin to her chest. "My new dad acts like I don't even exist."

Lottie's limbs got heavy. "I know how that feels." She silently wondered if two dads were better than the one who constantly battled with her mom. She glanced up toward the bright sky. "I wish I could play sports—you know, as a *job*. Men make lots of money doing that. I'm good at sports. If I could play something for a living, I could get rich. And then maybe I could help us all get out of this neighborhood."

"You'd be great." Rebecca pulled her shoulders back. "But what sport would they let you play?"

"I'd be happy to play almost anything, if they'd just give me a chance," Lottie displayed a wide grin. "I like them all—baseball, basketball, soccer. I'm good at them too."

"We know," Elsie Mae said with a laugh. "We watch you outrun the boys all the time. It's too bad there are no sports for girls ... are there?"

"Have you seen those roller derby gals on television?" Lottie asked, arching her brow.

"Yeah!" Rebecca raised a finger in the air. "They really move!"

"I bet they make loads of dough," Lottie thought aloud.

"They probably do," Rebecca agreed, "but wouldn't you be afraid of making a fool of yourself? What if you fell?"

"It wouldn't be any worse than the way the boys treat me when I play stickball." Lottie slapped her thigh. "At least I would get paid for it. *And* I'd get to be on television."

"You may be clumsy sometimes, Lottie ..." Rebecca began, rubbing one hand over her sweater pocket, "but you are definitely brave. Roller derby *is* a sport for girls. Have you seen Roughie Barclay skate? She's my favorite. She always sticks up for herself."

"Oh, yeah!" Elsie Mae sat up straight. "Roughie can really kick butt! Did you know that she's the daughter of a plumber? I read about her in a movie magazine. The article was in a summer issue."

"I got some new roller skates a while ago." Rebecca placed an index finger on her chin. "Then I went to the library to study up on things like roller derby."

Lottie let out a laugh. "Rebecca, you are such a librarian. So, what did you find out?"

"There wasn't much there," Rebecca answered, disappointed. "But I did read that roller derby is the first sport for women with professional teams and real body contact. You know, people bashing into one another on skates. They even have colored men on the teams."

"On television, the announcer said that the guys and the girls skate by the same rules," Elsie Mae added. "What would happen if one of the guys ran over one of the girls?"

"Those girls can take it," Lottie rocked in place as her chest tightened. "They're just as tough as the guys."

"I can't do *that* kind of skating," Rebecca said, massaging a shoulder as if it had just been crushed into a railing.

Lottie's mind was suddenly wrapped up in the future. She tightened her fists. "I bet you could." She jabbed one finger at Rebecca. "I could help you. I ain't afraid of those guys, and you shouldn't be, either. You know what? We could get together with some other girls and make a team. We might even get to skate on television."

Rebecca waved her off. "C'mon, Lottie," she scoffed. "Girls like us don't get on. Besides, I'm too shy for something like that."

"Don't have a cow, Rebecca," Elsie Mae said, leaning in and jutting out her jaw. "Lottie's right. You're a great skater, and I've seen lots of other girls in the neighborhood who skate all over the place. We should give this a try. We've got nothing to lose."

"Except maybe our teeth," Rebecca muttered.

"Or my virginity," Elsie Mae said.

"Please ..." Rebecca chuckled.

"Think about it, Rebecca." Lottie pressed both hands into a steeple. "This could be so much fun. We would make lots of new friends—and we could travel away from this place."

Rebecca raised one brow.

Lottie hoped that the thought of getting out of the Bronx would pique Rebecca's interest. Rebecca needed to get out faster than anybody else. Lottie and Elsie Mae could see the wheels turning inside their friend's head. A sly smile curled up at the edge of her mouth.

"I can skate a little." She shrugged her shoulders. "But I need to learn more."

"And I bet we'd meet plenty of cute guys along the way." Elsie Mae pushed her chest out, her eyes wide with delight.

"Oh, shut up about that!" Rebecca snapped. "Boys, boys, boys—that's all you ever think about." She snatched the red rubber ball out of Lottie's hand and tossed out the jacks.

Lottie sat back and thought for a moment. "You're right, Rebecca." She put a closed hand under her chin. "We would need to learn how to skate better. Especially me, 'cause I don't even have a pair of skates just yet. I'm good at sports, though. I bet I can learn fast enough."

Rebecca finished her turn with the jacks and rolled the ball over to Elsie Mae. "We should go over to the roller rink. They have a speed club. That's kind of like roller derby. We can try out for it."

"I'd adore that," Elsie Mae said.

"That's a great idea." Lottie thrummed her fingers on her thigh. "It would give us the practice we need."

"Where will you get the money for that, Lottie?" Elsie Mae raised one palm upwards. She sat back on her ankles and rocked with a renewed sense of vigor. "Do you think your dad would give it to you?"

"My dad doesn't have any extra dough." Lottie's brow furrowed. "I'm working for my own money. I've got a job, but I need to get a better one and make some real cash."

"That's so keen for you!" Elsie Mae squealed. "Where do you work?"

Lottie shrugged, knees pulled together keeping her body compressed and small while feeling both ears turn red. "I've been washing dishes and cleaning tables at Mason's Diner after school. I hate the job. The dishes never end and the tables are always a mess just a few minutes after I wipe them down. That's okay, though. I don't need a free ride. I know what I want—roller skates and lessons—and I'll clean all the dishes in the world to get the money."

"Mason's is a nice place," Rebecca tapped Lottie's hand. "They make the best chocolate malts. Besides, this will give us more experience when it comes time to clean up Elsie Mae's dishes in her movie star mansion."

The girls all laughed.

"That's right!" Elsie Mae clasped both hands to her chest. "I don't want any dirty dishes sitting around my mansion, you hear?"

"That does it." Lottie raised one thumb in the air. "As soon as I get a pair of skates, we'll all sign up for speed classes. It'll be a blast. We'll be like a trio of Sonja Henie's."

Lottie tossed the ball and scooped up the entire field of jacks with one quick, skillful move, winning the game.

"So dainty!" Rebecca made a delicate gesture with one hand.

"This is so boss!" Elsie Mae stood as she threw her hands up toward the sky. "We're going to be stars!" She stopped in her tracks and glanced around. "So, what should we do now? Play marbles?"

"Can't," Lottie groaned. "Bum finger." She showed the other girls her thumb and middle finger which she usually used to flick the shooter across the street to hit the opponent's box. She recalled the number of times she had bought candy for a nickel and then hung around the 154th Street store asking customers if they could spare an empty cheese box that she could use for marble contests.

One day, a group of boys had started picking on her after a marble game. "Hey, where'd you get those combat boots?" one yelled.

"You skinny curve!" another one jeered.

Lottie's cheeks were burning red causing her jaw to clench. Then she was suddenly shoved down onto the sidewalk. Her vision blacked out. She felt the marbles she had just rightfully won scatter in every direction. As she watched the boys quickly snatch up as many as they could, her legs stiffened and her breath collapsed. For a moment, Lottie remained sprawled on the cement, wishing the earth would just open up and swallow her.

As her memories stirred, Lottie wondered why bullies targeted her. She always turned her head away from these tormentors; trying not to catch their attention. Her mind flashed on an old image, maybe when it all started. When she was six years old, two older boys tackled her on the playground. They held her down, viciously tickling her ribs until they caused the tears to flow.

"You're nothing but a yellow-bellied chicken!" one of the boys shouted.

"Stop! *Stop!*" she begged. "You're hurting me!" Her breathing raced as her arms flailed in helpless movements.

"Big nose!" the other screamed.

She stared at both boys' faces which were radiating hatred and sadistic delight. Her stomach dropped as her heart went *thud*.

"Get up and fight back, big ears! You're such a coward!"

"And a weirdo!"

"Please stop," she pleaded, gasping for breath. Her cries for mercy only encouraged them. Lottie coughed and wheezed as she struggled to get free. "Somebody please help me!"

Nobody came that day.

Eventually, those boys left her like an abandoned household pet. It was a memory she would never forget. Now, after so many years, the pain was beginning to fade a bit; but the trauma that came with it would stay with Lottie for a lifetime and still there was no clear reason as to what might have caused this behavior. She gave her head a shake and managed to bring herself back to the safety of the rooftop and the company of her best friends.

"I have an idea," Elsie Mae announced. "Let's play Double Dutch. We can't be playing kids' games anymore. It's time for us to grow up."

"Let's play now," Lottie agreed. "Soon, we won't have time for games. We'll be too busy skating around in the roller derby and signing autographs for millions of fans!"

Elsie Mae grabbed one end of each of the jump ropes and tossed the other ends over to Rebecca.

"Here we go," Rebecca said through a laugh as she and Elsie Mae began twirling the ropes. "C'mon, Lottie! You think you can jump without tripping over yourself?"

"Just watch me!"

"Maybe you should take off those clodhoppers first." Elsie Mae pinched her nose and pointed to Lottie's big shoes.

"No." Lottie placed both hands on her hips. "If I can jump Double Dutch in these shoes, I can do anything."

The girls felt their spirits soar as they performed death-defying jump rope maneuvers: in, around, over and between the twirling twin ropes. Lottie didn't want the day to end.

That night as she lay in bed, the image of the injured little pigeon appeared again in her dreams. It perched on her rickety windowsill for a moment, moonlight weaving along the white feathers. Lottie's heart swelled as the bird spread its wings and flew upward. It swept across the sky, circling ever higher in graceful, fluid figure eights. Warmth spread through Lottie's body as the pigeon glided through the air without a care in the world, fluttering independently and sailing far away from all the misfortune below.

Chapter 4

ROLLER LUST

Wheels screeched and clattered. "Fly, Tommy, fly!" Elsie Mae's hands cupped her mouth as she yelled toward the center of the roller rink.

Rebecca laced her skates as Lottie giggled at Elsie Mae's spectacle, shouting encouragement to the wavy-haired boy.

Mesmerized by the varnished hardwood floor that was warped in some places, Lottie eyed the speed skaters whooshing by. Her heart lurched at the sight of the long-legged boy and there was a new type of stirring in her belly. She wondered what Tommy thought of her. Did he notice her? She knew she looked more like the rink's ratty seats which had been salvaged from an abandoned movie theater than someone he'd be interested in. She sat still, blending in with the surroundings. The familiar feeling of being an outsider burned deep until she brushed the sensation aside and let her mind linger on the roller derby luminaries from television. The threadbare skating rink, with its damaged banners and castaway furnishings, would fulfill her skating fantasy.

"What a blast. Go, guy, go!" Elsie Mae said.

Itching with hope, Lottie laced one roller skate and ignored the attention Elsie Mae was giving to the boy speed skater. Pushing a foot inside the other boot, she re-tore a once-mended sock. "I'll have to ask Mom to make another repair," she said to Rebecca. "I wonder if she can mend it again. My dad'll go ape if I need a new pair."

Elsie Mae stood at the barrier that separated the worn out seats from the skating floor. "Look how boss Tommy is!"

"Say, I thought you were seeing that Jason kid," Rebecca pointed out.

"Today ... Tommy's my number one."

Lottie wondered what it would feel like if Tommy held her hand or bought her a small gift. "How does she know his name?"

"You know how fast she can move." Rebecca waved one hand to the side dismissing even the effort to think about an answer to that question.

"I wish guys would notice me, too." Lottie's voice was laced with anxiety as she eyed Elsie Mae's strawberry blonde hair, rolled into bangs in the latest style. Lottie's gaze wandered down and stopped at the sight of Elsie Mae's breasts. Glancing at her own chest, she felt a wave of self-consciousness lap over her. Lottie looked away. "You know, I never noticed how, you know, *developed* Elsie Mae is." It wasn't just Lottie's flat chest that was wrong. Her hair, ears, nose, and everything else came together into one squirrelly nothing. She tugged an over-washed sweater around her boy-chest.

"Oh, big deal," Rebecca said. "Being stacked isn't everything. Elsie Mae makes the best of it. The boys always give her the eye."

"She just gets bigger and bigger." Lottie pursed her lips as her stomach hardened. Then she held both cupped hands in front of her.

"If she wears those sweaters any tighter," Rebecca giggled, "she'll bust right out of 'em."

Lottie flung her fingers outward from her flat chest. "Boom!"

"You ever think about boys?"

Lottie could only imagine what a boy would be like as a friend. She had wished ... but no. "Naw, never."

"Do you think you're ready to skate?"

She watched the speed skaters on the floor. "I gotta hold my horses. I can't wait to get out there and roll."

"Think you'll do okay?"

"Sure, it'll be a cinch. I'll get the hang of it, just like stickball."

"Take it easy at first."

Lottie called to Elsie Mae. "Hey Elsie Mae, the guys can really get the lead out."

"I know." Elsie Mae ogled the skating boys. "Look, Tommy's in the lead. He's more than ten feet ahead of everyone. What a heartthrob."

Wooden wheels skidded, careening around a sharp left turn then clattering as they rolled over a warped spot. Lottie's stomach fluttered as Tommy hunched down, long legs striding out over the right-hand corner.

"Floor it!" Elsie Mae's pupils widened. Tommy stroked left and right with power lunges. He built up speed, then roared down the straightaway. "He's so cute!"

"Sure, sure, cute." Lottie looked away. Tommy and Elsie Mae were everything she wasn't.

"We're next."

Anticipation boiled up her spine. She stood up, excitement causing the skates to start quavering. A few yards away, two other girls laced up their skates. "Only five of us," she said. "Kinda disappointing." So few girls were in the speed class.

"Where's Rebecca?" Elsie Mae asked.

Lottie searched, spotting Rebecca holed up in a corner, red hair in spirals, black-framed reading glasses sliding down her nose. "Reading again. Ya know what an Einstein she is."

"Girls, time to warm up," the coach yelled.

"The guys are done. We're next." Elsie Mae crooked a smile.

Tommy rolled past the two girls. Lottie's eyes locked onto him and she swooned. He bent over with his hands on his knees, breathing heavily, making Lottie's chest balloon. Passing in front of her, he cocked his head toward Elsie Mae and flashed a bright smile. He rolled up behind Lottie and Elsie Mae. "Greetings, guys," he said between gulps of air.

Lottie's pulse raced and she thought he sounded street smart, like those guys who worked on cars with greasy hands.

"Hi." Lottie waved to Tommy, who ignored her and eyed Elsie Mae's chest and legs. Lottie's heart went plop when Elsie Mae's face brightened. Tommy lost his appeal immediately. Skating toward the center of the rink, Lottie hung her head. She caught her reflection in the snack counter mirror and looked away. She pushed that ugly appearance out of her mind and focused all of possible attention on her wheeled feet.

Leaving her book and glasses, Rebecca rolled up beside her and the two struggled a half-lap around the rink. They didn't know the other gals who didn't speak a word or even look their way. All in all, it was a very awkward to start to their self-imposed training.

Elsie Mae followed Lottie's rattletrap lead with choppy steps up the straightaway. Lottie rolled her gawky frame around, arms thrashing in order to gain balance. One skate hit the other; she wobbled and crashed face first with a *splat*.

Elsie Mae winced.

The other girls rolled in lazy circles, squatting and stretching without saying a thing. At least they didn't laugh.

"Come on, Lottie." Elsie Mae watched Rebecca, who was closer, extend a hand. "You okay?"

"Yeah." Lottie rubbed her jaw where a raspberry-red bruise was forming. Looking unsettled, she clasped Rebecca's hand, pulled herself up, and clumped forward. "Guess it's not easy like I thought."

Elsie Mae drew back when Lottie furrowed her brow, stumbled and fell again. *Thwack.*

"You can do it," Rebecca said.

"Do what? Break my leg?" Lottie pushed her lower lip forward.

"No. Break your butt," Rebecca laughed.

Lottie stood up, trembled on her wheels, pin wheeled her arms in circles and flopped to the floor again.

Elsie Mae clutched her blouse button. "This is our first time," she explained to Tommy.

"I thought so." Tommy rolled his eyes at Lottie's hopeless practice run. "She's all wet."

"She's a little wild on her skates."

"Like a beanstalk lumberjack on wheels." Tommy slapped his thigh. "Is the greaseball your friend?"

"Yes. Zip it. That's Lottie, and my other friend Rebecca." Elsie Mae frowned and turned a half shoulder Tommy's way.

He ran a hand through his hair. "Don't blow your wig. She's wacky."

"Well, don't tell her you're making fun of her." Elsie Mae stared back into Tommy's eyes. "I feel sorry for her."

"Didn't mean to rattle your cage," Tommy finally said. "Hey, I hear the roller derby's looking for skaters."

"What do you mean, the roller derby's looking?"

"Sure, it's this sport down at the Armory; it's the roller derby. You get bread for skating." He patted his back pocket wallet. "I dropped in for a look last week."

"We know. It's on television," Elsie Mae said. "You'd be great, Tommy. You're the best here. And look how strong you are." She wrapped her fingers around Tommy's muscled bicep and watched him puff up to show off.

"They say if you get picked for a team, you get free room and board. They pay you every three weeks." Tommy stuck his chest out.

"Free food sounds good. Fat city."

"It'd be nice to have extra suds." He dropped his gaze and then looked up quickly. "I have to pay Pop back for the jalopy he bought me. It's fourteen years old, but it burns rubber."

"Kippy keen. It'd feel incredible if I was paid for skating."

"Mom and Pop want me out of the house next year." He drew a hand out of his pocket and jerked the thumb into the air. "They can't afford me, my brothers and my sister." Tommy's face fell at the thought. "If I don't get this skating gig, I'll have to take a job at the filling station. It pays ninety-five cents a day."

"That's impossible. It's not enough money."

"Yeah, sure ain't. And who wants to fill cars and clean windshields all day?" Tommy puffed out his chest again. "I'm better than that."

"I'm sure you'll get it—the roller derby job, that is. No need to work at the filling station." Elsie Mae drew her lips up into a smile, lifting his spirits. "I can't skate that well yet." She tottered on her skates. About to fall, she reached out to him.

Tommy opened his arms and caught her. "Whoa, there. You're so beautiful, you could be a star," he said with all the sincerity a seventeen-year-old could muster.

"A star? Really?" Elsie Mae brought a hand to her face and rubbed a cheek. "That's what I always wanted."

"A lot of producers and directors go to the games. There's a good chance they'd see you and give you a part in a movie. And they'll train you to skate better."

"I need the training."

"Once you skate really good, I know you've got what it takes. I bet, one day, you're going to light up the silver screen." He cocked his head to the side in a sexy way. "You'll outshine everyone else."

Elsie Mae stared intently, reached out and brushed his cheek with the back of her hand. "That is so nice to hear." She placed an open palm on her heart, wishing her mom and stepdad would show the kind of confidence in her that Tommy did.

"You know, Hollywood's making a roller derby movie right now with Mickey Rooney. It's called *Fireball*. And Bert Wall, a derby skater, is Mickey's stunt skater!" Tommy rubbed his head in a charming move that made Elsie Mae take on a flushed appearance.

"Just think, the two of us could be on television and in the movies." Elsie Mae looked toward the roof as if her imagination had soared into overdrive. It was as if she saw Tommy by her side through the din and squawking of the wheels against the hardwood floor behind where they were standing. She turned to see Lottie clomping awkwardly. "Hey, Lottie," she said. "Do you know Tommy?"

Nerve endings tingled inside Lottie like a wildfire. "Hi."

"Hi, sprout. I'm gonna do this derby skating next week. You want to go, too?"

Lottie took a deep breath and her heart beat wildly. "A sports date. Sure!" She smiled at Tommy's invitation. Maybe he hadn't seen how badly she had just skated. "I really like the way you get the lead out of your pants." Could this be real? The idea of going derby skating with Tommy thrilled her.

"We can all go," Tommy said.

Those words put the fire out inside Lottie's heart just as fast as it had flared up.

"Tommy asked me to go with him, and we thought you and Rebecca could come along," Elsie Mae added, tugging on Tommy's shirt collar.

Lottie sensed electricity passing between Tommy and Elsie Mae. A coldness doused the last romantic feelings clinging to teenage hope. Of course he liked Elsie Mae! Lottie felt like a fool and wished Rebecca were here to take some of the attention. She glanced at the floor awkwardly. "I watch roller derby every week." She raised her head. "I really think Roughie Barclay's boss; so does Rebecca."

"My favorite skater is Gerry Murphy," Elsie Mae said. "She's so beautiful. She's the roller derby queen. She must make tons of money. And guess what?" She turned fully to face Lottie. "Tommy thinks I'll be a big star."

"Of course you're going to be a star." Lottie pulled at her sweater self-consciously again. "You're pretty, like Gerry, and you could be a roller derby queen, too."

Rebecca rolled up, arms folded across her chest.

"I want to be as good as that short guy with black hair, Vinnie Christener," Tommy said. "He can *really* move it." Tommy shot one flattened hand forward. "Roughie and Gerry are the best ... for the gals, that is." He looked at Elsie Mae and winked.

"I bet the girls on the team are best friends." Lottie relaxed back and brushed her throat with gentle fingers, a self-soothing movement that helped to relax her.

Elsie Mae saluted one hand to her forehead. "Comrades."

"And they probably stick up for one another." Rebecca uncrossed her arms, relaxing along with her friend.

Lottie smiled at Rebecca's remark. "Tommy asked us to go to roller derby training."

"I'd be up for that." Rebecca cracked a big smile. "Except Lottie might need a nurse for all her bumps and bruises."

"Naw," Lottie said, waving her hand. "I'll get better here, and then I'll be made in the shade."

"It's at the Fourteenth Street Armory building in Manhattan. Let's all hop over there," Tommy said. "I can pick you up in my new tin can." His wide eyes bounced back and forth between the three girls. "Come on, whatcha say?"

"Jeez! What a kick."

"This might be our ticket to independence," Lottie said seeing Elsie Mae's enthusiasm.

Rebecca nodded her approval, then laughed. "Or a ticket to the emergency room."

"I've got copies of the release forms." Tommy dipped into his front pants pocket and pulled out folded sheets of paper.

"Forms? What are they for?" Elsie Mae asked.

"Our parents need to sign because we're underage." He separated two slips of paper and gave one to Rebecca and one to Lottie.

Fear curdled within Lottie's chest. She wondered what her father would think of the idea. How would she ask him? A knot tightened in her stomach. "My dad won't sign."

"What do you mean?" Rebecca asked.

"He won't let me do it. He won't understand."

"Sure he will." Rebecca nudged Lottie. "Tell him how much roller derby stars make."

"How much?"

"Hell's bells, let's at least try," Elsie Mae grumped.

Tommy handed the third paper to Elsie Mae. His hand hovered near hers and paused. "This is for you."

Lottie noticed his tone sounded as if he were kissing Elsie Mae.

"Well, I got to get outta here. I'll be seeing ya." Tommy pulled back and waved.

"Okey-dokey." Lottie waved with a goofy movement of her hand and head.

"Bye, Tommy." Elsie Mae cocked her head and gave a sexy wink that brought another wide smile to Tommy's lips. Rebecca waved absently.

The girls waited for Tommy to skate to the back of the rink. "Isn't he snazzy?" Elsie Mae turned to Lottie.

"You and boys." Lottie tugged a ratty strand of hair feeling the tension return a little.

"Let's be-bop down to this new derby with Tommy, okay?" Elsie Mae tucked the slip of paper into her bra.

"I don't know." Lottie shrugged.

"Sounds like a blast. Go with us, please!" Rebecca said.

Lottie shoved the paper into her sweater pocket. "I'm with you guys."

They all shook on it. The three felt a sense of new elation. They were going on an adventure. Elsie Mae's glassy-eyed gaze lit up again. "Maybe we'll be stars. Big stars—just like in the movie magazines." She batted her lashes in an attempt to resemble the starlets they read about so often.

The girls skated to the center of the rink. A few others joined them. Lottie and the other gals began to roll, inspiring a synchronized line. "Let's haul it!" she yelled. Her feet crossed and she careened outside the pace line. Stumbling, with her arms flailing in all directions, she flop-banged onto the hard floor in a heap.

Chapter 5

THIS AIN'T FOR GIRLS

Bam! Murray Zimmerman's hand slapped the kitchen table. Lottie cringed in surprise.

"What the hell's this?" Murray shouted, furrowing his brow.

Lottie's hopes dove into a pit of darkness, the familiar tension tightening every muscle. Lottie lowered her gaze, realizing that bringing the skater release form into the kitchen hadn't been a good idea. Or maybe this was the wrong time. Her dad rarely seemed upbeat, but she had hashed the idea over for hours. Finally, Lottie had skulked down the stairs, paper in hand. Now she was trembling next to her annoyed father, the paper release vibrating in her hand.

"What?!" Murray shouted again as Lottie's insides quavered.

"What is it? Um ... it's roller skating on a banked track." Lottie tilted her head to one side, giving her father an awkward glance. She tried to look and sound uninterested. If she seemed excited, he might quash the dream just because.

Murray sat at the Formica table as if on a throne, smoking and reading the newspaper. He dominated the sparsely furnished room. Esther puttered behind him, bringing him food or a beer on command. The stuffy kitchen was filled with the smell of ham hocks and navy beans from Esther's soup. "What's it pay?"

"I'm not sure."

"Then why are you doing this?" Murray pressed his lips into a fine line.

"It's something I finally like to do." Lottie stood rigid.

"Aren't you a little small for this sort of thing?" Murray stared deep into Lottie's eyes. "Let me see." He snatched the paper out of Lottie's fingers, turned away to drag on his cigarette and stared at the paper for an eternity.

Lottie held her breath, and finally pointed to the signature line. Noticing her finger shake, she hid her hands behind her back. "You just have to sign at the bottom."

"You're not even sixteen years old yet."

"That's why you need to sign."

"But you're a girl." Murray dismissed the idea with a wave of his hand.

"This is for girls *and* boys," Lottie attempted, undismayed.

"Well ..." Murray fiddled with his cigarette. "What's this going to cost me?" The veins pulsed at his temple and the lines between his brows deepened. "I don't have money for nonsense!" He jammed the Lucky Strike into a plate, crushing it to bits with his big hand. When he raised his head, his dark hair quivered; his eyes penetrated Lottie, who shrank deeper inside herself.

"It won't cost a thing. Me an' Elsie Mae are going down to the Armory this Friday." She grinned, hoping to reach his good side.

Murray slapped the paper onto the table and glared. "Who said you could go there? Ain't you working at Mason's? You know he only gave you that job because me and him go way back."

"Mr. Mason doesn't need me Friday. His nephew's coming to town." Her father might have thought she lost the job to the nephew, so Lottie quickly added, "But he's leaving on Sunday, so Mr. Mason told me to come back Monday."

Murray grumbled, "This is that damn television roller derby, ain't it?"

"I think so." Lottie shrugged big; shoulders to ears. "Rebecca's going along, too." Lottie looked at Esther, wanting support but knowing it wouldn't come. In an eerie moment of precognition, Lottie saw herself becoming her mother, something she knew would inevitably happen if she didn't do something to get out of this place. So much hinged on this.

"This ain't no way to make a living." Murray rubbed the back of his neck without making eye contact.

Lottie smelled beer-tinged breath. Murray's eyes narrowed and she felt herself shiver. "I just want to try it. It might be?"

"Women don't do these kinds of things. You could get hurt." He glanced at his wife for agreement. Esther turned her back to the scene, stirring the big pot on the stove. Lottie thanked her silently. Mom might not help, but she wouldn't hinder this dream, either. Murray turned and read more of the slip. "What about school?"

Lottie's chest ached; she felt out of place at school. The kids made fun of her and the way she looked. She never caught on to the things the other girls did to look boss and pretty, so they stayed clear of her. Elsie Mae had it all: good looks, friends, nice clothes, and boyfriends.

"I'm doing the best I can." Lottie knew she was different from Rebecca. She wanted to get away from the school grind. She had stopped thinking about school the moment she started playing sports, even the ones she wasn't good at. She didn't know any other girls who wanted that except her two gal friends ... and Tommy.

"Work harder. This damn skating is dangerous."

"But a bunch of us are trying out. I can keep up my school, my job at Mason's, *and* I can do this." The shakes quavered inside her. She hoped her dad understood that getting a different job, especially *this* job, would be better than the job at Mason's Diner. This was more important than finishing high school; she could become independent and not be a burden on him anymore.

"These ideas ain't for everyone, especially girls. Why don't you help your mother around the house?"

It was a question Lottie couldn't answer. Women's work was boring. Becoming a housewife sounded disgusting. What a drag. She knew there wasn't a boy in the world interested in a plug-ugly tomboy like her, so maybe she didn't *need* to practice homemaking skills.

"I don't know." She felt a little sorry for her mother, but if things went that way now, she'd end up being a slave to a man. Mom would never experience the thrill of hitting a homerun. Housework ... yuck!

"You should learn to do household chores. Can't you find a man?" Murray leaned forward.

Lottie's heart stopped. She wondered what boy would ever marry her. She looked down at her shoes.

Murray sat quietly in thought. To Lottie it seemed like the whole idea burrowed deep under his skin. What was taking so long for a yes or no? He glared at her with hardened eyes, snarled and lurched forward. "You shouldn't chase this foolish idea. You can't eat glory for food! You'll starve!"

Lottie cringed at those words without totally understanding them. She said nothing. Then, "What do you mean?"

"Skating can't pay the bills!"

Lottie held her breath a moment. "I just want to try."

"This'll never go anywhere."

Lottie's hopes crashed to the floor. Her mother's reddened eyes darted away as if her own hopes were being dashed to bits as well.

"Please Dad?"

"No."

"But ..."

Murray went silent, his jaw clamped shut. Lottie felt like hiding somewhere; a hiding spot no one could ever find. With shoulders slumped forward, defeated, she pushed the slip of paper and watched it float down to the floor. "But ..." Arms hanging by her sides, she slowly turned and walked away. What would the future be now? Silence followed her until she reached the foot of the stairs that led up to her sparse bedroom.

"Get back here!" Murray's voice bellowed from the kitchen.

Lottie's heart skipped, and she stopped in her tracks. Was he going to punish her for even trying?

"Now!"

Her pulse raced as she slowly turned and returned to the kitchen table.

Lottie jumped when Murray snatched the paper up off of the ground. Minutes ticked by while he adjusted himself in his chair. He rubbed two fingers over the deep lines between his brows, as if trying to rub out a bad headache.

"Yes?" Lottie said quietly.

"You know how rough things are out there? The world is full of dangers for a young girl."

Lottie's imagination saw herself among beloved television mentors, everyone skating on the track as best friends. Nothing else. "I know."

"I *don't* know." Murray paused. "Well, give me a damn pen."

Esther fumbled for a pen in her ragged apron.

"I'm telling you, you'll starve. You'll eat peanuts." Murray scrawled a signature onto the paper and flung it toward Lottie, then slammed the pen onto the table with a *whack*. "When you need money, don't come running my way." He shook another Lucky Strike out of the pack and flicked a match.

Two hours later, Lottie couldn't sleep. Her head swam with the smiling faces of famous skaters from television. They were the most important people in her life. Vinnie Christner, Roughie Barclay, Eve Belzak, Charlie Samuels, Gerry Murphy and all the others greeted her. They welcomed the new skinny girl into their world.

That night, the pigeon flew on quiet wings and perched outside her windowsill. Lottie gazed as if in a dream. Her special friend suddenly rose, flying in transparent silver ovals until it was out of sight somewhere in the dark sky. It swirled like a comet on wings to the center of the universe.

Rebecca squirmed at the supper table, heart pounding. She was boiling over with news.

"There we go." Her mother placed the last dish, a bowl of salad, at the center of the table. "Okay, let's eat."

With her two older brothers and parents seated at their usual supper places, Rebecca listened while everyone talked about their day. Rebecca, for once, had something to share with the family.

"Sit up to the table, young lady." Rebecca's mother scooped spaghetti onto her plate. Rebecca wiggled back and forth in the chair, pushing herself and the chair's legs closer to her place setting.

"Okay, Mama." After spooning a dollop of salad onto her plate, she forked a spiral of noodles into her mouth and listened to the conversation unfold.

Halfway through supper, Rebecca made her announcement. "I'm going to go down to skate on that banked track!"

"That's good, sweetie," her dad said. "Just keep your school grades up." Beneath the table, he placed one hand on her knee and turned his head in the other direction.

Rebecca froze. His touch paralyzed her. She hid the shame that flushed up from her belly. "I will, Daddy. You know I get all A's, and I'll be graduating soon," she said. "Besides, skating will just be in the evenings and on weekends." She prayed he'd move his hand. More importantly, she didn't want anyone to detect the disgust whirling inside of her.

More silence.

"What's the matter, Rebecca?" her mother asked. "You seem nervous."

"Oh nothing, Mama. I'm fine." Rebecca leaned over her plate to scoop up more spaghetti. "Just excited to skate." She tried to hide her trembling.

Philip Peterson lifted his hand away from his daughter's leg after giving it a short, firm squeeze high up where knee started to become thigh. Rebecca picked imaginary lint from her shoulder.

"I just made the first-string football team," her older brother, Philip II, piped up.

"I'm so proud of you, son."

'P.P. Two' was the family's affectionate nickname for their oldest, though Rebecca thought it sounded stupid. P.P. turned red at his father's praise. He seemed set afire by making his dad happy.

"When's the first big game?"

"Two weeks from Saturday."

"Who're ya playing?"

"The Wildcats from East Bronx."

"I'll come and watch," Philip the First said. "I remember my school football games. That was the first time I saw your mother. She played a piccolo in the band."

Rebecca lowered her head to fork more spaghetti from her plate. She looked up at P.P. who appeared big and strong. She was proud of him, too.

"Does anyone want to go squirrel hunting with me tomorrow?" Philip the First asked.

"Me," P.P. Two said.

"I do. Me, too!" said Rebecca's other brother, raising a hand as if he were in school.

Rebecca said nothing. Her father never invited her to tag along for sports, hunting or fishing. She preferred it that way. Invisibility kept her father from asking favors, from getting too close when no one was looking. She cleaned her plate and listened to the supper table conversation. She scooted a slip of paper along the table toward her mother. "Would you sign this, please? I can pick it up tomorrow."

"Sure, honey."

Rebecca left the table. Working her way to her room, she could still hear her dad and older brothers talking about sports. She was certain her mother would sign the paper before morning. Her mother made those sorts of decisions without any browbeating.

Closing the bedroom door, Rebecca looked around the warm surroundings relieved as the mumbling table voices disappeared. She had filled her room with drawings hung carefully on the walls. Her shelves were lined with books and trinkets. Her spirits brightened when her hand lingered over a locked box on the dresser that she'd decorated with small bits of glitter and plastic jewels glued to its top. Rebecca had neatly organized everything in her room; except for the sloppy clothes strewn helter-skelter in her closet.

Tap. Tap.

So many times she had heard another light tap on her door. *Tap. Tap.* Right now she pretended not to hear.

"Princess, it's Dad," he would say. She always let him in, she was terrified not to. Then he would do those things he did. It turned her stomach, and now she wished she'd said no long, long ago. Like Lottie had said, she wished she had told someone about how dirty it all felt. Now, she just wanted to get out of the house.

Rebecca flopped onto her bed, exhaled and pulled out a special drawing from the sketchbook under her pillow. She placed it and an orderly box of colored pencils in front of her. She gazed at a picture of a woman on roller skates, her favorite of them all. It had taken four days to draw the athlete's skates, erasing and redrawing them over and over. She loved it. Every day she conjured another detail to add or another line to darken. Reaching for a brown pencil, she gently added swishing lines behind the skater to indicate speed. She rubbed the lines with a hankie-covered finger to blur them. She could spend hours shading in the uniform's flowing folds, lovingly completing her rendition of Roughie Barclay.

Three light taps sounded against Rebecca's door again. "Princess, its Daddy."

Rebecca took shallow breaths. She ignored the sounds and let her eyelids close. There must be something better than this.

Elsie Mae looked up from the television after becoming engrossed in a new show, *Search for a Song,* which had come on after *Texaco Star Theater*. On the kitchen table, the release form rested untouched and unsigned, exactly where she left it.

The fact that no one read or mentioned the release form ate away at Elsie Mae's gut. Why didn't anyone care? Her mother spent most of her time with that new husband. Little attention was given elsewhere. Elsie Mae had everything she wanted. Money and the latest clothes were always available, but she felt alone, abandoned.

The television show ended.

"We're going to bed now," her mother called.

Elsie Mae didn't answer. She turned off the television, scampered to the table, snatched the release form, scurried back to her room and plopped onto her bed. Lying on two big pillows, she picked up a movie magazine, ignored the release form, and escaped into her dream world. She read the stories of the stars over and over again. Images spun like cotton candy in her head. "So groovy," she whispered, poring over a feature on teen idol Tony Bennett. He reminded her of Tommy.

"If I were a star, people would adore me." She waved her luscious locks. "If only I were someone." Her eyes glazed and her thoughts roamed like clouds. Suddenly, she tossed the magazine onto the covers and grabbed a Parker pen. Pulling the release form close with a spike of inspiration, she smoothed it out in front of her and forged her mother's name. "There. No sweat. I'm going to be famous."

Chapter 6

LOVE MARATHON

At thirty-one years old, Buddy Wilson was enjoying his retirement from the professional circuit. He had visited hundreds of towns and cities as a top skater; sleeping in the men's group quarters, skating rugged games every day—and sometimes a matinee, too. He helped set up the monster track and did promotion for live bouts. Now he operated the roller derby training center at the New York Armory. He did almost everything in the makeshift office: paperwork, phone calls and the training of all levels of skaters. He was happy to be an important part of the sport he loved. He opted for short hair which complemented a round face and olive skin. Sitting on a dilapidated folding chair inside the darkened Armory, he waited to open the old backstage door.

"It's almost time. See, here it says it opens at 7:30," Buddy heard a voice say from outside the old door. He felt an excited brain buzz and smiled almost noticeably. Buddy relaxed with an unfocused gaze, letting his mind reel back some thirteen years. With a shallow sigh, he was a young skater again, like those eager beavers waiting outside. He could smell a whiff of sea air from the rickety Coney Island-style wharf that materialized in his memories. That would have been ... what ... 1936?

"Look, the sign," a young Buddy said. "Work." Banishing feelings of hopelessness, he pointed to a handwritten sign marked *Roller Marathoners Wanted*. "See, I heard they were hiring. Soon we'll be on easy street."

"I sure hope we can get in. Do they hire girls?" Gloria Wilson placed one hand on her heart. Dirty blonde hair stood tousled up high to make her look taller, like Buddy's wife—not the seventeen-year-old newlywed she really was.

"I hear it's the only place in town looking for gals." Buddy clasped one of her hands in his. He loved her milky white skin and the round beauty mark on her left cheek. He told her every single day how he adored those lavish red lips.

"I sure hope we get a break. We need the work." Buddy placed a quick kiss on Gloria's cheek. Just the other morning, they ran out of money. "I feel rotten about losing all the yard cleaning jobs I had. I never thought I'd be out of work."

"My parents had me going door to door begging for pennies." Gloria wrung out a smile as if that had been an enjoyable time. "I got so embarrassed when I turned thirteen. I tried to act young, but don't think it always worked."

"Those days are over for us." Buddy pulled her close.

"Not even President Herbert Hoover knew so many jobs would be lost. Seems like everyone is out of work."

"There's a line of people." Buddy wiggled his fingers while they waited next to the boardwalk galleries. They were closed now, circled with dirty ropes that tied down torn canvas used to hide the games inside. "The Ferris wheel's kind of old and rusty." He pointed.

The couple scooted along the unpainted boardwalk, moving a few feet at a time, edging closer to the dance hall for the audition.

"Looks like the Ferris wheel might crumble and fall apart." Gloria pulled two fingers to her lips.

Buddy put both hands in his pants pockets. "What if it kills the riders?"

"Let's not think about that. It's not like we're going to ride it."

"See, we're closer now." Buddy nodded toward the front of the line, and took three baby steps forward. "No more fretting about being an Apple Annie."

Finally inside the building, Gloria glanced around. "This used to be home to those marathon dance contests."

Roller Babes

"A rattletrap of a dance hall," Buddy remarked, nearing a man seated at a table next to a younger, red haired gal. "The place stretches over the ocean on those tall pilings that plunge deep into the sea." Buddy waved his hand like a wand, presenting the dance floor's wooden surface. The ocean currents rolled relentlessly beneath. "Hear the ocean?"

"Creepy," Gloria shuddered as the waves battered the pilings, vibrating the rickety amusement pier and sending a renewed shiver of nervousness through Buddy.

"Just a few more people to go, then us," he whispered. "Let me do most of the talking." He closed his eyes and said a small prayer to ease his worries. His goal was to take care of his wife.

"Sure, I'll be a dainty flower."

Buddy eyed the floor. He guessed it measured some seventy feet wide and two hundred feet long. Loge seats lined three sides and behind these ran circus seats nicknamed 'the peanut gallery.'

"That must be where the master of ceremonies stands." Gloria motioned to a nearby bandstand.

"They look so young." Buddy nodded at two floor judges, two nurses and a doctor at the center of the dance floor.

"They must be the same people who worked the dance contests," Gloria joked.

Buddy chuckled. "The medical people look kind of young. The doctor's about our age."

"Think it's a chizz?" Gloria asked.

"If it is, then it's a *dilly*," Buddy wiggled his fingers.

The auditioning couple directly in front of them were quickly dismissed. Buddy held his breath as the rejected couple hung their heads and exited back through the same the line where all the other hopeful applicants were waiting to enter.

"Oh, no!" Gloria whispered.

Buddy's hopes faded. He wondered why the couple hadn't made it. *Were they too old? Maybe they weren't married? Or were they married?* He began to shake. *Will the boss think my wife is not attractive enough for the show? What's the race owner looking for?* He steadied himself. *God, I hope we get this gig.*

"I'm worried," Gloria whispered under her breath.

Buddy took Gloria's hand. "Come on, smile. Let's give it our best." Buddy and his wife stood in front of the owner who looked about twenty-five years old. He wore a big suit, a gold ring and a broad-brimmed fedora. He reminded Buddy of the comic strip hero Dick Tracy.

"How old are you?" the owner thumped one forefinger on a makeshift table where he sat next to a young redhead.

"Old enough to know better." Buddy wrung the rim of his hat and clutched at his waist. He wanted to impress the owner.

The owner smirked, exhaled, pushed some papers aside and waited. Buddy's fingers wiggled. The ocean crashed against the pilings, wracking the building with creaking sounds. Another shiver jolted through Buddy.

"Well sir, we're seventeen," Buddy said with a humble yet theatrical bow.

"Married, huh?" The owner scratched his chin.

"Yes, sir."

"Can you skate?"

"Sure can."

The owner looked them over while the redhead next to him eyed Buddy up and down, drinking in his every move.

Buddy thought the owner looked equal parts carnie, car salesman and businessman. He liked him right away.

"Let me be honest," the owner said with a long sigh. He pushed a paper aside. "Hundreds of kids, the same as you, jump the blinds or make it down here to the pier."

Buddy's breathing clambered to a stop; his gaze ping-ponged between the owner and the watching woman.

"They wait in line for hours, just like you did, in need of grub and a place to sleep. They tote skates and a few changes of clothes. They have big dreams."

"We understand, sir." Buddy forced measured breaths as a sinking feeling growled in his stomach.

The owner sat back in the chair. "Most don't have talent or work skills. Some ran away from home or they lost their jobs when the Depression hit. Understand?"

Buddy and Gloria nodded their heads and clasped each other's hands even tighter. Buddy prepared himself for the letdown. They'd get no work.

"After a race or two, nearly all leave in a worse situation than when they came in." The owner caressed his forehead and covered his eyes.

Buddy's heart hammered in his chest.

"It's hard work. Still interested?" The owner looked up.

Buddy's eyes widened. He looked at Gloria's pleading gaze. He knew she hadn't eaten for over a day. "Do we get to eat and sleep here?"

"Yes. And you'll work real hard."

Gloria whispered, "Yes, Buddy. Say *yes*."

Buddy straightened his back and stood straight. "We're ready to go to work right away."

"You're not in any trouble with the cops, are you?" The owner wagged a finger.

"No, sir."

"And we don't make trouble." Gloria leaned forward to look the man right in the eyes.

The owner pulled his hat off and scratched his head. "All right." He smiled wide. "You're an attractive couple." He put his hat back on and paused to jot down their names. "You're in."

Buddy's heart jumped and Gloria exhaled.

"This is Roxie Harris." The man gestured to a gum-chewing girl with shocking red lipstick and deep black hair. "She has your registration tags. Roxie, babes, can you show the new kids their living quarters?"

"Sure." Roxie popped her gum.

"My name is Oscar Wentworth. I run the races."

"Thank you, Mr. Wentworth." Buddy was breathless and bowed deep, for real this time, no flippant attitude now. The wavering in his gut became weightless. "You won't be sorry."

"I hope not."

"From the layout of things, you must have some passion for this marathon idea." Buddy's eyes roamed around the hall and ceilings.

"It's the Depression, kid." Oscar moved another application form under his eyes.

All Buddy knew was that Gloria would finally eat.

"I'm one of the skaters, too. C'mon, follow me." Roxie swished her hips from side to side in exaggerated movements. Her adenoidal voice pricked under Buddy's skin. He and Gloria followed.

"I've been here two months now. I got dreams, see." Roxie handed them registration tags. "You put these on the right-hand side of your blouse and shirt, so the audience and judges can see your number, even though one judge's eyes are so bad he won't be able to read it. He needs glasses." Roxie chewed a mass of gum like a cow.

"Okay, sure." Buddy took two pieces of cloth with number eleven written on both.

"This a-way." Roxie cocked her head and escorted the couple behind the orchestra platform, past a tall curtain where a cavernous room loomed.

"They say the boss's family owns a skate factory in the Chicago area and this marathon's some sort of PR idea." She shrugged her shoulders.

"Brilliant idea!" Buddy said.

"Really? I don't get it." Roxie tapped a foot and inspected red fingernails. "Here it is. Your new home." She gestured with one open hand in the air.

"Oh, my." Gloria smoothed a wrinkle in her blouse.

Buddy stopped short at the sight of twenty old cots with inch-thick mattresses. Each cot had a three-foot space between, stuffed with old cloth and garments. Other contestants lounged or lay sprawled from exhaustion. There were draped sheets and improvised clotheslines hung clumsily. Some people listened to muffled wireless broadcasts. The water-stained walls sickened Buddy. Four rickety windows let muted motion-filled ocean light seep into the gloomy backstage room.

"Girls are to the left. That's where you and I sleep, hon." Roxie looked at Buddy and winked. "Some of the girls are friends." She sucked in a wad of gum between her lips with a *clack*.

"Friends?" Buddy asked.

"Sure, you know. Say, what's your name again?"

"Buddy."

"Listen, Buddy. My partner cracked an ankle two days ago, so he's gone now. He had that cot over there." She pointed. "You wouldn't wanna be my rollin' partner would you? You look like you're a strong one."

"I'm sorry to hear that about your partner, but I have a partner here." He tapped Gloria's hand, then reached an arm around her waist and pulled her close.

Roxie shot back, "You never know when one of you'll get knocked out with something and need a partner. I'll keep looking till the next grind." She eyed a few other contestants in the room. "No offense, hon," she said to Gloria.

"No offence taken," Gloria said.

Buddy inhaled the odors of stale food and mildew. The cots must have been left over from the dance marathon. So much time and neglect must have gone by that the ocean's salty air had penetrated them. "This smell of salt and mildew makes me woozy," he said.

Roxie pointed at Buddy's nose. "See what I mean? Don't get sick now, or Gloria will be looking for another man. On the right side of the room are the guys."

"But we're married," Buddy said.

"No matter. Orders from the chief. No mixing even if you're hitched." Roxie shook her head with a wicked laugh. "It won't take you long to get used to the family here."

"Okay." Buddy gazed around.

"There are some nice people, and just a few kooks."

"But how do we ..." Buddy's question lingered unfinished.

"Get together?" She crossed two fingers. "Trust me. You'll figure that out. I know all the tricks when it comes to a getting a little hooch."

Gloria cleared her throat.

"Worse than a Hooverville shantytown," Buddy remarked while noticing the blankets and clothing sagging over stopgap ropes—an attempted partition for the marathoners to give them some privacy. His mind had already worked out ways to meet up with Gloria. He inspected a shaky desk and chair that someone had tossed out with the trash, right near Gloria's cot.

"You want those?" Roxie asked.

"Thanks, that would be fine," Buddy figured Gloria could use it for applying makeup.

Gloria wrinkled her nose.

"*My* pleasure." Roxie swished back across the darkened orchestra pit toward Oscar's table. Buddy and Gloria settled into their new digs and ate in silence with a group of Oscar Wentworth's other roller racers.

Three days later, Roxie disappeared. Buddy wondered if her dreams had ended, shattered to bits like the never-ending waves that bashed against the dilapidated pilings below. His knees were weak thinking about the possibilities. She had seemed so confident, like someone who would last. Still, he remained; waiting with the other roller contestants for the race of his life.

Buddy and Gloria held hands, following the other twenty competing pairs. Music blasted from above. They raced nonstop all day long, except for a morning break.

The victorious couple in each day's big race won a small cash prize—or at least that was what the audience was told. All that skaters really rolled for was a food break.

"It's like Oscar told us." Buddy arched his back. "Most of the contestants take a beating and leave more desperate than when they arrived."

"I'm just glad the promoters have food and beds." Gloria gobbled down a half-stale beef sandwich. "We'll manage to find time for ourselves. The other married couples must have figured something out."

Buddy knew Gloria never complained about how hungry she felt, though she was practically starving. If she complained, the burden on Buddy would be too much. Everyone was suffering through these Depression years, and this was their portion of the hardship. Buddy saw his wife acting happy, skating miles and miles a week for a meager existence.

"I'm starting to take a liking to this skating," Buddy said.

"At first, I wasn't sure."

"And that fella with the long black hair almost covering his eyes," Buddy brushed aside invisible hair strands off his forehead. "When he starts to stagger and drag his feet like an old man ready for the ambulance ... it makes me laugh every time."

Life was exactly what Oscar had said. Buddy worked hard so that he and Gloria could keep their paltry job and the impoverished sleeping quarters it provided.

"The first days were hard; my dogs were barking." Buddy curled his toes.

"My feet are still swollen," Gloria said.

All day and night, the ocean pounded below. It rolled in lengthy swells that made Buddy's stomach turn. He and the other marathon skaters struggled with physical pain while humiliating themselves in front of a few dozen spectators sitting in the cheap seats. It was part of the daily grind. He swallowed any pride he had left just to survive.

"Did you hear?" Gloria asked in a quiet voice breaking into his thoughts. "Last night, Earl Miller walked to the end of the pier and shot himself in the head. The riptides swept his body out to sea."

"Poor guy."

"Gives me the heebie-jeebies."

Buddy looked at Gloria lovingly. She was nursing bleeding feet and massaging the knots out of sore calf muscles. "Don't that beat all? It's the talk of the day."

"Suicide."

Buddy rolled off to sit on the john and brush his teeth at the same time. "Not to worry. We have about two minutes."

"Earl left a note ... saying it wasn't worth it anymore. 'What's the use of it all?' Stuff like that." Gloria swallowed the last bit of cheese and washed her face in a tarnished tin water basin.

The toilet flushed. Buddy appeared in skates, buckling and zipping and skating. "I used to love the ocean, its size and salty smell." He inhaled deeply. "Now I hate it. I don't care if I ever see it again."

"I guess the note and some blood were all that was left on the pier," Gloria whispered. "His partner, Laura, is going back home to Albany."

"I wish her the best."

Gloria's tiny fingers trembled while reaching over a set of worn-out cosmetics on top of the ragged desk. "I need to put on my face."

"We've got one more minute." Buddy bent over a shard of a mirror and raced a comb through his hair.

"You'd never do that, would you?" Gloria searched Buddy's eyes.

"Of course not, babykins. After two weeks, we're doing pretty good here."

"Good." She powdered her face.

"Here." Buddy tossed a few wads of rough toilet paper onto Gloria's desk. "I stole this from the crapper." He smiled and blushed.

"Some added curves—what do you think?"

He nodded. "We don't want this thing to be a flopper."

"More of a glamour girl, huh?" Gloria divided the toilet paper, packing it into two mounds. "There." She pushed one into the left cup of her bra. She stared into the mirror and finished by tucking the other into her right. "What do you think? Quite a femme, huh?" She sat back for a moment.

Buddy howled like a coyote. "Nice tickets."

"The audience will think I skate as good as Ginger Rogers can dance," she forced a laugh.

Buddy heard the master of ceremonies pipe in *Pennies from Heaven* from the antiquated wireless receiver. The tune bellowed through an amplifier system turned up way too loud.

"Almost time." Gloria adjusted her bra and butt.

"All right, kids. How about a little spirit?" the emcee yelled to wake the small, sleepy audience. "Welcome to the nineteen thirty-six transcontinental roller marathon!" his voice screeched.

"Come on." Buddy finished a quick shave. "I found this newspaper along the pier, in a trash can. Its two days old, but I've got a new idea."

"Just a half-minute."

He watched Gloria take a pencil and scrape the last bit of the lipstick out of the cylinder, rub it onto a thin finger, and apply it to her lips. "What'll I do for tomorrow's race?" she asked. A tear appeared in the corner of her eye. She dropped the empty lipstick tube into the trash, tilted her head back and dabbed the tear dry.

"Luscious!" Buddy complimented her with an affectionate rub on her shoulders. "They're going to love you! Just the way I do." He hoped his new idea would make a little extra money tonight.

"Maybe I can use water and rouge on my lips."

Buddy kissed her. "Don't worry now. We have to do our best."

The emcee's voice echoed, thinned through metal horn speakers, "A little spirit. Look at these kids, ladies and gentlemen. Over one thousand hours and forty-one days, they're still going and going."

Buddy and Gloria rolled, listening to the amplified voice and the drone of roller skates that filled the hall, drowning out the pounding of the ocean below.

"Who will survive the monster roller marathon?" the announcer questioned.

Big red, white and purple spotlights dizzily roamed the hall and splashed against Gloria's dress.

The emcee directed the small crowd's attention to the numbers above his head. The people were noiseless as sleepy eyes watched. "The number on the left represents the number of hours elapsed in the race, and the other the number of miles the lead skaters have put on their wheels." He revved his voice like this was amazing. The small audience sat still.

"Some people are asleep," Buddy noticed.

"Just to remind everyone about the rules," the emcee said. "Each couple must always be touching one another, and never skate outside the boundary lines. If they don't touch one another, or don't stay inside the lines, they're disqualified."

The audience listened quietly, hypnotized by the droning roll of the skates, falling into a lull. Buddy whirled Gloria as the circling dance partners made everyone dizzy.

"Look how they struggle. Look how they fight. All of them exhausted. I'm calling on couple number eleven," the emcee announced. "Gloria and Buddy Wilson. I feel a spark of romance in the air, and they're in second place here at the transcontinental roller marathon!" The emcee pointed to the young couple, a purplish spotlight shone in Buddy's eyes.

"Smile," Buddy reminded Gloria with a whisper. Gloria put on a pretty face.

"That's it. They love the girls."

"Round and round they go. Who's going to win the race?" the announcer beckoned.

Buddy coached a move and pulled out a newspaper. "Look, little Gloria's carrying the load, while Buddy catches up on today's news." Another searchlight outlined the couple. "Checking today's stock quotes?" The announcer finally charmed the audience.

Someone clapped. A few pennies flew from the audience and tinkled on the floor.

"It worked!" Buddy leaned on Gloria and tucked the newspaper under his armpit. He maneuvered around others and scooped up the coins.

"How much?" Gloria asked.

"Not enough. Keep smiling."

Whenever the emcee focused on the married couple, Buddy and his young wife became animated.

"Give! Isn't that a cute pair? Give!" the emcee begged over the microphone. Then a spotlight shone on the couple again. "Come on, ladies and gentlemen, give!"

Buddy whirled Gloria in a small circle. He hugged her and she smiled toward the audience. No more coins came. The announcer and the lights swung toward another couple.

After a minute, Buddy bent over and grabbed Gloria's arms. "Rest your elbows on my back, and smile."

"And look, now Buddy's pulling Gloria. Isn't he a good hubby?"

Faces ogled. Buddy struggled to pull the two of them. They resembled a steam engine as he chugged his feet as if hauling a freight car. A few people clapped. Gloria rolled along without having to move her legs. She showed every sign of exhaustion while they kept the second-place position in the race.

Little reaction came from the crowd. Buddy's stomach sank.

"Come on, folks," the emcee beckoned. "These newlyweds need to eat tonight. Let's see if their tortured feet can make it all the way to become our first-place winner!"

The audience sat, unmoved.

"And the good news ... the little lady is expecting! Give!"

"Touch your belly," Buddy whispered to Gloria.

Gloria put two hands gently on her tummy.

Several people clapped. A few more pennies came flying out from the sparse audience, falling right under Buddy's skates.

"Quick, Gloria." Buddy, edged around and scooped up the coins. He counted to himself as his heart raced. The big lights roamed to other couples.

"More pennies," Gloria whispered and she snatched a few.

"Don't miss any."

"Here." Gloria handed Buddy four pennies. "Did we make it?"

Buddy felt his face flush. *Just one more penny.*

"What next?"

"I've got it!" Buddy's stomach froze. He inhaled and lifted Gloria off her skates, holding her high in his arms. "Lay your head on my shoulder and rest." His legs wobbled with her weight as he puffed and pushed his muscles to the limit.

A single penny clinked to the floor.

Buddy's eyes widened in amazement. "We did it! It's the cat's pajamas," he huffed. "We can get you some new lipstick." He lowered Gloria onto her skates, and with their hands still clasped together, he scooped the penny off the floor. Buddy stuffed the coins into his pocket, proud to be able to get his wife a small gift she needed so badly. "Sell it!"

Gloria raised a dainty hand toward the watchers of the race. The beacon of light found her. She patted her belly with one hand and waved with the other. Buddy smiled and wiggled his fingers.

"And the little lady says 'Thank you!'" the announcer blared.

Someone clapped.

Gloria whispered to Buddy. "If there's any money left, can we get an ice cream?"

"Of course, babykins." Buddy bowed as the colored beacons went dim, receding back into a fading memory.

Buddy had a million fond memories of those early races, but today, he lowered his head as the memories bleached away. The swells of the ocean rolled one last wave against the pilings. Foam splashed, bubbled and dissolved. Buddy's dream state broke into fragments. The loud droning of skate wheels speeding against the dance floor softened and disappeared. The sights and sounds of the roller marathon vanished from his mind. He blinked, chuckled to himself and rubbed his eyes.

Buddy raised both eyebrows and wiggled his fingers, realizing the time had come to let in the new trainees. He pushed himself up from the chair and opened the backstage door, oblivious to the scratching sound it made on the cement floor. "Time to train new skaters," he mumbled.

Chapter 7

THE ARMORY HEEBIE-JEEBIES

Lottie nudged Elsie Mae and marveled at the immense building, wondering what was going to happen once they were inside. The dark bricks and turreted rooftop reminded her of a fortress. The little hairs stiffened on the back of her neck. The friends joined a line of other skaters, all casually standing with skate bags and cases at the Armory's stage door. "Our first practice. I'm getting scared."

"I feel sort of wacky." Elsie Mae tightened her shoulders.

"I didn't expect this. It's like Fort Knox." Rebecca shuddered.

Would its thick walls protect Lottie from what lay ahead? A wave of dizziness flooded her brain. Waiting in line, each moment brought another nagging question. *What if I fall on my face? Did I make the right decision to do this roller derby?*

"This sounded like a boss idea when we were on the roof," Rebecca bit her lip. "So many other people, making me feel out of place."

"I hope I do okay." Lottie's anxiety bubbled up from within.

"Couldn't do any worse than the spills you took at the roller rink," Elsie Mae laughed.

"Very funny. After school, I worked at Mason's Diner. I'm tired, but I hope I do better at this than I did at speed skating." Lottie dragged a hand through chopped brownish-blonde hair.

"Hello, Joe, whaddaya know?" Tommy greeted two school buddies standing in the front of the line. Lottie watched them turn and glance back.

"What's buzzin', cousin?" one boy asked Tommy while looking Elsie Mae up and down. His eyes searched every curve. Elsie Mae returned their leers with a wink and a hand on her hip. Tommy's buddies chortled and slapped one another on the shoulders.

Suddenly, Lottie felt Tommy's friends looking in her direction. She quickly turned away. It sent a rush of numbness through her, and she felt invisible.

"There's more people makin' the scene here than I expected," said Elsie Mae as she moved closer to Tommy.

Lottie studied the line of skaters while dusk ate slowly away at the blue sky. "Competition. I'm going to give it my all, you know—skate flat out."

Just then, a light above the battered door cast a faint glow, constricting Lottie's pupils.

Tommy took out his comb and smoothed back his hair. "I hope some of these skaters are dead hoofers."

Rebecca hunched forward, buried her nose in a book and kept a few feet between her and everyone else.

"How can you read in this light?" Lottie asked.

"Why don't you mind your own business?"

"Okay. Don't get evil on me." Lottie felt a chill and shook her head. She understood why Rebecca found books interesting. Lottie wrung her hands and realized that Tommy's never-ending stares at Elsie Mae with his big brown eyes bugged her. And now Rebecca was turning snippy.

"I wonder what the training will be like," Elsie Mae piped up.

"Skate our butts off." Lottie slapped Elsie Mae's backside.

"Do you think there'll be a motion-picture producer in there?" Elsie Mae poked her head sideways, scanning down the line of people as if she could recognize a producer among the skaters.

"I hope not yet," Lottie said. "Not the way I skate."

"If there is, he's going to spy you right away." Tommy nestled his shoulder against Elsie Mae's. "I heard that Beverly Tyler and Pat O'Brien are in that new motion picture with Mickey Rooney."

"Kooky keen!" Elsie Mae fake swooned. "I can't wait till I'm a star."

Even in the cold air, Lottie's hands were sweaty. All four waited. Lottie still hurt, with skid marks on her butt and knees. A blister on her foot from the roller rink's speed club practices shot pain from the bottom of her foot all the way up her leg.

The only colored girl in the line pulled back her jet-black hair to form a perfect ponytail. She had a solid athlete's body. She turned to look at Lottie. The girl smiled, showing delicate dimples. Lottie sensed real friendliness, and smiled back. *One friendly face,* she thought.

A dull thud came from inside; someone was at the door. Lottie's spine went rigid as the door's shoving sound—metal scratching on cement—scared her. "They're open," she said as her breath caught in her chest.

The group filed in one by one. Rebecca pulled at the shoulder of her sweater. "I don't know about this." A line of sweat formed along her upper lip. Rebecca looked like she wanted to turn and cut out.

Lottie tugged Rebecca's arm. She wanted to say something reassuring. Instead, she blurted out, "Ain't no turning back now."

"I'm not sure I want to." Rebecca stiffened straight up like an icicle.

"You can't drift," Elsie Mae reminded her.

Lottie withered. Aside from the colored girl, she felt out of place. "I might want out, too."

"Don't agitate to the gravel," Tommy frowned.

"Sure, don't be cubes. This'll be a big tickle," Elsie Mae plastered on a closed-lipped smile.

Lottie recalled the veins that pulsed in her father's temples. She pulled her shaky nerves together. She took a deep breath and nodded her head toward the door. "Okay. We're right here with you. All together. I can do this."

"Okay, okay," Rebecca said with a wheeze. "I'm with you, Empress Lottie."

"Comrades." Elsie Mae saluted.

Lottie, feeling like a steer in a herd of cattle headed for slaughter, followed the others through the old door: young guys and gals from all the boroughs, all sorts and sizes. Rebecca followed. Just inside, Lottie noticed a folding chair and a telephone. The items seemed out of place and she wondered why they were there. She peered down the darkened hallway, catching a glimpse of the skating track. The sight twisted her gut.

"Now I'm really feelin' creepy, Rebecca."

"I know. I see it." Rebecca put two wobbly fingers on her lower lip.

"Underage skaters, give me your releases and then follow this corridor to the arena," Buddy yelled to everyone, pointing the way.

"I'm cranked, you know? Going ape!" Elsie Mae said.

"You'll be the best!" Tommy held her hand.

Lottie's stomach tensed. "We'll all be great."

"How ya doing, pipsqueak?" Buddy winked as he took Lottie's paperwork.

Lottie looked behind her, then realized he was talking to her. "Me?"

"Yes, you," Buddy winked.

Lottie bit the inside of her cheek and nodded. Then she followed the others through the dank, low-ceilinged walkways beneath raised bleachers that wrapped along the paths made for the cleaning crews.

"Cast your eyes on that." Tommy pointed to the walls of the corridor where paying audiences walked through to get to their seats.

Lottie squinted at the large-framed pictures hung there. She recognized different sports stars; the hornets in her chest hummed harder.

"Wonder if our pictures will be up there one day?" Elsie Mae asked.

Lottie shivered. "I'm standing where so many famous people have performed." She thought she'd never measure up. The buzzing in her stomach wrung into overdrive. And then ... *whoa*! She shrank like an insignificant speck underneath the dizzying rafters of the arena's roof. Four pigeons fluttered and rested on the large, domed light fixtures. Lottie focused, and watched a white one chirp out a cooing sound. With wings spread, the bird raised itself from its perch and circled the entire ceiling. Lottie took a slight step back with a surge of new energy.

Chapter 8

WILD HORNET'S SWIRL

A growling rumbled from the back of the building, it worried Lottie. Big furnaces were burning, sending unnecessarily warm air through the colossal space. It made her mouth dry and body swelter. She stared up at the ceiling. The pigeons were gone. Six oversized bulbs hung between the rafters and catwalks. The lights threw scattered rays across the banked racetrack. Everything looked gray and shadowy.

"It's giving me goosebumps." Lottie trembled. She tasted the faint odor of a million different shows and circuses; the scent of stale popcorn still lingered.

"Look how far out and up the seats go." Elsie Mae pointed, counting the rows. "Miles of seats, filling all four sides of the arena."

Lottie noticed the seats rippling down toward the center, looking like a hundred stair steps. "Too many."

"How many people will this place hold?" Elsie Mae asked.

"Thousands." Tommy's eyes twinkled.

Rebecca fidgeted. "They'll all watch us fall over ourselves on that track."

A chill ran through Lottie, as if dead athletes were haunting the timeworn seats and rafters. She sensed there were spirits keeping guard over sacred territory. "I wonder if there are ghosts."

"Don't give me the willies!" Rebecca pulled her arms around her chest. The group's footsteps echoed through the empty arena.

"What did we get into?" Lottie asked, as prickles ran up her arms.

"You're making me crazy!" Rebecca hunched down and crashed a shoulder into her friend.

"Don't be a pill. Look at that track," Elsie Mae stared bug-eyed at the alluring track. It loomed before them like a majestic dragon. Lottie counted six benches and two massage tables in the center of the angled oval. On the other side, another straightaway started a few feet off the floor, then twisted upwards, forming another monster bank.

"It really kills!" Elsie Mae dropped her mouth wide.

"I'm not sure I can do this." Rebecca leaned close to Lottie's shoulder. "I feel like a misfit again. Those banks are nothing like the roller rink."

"I can do it." Tommy hooked one thumb into a belt loop and thrust his pelvis forward. "I'll be on cloud nine."

"It's so crazy-keen." Elsie Mae lifted her heels and teetered on her toes. "I just hope I don't get blisters on my feet."

Lottie edged toward the high part of the track. Her breathing constricted. "It's way taller than me—way bigger than it looks on television." A corkscrew turned in her stomach.

"Looks dangerous," Rebecca whispered, shrinking back from the others.

"How *does* anyone skate on this thing?" Lottie frowned.

The man walked in front of them. "Welcome to roller derby training. I'm Buddy Wilson, your coach and trainer." He gestured toward the track. "The banked track is one hundred and fifteen feet long and sixty feet wide. The highest banks are at forty-five degrees."

"High enough to break our necks," Rebecca muttered.

"You might break your neck, or any other bone," Buddy responded without anger. "But for sure, you'll rub raw the skin off the bottom of your feet." Buddy guided the group to the front rows of empty seats where they could take in the entirety of the track. "Take a seat everyone; change into your skates. If it's your first time, you're in the beginners' class. Whether you're a guy or a gal, all beginners skate together."

"Oh, good." Lottie liked that idea.

"I'm not so keen on that," said Rebecca.

"Don't worry, we ain't gonna bite you," Tommy giggled.

Buddy stopped the small talk. "This is going to be easy compared to when I began. You'll alternate an hour with the other group. When I skated, we would go nonstop for hours."

Lottie swallowed as they took their shoes off and put skates on. The small sounds of shoes being set aside and laces being tied became a cacophony in the still air.

"I want you all to know, this isn't for everyone. Some won't make it. It takes determination to be a roller derby skater." Buddy paused with a deep inhalation. "Let's see if you have the drive! Beginners first—warm up."

Lottie's dream began to shatter like a broken coffee cup. *What if I don't have what it takes? What if I just slide down that steep bank?* She needed to be good at this. Looking around at all the people, she doubted she'd be one of the fortunate ones. She dug deep to urge the competitive drive from within; forcing the memory of that homerun to sharpen and be a mental guide.

"You've got just ten minutes to get your skates on. Get up there before the first exercise. Beginners, take it slow, and be ready to work hard."

Buddy's face reminded Lottie of her father's, but without the anger lines or clenched jaw. She shook the crazy idea from her head.

Buddy clapped his hands. "Hurry up!"

Lottie didn't recognize any of the skaters. They dressed in loose clothing and busied themselves with preparation routines—nothing like the constant excitement of television.

"Hurry up, Lottie," Rebecca said. "You heard Mr. Wilson." She had her skates on and was standing up, ready to march toward the big track.

"Come on, beginners, let's go!" Buddy called out.

After tightening her laces with shaking hands, Lottie glanced at the other skaters. They rolled awkwardly around the big track. Each skater's unsteady movements made a low rumbling sound that reverberated throughout the Armory. Skates pounding on the wooden surface made it difficult to hear normal voices. The skaters glided and stretched their legs; up on the track, each person appeared larger than life. Lottie noticed that the guys looked bigger and faster than the group of girls. *Maybe,* she thought, *my father was right. Maybe this isn't something for girls.*

Rebecca made it to the track and rolled shakily for one lap. She wheeled into the infield. "It's steep!" She waved at Lottie, encouraging her onto the track. "Come on! Don't be a chump!"

"Let's get out there!" Buddy yelled directly at Lottie, waking her out of the daze. She stood, tossing her sweater onto a seat, and clump-walked toward the entrance of the track.

"I can do this," Lottie said to herself. Holding the guardrail tight, she positioned her left skate and then the right. Her hands let go. "Just like stickball." With her weight full on the skates, the wheels unexpectedly turned down the bank. Her skates sped toward the center floor. She rolled with jerky movements, flailing her hands as if a bumblebee just landed on her right elbow and shoulder. She tumbled over and hit an infield bench with the middle of her back, landing on the floor with a wince. "Ouch! That hurts."

Rebecca laughed. "Told you it's steep."

"You'll get it!" Elsie Mae waved Lottie on.

"Warm up's over. Let's go! Let's go! Fall in!" Buddy hollered. He waved his left hand up high to get everyone's attention. He gestured for the skaters to form a line behind him. "Time to learn the five-stride!"

Blood rushed through Lottie's head. She pulled herself up onto her skates, ignored the others' rolled eyes and coasted toward the banks. From the ovals inside, she tried to skate up the bank toward the guardrails. She felt like she was struggling up a steep hill. Halfway up, gravity pulled her back. She reeled, splattering butt-first directly into the infield again. Scooting backward like a fish out of water, she tripped over the same bench from her earlier fall. She repeated her painful wince. "I can't believe I did it again."

"Come on!" Buddy said encouragingly. He watched. Lottie awkwardly stood again. "Get into the pace." Buddy's gaze gave her a comfortable feeling, unlike the looks the other men and boys gave her. She shook it off, frowned in concentration and regained control of her wobbling skates.

"Come on, Lottie. Floor it!" Elsie Mae thumbed-up as she rolled clumsily past, following the pace line as best she could.

"Get the lead out," Rebecca said.

"I know now. I'm such a mutt-head." Lottie smacked her forehead and studied the situation. Her chest pounded; a plan etched itself in her mind. She built up speed inside the flat center to give her the momentum needed to roll up the banks. "I've got it," she huffed through clinched teeth. Pushing along on the floor, she edged one skate onto the track at the lowest bank, then bumbled and clumped up to the guardrail. "Phew!" She wiped her brow.

The skaters whooshed past her. They rolled in a long pace line, attempting to coordinate a rhythm. As they passed by, a gust of air brushed against Lottie's face. They skated faster, working as a unit. Tommy and Elsie Mae rolled along in the middle and looked sheepishly at Lottie. Rebecca skated at the end of the line.

Faces burned red with heat and concentration. Each skater focused upon the skater directly in front of them, copying every stride, with Buddy in the lead.

Lottie's skates squeaked. She staggered and picked up speed. The end-of-the-line of skaters passed her by. *If I can get behind the last skater, the wind will get me into the groove.* She fell in behind Rebecca, but her lumbering movements couldn't catch up with the others. The line glided away while she stumbled, unable to gain any speed.

Lottie's feet twisted up again. "HEEEYYYYY, get outta my way!" Her face contorted into a snarl as she crashed to the hard track floor. She spun awkwardly before skidding headfirst down the steep bank, hitting the infield once again. "Ouch!" She felt the skaters' stares and giggles. She was a bumbling failure. Half her body lay on the track, her wheels spinning and pointing toward the guardrails. Her head, face up, dangled over the edge, onto the infield floor.

Buddy smiled sympathetically.

Lottie felt pain in her jaw and rubbed the back of her neck. She eased her head back and up as the line of skaters clipped along faster than anyone she'd ever seen. How could people go that fast on skates? The sight made her angry. "Darn it, I'm really a louse at this." She grunted and hauled herself upright. "I ain't going to get it." Yet she redoubled her effort, focusing so she could learn to skate on these damned banks. The marathon pace lasted thirty minutes, and Lottie fell another ten times. Her body was as banged up as if she had been tumbled inside a cement mixer. She had knots from the falls and sore muscles from the stress of staying atop the inclined track. Brain-dead and unworthy, she felt her body aching with pain.

After the first beginners' pace, the advanced group took over to practice breakaways and blocking. Lottie didn't notice; she sat, exhausted from the first go-around.

Time zoomed along with doubtful thoughts inside Lottie's brain. Was this a train wreck? "Beginners, second workout!" Buddy yelled.

Lottie's heart pumped. She didn't want to humiliate herself again, or see her dad's angry face. Determined to show him she could do it, she forced herself onto the track once more. The training ended with more struggling and falling.

"All right, that's it for tonight," Buddy said after he blew his whistle.

Slumping in a front row seat, Lottie caught her breath and bent over to unlace her skates. Thinking of her terrible job at Mason's Diner and her piss-poor school grades, she pushed down a choking cry. They were bad, but maybe this was the wrong thing for her, too. She looked at a blood-soaked sock. The blister from speed skating at the roller rink had been replaced with a new one. It hurt, like everything else in her life. Sobs waited just beneath the pain. She kept quiet.

"What's your name?" Buddy asked, sitting down beside her.

"Lottie," she managed to answer without crying. She watched the older man eyeing her wrinkled, baggy pants where they sagged, four sizes too large. She knew she looked like a rawboned sack of potatoes in a crumpled paper bag.

"Your moves on the track remind me of someone," Buddy said, smiling. "You could be in the Sunday funny papers." He laughed with the gentleness of an older man.

Lottie's stomach clenched. She looked left and right nervously. She felt like a freak, sensing every eye spying down upon her.

"You looney, huh?" Buddy gave a friendly nod. "I'm going to call you the Little Lunatic."

Her chest fell. She was a spazzed-out freak and a lunatic on the track to boot. She would never become a pro skater. She was a half-portion.

"The Little Lunatic," Rebecca said with a laugh.

"Yes, the Little Lunatic," Buddy repeated. "Keep on training. You're required to learn to stay on your skates." He left.

"Really?" Lottie stiffened her posture.

"Lunatic," Rebecca said. "I think he approves of you!"

Lottie laughed lightly. "I guess he thinks I should be in the booby hatch." Her nose crinkled.

"Naw. Really! He likes you," Rebecca said.

Lottie thought for a moment. "I suppose it's not all that crummy a nickname."

Tommy put his skates inside a case. "That was some workout. I've never skated so hard before."

"My calves are killing me," Elsie Mae said.

Tommy reached over to massage her shins.

"I'm so beat," Rebecca said. "Like someone whipped the tar outta me."

Lottie pushed herself upright with one hand on her aching back. She felt her eyes well up with tears. The dream of a life in sports had died. She grimaced and ignored the pain.

"More fun than all get-out," she suddenly exclaimed. "Like makin' lemonade. Let's come back tomorrow!" Some spark inside set aside embarrassment and defeat, determined to get on a team and see the world. If she didn't act on this now, she'd never have another chance.

The sound of feathers ruffling woke Lottie that night. The pigeon was visiting like a silver ghost. Locked inside a small wire cage, the bird sat motionless except to take shallow gulps of air. Lottie barely saw its chest expand and slowly contract. She held back a scream. Unable to stretch its wings, the bird's hollow eyes could only stare from within its wire jail. Lottie gulped down breaths to keep quiet while the pigeon's jail-keeper, a man with a white face dressed all in black, ogled the bird. Coarse lines etched themselves deep into his face.

Chapter 9

AN ACCIDENT EVERY NIGHT

Peering out the dirty window of the Armory's back door, Buddy recognized the new girl, Lottie. She had stuck with training for several months now. Lottie always stirred memories within him. It wasn't her looks, but tiny waist and determined spirit that reminded him of Gloria.

He recalled one night at the marathon. Gloria had never looked so beautiful. His eyes began to prickle with tears, so he closed them. On that unforgettable evening, his roller-racing career had taken a dramatic turn. The memory and sounds of the ocean seethed into his mind. The waves grew louder, and he could hear them crash into the pilings beneath the amusement pier. Oscar Wentworth was in front of him again.

The tall boss man called out, "Okay, kids. Gather around." Oscar towered over the backstage clutter of scattered cots and canvas walls that created cubicles for the marathoners.

Gloria had just washed their clothes in a dirty sink. She pushed the drying underwear aside on the makeshift clothesline so she and Buddy could watch and listen.

Oscar stood still with his hands folded in front of his hips. He thought for a moment. "We're in some desperate times."

Buddy felt surprised to see Oscar decked out in a wrinkled suit that hadn't been cleaned for weeks. "This don't sound so good. Oscar's been working day and night."

"I heard a rumor we're shutting down," one of skaters called out.

"I hope not." Gloria gave Buddy a worried look. "This is where we eat and sleep. It's our home. What'll we do?"

The hopeless sound in her voice wrenched Buddy; a sense of fatigue came over him. He knew there were no other jobs for them and he loved his wife too much to see her suffer. The roller races were now all he knew. Most of the skaters had become family.

"Don't worry, babykins." He put an arm around her and hugged her close. "Let's do what Mr. Wentworth says. I'm sure everything'll work out."

"Listen up, kids." Oscar motioned for the troupe's attention. "Don't none of you get discouraged because people ain't coming to the races. Most days, there's more skaters here than people in the audience. But it takes time to get these things going." He inhaled deeply. A solemnity drew across his eyes. "So we've decided to start a little novelty that'll jam-pack them in."

Buddy gave Gloria a love nudge with his elbow. "That's what we need. I hope he's right."

"Even if he ain't, we've got to do what the boss says."

Oscar stretched his arms open, held out his big workman's hands and flashed his teeth. His face brightened. "We've got to jazz things up a bit if we're going to make some dough."

"Sure do!" the skater next to Gloria stood up.

Oscar directed a fond look at Gloria and Buddy. "Now here's what we're going to do." He leaned forward.

Everyone scooted toward him.

"Near suppertime, a minute or so before the end of the two-hour period, there'll be an accident."

"An accident?" Gloria questioned.

Skaters murmured.

Oscar smiled, looking slowly from left to right, making eye contact with everyone. Even those smoking cigarettes stopped in mid-breath to listen. "We're going to take 'em on the ride of their lives. This is just within the derby family, you hear?"

Buddy couldn't wait to hear Oscar's plan. "Of course, boss." Skaters nodded and leaned closer.

Oscar raised an index finger in the air. "No one's going to get hurt, see? Copasetic!" Oscar moved the raised finger and pressed it to lips with a shush sound. "But one couple will 'accidentally' trip the team that's in the lead." He paused, and slowly, a smile of hidden knowledge formed on his lips. "Get what I mean?"

The skaters looked around at one another. A few laughed and nodded. "Oh yeah! I get it!" Buddy raised his head, acknowledging his complicity in this new and devious plan.

"You'll need to sell it. Make 'em feel it!" Oscar pumped a fist against his chest.

"I know what we can do." Buddy placed his attention on Gloria's fake pregnancy and tapped the tummy-stuffed area lovingly. "Babykins, understand? You're going to take the fall and act hurt. The crowd will sympathize and start rooting for you."

Oscar wagged his finger in a small circle. "That's right! I guarantee that this'll bring in the crowds! When they think they're going to see blood and gore, there'll be no stopping us! And you kids will be the winners, because the crowds will get bigger. And when the Hollywood and Broadway bunch start to come in the doors, we'll have 'em packed to the rafters." Oscar leaned back on his heels.

Skaters exhaled a collective *ahhh*. They smiled with delight. Buddy looked around the moldy room, noticing people nodding at one another as couples embraced.

"It'll take a little showmanship," Oscar warned. "Those with ability can become big stars." His grin sagged and he pointed as if scolding each individual one at a time. "And, keep this under your hats. Each and every one of you! All right?"

Everyone nodded. Gloria zipped her lips.

"Then let's go, kids!" Oscar eyed his troupe as they gathered themselves for the race. Buddy's adrenaline spiked. The skaters trickled out of the living area in groups of two and entered the sparsely attended hall. Large searchlights shone on each couple when they appeared.

"It looks like only twenty or thirty people," Gloria said. "This whole thing might be hopeless."

Roller Babes

"Empty as a dead library." Buddy took his wife's hand. "Oscar knows what he's doing."

The emcee played the song *Pick Yourself Up* from the radio through a cheap tinny sound system. The contestants stilled, poised to start.

"Hi, Buddy and Gloria," called out a wrinkle-faced woman with dark-rimmed glasses. She waved a dirty hankie from her position in the peanut gallery, frantically trying to get the couple's attention.

"Look, she's still here." Buddy waved nicely back. "What a character."

"She must be seventy years old." Gloria leaned closer to Buddy. "She's been in that same seat for three days now." Gloria waved and smiled at the woman.

For Buddy, it felt like having a family member trackside, cheering them on. He waved again, adding a blown kiss. The old lady unfolded the dilapidated plaid blanket she brought along each night. She sat up straight and kept rheumy eyes on her favorite skaters.

Buddy and Gloria positioned themselves at the starting line along with the other couples. The ocean surging beneath the creaking pier was the only sound to be heard throughout the mostly-empty dance hall.

"Yowza, *yowza*, **yowza**," the emcee suddenly called and the arena walls trembled. The siren sounded, causing Buddy's heart to jump. "Let's go," Buddy yelled.

Inside the antiquated wooden structure, wheels rumbled to life. In no time, the roller race thrummed into existence, filling the hall with the sounds of the marathon for life.

Buddy and Gloria alternated between first and second place with another couple throughout the day, while the emcee addressed the audience.

"Let's see some spirit!" came the calls. The small audience sat on their hands, unmoved. Like the dilapidated building, the onlookers were dead.

"I see couple number eighteen from Jersey City," the emcee said. "And look! There's couple number six, all the way from Dixon, Illinois."

The audience was silent.

"It's *the* race of destiny. Where will it stop? How will it end?" His voice book-echoed back and forth and around and around.

After hours of nonstop racing, the older, unemployed men were replaced by a few new teenagers on the bleachers. Buddy and Gloria heard the emcee say, "It's late in the day, and Buddy and Gloria Wilson, number eleven, are still in first place. Good going, kids. Wait! Wait! Just a minute."

"I think this is it," Buddy whispered.

"I'm ready."

"It looks like they're about to be passed!" shouted the voice.

A few people in the audience turned their attention to the leading pair while spotlights swung toward Buddy.

Buddy felt the heat of the lights on his face. "It's almost time."

Just then, there were sounds of roller skates clomping on the dance floor. The crowd looked. The second place couple came speeding forward, then tried to break. "No!" someone shouted. The sound of clattering skates pierced the air and the second place couple careened into Buddy and Gloria.

"Look out!" Buddy yelled. His screams came too late; the couple crashed directly into little Gloria.

"And—*wait*—it looks like there's been an accident out there!" the emcee yelled into the microphone. Skaters wobbled, screeching to a halt.

Just then, Gloria's hand left Buddy's; she fell and slid painfully along the floor, worn smooth by millions of wheels. She landed half on her belly. She wheezed and went limp, appearing unconscious.

"Gloria!" Buddy screamed, reaching out too late with his empty hand. Every eye in the place stayed with couple number eleven. The floor judge blew his whistle.

"Oh, no!" Buddy and Gloria's favorite fan shouted.

Buddy swiveled in unbalanced circles. He pointed a finger at the couple that had crashed into his Gloria. With an exaggerated frown, he yelled, "Hey! What's wrong with you? You trying to kill us?" A vein on the side of his head pulsed.

The patrons stood and gasped in hushed, worried voices.

"It doesn't look good," the announcer said.

The old woman held both hands to her cheeks. Buddy could see tears welling up in her eyes. "Oh, my God." He saw her mouth whisper and tremble.

Buddy raised a fist. The hall went still as everyone gawked. The smashing waves sounded louder in the deadness of the rink. Gloria lay sprawled out on the floor, motionless. Seconds passed like minutes.

"Now, now, don't worry, ladies and gentlemen. I'm sure everything's going to be okay," the emcee promised.

Buddy regained control of his skates and his rage. He whirred to Gloria's side while the offending couple took the first place lead on the rink and the leader board.

"Couple number eleven, Buddy and Gloria Wilson, have lost their lead!" the emcee shouted. "And couple number nine are the new lead skaters."

The crowd booed, disgusted with the new lead couple. Paper cups were tossed onto the race floor. "Cheats!" the onlookers yelled.

"Gloria, you okay?" Buddy shouted, leaning over his fallen wife. His drawn face showed exaggerated, deep fear.

The audience looked on while Buddy hovered lovingly over his hurt wife. An official-looking doctor in a white coat bent over Gloria, waving smelling salts beneath her nose. A nurse came running to massage Gloria's legs and ease her skates off.

"My God! Is she okay?" someone screamed.

Rocking her head groggily from left to right, Gloria finally opened her eyes. She pointed at Buddy, who bent over her. Gloria raised a limp hand to her forehead, as if barely able to comprehend what had happened.

"Gloria, Gloria!" Buddy used a single hand to brush a stray hair from her forehead and gently kissed the spot.

Gloria's pained face angled itself toward the peanut gallery, and she used both hands to grasp her belly.

"Just goes to show you, there's action every minute here at the transcontinental roller marathon." The emcee's voice lost its false concern and resumed its professional tone.

The little old lady with the blanket cried and removed big glasses to wipe tears off while the rest of the audience watched sympathetically.

"It looks like everything is okay, after all. Give! Give!" the emcee bellowed. "To couple number eleven. Mrs. Wilson is with child!" The crowd let out a moan. "Give!" the emcee begged.

The little old lady patted her tears dry with the dirty hankie. With a shaking hand, she pulled out a tattered change purse. She dug out a penny and looked at it. She wiped another tear, dropped the penny back, and found a shiny nickel. With trembling fingers, she tossed the coin from the peanut gallery to the floor next to her beloved couple.

"Let's hope the little one's okay." The emcee's voice cut through the mayhem.

"A nickel!" Buddy whispered and grabbed it. He put it against his chest, then kissed it and motioned his hand towards his favorite fan.

The little old lady threw a kiss back. Gloria gently held the pillow beneath her jersey with both hands, making the couple instant stars.

Buddy helped the doctor haul Gloria by the arms and drag her to the dressing and sleeping area. He felt the crowd's rush of sympathy go out to him and Gloria. Three more pennies clinked onto the floor.

"It looks like couple number eleven are out of the race. Gloria's being taken to the dressing area for medical attention," came the official-sounding announcement.

Groans of anguish came from the crowd, and one last penny trickled onto the worn out dance floor.

"Yowza, yowza. *Give!*" the emcee's muffled voice rattled inside Buddy's brain while the nurse followed the injured procession, picking up the pennies. Backstage, the couple rested on their cots, relieved to have a break from the skating. Gloria's face glowed. She and Buddy burst into giggles that turned to full-throated laughter.

The nurse handed Buddy four pennies.

"You did good!" Buddy eagerly counted the pennies. "And a nickel!"

"I thought our favorite fan in the peanut gallery was going to faint!" Gloria said.

"Maybe this'll get more people to the races, like Oscar said."

"A lollapalooza!"

The siren blew out on the racetrack, signaling the end of the grind; the contestants rushed for the dressing and living areas.

The size of the audience doubled the next day. Buddy treated the new visitors to another accident between the skating couples. The crowds grew day by day, race by race. Buddy remembered the different ways he and the other marathon couples invented accidental collisions into one another. He had kept the audiences charged up with grudges and retaliation. One night, the designated offending couple crashed into Buddy and Gloria. Buddy jabbed out his elbow and sent a body blow into the other man. It looked to the fans like his elbow had put the man's eye out. The spectators loved it. They stood, cheered and yelled. Never had Buddy seen such a reaction. He learned what sold tickets.

Within a month Oscar announced, "I've authorized building a big-banked track. It'll be portable, and I'm changing the game to something called the *Roller Derby*."

"That's the name of your family skate business in Chicago," someone said.

"Ingenious!" Buddy said.

"The track has some *give* to it, so you won't get so banged up when you fall," Oscar explained. "We'll separate the men from the women, and alternate twelve-minute races. Men against men, and women against women. A playwright friend and I invented rules, so the audiences will have something to read at the games."

Buddy knew that his elbow block had inspired Oscar's body contact races. He and Gloria found themselves stars at the banked-track events.

Buddy's marathon of memories began to freeze and fade. He had lost track of time. The Armory's back door needed to be opened for today's hopefuls who were waiting for the night's training. His recollections gave way to the current day. When he opened the back door, he thought, *Lottie will come walking in.*

She was the small and awkward girl who'd improved over the many training sessions. *She's determined,* he thought. Her skating was at the point where she could stay in the pace line all night long, graduating into the advanced class. It wasn't her natural skating talent, but the core of grittiness and determination that was making her into a good skater. His heart was cheering for her to make it.

Buddy tossed aside the board that acted as an added brace and screeched the back door open to the waiting faces. Eyes widened. Wide, smiling grins appeared. It was time to teach new skaters about the roller derby.

Chapter 10

CAROLINE AND JC

Lottie's legs ached as she stuffed swollen feet into her old skates. Exhausted after the night's two-hour pace, she flopped a wrecked body into a front row seat, yards from the big track. Buddy walked past and smiled; the pleasant feeling from that helped to dull the pain just a little.

Rebecca collapsed into the seat next to Lottie. "I don't think I can take much more of this. Some of the fellas are so much stronger."

"But they don't have much finesse," Lottie said. "And I can tell by how everyone looks, we're all getting stronger, in shape. All of us except for the dozen skaters who've dropped out over the months."

"You've always been as good as the boys. And Elsie Mae over there has her boy, Tommy, to help her. I'm all alone."

"You've got me. You'll always have me." Lottie gazed into Rebecca's sad eyes. "Besides, I'm having trouble keeping up with my homework. I hope I don't flunk out," she said. "But I need this roller derby job more than ever."

"You're getting behind the grind?" Elsie Mae smirked and plopped down next to the two.

"I can't keep doing all this for much longer." Lottie sat back. "I wonder how good my grades have to be to get into this sport."

"I'm keeping my grades up," Rebecca said. "It's our last year. Lottie, I can help you out with homework if you give me a little help with skating."

"I can spare about an hour a night," Lottie said.

"Lottie, you have to keep trying. I'll keep going if you do."

"I'll try. Between skating, Mason's and school; sometimes I feel like I'm falling apart."

"Don't curve out. Without a little help from Tommy, I'd have nothing." A solemn expression came across Elsie Mae's eyes.

"Stay earthbound. Your dad won't like it if you drop out of school," Rebecca said.

Lottie knew Rebecca was right. The work and harried schedule was brutal, but she promised herself to skate and work hard. She needed to keep things smooth with Dad. She'd stick it out with Elsie Mae and Rebecca.

Elsie Mae patted her hair into place. "I might not need school if I become a star. Or what if I get married?"

"I can't worry about that," Lottie said. "I'm bad news, there ain't one guy who ever took a second look at me."

"Maybe you like girls," Elsie Mae laughed.

Lottie frowned. "I'm killing myself to learn to be a skater. It's the toughest thing I've ever done."

"Anyone have any new stories?" Tommy asked. The four of them looked around at each other.

"See that couple one, two, three rows down?" Elsie Mae pointed. "She's always with that boy with the small nose and greasy black hair. Those two." Elsie Mae motioned at the boy and the pretty girl. "They're the cutest couple here. That's the best, see?"

"Don't point," Rebecca scolded. "Besides, he's got a cute face but his body looks like a grungy laborer with a farmer's tan. You know, only his arms and face are tan. I bet the rest of him is sheet-white."

Lottie sat up. "They might be lovers." She felt a touch of envy.

"Big deal," Rebecca said.

"Okay, here's the baked wind. Listen to what I heard," Elsie Mae said. "They actually owned a sandwich shop and needed to close it down. You know, they couldn't pay the bills? One day, the place was set on fire. They say *he* started the fire to collect on the insurance money. A week later, both of 'em showed up here."

"Arson?" Rebecca asked. "That sounds like trouble."

Roller Babes

"Who cares? I still say they're the cutest couple here. She's a flame, and the word is they're going to go pro."

The blonde turned to look at Elsie Mae, and furrowed her brow. She snapped her head back and turned away quickly, causing her perfect hair to sway back and forth.

Elsie Mae's mouth hinged open. "Why'd she do that? See her face get all hard? What'd I do to her?"

"Now you know how I feel when boys look at me," Lottie mumbled.

"What's she so frosted about?" Tommy asked, putting an arm around Elsie Mae.

"Maybe you shouldn't gossip and point, like I said."

"Rebecca, they can't hear us," Elsie Mae said. "They're also ringed. You know, married."

"Married? Yuck. How dreamy," Rebecca said sarcastically. "There're other things in life besides marriage."

"What other things? Like what?" Elsie Mae asked.

"I don't know ... skating ... college ... and stuff," Rebecca said.

"You know how the married couples get so much attention on the roller derby show? It's romantic." Elsie Mae rolled her eyes upwards. "All the little girls watching television want to be a skater who's in *love*."

"Not me."

"Yeah." Lottie put a fist under her chin. "I'll never have a skating husband. You and Tommy will get on teams. But I ain't getting married just to be on a team. I'll do it by being the best skater here."

"Don't be a jelly bean. You never know," Elsie Mae said without taking her eyes off of the couple.

The blonde girl turned once again to stare down Elsie Mae. The young wife wrinkled her nose, as if smelling a bad odor and then turned away.

"That's it. I'm going to send her to the moon next time we're on the track." Elsie Mae straightened her back.

"Don't be silly. You're a lover, not a hater." Tommy pulled Elsie Mae's shoulders into his chest.

"What was that about? What did we ever do to them?" Rebecca searched anxiously over her shoulders, looking for invisible lint again. "She's making me nervous."

"She's just being a party-pooper. She can skate, and she's a real Marilyn Monroe. But he's a cement mixer. You know; a square. I guess she thinks she's prettier than you, Elsie Mae." Tommy scooted a little closer to his girl. "They're begging for a tune-up."

"Anybody know their names?" Rebecca asked.

"The Marilyn Monroe's name is Dumbrowsky." Elsie Mae frowned at Tommy. "Caroline Dumbrowsky. They call her husband JC. No one knows his real name. They just call him JC."

"JC the arsonist," Rebecca muttered. "Whadda a pill."

"Don't worry honey, you're the butter-and-egg fly, a real dolly. She's just jealous," Tommy said to Elsie Mae.

Lottie saw Elsie Mae swoon from the sweet talk. "If anything happens to either of them, guess who'll be next in line?"

"Say, you two are getting pretty lovey-dovey. What's going on?" Rebecca asked with a frown.

Tommy threw both arms around Elsie Mae. He kissed her rosy cheek as an answer.

"Well, why don't you two get married, then?" Rebecca asked.

"We haven't even talked about it." Elsie Mae gazed into Tommy's eyes.

"Then why are you always all over each other?" Rebecca said. "I know you're playing backseat bingo."

"Don't be an oddball." Elsie Mae stuck out her lower lip in a cute pout.

"I'm not an oddball." Rebecca adjusted herself in a fake huff. "I'm just a misfit." She stood and did a dance in a circle, and then dropped back to her seat.

The others laughed. Lottie relaxed a moment longer to let her tired muscles recoup. Rebecca pulled out a book, pushed her black-framed glasses onto her nose, hunched over and buried her face in the pages.

Lottie rummaged through her skate bag in search of something. She found it: a thick sanitary napkin wrapped in brown paper. She hoped the napkin would reduce the searing foot pain from the never-ending blisters. She'd do anything to keep going and be picked for a team. "What did ya hear about her?" Lottie nodded toward the athletic Negro girl.

"Oh her," Elsie Mae said. "I heard she had a boyfriend in school two years ago. Something terrible happened. Someone pawed her up or something," she whispered. "No one talks much about it. And see that other white girl?"

Lottie looked at the two girls sitting together. "Yeah?" Lottie waited for the dirt.

"She's with her. They live together. You know ..." Elsie Mae said, "... *together.*" She put her two fingers from both hands together at the tips. "They went out and bought curtains for their place."

"What?" Lottie scratched her head.

"They share each other's garden tools," Elsie Mae huffed.

"What's wrong with that?" Lottie asked.

"Never mind." Elsie Mae gave up.

"I read a book the other day about the women who play professional golf." Rebecca looked up from the pages of a thick book. "They mentioned that some of the gals weren't married ... and lived with companions."

"*Companions?*" Lottie grabbed the fluffy napkin and hid it, waiting for the right time.

The Negro girl flashed a dimpled smile at Lottie. The girl's hair resembled black wire, all pulled back into a tight ponytail. Her face was the color of caramel, with bright, almond-shaped eyes.

Lottie smiled back. "I like her."

"Um huh?" Elsie Mae smiled.

"Drill number two!" Buddy Wilson called out and blew his whistle.

The rest period ended. The advanced group came to attention while Lottie shoved the sanitary napkin inside her skate to form a cushion. She packed the bloodied mess of a foot back into the skate boot and grimaced.

"We're going to practice falling on our backsides without breaking a wrist," he said. "Trust me, if you want to be on a professional team, you'll need this skill."

"Here's a trick I just heard that the pros use, Lottie." Elsie Mae pointed to Lottie's skate. "Don't lace your skates up all the way. Keep them loose." She tugged on Lottie's laces. "That helps cut down on blisters and cramped muscles. And loosen your front wheel trucks. You'll be able to move up and down the banks better."

"Sounds screwy." Lottie did what Elsie Mae suggested. Then she stood, favoring the blistered foot, and toppled over into the seat next to her. Holding one hand out, Elsie Mae pulled her friend to her feet. Lottie braced herself to struggle through the rest of the evening's training. "That's better, I think," she said, wobbling side-to-side on newly adjusted skates. She could barely stand, let alone skate. "But my feet still feel like raw hamburger." With pain tightening on her face, she followed the others onto the track, ready to fall and embarrass herself over and over again.

Halfway into the drill, JC took a tumble and stretched his arms out to take Tommy down, too.

"Hey!" Tommy yelped. His wrist hit the side of an upright. "Ouch."

Buddy blew his whistle twice. "No screwing around out here you too. You're going to need each other if you're on the same team. So no more *accidents* like that."

Tommy pulled upright onto his skates, rubbing his twisted wrist.

The skaters training for a future job had become a family of competitors, struggling for a role on the golden-wheeled derby circuit. Everyone knew one another, but they also knew that only the best would get the financial rewards of a fulltime job.

Chapter 11

MINOR LEAGUE

With shoulders hunched in worry Rebecca asked, "What's going on tonight?"

Lottie had fallen into the daily routine of school, work and training. "What d'ya mean?"

"See, out there, on the infield benches? There are our team helmets."

Buddy appeared with both hands on his hips. "You all know the rules to the game, don't you?"

Some said "Sure!" Others nodded "Yes."

"Well, you better. Management reads the rules at each game and places printed rule guides in the programs. Tonight, and for the next week or so, the advanced skaters are going to play scrimmage games. Nobody makes it to the professional ranks without working out in the amateur games. We call it the Minor League."

Rebecca's lower lip trembled in excitement.

"This should be a blast." Lottie straightened and repeatedly ran a hand through her hair.

Buddy started writing names on a chalkboard that sat at the end of the front row bleachers. "I'm selecting names, so I think each squad will have at least one good jammer and one leader or captain type."

He listed the girls with Rebecca, Caroline, the colored girl, and Elsie Mae all on the same team.

"You're our teammates," Lottie said happily to Caroline and Elsie Mae.

They smiled, but Caroline gave off no expression.

Then Buddy scrawled the boys' teams on the old board. "If your name isn't up here, you're not ready to scrimmage yet. Don't worry. Watch to learn. Keep working on the basic skills and you'll be up here in a jiffy."

"Girls, are you ready?"

"Not really," someone joked.

"You're ready. Get into your teams on the infield, and one person on each team pass out the helmets. Striped helmets are the jammers."

The chitchatting ended when Buddy called both teams to the starting line. Lottie wobbled to the line, holding her trembling body still until the whistle finally sounded to start the play.

Skates thundered as the whistle shrilled. Lottie's hair stiffened on the nape of her neck as she kicked another skater's wheels. Legs scattered recklessly, and Lottie saw the hard metal of another skate jab a player. Skaters tripped over each other, even among team members. Two players went down, and the rest of the eight skaters tumbled over them, crashing into a heap.

The whistle sounded.

"Stop! See why you need this?" Buddy said loudly. "Get up, on the line again, and learn to stride alongside each other without tripping over everyone's wheels!"

Lottie's face reddened. It took two more repeated attempts before everyone started off the line without tripping each other.

"I don't like this," Rebecca's hands moved in jerks. "Why can't we get a jammer out?"

"This is the showdown I've been waiting for, but it's nothing like I thought," Lottie's voice wavered. "And that Caroline keeps elbowing me in the ribs."

"Again, girls!" Buddy sounded exasperated.

This time, a jammer soared out in front of the pack. "Good!" Buddy yelled, but the pack stretched out like a long line of lone skaters. Everyone skated yards from each other. There was no way for the audience to tell where the pack started and stopped. Skaters were straggling all over. No one knew how to form a pack.

"Stop! Stop!" Buddy called. "Two more jams, then the boys are up."

"We're lame ducks," Elsie Mae said. "But I'm looking sexy doing it, ain't I?"

Lottie's belly looped and she took a place at the starting line waiting for the whistle. When it blew, she pushed the backside of her jammer, who took off away from the rest. Then she called out, "Form the pack. Here!"

To her amazement, the other skaters did what she said. They looked at one another and tried to skate in and alongside each other. Suddenly, everyone bashed, jabbed and dodged vicious attempts at body blows. It felt like a real game to Lottie. She put her head down and plowed over every pack skater in her way, pushing and shoving the awkward clump back and forth. She even bashed into her own players.

One of her teammates became incensed and pushed Lottie into the rail, eyes glaring like a psycho demon. She squared off with Lottie and slapped her. "I'm sorry! I was just getting confused about who's on what team," Lottie stammered. It stung like hell. She felt like crying, but it was just a girl slap—nothing like what the boy bullies had done to her for years.

The whistle sounded. "Jam over," Buddy bellowed, jumping into the middle of the skirmish. "Break it up. Everyone come to the infield."

Amid heavy breathing and aching ribs and feet, evil stares surrounded Buddy. "So, you think this is hit or be hit, right?"

"Yes," one girl sounded out. "If I don't get them, they'll get me."

"How many others feel that way about pack work?"

Most raised their hands.

"No! You're wrong. None of you have any idea what you're doing in that pack. There's strategy, like late chase or back-stop positions. This is about *teamwork*, like pulling the pack, lifting it. You're all missing the point of what pack work is."

Lottie looked around, wide-eyed under a sheen of sweat on her face. "Strategy?"

"You're all playing like amateurs, just hitting because you seem to think it's a free-for-all. To get to the major league, there's a lot more to learn. Skaters from as far back as 1935 have slowly developed these strategies. I hope some of you can respect those who went before you and pick up where they left off. None of them are documented in the rules of the sport."

The girls looked at their skates, each running the words over in their minds like confused kids in a big candy store. Lottie muttered, "More homework."

"Alright, boys next," Buddy announced. "Watch the boys and see if you can use teamwork in your next scrimmage."

"I feel like a failure." Lottie's chest sank.

"What's new about that?" Elsie Mae laughed. "You've got to start feeling better about all you've learned and are learning. I'm telling you the truth. You're great at this."

"I suppose so. I'll get the hang of it."

"Promise me? Go easy on yourself."

"Pinky promise."

"Pinky promise." Elsie Mae extended her little finger, twisted it around Lottie's and shook.

The gal pal trio from the Bronx doubled down and trained as often as possible. Once in a while, one of them might miss a day, and there were strains and sprains, bumps and bruises. Still, Lottie was enthused about learning teamwork. Each day saw improvement in their skills; new careers seemed to be blossoming.

Chapter 12

A DESPERATE MOVE

Lottie fidgeted beside Elsie Mae. "Rebecca's going to miss tonight. She's gonna work on homework."

The evening had turned cold. Lottie's breath frosted and hovered as soon as it hit the air. The skaters shuffled uneasily in line outside the Armory door, waiting for evening training. Swirling snowflakes created a drowsy, hypnotic effect in Elsie Mae's eyes and made Lottie's gut ache. "Hey, what's wrong with you?" Lottie asked. "You've been acting kinda loony for weeks now."

"I've been feelin' like a wet sock." Elsie Mae's shoulders slumped and her arms hung loosely to the side. "My feet and legs are killing me."

"Is that all? All of our hocks are beat to a pulp. All these months, my legs are heavy as lead." Lottie's own body protested just at the thought. "You sure it's the aches and being tired? I never seen ya look so down like this before."

"Umm, well ... something's happened." Elsie Mae's voice sounded low and her eyes were void of emotion.

"Well, what? What happened?" Lottie edged closer and noticed that Elsie Mae's chin was trembling. Lottie felt light headed with fear.

"I can't say."

"You and Tommy have both missed a few practices," Lottie whispered so the people in front of them couldn't overhear. "That's not like you guys."

"Me and Tommy ..." Elsie Mae swayed back and forth, then stiffened and stood deathly still. After a moment, Lottie saw her eyes well up with tears, about to cry.

Lottie put a hand to her mouth and took fast short breaths. "You and Tommy what?"

"Ain't no ... never mind."

Lottie's chest hammered. She wanted to reach out and touch Elsie Mae. She leaned her head closer. "Then what?"

"I guess we're getting married," Elsie Mae said.

Lottie's mind went into a tailspin. She raised her brows and excess saliva twizzled in her mouth. "That's good. Ain't it?"

"I guess. I just feel shot down." Elsie Mae's once vibrant strawberry blonde hair hung forward to hide her face in a limp mass.

"You'll get on a team for sure, now!" Lottie said. Then she stopped short, her eyebrows knitted together with worry. "But what's wrong? Why do you look ruined?"

Tears slipped from Elsie Mae's eyes beneath strands of hair. "Oh, Lottie."

Lottie's stomach rolled; underarms breaking out in sweat. "God, what? No. What?"

"I'm, well, you see ... I'm P.G." Elsie Mae's voice quivered while averting sad eyes from Lottie's stare.

Lottie's mouth gaped open. That barbed word stung. A hunk of metal clunked inside her gut. "P.G.?"

"Everybody's having babies," Elsie Mae shrugged.

Lottie looked aside, a sour taste in her mouth. This wasn't the Elsie Mae she knew, her best friend. Something must be wrong. "Oh, not everybody. Why have a kid if you don't have the dough to take care of it? I mean, what are you going to do?"

"We'll all be cooking for our husbands, pressing their shirts and taking care of the kids someday." Elsie Mae weaved in place as one arm clutched her belly.

"That sounds peachy for you and Tommy," Lottie said. "I'm not sure what else there is, but I ain't ironing no shirts."

Elsie Mae gripped her ring finger with one hand and stared at it. "We can't afford an engagement ring," Elsie Mae looked up. "Tommy's going to quit skating and work at the filling station."

Lottie was numb with shock. Things were moving too fast. "You can't skip out now! Rebecca and I need you.

We made it to the minor league scrimmages. Ain't you thrilled?" She felt paralyzed. "Tommy's the best guy on the track. He's sure to go pro."

Elsie Mae shook her head *no* and closed her lips tight.

"No? What are you talking about?"

Elsie Mae's voice cracked. "Well ... we think we can raise the baby on ninety-five cents a day."

"The baby." Lottie thoughts felt fuzzy and blueish. Her own dream melted, and Elsie's words flickered vague images in her head while the realization the new mother's dreams of Hollywood were also dying. "Baby," she said again. "That's right ... the baby. Ninety-five a day; oh, God, how?"

"I don't know." Elsie Mae sounded out of ideas. "The doctor says it's too dangerous to skate with the kid inside and all. And how could we travel with a baby?"

"But you have so much talent. What about being a star?"

"I guess I'll have to trade my movie magazine subscription for *Better Homes and Gardens*." Elsie Mae forced a smile.

The uneasy humor stopped Lottie's thoughts. Breath tightening, she sorted through ideas. "Don't worry, we're all in this together. Comrades, remember?"

"Well ..."

"Hi, Lottie," a Negro girl unintentionally interrupted Elsie Mae by joining them at the end of the line.

Tommy entered the line a few feet away. Lottie glanced over in that direction. His dejected look hurt. She looked back at the girl with a jet-black ponytail. "Oh, hi," she said, plastering a grin on what must have been a sheet-white face. "What's your name?"

"My name's Ruby. Ruby Johnson." Her smile widened. "I've seen you here the last few months. I like the nickname that Buddy gave you. He likes your skating."

"Oh, yeah." Lottie laughed awkwardly. "I don't know where he got it. I guess I skate kinda queer. Like a loony."

"Doesn't matter, I like it," Ruby said. "I remember when you started. You been getting better."

"I can stay in the pace now." Lottie perked up. "And I'm getting better at the blocking. I'm in love with this sport."

"Me too. I've never had something like this in my life. The feeling of the banks; it's hard to explain."

"Like a bird, flying, ya know."

"Yes," Ruby looked upwards. Both paused a moment. "The New York Yankees defeated the Dodgers."

"Great, huh? My dad don't want me to do sports." Lottie tucked her head.

"My dad's a janitor at the bank. He works nights and he thinks this skating thing's a frolic. Just some nonsense." Ruby shook her head. "When I told him I was trying out for the roller derby, he kicked me out of the house. He can't read and write much, you know. He thinks I should get a job cleaning houses or become a maid for some rich family. So for now, I'm staying with a friend."

"Sometimes I wish I could up and leave home too." Lottie sensed a sinking feeling in the pit of her gut hearing all these stories from other skaters.

"Lottie, take this from the bird with the word. It's hard on your own. I miss home. Even my strict dad. I'm lonely without my family and I don't have many friends. Never *did* have many friends. My dad don't think these sorts of dreams are for a colored girl. I do real good in school, but there aren't many jobs for us coloreds."

"It don't seem fair." Lottie tapped Ruby's wrist in a gesture of empathy. "I'm not much in school and my dad's not crazy about this idea either. He don't think it's anything that girls should do. He says it'll never pay. Something about how I'll eat glory for food."

"Sounds like my dad." Ruby put a hand on her mouth and giggled.

Lottie laughed.

"Just stay home as long as you can." Ruby nodded.

Lottie looked up at the top of Ruby's head. "You look like you can take care of yourself; you know, you're athletic. What are ya, a foot taller than me?"

"I'm five foot-ten. And don't let all this toughness fool you. I'm really a softy." Ruby put one finger up to pursed lips. "Don't tell anyone. When I was in the fifth grade, I was so shy I couldn't ask to go to the bathroom. I sat at my desk, watching the clock. I only had ten minutes to go before school would be out. I couldn't wait for those ten minutes to get over." Ruby's cheeks blushed. "I crossed my legs and held on tight. I couldn't hold it. Then, I peed my pants."

Lottie laughed. "That must have been embarrassing."

"God, was it ever!" Ruby ducked her head between her shoulders. "Luckily, I had a coat in the back of the room and I hung it around my waist so no one would see."

"You're funny. I see shy ain't a problem no more. How'd you get interested in skating?"

"The kids in school never liked me. But when I went out for sports like the track team, all of a sudden everyone did. I guess if you're just a Negro, people don't take you for much. But when you can do something like basketball or track, they accept you."

"I liked sports, too. But still, no one liked me."

"One night I saw *Roller Derby* on television. There was one colored fella on the teams, so I thought, *What the heck*?" She raised her shoulders. "*I'll give it a try*. If I lived through wetting my pants, I can do this. I love to skate. Besides, when Dad asked me to move out, I found a friend living close to the Armory. We're both training."

"What's her name?"

"Laura Miller. She's up the line a little." Ruby pointed.

"I'm from the Bronx. We got lots in common," Lottie said.

Ruby swished from side to side like a schoolgirl. "Things never felt right about liking sports. You know, I don't see many girls doing them. Right now, I really need to get on a team, seeing that I've left home and all. If not, guess I'll get one of those cleaning jobs, like my dad wants."

Lottie looked at Elsie Mae. "This is my friend, Elsie Mae."

Ruby extended her hand. "Hi, Elsie Mae."

They shook hands and looked on with blank eyes. Lottie noticed that Elsie Mae couldn't manage her normal greeting.

"Whatcha thinking about, Elsie Mae?" Lottie asked.

"Nothing much. Not now."

Awkwardness settled over the group until the door opened with a loud scrape. Lottie felt terrible seeing Elsie Mae with her head hanging low. She knew there'd be hard times ahead for her friend.

Ten minutes later, Lottie and the other skaters changed into their skates, got onto the track and followed the instructor's commands. Lottie focused on staying in the race line, personal lives set aside for a few hours.

"Go!" Buddy shouted. Lottie broke away from the front of the line. Halfway around, he threw a folding chair onto the track, eight feet in front of her; there were only seconds before a crash. "Come on! Jump!" he said. "With this, you'll learn how to avoid fallen skaters!"

Lottie swerved to miss the chair, but couldn't. She crashed face first again. "Oh, brother!" she exclaimed. Ruby covered a smile with a hand. Without thinking, Lottie scrambled onto her skates and labored forward, at it again. It was another day of learning by getting banged around.

During the break, Tommy and Elsie Mae put their shoes on and left. Lottie's chest sank watching the couple exit. She pulled in and then released a breath, wondering if she should follow them. She sensed stiffness in her neck. At the backstage door, Elsie Mae and Tommy vanished, disappearing into the cold night.

"Where'd your friends run off to?" Ruby asked, noticing they were no longer training.

"Don't know. They're in love, ya know." Lottie noticed Sammy Kyle—black, curly hair tousled atop his head—talking to another man.

"Look, it's the go-go skaters. They never get tired. They just go and go," Ruby said.

Lottie couldn't believe that her all-time favorites, beloved by her hometown fans, were sitting just yards away. Lottie wanted to be as good as they were one day. "Do you think they know we're staring?"

"I guess so. It seems they don't pay it no mind. They're actin' downright lofty," Ruby said. "My dad would love this!"

"Blocking!" Buddy Wilson called. "Listen up, because I'm only going to explain this once. The purpose of blocking is to stop or slow your opponent's forward movement while maintaining your own progress. You can use your right or left hip, knee, elbow or shoulder to throw a block. If your body position's off or wrong, you'll fall. If you're off balance, you'll bounce off the other skater and be thrown forward. Got it?"

"I want to know everything he knows." Lottie crammed the information into her head.

"He's been doing this since the 1930s. Just how you going to learn all that, Missy?" Ruby asked.

"Everyone on the track!"

"C'mon!" Ruby half-towed Lottie toward the track. "Don't make Buddy wait."

Skating in single file, ready for the blocking drill, Lottie's heart stammered as she looked behind her. There was Sammy Kyle! She quaked in her skates and wobbled in front of the star.

He's twice my size and weight; what if he hurts me? Surely he ain't going to block with me?

The whistle blew and the two of them sped away from the line. Sammy wheeled smoothly close behind while Lottie swerved all over the track. Sammy's heavy skate-pounding rode on her heels. She heard him laugh. He stepped to the inside to pass and missed her with an easy elbow block. In a flash, she came back with a strong-arm blast. Bouncing off him, she thrust herself forward. She reeled out of control and fell on her face ... *thwawmp!*

Now I know what Buddy meant.

She struggled onto her skates and joined the back of the line, only to see a smiling Sammy Kyle following immediately behind her. "Not again," she wheezed. The whistle blew and the two sped away for a second time. This time, when Sammy passed her, she felt a hard push on her shoulder. His elbow threw her shoulders back causing her arms to whirl like helicopter blades. Her legs flew up in front of her; she slammed onto her butt ... *bowmp.*

"Ha!" he yelled.

Dazed, she saw the backside of the hulk swaying away with cocky movements. She clambered back up. Cursing, she skated back into the line of skaters. Sammy rolled right up behind her again. She rubbed the knot out of her butt muscles right in his face and gritted her teeth.

When their turn came again, Lottie pushed away from the line of skaters. She sharpened her ears and kept one eye open for his shadow from behind. Her anger at his cockiness had turned to rage.

He stepped in to pass her, throwing a body block. At the last millisecond, she pulled her head and shoulders backward to avoid his body check. He missed. Caught off guard, he teetered awkwardly. He staggered off balance!

"Way to go, Lottie!" Ruby said.

"HEEEYYYYY! Get outta my way!" Lottie yelled, visibly shaking Sammy. She rolled to his left and wound up one great elbow blast with her shoulder, as if winding up to pitch a baseball. Connecting with his left shoulder, she felt strong, pure contact. She used her elbow for a hook and slung him backward, flipping her tormentor into the air.

"*Yow!*" he yelled.

Through the corner of her eye, Lottie saw his skates and legs fly into the air. His wheels spun, airborne, going nowhere. She heard no sound. The world seem to hold still for one second as a golden hue covered the rink. Then the rattle of skates on wooden planks seem so loud it was deafening. His butt hit the track with a *thawnk.* He let out a hissing breath. "What the ...?"

Lottie whirled away, crouching over with a sense of satisfaction as speed was now the only concern. She'd never shown such aggression before. It felt great.

"That's it!" Ruby cheered excitedly from across the track. All of the others clapped.

Sammy Kyle shot an angry look at Lottie as he got up and rubbed the kinks out of his buttocks. But the cheers were for one their own that had slayed the hulk! A small flame of self-fulfillment burned inside her.

Buddy pulled Lottie aside. "When you block, use your whole body. Start with pointing your front wheels up the banks. That slows you down while your opponent is moving faster, see? Then leverage your legs, waist and torso." He gestured the move.

"That's better. It took us years to learn that move. It's like a pro golfer who puts his whole body into the swing. But don't give away the move to the other player." He patted her shoulder.

After the training session, Lottie's adrenaline still pumped through her body. She found the Armory's back area blanketed with more snow but none of the cold sank in past a tattered long sweater. Gazing through the white winter wonderland, she spotted Tommy's car twenty yards away. A few people stood near it. *Did they wait to take me home, after all?*

She walked closer; three police cars surrounded the old Ford coupe, what Tommy called his 'tin can.' Her euphoria pounded high inside, so much that she missed the sound of a siren scream in the distance, not processing the implications of the police cars.

She couldn't wait to tell Tommy and Elsie Mae about this victory. She noticed two motionless people inside the car. Cold slammed around now, all warmth gone while the night air seemed to darken to pitch black with only a spotlight brightness under each streetlamp and the car washed in pulsing red and white light.

"What is it?" she whispered in ungodly anguish. Her adrenaline soured, a pain stirred someplace deep in her stomach. Dread moved like a speeding freight train, straight toward her heart. "What happened?" she asked, pushing her way through the bystanders.

"Have some respect for law and order around here. Stand back, everyone." A policeman attempted to hold her back, but she pushed closer. Her eyes spotted a runner hose stuck into the tailpipe of Tommy's car which led into one small window vent. The other windows were tightly closed.

"Back, everyone."

Her stomach clutched. She felt tears forming. Her ears pounded. "It can't be!"

"Break it up. Keep it moving, folks. There's nothing to see here," the policeman said.

Inside the exhaust-filled car, Lottie saw two people, heads close together, lifeless. Lottie's knees weakened and she began to wave people away as if she couldn't see right. She squinted, and then her breath hitched in her chest. She recognized the long, wondrous hair. It *was* Elsie Mae's head that lay motionless, tucked into the arms of the other.

"No," Lottie gasped. The sight ripped through her. Her heart felt like it had crashed onto the cold, snow-covered ground. Sagging like an orphaned ragdoll, she moaned. "Oh, my God!" Her entire body gave way to numbness. Wanting to breathe life back into Elsie Mae, Lottie knew it was too late so there was an overwhelming feeling of helplessness.

"Elsie Mae! Tommy!" Her breathy gasps left her lips and froze in the shivering air. She backed away with shaking hands held to her mouth. She fell to her knees in a quiver.

"Get back, folks," the policeman barked again.

Her mind ballooned with memories of Elsie Mae cheering in a pink felt skirt, tossing jacks and catching a red rubber ball on the hot tar rooftop. She saw Elsie Mae laughing with Tommy, skating around the track with laughter and a bright blue dress bought just for skating because it flared out with the slightest breeze. Lottie remembered how she loved to read movie magazines. Lottie couldn't reconcile the lively sprite she remembered with the sight of Elsie Mae's stiff body nestled in Tommy's arms.

"Oh, honey." Ruby put an arm around Lottie just as the muffled sobs sneaked out from the very depth of her being.

"This can't be happening. They can't!" Lottie's voice broke. "They can't be gone."

"I'm so sorry." Ruby lowered to her knees and embraced Lottie until her own tears welled up.

"Why'd we ever do this darned roller derby?" said Lottie. "It killed her."

"Now, you can't think that way, honey," Ruby said.

"She wanted to be a star." Tears stung Lottie's eyes.

"I know. I know." Ruby held Lottie close, actually rocking them both.

"Dad was right! I'm never going to skate again!" Lottie's world had ended.

Ruby stroked her hair and looked toward the black sky as the bystanders slowly disappeared. "I know."

Moments passed until Lottie could think again. "What should I do?"

"Let's stand up, okay?"

Lottie nodded as both girls wobbled to their feet. Ruby turned Lottie around and placed one hand on her shoulder. "We need to rest. When the morning comes, we'll know what to do. For now, just rest."

Lottie couldn't understand. Her mind was a void. Dad's warnings were nothing compared to this. Ruby and Lottie dragged themselves back to their respective homes.

Once inside the house, with shaking limbs, Lottie flopped into bed, still dressed. She held back a scream, then slept for a long time in sheer exhaustion. The world was dangerous, just as Dad had warned her. She couldn't return to the Armory, back to the scene where death had taken Elsie Mae and Tommy. She couldn't experience it again. How could she escape? Lottie didn't want to go anywhere or do anything without her friend. She stayed away for five days.

On the fifth night, Lottie heard a light pecking sound. The white pigeon was on the windowsill. It cooed and pecked at the wood. Lottie watched. The bird seemed to be using one eye to look at her; then it would turn its head to look with the other eye. Suddenly, it lifted one foot and placed it down. Her white pigeon-dove poked its neck forward, lifted the other foot, and tapped the wooden window's edge. Lottie's gaze ping-ponged from the pigeon to her skates on the floor, feeling close to this moon-silvered bird. It was her friend and she was happy it had visited. The friendly dove repeated the movement again and again. Lottie's eyes danced as life and energy flooded over her again.

Chapter 13

THE WEAKER SEX

Finally, after a rough week, Lottie slipped back into the training ritual. At first, when she gazed at the other faces, there was only Elsie Mae's face looking back. She remembered how Elsie Mae had brightened every situation with a big smile, with movie star appeal. *Why did someone like her have to leave us?* she wondered.

Lottie took her usual seat at the Armory by second nature. She plopped down next to Rebecca and Ruby, ready for another practice, but she was still questioning what life was all about.

"You're thinking of Elsie Mae and Tommy again, huh?" Rebecca asked softly.

"Are you doing okay, Lottie?" Ruby asked.

Lottie had a falling sensation, and wiped a tear aside. "It's not the same without 'em. It's not fair."

"I miss them, too," Rebecca said.

"Sure. And me too." Ruby slumped her shoulders.

Lottie gazed in and out of the dusty Armory ceilings. She searched between the rafters and catwalks, slowing her eyes, looking into every shadow and dark corner.

"What do you keep looking for?" Rebecca asked.

Lottie blinked as her chin trembled. "Oh, I don't know. I guess I keep thinking they're still here."

"You mean *spirits*?"

"I think I feel them. Sounds crazy, huh?"

"Sure does!" Ruby pulled her head up.

"Gives me goose bumps." Rebecca shivered and tugged her sweater close to her core.

"I hate it." Lottie wondered what Elsie Mae would be thinking if she were a spirit.

"If Elsie were here, she'd be cheering us all on," Rebecca's voice broke.

"They'd be here, alright. Remember how Tommy loved her?" Lottie asked.

"That's life's most precious gift. People never leave. They stay in your soul." Ruby gently tapped Lottie's shoulder and lingered. "Can you feel 'em?"

Lottie rested one hand on Ruby's. "Love," she whispered, searching for a feeling and staring across the catwalks. In the dusty shadows, she thought she saw the outline of Elsie Mae in a pink poodle skirt and tight cream sweater. Then she felt a smile as tears rolled down her cheeks. "You're so right. She'd want us to do our best. I can feel her."

"You feel the spirit inside?" Ruby asked.

"Yes."

"That'll never go away." Ruby watched Lottie's face change. "Did you hear the latest rumor?" Ruby changed the conversation.

"Never," Rebecca chimed.

Lottie paused and extended both hands toward her friends. "Wait a minute." She exhaled, closed her eyes. Setting aside the grief by drawing a box around it inside her head. Making the box smaller, she pushed Elsie Mae's pain to the back of her mind, letting her own roller derby dreams seep back into the foreground.

"Ready to practice?" Rebecca asked.

"I'll never forget. I think I'm ready." Lottie exhaled a long breath.

"Do it for Elsie Mae and Tommy," Rebecca said.

"Okay," Lottie exhaled.

"Well, did you hear?" Ruby tapped Lottie in the ribs, waking her. "They're saying someone's going to get picked for the teams tonight!"

"Yikes." Lottie straightened. "What if ..."

"You mean, tonight might be *the* night!" Rebecca squeaked. "Empress Lottie, remember? We're *not* going to take over the world by staying home and knitting!"

"It'd be good news. We need some good news, even if it is just a rumor." Lottie lifted her head.

"That's what I heard, and that is for sure," Ruby agreed.

"The teams! I knew it!" Rebecca said. "It could be another tall tale, but it might be true."

"I don't know if I can stand it." Ruby's eyes gleamed. "There ain't no Negroes on the girls' teams. Maybe my turn?"

"You're a good skater, Ruby," Lottie said. "I don't see what you have to worry about. Besides, look at *me*. How many scrawny Jewish girls are on the teams?"

"See any bookworms out there?" Rebecca laughed. They all paused and then laughed.

"Go on." Ruby waved a hand. "We just might all be crazy, huh?"

"Well, this is the kookiest thing I've ever done," Rebecca said.

Lottie stopped laughing. "I'm the one that won't make it. I'm a bonehead," she said. "It would be nice. But my big, clumsy feet …"

"Don't say that," Rebecca said. "All those wacky tumbles and falls you've been pulling on the track have to be worth something!" She elbowed Lottie in the ribs and cracked a small smile.

"So far, all they're worth is a bunch of bruises and scrapes."

"Besides," Ruby said, "you've got what it takes. You're a scrappy little fighter!" She raised both fists and sparred with the air like a prizefighter. "You can take it."

Lottie's stomach twisted in hope and despair as she pulled on the old familiar skates, grimacing at another blister that had broken under the pressure of the leather. She shuddered at the idea of the rumored announcement. She forced all thoughts to focus on a scene: being on the road with the derby. "I hope you're right."

"You been dragging your behind to this old Armory for a long time now. And working at Mason's! Suffering pain from head to toe, putting up with ugly bumps everywhere, you deserve your break!" Ruby said.

"Besides, we just graduated from school," Rebecca said. "I'm seventeen. We got our whole lives ahead a us."

Lottie pushed herself back in the hard chair. "Just barely graduated," she corrected. "I got all Cs and Ds. Not much to brag about." She took two deep breaths. "Okay, I'm ready."

"Look, I have a blister on top of another blister on my heel," Rebecca said with a laughing moan.

"That's nothing," Ruby scoffed. "I have one big scrape of skin for a butt. Oh no, look!" She hunched her head downwards. "I mean, look, but don't really look."

Bent over, ignoring nagging back pain, Lottie laced up skates. "Look where?"

"Over there." Ruby angled her head to the right as if pointing.

"Who is it?" Rebecca asked.

"Over there. Right there." Ruby nodded again still hunched down.

Lottie saw most of the same skaters every night. Tonight, she strained to look past the familiar faces to see who might be new. While Rebecca craned her head toward the entrance, Lottie twisted around to push the kinks out of knotted muscles. She caught a glimpse of the black-haired Vinnie Christner and Charlie Samuels. "Those television skaters! They're two rows back and a few seats behind us!"

"Is it really them?" Rebecca asked.

"Shhh! Don't let them see you staring," Ruby said.

"It's Vinnie and Charlie, all right. What do we do?" Rebecca hissed in excitement.

"I don't know," Lottie said. "Just listen. Don't stare." The girls straightened in their seats and Lottie strained to overhear the men's conversation.

"The fillies just can't skate as good as the fellas," Vinnie was saying. "They're the whole problem with the game."

Lottie faced straight ahead and forced her ears to pick up on the men's words.

"It brings the game down," Charlie Samuels said.

"There're going to be big changes. I heard management's going to get rid of the gals," Vinnie said.

"Good. I heard that, too. They wanted to do it last year."

"Watch how they flirt with management and stay with the game. They'll be full of honey coolers, you know."

"Power-hungry bitches. They got to get rid of 'em this time."

Ruby, Rebecca and Lottie turned to one another. Lottie's friends' faces were agog.

"If they did, it'd be the best thing that ever happened to the derby," Vinnie said with a sense of contempt. "It'll legitimize the game for the fans, once and for all."

Lottie's eyes darted back and forth, catching glimpses of the two male skaters. "That can't happen. We gotta get derby jobs," she said.

Rebecca stared straight ahead at the track, her cheeks hollowed.

"Humph," Ruby sniffed. She frowned and crossed both arms; her back straightened up.

"I don't believe it," Lottie said under her breath. She lowered her head and pretended to work on her skates.

"They want the girls out," Ruby muttered. "What'll we do?"

"Shhh, listen."

"They look so off-the-cob out there," Charlie said.

"Some of 'em are as ugly as gorillas. You know the ones I'm talking about."

"Yeah, the ones who stick with other gals."

Ruby clenched one hand into a fist. "Those two are just pecker-heads. They better cool it before some gorilla beats the crap out of them."

Lottie's rage boiled from her belly. She remembered the boys who'd attacked her at the playground, how she'd ducked and run when they tossed rocks at her. So many years of hateful taunts filled her gut. She knew she was as good an athlete as any of them. She strained to listen.

"If the press finds out how phony it is ..." Lottie saw Vinnie slice one hand across his throat. "The news will crush us."

Lottie's nerves coiled.

"That'll kill the game for good. We'll all be beating the sidewalks, looking for work," Charlie finished.

Lottie nudged Ruby. "They look so small compared to how they look on television."

Ruby unfolded one arm, extended a hand and measured an inch between thumb and pointer finger. "Yeah. About this big."

Lottie giggled and then stopped herself by placing a hand over her mouth.

"Vinnie's no Clark Gable," Rebecca said.

"Not like that cute Elvis Presley," Ruby muttered.

"Who?" Lottie asked.

"He's this white cat from Memphis," Ruby said.

Lottie looked back with a blank stare.

"Good sounds." Ruby bounced her head. "Oh, never mind, you'll see. He's got black soul. We Negroes keep up on the new singers. He's rock n' roll, and he's going to be big. Shhh, cut the gas."

"I hate it when they play up to the cameras," Vinnie said, "A bunch of lousy actors."

"I know. And they just bum the gums!" Charlie said. "They're bitches!"

"Yammer, yammer, yammer! Booshwash. Talk, talk, talk. Besides, they're smaller and slower than us."

"They can't even throw a block like us men," Charlie was ranting, raising his voice.

"Our game's twice as fast. And rugged. The gals are so—tired. Time for them to go."

"With them out, the game will finally be *legitimate*."

"Like the other major league sports."

"They're the weaker sex, you know?" Charlie said. "Just flirts in skirts."

"Their bodies are made for one thing," Vinnie said, making curved girl-body gestures with his hands.

"They belong at home, raising kids and pregnant."

Lottie's quick glance caught Charlie's sleazy gesture: one clenched hand, pushing forward. Both men chuckled.

"Say. I shacked up with Eve Belzak last week," Vinnie said.

"Me, too!" They both laughed.

Lottie's jaw dropped. "Are they really saying all that about the gals who skate on their teams?" she asked Ruby.

"Sounds that way. I heard that Vinnie's wife wants him to leave the derby."

"Why?" Rebecca asked.

"Envy, I guess. Vinnie chases the women. And I heard that when ol' Charlie over there started, he was nice and polite. Now he's a big drunk, and he tries to elbow rookies in the face to see if he can break their noses and teeth."

"Why do that?" Rebecca asked.

"So the rookies take a dive for him whenever he wants. That is, if they don't quit after he bashes their faces in."

"I've got an idea. What if they got rid of the men?" Lottie said.

Ruby smiled. "Now *that* would be something."

"That'll never happen," Rebecca said.

"I'm getting out of here. They make me sick." Ruby stood up, ready to skate it off.

"I'd like to see those fellas barefoot and pregnant," Rebecca said. "Wait, Ruby; I'm going with you. Don't leave me here with these dead hoofer barbarians."

Lottie sat and stewed. She let her mind wander. How could she get a job when it sounded like the guys, and maybe management, were against girls? A revulsion stirred inside while thoughts on how to salvage this career appeared and faded, appeared and faded. Soon, the two men left for their workout.

Lottie's fury melted into a frazzle with the night's battle-ready workout. She struggled through a drawn-out pace and then a quick breakaway-and-blocking drill. At the end of practice, the three friends flopped into their usual seats.

Lottie noticed a flurry of activity when Buddy stood in front of the group, using his arms to get everyone's eyes on him.

"Attention, everyone!" Buddy called out. "Attention, everyone. I have an announcement."

"This could be it," Ruby said. "I'm about ready to flip."

"Don't flip out," Lottie said. "It might be good *or* bad news."

"What if they announce no more gals?" Rebecca asked.

Heads turned to face Buddy who stood next to the highest end of the track with another man at his right. The other man stood tall, wore a new blue suit and had gray streaks of hair at his temples.

"Now listen up a minute. We have with us tonight the owner of the derby: my old friend, Mr. Oscar Wentworth." Buddy gestured to the stranger. "He's here to bring on the new skaters who'll be our new professionals."

"See? The rumor was true!" Ruby sat upright. Lottie's mind muddled into a fog of confusion and hope.

"All right. Now, listen closely. I have a list of skaters here," Buddy said, unfolding a piece of paper. The entire building went silent. Lottie heard motorized fans humming deep backstage. Her hands trembled.

"You'll report to me if your name's on the list," Buddy said. "You *must* train tomorrow. Then you'll be going to New Jersey this Saturday to work in Unit A."

Trying to find a distraction from the overwhelming apprehension about being left behind, Lottie looked at the face of the man standing next to Buddy. She'd never seen him before. He towered over Buddy and seemed older and accustomed to being in charge. The blue of his jacket exactly matched the blue in his slacks, an expensive suit. He was the real deal. Anticipation rested thick in the air. It hovered like the dust that had been worked up from hard skating which was slowly settling onto the cement floor, rafters and ceiling bulbs.

"You got it?" Buddy looked up from his paper. "If I call your name, come see me." He paused. "If your name isn't called, don't worry. Pack up and go home tonight. Come back and work harder. You might be the next one called to be on a team later this year."

Lottie's blood raced. She took a gulp of air.

"Here we go. Two boys. Andy Gleason and Dusty Miller, come over here." Buddy raised his eyes from the paper and searched for the chosen skaters.

Lottie shivered.

Skaters' heads spun to look at the two lucky boys who rolled toward Buddy and Oscar. The boss man shook their hands and gave each of them papers.

"What the heck are they saying?" Ruby asked. Everyone watched the boss talking to the new skaters. They grinned and nodded, and then the boss returned his attention to Buddy, nodding for the call to continue.

Lottie's hands were clammy. All she could think about was how she'd teetered and stumbled around the track for months. Her ears grew hot.

"Okay. For the gals!" Buddy shouted and raised one hand like a stop sign. "We need four gals." He looked down at the paper.

"Oh, God," Lottie said.

Ruby sat motionless. Rebecca lifted both hands and crossed her fingers. Lottie closed her eyes visualizing a white dove, it wasn't flying. It was just staring.

Buddy cleared his throat and wobbled his fingers. "Caroline Dumbrowsky, Ruby Johnson, Rebecca Peterson, and ... Lottie Zimmerman."

Silence.

Impossible.

As the news sunk in, Lottie's heart raced up to her throat and did a flip, nearly choking her. She opened her eyes and took in a big gasp of air. She didn't know whether to cry or yell. Ruby flung back her head in disbelief, and it hit the back of her seat. Rebecca cringed.

"Let me call out the names again," Buddy said.

Lottie didn't hear another word. Her heart soared, pounding out of her chest. The idea of performing in a real match rattled her. Shaking, she clump-scooted in her skates over to where the boss man stood. She didn't notice Ruby and Rebecca right behind her with Caroline not much farther behind.

Lottie and the three other newly-chosen girls milled around Oscar Wentworth. He spoke to each one, greeting them with a big smile, nodding, and giving directions. The words went right through Lottie's head without registering. "This can't be happening," she said in a quiet voice.

"It's happening," Buddy said.

"Congratulations, Caroline," Lottie said. Caroline fake-grinned and ignored the other girls.

Oscar passed Lottie a paper and flinched when he saw her up close. She saw his eyes looking at her ratty hair, eyedropper nose and skinny face. "Are you sure?" Oscar asked Buddy.

"She's the best. Fearless." Buddy looked directly into the boss man's eyes.

"Good." The boss turned his attention back to Lottie with a small frown, still eyeing her face and clothes.

Lottie looked down at skinny ankles under the mended socks stuffed into battle-scarred skates. She knew he disapproved of the whole package. She looked at the other girls, and thought how much prettier they were.

"Oscar, I'd like you to meet Lottie Zimmerman, a.k.a. the Little Lunatic. She earned her name from the haphazard moves she pulls out there on the track. She's taken lots of tumbles, but nothing can stop her from getting back into the race. She's got what it takes, that's for sure."

Lottie cracked a wide smile.

Oscar took a deep breath. "Hello, Little Lunatic. Be here to practice tomorrow. Then Saturday, at 9 A.M. someone will pick you up and get you to Trenton, New Jersey." He spoke each detail slowly, enunciating every syllable.

With shaking fingers, Lottie took the paper from Oscar's large hand. She straightened her spine. "Thanks, Mr. Wentworth."

"Call me Oscar. You'll be assigned roommates and you'll get three meals each day. Welcome to the derby girls."

She pulled the paper close to her body, hoping that it would halt the shaking. Her heart flipped endlessly.

"Don't forget, you need to train again tomorrow," Oscar finished.

She anticipated the pigeon visiting her dreams again, struggling higher than ever. Soaring above lousy weather and darkened clouds, fluttering freely over treacherous winds and reveling in gracious blue horizons kissed with morning sunshine: it would never stop flying! "I won't forget. I'll be here tomorrow," she said, turning to see Ruby who opened her arms to give Lottie an energetic hug.

"We made it!" Rebecca said.

"I can't believe it." Ruby opened her mouth and let out a small yelp.

Rebecca clutched the paper close to her chest. "I'm so excited. I can't wait to go home and tell everyone."

"Guys, we're on a professional team. We got jobs!" Lottie jumped once into the air. When she landed, her skates wobbled and arms flailed.

"Don't go fallin' and breakin' a leg, now," Ruby said.

"I can finally get away from home," Rebecca whispered, her eyes filling with tears. Lottie knew what she meant and felt joy—as much for Rebecca and Ruby as for herself.

"Me, too." Lottie watched Caroline Dumbrowsky take her papers over to her husband, JC.

Lottie, Ruby and Rebecca held one another's hands briefly. The warmth of Ruby's hand felt the dearest of all. Nearly exploding inside, Lottie hurried home to find her parents at their kitchen war stations: Esther bunkered behind the table and Murray at his chair, smoking and reading the newspaper.

"Look!" Lottie pushed the paper forward with one hand. "They hired me for the derby!"

Esther's eyes widened. She moved aside a big pot on the stove and brought one shaky hand up to her lips.

Her dad slapped the newspaper down on the table. He grabbed the paper out of Lottie's hands. Head down, brows furrowed, he read it, remaining silent.

Esther rubbed her hands dry on her apron and moved closer to Lottie. Her eyes shone with tears. "Oh, Lottie, this is wonderful."

Lottie's soul filled with confidence for a split second. "We leave this Saturday morning. My first bout will be in Trenton, New Jersey."

A single tear ran along her mom's cheek. "Where will you stay?"

"They put us in hotels and living quarters, like that. They even have a cook who makes our meals. It's perfect."

"You'll eat well," Mom said.

"Oh. And Rebecca and another friend, Ruby, got picked too. So I won't be alone."

Murray shoved the paper aside. "Humph," he grunted his disapproval. Lottie wanted him to be proud. It had taken so many months of treacherous work to get into the derby. Instead, her father pulled the newspaper open and put it up to his face like he was blocking out the world. "You'll be back in a week," he finally muttered. "Goddamn roller derby." He shook the folds out of the paper, closed it around himself, and continued reading.

Later in her bedroom, Lottie heard a small knock. Her mom slowly entered, the family's beat-up, stained suitcase dangling from one hand.

Esther struggled to find words. "Are you sure this is what you want? Going off to join the roller derby?"

"I'm sure. Skating is so much fun. And I think I'm pretty good at it."

"I thought so. You must be. And they hired you, right?" Mom's eyes sparkled. "Not everyone gets to do something they enjoy. I'm happy for you." Mom held out the suitcase. "I thought you'd need this."

Lottie took the suitcase as if it were a piece of delicate Tiffany chinaware. Esther sat on the edge of the ragged bed while Lottie opened the suitcase. A cute lady's hat, decorated with yellowed flowers, was nestled inside. The white fabric had faded during years of storage.

"Your dad gave me that hat as a wedding gift. It's a Betmar Sylvie style, made of wool, with a yellow headband and dark satin veil."

"It's beautiful." Lottie expanded her lungs, picked the hat up and examined the shiny silver hatpin that was pushed through the back with a big pearl blob on the top end, it was stuck in behind the veil attachment. "Fancy, and so classy."

"It's not much."

Lottie sat tall, examining her mother's eyes, understanding how much the hat meant to her. Her throat thickened, knowing that this was Mom's cherished keepsake. Lottie imagined a sensitive side to her dad, giving his new bride this gift. She felt warm and surrounded by a glow of support. "I love it." She ran two fingers around the brim slowly. "Really, Mom ... it's rag ... the best!"

"Maybe it'll give you good luck."

"Oh, Mama, I'm sure it will! I'll keep it close." Lottie placed an open hand on her chest.

"Be a good girl."

"I will. Don't worry. I'm sure going to miss you, Rhoda and Betty. And even Dad." her voice almost cracked. She knew that Betty would look after little Rhoda, just as Lottie had looked after both younger sisters for so many years.

"We'll miss you, too. My little girl, leaving to go off to work." Esther stood tall and sturdy for the first time Lottie could remember.

"I hope I can stay with it," Lottie said.

"Just keep working hard."

"I will. I'll work real hard, Mom."

She packed all her underwear, a couple of faded dresses, a pair of pants and all the mended socks. She opened a few drawers and pointed to the clothes she wanted to leave behind. "Be sure to look over the two little ones for me, and tell them I'll miss them and I love them," Lottie said.

"They'll need the clothes. They're getting taller every day."

Lottie pulled her raggedy roller skates from the floor and placed them over the clothes in the suitcase, pressing them down and testing to make sure the case would close. Then she put the lucky hat in, running two fingers around the yellow brim one more time.

"There. I'm ready. I have one more training session tomorrow, and then I'm off!"

Her mother opened her arms to give her daughter a loving hug. Warmth washed over Lottie. But as life had shown her so far, it was a pleasure that would turn chilly just hours later.

Chapter 14

I'LL KILL FOR IT

Ruby bounced on her toes and shot a thumbs-up at Lottie and Rebecca. "I can't believe it! We're done for the night! And tomorrow we start a real career!"

"It's the dreamiest." Rebecca's eyes danced. "We'll be bringing home the bacon."

"Money made from sports ..." Lottie was breathless. It was deep in the evening in the arid Armory. Lottie's last night of training. Nothing seemed real. Life charged forward on the wings of a dream. Her mind struggled to latch onto all that was happening. "My dad thinks I'll be back home in a week."

"I doubt it—not with all those months of killing ourselves!" Ruby loosened tight braids.

Rebecca poked Lottie's arm. "Besides, we'll have all sorts of new friends from our teammates."

"You're right. We made it." Lottie's face blazed from the night's workout. Her spirits were high.

"Where's Caroline?" Ruby looked all around.

"She's supposed to be on the team with us," Ruby said.

"This is it." Rebecca rocked back and forth in her seat. "I feel like I'm going to pop!" She made a popping sound with her mouth and sat upright.

Ruby laughed, pulling back her red hair. "Girl, you done popped long ago."

"And you're a good skater now," Lottie said.

"I don't know ..." Rebecca arched her back.

"I hear something," Ruby said.

"What's going on?" Rebecca stared toward the skaters' entrance.

Lottie grimaced, taking her skates off bandaged feet. She threw them inside her skate bag, straining to hear the voices in the background.

"Can't you hear?" asked Rebecca. "Sounds like arguing."

Lottie stopped and listened.

"Why wasn't *I* good enough?" The voice received no answer.

"I want to know! Now!" the voice grew louder.

"I think that's JC," Rebecca whispered.

"Yeah, sounds like his voice." Lottie peered between the high banks and the seating area. She spotted him. His lips curled and his blazing eyes met hers, furrows etched into his cheeks and forehead. Her friends tittered.

"Look at his hair—it's all wet and hanging in his eyes. He's drunk—he's throwing his arms around!" Rebecca fidgeted.

"Wait a minute, JC." Buddy was holding his hands up like a shield.

"You're part of this! You did this!" JC yelled toward Buddy.

Lottie's heart skipped a beat.

"Let's just settle down," Buddy commanded.

"I won't settle down!"

"Oh, no." Rebecca tugged at her blouse nervously.

Lottie couldn't swallow. Her heart went *thud* as JC pulled a gun out of his pants.

"Can't be!" Ruby winced.

Lottie froze in place.

The three watched as the pistol rattled Buddy's calm. He leaned back, away from JC, eyes glazed and hands shaking. "Son ... alright, now ... get yourself under control."

"What should we do?" Lottie's mind raced. She looked left and right as sweat beaded on her forehead.

"You did this!" JC yelled.

"I'm just a trainer." Buddy lowered his voice and held out one loose hand. "Take it easy ... just ... let me have the gun."

"Hell, no, you bastard! I hate you!" JC jabbed the gun at Buddy's chest.

"No!" Lottie couldn't hold back her voice.

"Wait, wait!" Buddy's voice wavered. "We can work this out!"

Lottie's gut twisted.

JC's lips moved without producing a sound. All of his attention was directed at Buddy. He spat. "Someone wants her for himself!"

"No, son."

"Who's after her? I'll kill him, too!" JC demanded.

Buddy shook his head in a gentle *no*. "Son, you have this all wrong."

JC shoved Buddy's shoulder with his free hand. "You ass, you're gonna pay!"

Buddy staggered back, his feet racing to keep from falling.

Suddenly, Lottie's body reacted. She trotted in her socks toward the scene. The other skaters didn't move, just watched them in a haze.

JC moved his lips, jabbed one finger at Buddy, and waved the gun. His face ballooned. "Why did you take Caroline and not me?"

"Look out!" somebody shrieked.

JC pushed the gun like a knife into Buddy's chest. Lottie cringed as Buddy doubled over in pain. JC pulled the gun back and slammed it with a nauseating *thwack* against the side of his head.

Lottie stiffened, her hand outstretched in a feeble attempt to help. "Stop ..." she whispered.

Buddy recoiled and a trickle of blood seeped down his cheek and throat. His mouth opened in pain and he staggered two steps, then fell.

JC's upper lip curled, "You have to take both of us! You have to take both of us!"

Buddy hid his face inside of an elbow and raised a pleading hand. "No, please."

Lottie screamed, "HEEEYYYYY! Get outta my way!" She held both hands out to her sides. JC jerked his head up, eyes blazing with drunken hate. "Stop it!" Lottie screamed.

JC looked at Lottie for a brief instant. It was enough time for Buddy. He kicked the gun out of JC's hand. The weapon skidded across the floor to rest in front of Lottie. JC blinked at his empty hand. His eyes opened wide as he gulped a long lungful of the stale Armory air, as if he hadn't breathed in a long time.

Lottie picked up the gun like it was a dead scorpion. She feared it, but couldn't let it sit at her feet.

"Lottie, thanks," Buddy whispered.

JC's eyes relaxed. His face sagged as his breathing broke down into small sobs. He dropped his head and his sinking shoulders shook. "Oh, God," he moaned. He crumpled to his knees. "No, no, no."

Buddy placed a shaking hand on JC's shoulder. JC went limp at Buddy's touch, curling into a fetal position. Buddy leaned over the boy; sweat dripped from the trainer's bloodied brow. "It's going to be okay, son."

Lottie finally breathed, watching Buddy stroke the whimpering JC's head.

"Son, you're going to be just fine." Buddy rubbed JC's arm.

Lottie felt her body relax.

"It's going to be okay," Buddy repeated.

A warm feeling washed over Lottie as Buddy caressed the boy. Buddy peered up at Lottie over JC's prostrate body and stretched one hand between his ear and lips to mimic a telephone, mouthing po-lice.

Lottie nodded. She turned and raced through the halls and walkways, gun still in hand, remembering the phone near the back entrance next to the folding chair. Shoeless, she hurried to make the call.

By the time she returned, Buddy and JC were reclining, exhausted, in two seats at the edge of the arena. JC's nose looked cute again. His eyes were dazed, anger gone, leaving his spirit fatigued, empty. Lottie stayed back, not wanting to put the gun anywhere near JC. Nodding to Buddy, she indicated the police were on the way.

The tension in Buddy's face had eased and the trickle of blood seemed to be drying.

"Let me get a rag." Lottie ran to the bathroom for a wet paper towel.

The police arrived promptly. When Lottie returned, one officer snapped handcuffs onto JC and led him away. She handed the gun to the officer's partner and carried the rag over to Buddy, who dabbed at his wound. The horror show was over and the other shocked skaters went home for the night.

"Lottie, good going. We have to go." Ruby and Rebecca sheepishly passed Buddy.

At first, Lottie didn't register what they said. As they eased through the exit area, Lottie called, "I'll see ya tomorrow!"

"Okay."

Buddy sat back in the seat. "Phew. Thanks, Lottie. I think you saved my life tonight."

"Oh. It's nothing," she felt taller and stronger. A sense of fullness hammered inside, but she felt shyness creep over her face. "Are you okay?"

He exhaled. "I'm okay. Don't worry about me."

"Let me help." She gently wiped the blood dripping down Buddy's neck. He moaned, echoing it across the evening silence that filled the hall. Lottie ran the events over and over in her mind, becoming calmer while Buddy seemed to do the same.

Buddy took a deep breath. "You know, this business is full of drunks and crooks."

His words wounded Lottie. "I would never have guessed."

"And con men."

"But why did he have a gun?"

"You just never know. So many problem people. Everyone sees those professional skaters on television, not knowing that over half of 'em owe me money for training, equipment and skates. I'll never see a dime of it. The derby's always been full of chiselers."

Lottie was solemn. "I'd never do that."

"Like the skater in Unit B who got drunk. His wife chased him with a rolling pin, and he jumped off his roof, breaking both ankles. He used Oscar's insurance to pay the hospital bills. Then he got addicted to pain pills, swallowed about fifty of them a day. When he couldn't afford the pills anymore, he sued Oscar's company to keep feeding his addiction."

She tilted her chin down and frowned. "Someone we know?"

"Oh, he's a top skater; no need to mention names. So many con men." Buddy pulled his shoulders back. "Anyway ... I have a feeling about you. I think you're going to do just fine." He looked up, a spark finally glistening in his eyes.

Lottie felt her ears grow hot. She looked down and saw her patched socks, kicking nervously. "I hope so."

"You remind me of someone I knew twelve years ago. Her name was Gloria."

"Gloria? Was she a skater?"

"Yeah. One of the best." He grinned. "My wife. We skated in the original derby in the thirties." His gaze was unfocused, clearly remembering his wife and their times together with fondness.

"What was she like?"

Buddy's eyes searched to the left as if dredging up far-off thoughts. "She was small, like you." Buddy looked at Lottie. "Things were different back then. I remember the night Oscar Wentworth held a meeting and asked Gloria to start a fistfight with another skater. He told us we needed more color in the game."

"Color?"

Buddy let out a subdued chuckle and scratched his chin. "Yes. The fans went crazy that week, every match. They loved the fighting. You see, Gloria and this one other gal fought every night. Some of the skaters didn't want the hijinks; they said they just wanted to skate. But Mr. Wentworth knew what the fans wanted."

"You mean a show."

"It was in St. Louis. One night after a game, we took two buses to Cincinnati. I took the bus with the smokers and pinochle players. That old bus was a barrel of fun. And Gloria, well, she rode in the other bus. She didn't smoke, and she never had a head for cards." Buddy's eyes danced and he spoke a little faster.

"How far was it from St. Louis to Cincinnati? Was it far?"

"The ride took about five hours. All the way, we played cards, smoked and laughed over how the fights were going between Gloria and the other skater. Funny, now I can't even remember the other gal's name. Anyway, all the way to Cincinnati, we yammered about how the other gal took a left hook to the jaw. She would throw her head back like she'd been hit by Sugar Ray." Buddy grinned.

"Ouch."

He smiled again at the memory. "When her head snapped back, she'd squint her eyes. The whole audience yelled and stood on its feet." He put a hand to his mouth, chuckling. "Of course, she wasn't hurt a bit."

"It was fake?"

"Oh sure; all ... well, most of the fighting was fake. Anyway, when our bus pulled into Cincinnati, Mr. Wentworth was waiting to give us the news." Buddy squeezed his eyes shut and moaned. "Oscar told us that the other bus had blown a tire, crashed and exploded into flames." Buddy's eyes prickled, as if his emotions had finally caught up with the memory. "Fourteen of the skaters died in the crash." His voice was low and slow. "Including my Gloria."

Lottie's hands trembled, heaviness nagged at her stomach. "God. I'm so sorry. How terrible ..." Her eyes watered thinking of Elsie Mae and Tommy.

Buddy hung his head. "It was something terrible."

Tears rolled down Lottie's cheeks.

Time stood still. Thoughts swirled and settled. Finally, Buddy inhaled deeply. He looked up. "Listen here." He straightened, his voice sounding father-like. "These things happen, and life goes on."

Lottie wiped her eyes with the backs of her hands.

"I get a kick out of helping the new kids these days," he said. "And you. I have a feeling about you. You have something special. Here's my advice: go out there and make a name for yourself, you hear?"

"Sure, Buddy." Her smile quivered.

"You'll be able to skate for the home or the visiting team. You're versatile."

"I guess that's good."

"They'll probably start you out in the pack. But trust me, I have a feeling about you. You have something special. You'll be a better jammer and captain. It'll take time. You hang in there kid, do your time and you will shine."

The other skaters had left. The evening was over and the weather had turned colder. Lottie's last night ended with a shock she'd never expected. Oddly, she didn't want to leave. She felt at home at the Armory with Buddy. It was the place where she had adjusted to skating, found her bearings and balance. She'd also tasted moments of terror. She wondered if she'd ever see Buddy again. Her young heart ached all the way home.

Chapter 15

LOCKER ROOM DRAMA

Lottie's face reddened as the locker room door in Trenton, New Jersey, opened. The hair on the back of her neck stiffened. Then she heard a voice from inside the gloom.

"I'm not wearing this jersey!" someone yelled.

Lottie stopped in her tracks beside Rebecca.

Heads turned in Lottie's direction. She and her two friends stood still and gaped at the insides of the moldy locker room. It was half-filled with cigarette smoke. Lottie swallowed uncomfortably and choked at the odor of dirty socks and ripe bodies. Her heart thrummed.

"We're here," Ruby exhaled.

Lottie had never been behind the scenes of any sport. The backstage room sent a chill up her spine as she heard a rash of loud talk.

"Remember that poor, skinny guy, Johnny Kazar?" a voice bellowed. "Well, he died on the track. I can't wear this number. Give me another jersey!" The woman with the scratchy voice threw the jersey back at a plump, blonde woman.

Lottie leaned over to Rebecca's ear. "All the people I saw on television. They're right here!"

The voice continued like spitting nails. "You're not in charge here! Who put you in charge, *Patty whatever-your-name-is?*"

Lottie's muscles tensed. The woman's face contorted with bulging neck veins and a lined forehead when she spoke. Then she tossed a jersey. "I *am* Eve Belzak."

"Wow," Rebecca pushed her shoulders to her ear lobes.

"Look, guys! It's Eve Belzak." Lottie pulled her brows in. She watched Eve's face furrow and stretch taut.

"What she be angry at?" Ruby plastered a *how-did-I-get-here?* smile on her face.

"Yes, Eve, and *I* am Patty Carlson. You're always complaining about your uniform. Ambitious or not, we can't keep doing this for you." Plump and blonde, Patty waved a finger at the sexy-looking Belzak who held the rejected jersey at waist level and out like it was contaminated.

"I'm thirty-one, and I've been around the derby longer than you. There's only one person who's ever been killed in the game. That number's jinxed!" Belzak pointed a finger directly at Patty's forehead.

Rebecca put a hand to her mouth.

"Alright, alright ... we have the new kids here today and we need to make do," Patty huffed.

"Never mind them, I need to look good out there."

"Well, can't you use scarves, pushed-up elbow pads, attachments on your helmet? Be like the other gals!"

Belzak furrowed her brow. "Hell, no! I'm not like the other gals! And I see the new kids, a bunch of wet rags. Wheat, right from the fields." Belzak angled away from Patty and searched Lottie up and down with narrowed eyelids.

Lottie looked down at her feet, noticing the secondhand combat boots and the washed-out, crumpled dress that could have been tan, could have been gray. Her insides turned to jelly. In that second, she noticed that the women in the locker room wore the latest styles: long dresses with bright trim of greens and yellows all with large shoulders. Two women were finishing changing their hair color at a back sink and others were fixing makeup that brought out their beauty. The may have stunk, but it also glittered with color.

"Oh, no," Ruby moaned.

Belzak turned back to Patty. "If you want me to sell my ass out there tonight, I ain't doin' it in that jersey! Don't cross me."

"Don't worry, gals. Come on in. I've been expecting you." Patty motioned everyone to move past the door and into the dressing area.

The other skaters in the dimly-lit room continued to hang clothes inside their lockers, adjust their individual looks and put on their uniforms. Some of them smoked while preparing for the match. A few laughed when Belzak shouted, "What are you trying to do, kill me?"

"Kill you? You go through uniforms the same way you go through men," Patty remarked not backing down. "If you're not careful, one of 'em might haul off and mug you. Not that I would care."

Lottie's sight bounced from one small part of the room to another. She took two steps and stood still again.

Ruby stopped and whispered, "Men?"

"That ain't none of your damn business. I got blinkers for the fellas, and I enjoy my men! Besides, I keep ol' Bessie right here, in case one of them gets outta hand." Belzak dug through a flashy red handbag and pulled out a small revolver, waving it as if to make an impression.

"Oh my gosh, another gun," Lottie's muscles tensed. Her fingers trembled against the strap of her skate bag and she took a step backward.

"Put that away!" Patty ordered like a warden. "If you'd be more discreet with men, you wouldn't need that."

"What would you know, ya old cow? I don't need your help. I've got ol' Bessie." Belzak plopped the gun back into her bag and lovingly tapped its side. "In fact, I have a date with a professional *baseball* player tonight. I only date men of a superior stripe. Now, give me another uniform!"

"Here, gals." Patty pulled out three canvas duffle bags. Each bag was marked with the American Roller Derby League logo. "First, you get your own league bag for your skates and other things."

Patty examined Belzak's rejected jersey. She frowned and pulled another one out of the box. "A *base*ball player huh? I guess that's the fourth baseball player this week. Five more and you'll have your own ball team." Patty laughed with body relaxed; no hunching or slouching as she moved around the room. There was no apology in her body movement.

Belzak's brow knitted and her mouth opened wide. "Mind your own kiss-ass business, and I'll stay out of yours."

Rebecca put one finger in her ear. Lottie's eyes widened as she gently opened her skate and equipment bag.

Patty tossed out another jersey for Belzak. "Here. This one's torn. Will it fit?"

The women prepping and fussing and soaking in the entertainment between Patty and Belzak looked only a few years older than Lottie and totally unruffled at the exchange. Lottie easily recognized the plumber's daughter, Roughie Barclay, putting patches of orange-tan makeup on her face. "Look who it is." Lottie tapped Rebecca's hand.

"Yes," Ruby tapped back.

Belzak yanked the jersey over her chest. "Besides, I'm not like a few of the other bitches around here that act like they're part of a Mothers for Morality committee or something."

"If you had some morals, you'd get more respect," Patty said.

"I don't need your respect!"

"Okay, Miss Superstar," Patty laughed.

Ruby pinched her bottom lip.

Lottie inhaled a short breath as she spotted everybody's favorite skater, Gerry Murphy. She had a gold scarf around the neck of her white jersey. She had an *appeal* that made everyone feel close to her. Lottie felt she had known Gerry all her life. "The queen of the roller derby," Lottie whispered.

"I know," Rebecca said, and Ruby nodded.

Belzak was exasperated. "Up your wazoo. This one's too big." She turned to one of the big girls and threw the ripped jersey at her. "You can wear this one; you're a *fat-assed* girl."

The big girl reluctantly took the jersey with rolling eyes while Belzak stuck her hand out for another. Lottie and everyone else watched in silence now; the scene seemed to finally cross a line.

"All right, all right," Patty said. "Take this one." She threw another jersey at Belzak.

"I'm telling you, I'll quit before I use that jinxed jersey or one that's too big." Belzak pulled the new uniform over her head in one swift movement. It fit snugly.

"Unfortunately, you'll never quit. You've got derby dust in your fucking blood."

Ruby chuckled softly at the grown up swear word.

Belzak used both hands to cup her breasts. She packed them upwards until they bulged, making them protrude, big and obvious. "Got to get my tickets ready."

"Jesus!" Patty shook her head and turned toward the door.

Lottie, Rebecca and Ruby ignored Belzak and watched Gerry Murphy, instead. Gerry sat with a Marlboro tucked between ruby lips, taking short puffs. Smoke trailed up from the tip and drifted into her green eyes. Unflinching, she puffed, laying out her skates. Smoke climbed through the air, wrapping around the golden scarf and then drifting to the ceiling. One and a half inches of ash grew at the end of the cigarette, and suddenly fell to the floor in a quiet splash. Lottie envied Gerry's statuesque body; wide shoulders and strong but feminine arms.

"She's a leader on the track," said Ruby, "but she looks shy and kind of quiet in here. Don't you think?"

"She's smaller than she looks on television." Rebecca squirmed at saying something not so nice about such a glamourous gal.

"Now where in the Sam ... where'd my scissors go?" Belzak shouted. "I need to deepen this neckline. And look what the cat dragged in." Belzak motioned to the Lottie and the two new girls, who still stood motionless at the door.

"Or what Buddy Wilson dragged out of the sewers of New York's skid row," another voice said as the others laughed. "That Buddy Wilson's a drunken liar," the voice scratched.

Lottie's chest stung. "No," she gasped.

A number of eyes fixed on Ruby. Ruby clutched her skate bag close and fingered the embossed red-white-and-blue A.R.D.L. letters—the American Roller Derby League's simple logo.

"A new group of whiney brats," Roughie Barclay said in a guttural voice.

"A colored girl and a Jew. What next? Skating cats and dogs?" Belzak barked in her gravelly voice.

"Well, we already have skating sluts," Patty remarked.

Lottie shifted her weight from one foot to the other. Everyone in the room ignored Belzak and puttered on with their bags and uniforms, adjusting things here and there, pulling out combs, cigarettes, purses and clothes from their skate bags. Three of the skating stars grouped close together. One opened a purse, offering another skater a cigarette. She grabbed the Camel, lit a match and took a deep drag. "Let's see if we can get that Julian jam right tonight."

Lottie didn't understand but turned on listening ears.

"Yeah. Last night's was no hay burner," Roughie said from the front of the room.

"Find yourselves a place to change and suit up. It's always like this in the locker rooms." Patty bent over and rummaged through skating tights.

"Always like this?" Rebecca searched for a quieter corner.

Belzak stuck her chest out. "That jam needs more razzle-dazzle."

"We could do the leap-frog play," Roughie said in a voice like an unoiled water pump.

Belzak adjusted a big hoop earring. "No, we did that two nights ago."

Lottie wondered how Belzak could skate with such big earrings. She noticed that some of the other skaters wore jewelry, too.

"Here you go, new skaters," Patty warmly presented the three with two jerseys each. "My name's Patty Carlson. I'm your unit manager." She patted the folded jersey material. "But remember, I get these back after the game. You don't get ta keep 'em. You do keep the duffel bags."

"Thank you." Lottie's chest swelled, touching the jersey she might have seen on television.

"Thank you ma'am." Ruby dipped her head.

"Any questions? Just let me know. I've been around every season for eight years now, and I can tell you what's going on. Here." She handed over the remaining parts of the girls' uniforms: jersey, tights, trunks and socks.

"Lottie and Ruby, you're on the visiting team, the red shirts. Your captain is Midge Barclay. You know her, I'm sure. They call her Roughie. Make sure to listen to her." Patty gestured nonchalantly toward the older woman near the front.

"Yes, ma'am."

Lottie didn't realize the skaters were managed by the captains on the teams, but it made sense. Roughie was small and stout. Short legs made her look deformed, but Lottie knew she could paddle them fiercely and pick up speed, lickety-split. Roughie had dirty blonde hair. She had a thin blonde mustache and an angry expression that wasn't noticeable on television. Her eyes appeared glazed-over; sickly skin looked blotched and yellowish, so she added orange makeup smudges along one cheek to bring out an even more evil appearance.

"Roughie." Rebecca's knees shook.

"You're favorite," Lottie whispered to Rebecca.

Rebecca rifled through her old carrying case and pulled out a book. Inside the cover was the drawing she'd made at home. She eased toward her mentor. Roughie looked up while wrapping a wrist with white tape.

Rebecca stood a yard away from the skater, and held out her delicate drawing. "I ... I wonder if I could get your autograph."

Roughie stared at the picture.

The room fell quiet.

"What's this?" Roughie asked in a sharp voice, grabbing the drawing.

"Well, I've watched you for the past year," Rebecca said quietly, ducking her head.

Roughie's eyes narrowed. She tossed the drawing to the floor. "Get away from me."

Rebecca's face turned white. As she backed up, her wispy red hair slipped forward, covering her eyes. Slowly, she squatted to the floor to pick up her drawing and moved away. With both shoulders curled over her chest to be as small as possible, she squeaked back to her dressing area and quietly tucked the drawing safely inside the new skate bag.

"It's nothing, really; just a silly drawing." Rebecca looked over her shoulder, searching for pretend lint.

"You're a white shirt," Patty said to Rebecca. "Your captain is Gerry Murphy. If there are no questions, I'm taking the lineup changes to the trackside announcer and television broadcasters. So suit up." Patty disappeared.

The idea of television spiked the jitters up from Lottie's toes. She took a seat at the front of the room near two of the experienced skaters. She put her skate bags down. Bobbie Beal, with a Lucky Strike hanging from pink lips, bent down, grabbed the bags and flung them back to the corner. "You go over there, kid."

Roughie grabbed the bag out of Rebecca's hand and threw it to the rear of the locker area. "You sit back there with Blackie."

Amid chuckles, Lottie, Ruby and Rebecca crept past the scarred wooden lockers and banged-up benches to a small dressing area at the back of the room. Walking past the group, Lottie felt an icy chill of embarrassment and vulnerability. She found a private area in a corner of the room.

"Wow. This is sort of neat." Ruby's hand shook as she tinkered with the tie that held her ponytail tight. "Did you notice how friendly Gerry looks?"

"She looks like a good egg on television, too," Lottie said.

"And Caroline Dumbrowsky didn't even show?" Rebecca picked up a book that had fallen from her bag onto the dirty floor. She unruffled its pages, patted it clean and placed it inside her duffle bag.

Ruby nervously untied her shoes. "Yeah. What the devil happened?"

"I don't know," Lottie whispered. "But so much for making friends on our first day."

"It'll be fine." Ruby tightened a lace.

Lottie saw a skater across the room staring at Ruby. "I'm getting edgy. I can hear the sound of the crowd."

Murmurs from the audience wafted into the locker room from the dust-filled ceiling vents. The noise cascaded down through the smelly room and buffeted Lottie's ears. It sounded like loads of people milling around in the arena.

"What have we done? Lottie's hands quaked while she suited up in the remnants of the uniform Patty had given her.

Ruby tried to bind up the extra folds of her jersey. "These don't fit very well. But maybe I can tighten it here around my waist."

"That looks better. Better not complain," Lottie said.

"There must be hundreds of thousands of people out there." Rebecca forced her body to uncurl while trying to relax.

Lottie opened her old skate bag and ran two fingers slowly around the brim of the cream and yellow good luck hat. The Betmar Sylvie style and soft yet solid wool steadied her pulse. Her eyes sparkled at the yellow flower and sash. She inhaled its familiar feeling. She closed her eyes and thought of home, and knew everything would be okay. A warm remembrance of her mother's support filled her. She knew her mom was proud of this new job and how she'd found a special place in the world. Those weekends in front of the television watching roller derby were because of Mom. What Lottie was doing might have been something Mom herself might have wanted to do, if times had been different. How meaningful her mother's gift felt at that moment. She rested the hat into her new equipment bag.

"Hey, you new kids, just sit on the bench and stay out of the way," Belzak shouted, pushing her breasts up and puffing her chest out again. "You know who I am, don't you? I'm Eve Belzak."

Lottie's face gave off only blank emotion. "Sure, we know who you are. We'll do whatever you say." Lottie made her voice flat. She pulled her skates out of her bag; not having decided if she wanted to push back or just take it for now, but that same old rage at bullies swirling around inside.

"Just do what you're told," Roughie said, "and no obscene gestures in front of the cameras. Hands off your bra straps!"

"If you skate and get tired, keep going. And stay up front," Bobbie Beal said.

"That is, *if* you skate," Belzak added, with lines deepening in her forehead.

"Learn to think on your skates." Roughie tipped a flask up to her lips, threw her head back and gulped.

"And whatever you do, don't let anyone from the other team pass you for a point," Belzak insisted.

"Isn't there going to be a team strategy talk?" Ruby asked Lottie.

"Don't look that way." Lottie tucked her jersey in. It sagged in all the wrong places. She looked away from the mirror. "Just a lot of bickering in here."

Patty poked her face in the door. "Red shirt warm-up! Come on, girls!"

"Here." Belzak held out a brown stuffed teddy bear with a red bow tied around its neck. "Give this to the announcer."

Patty took the animal and clutched it along with a clipboard and pencil. "I'm on the way to the announcer's table. Red shirt warm ups." She disappeared again.

Lottie and Ruby stood, but no one else moved. So both sat down again. Ruby rocked back and forth on her butt. One of the skaters lit another cigarette, smoking it in three quick breaths. Seconds turned to minutes as Lottie and Ruby perched on the edge of their seats.

"Red shirts! Let's go! And don't forget to take your valuables; remember there's no lock on this door," Patty shouted from outside the locker room. She called two more times before the skaters responded.

Lottie grabbed her tan purse. Wheels squeaking, stumbling over cracks and bumps in the floor, she followed her teammates through the dark and winding back passages of the arena. She smelled stale beer and popcorn. Her eye caught slender slices of the bright light that broke through big curtains and wooden slats, shining from the main arena. When she entered the stadium-sized gymnasium, it purred with electric energy. She swiveled her head and gawked at the swollen crowd, adjusting her eyes to the brilliant television lights.

Swarms of well-dressed men in suits and women in long patterned dresses filled the seats. Lottie had never seen so many well-heeled people in one place. She rolled along with ears closed to the deafening yells of the crowd, suddenly scared to death. Her palms sweated as the home team entered to cheers. Lottie was oblivious to what was happening and the warm-ups ended in what seemed like seconds.

"Ladies and gentlemen, welcome to tonight's American Roller Derby League game!" the announcer's voice boomed. Instantly, the crowd rose to its feet, subdued excitement now growing louder into cheers.

Bright lights flashed around Lottie, making her dizzy. The sounds of skaters taking their places echoed through the stadium. She lost the ability to see straight or hear distinct sounds.

"Eve Belzak, please come to the announcer's table. You have a gift from a fan," the announcer crooned over the loudspeaker.

Belzak skated to the center of the track, pausing one last second to revel in the crowd's attention. Members of the audience bellowed, "*Boooo*," and motioned with thumbs down while a few applauded. The announcer reached up with one hand from the table alongside the straightaway to deliver Belzak a stuffed animal with a red bow.

"Isn't that the same stuffed toy she gave Patty in the dressing room?" Ruby said under her breath.

"I think so," Lottie said.

Belzak feigned surprise and took a long minute with the audience. She waved thankful gestures to no one in particular.

"What's she doing?" Ruby asked.

Once Belzak rolled back into the infield, her face beamed full of life. Her mouth was small, her nose upturned. Eve adjusted one of her dangling earrings. She lingered on her skates and rolled the arms of her jersey up as high as she could. With the low V-neck and exposed arms, she showed off as much skin as possible.

The announcer started again. "And sitting in the front row tonight is the legendary movie star, Mickey Rooney. Perhaps he'll take a bow?"

"From that new movie!" Lottie strained her neck to catch a glimpse of Mickey.

"Sit here, and don't get in the way," Belzak said. "This ain't about you!"

Lottie sat back obediently.

The large television cameras trolleyed along, filming the preliminary action. Every once in a while, the long alien tube of a camera hovered by Lottie. Her heart jumped into her throat.

"You're as white as a ghost," Ruby said. "What about me? Do *I* look white?" That broke the terror-driven ice a little and they chortled, trying hard to look casual and like they belonged.

The two teams went to the starting line.

"And here we go with the start of tonight's big game!" the announcer shouted. The yelling, booing and applause increased. Lottie realized all this excitement was for women; there were only women up there—only paid, professional women working a huge crowd. This was *IT*.

"I'm shaking." Ruby displayed a trembling palm.

"It's so loud in here," Lottie said.

Thundering skates rumbled around the track. A low roar came up from underneath and reverberated out toward the audience. It rose to a loud crescendo behind Lottie, then moved to the right, then back up front, echoing like a death-whirlwind. The shattering ruckus was nothing like what she'd heard on the little Philco television at home.

"Come on!" a voice from the track yelled. Lottie could barely hear over the relentless cyclone of applause circling all around the infield. A big bluish beacon was shining back and forth. Skaters talked and yelled at each other. Track sounds pounded incessantly, blanketing her brain with low-pitched throbs of thunder. Each time the group of skaters whisked past her, wind-gusts buffeted her face and burned her eyes. The relentless rhythm engulfed Lottie, until the rhythms of her body felt like part of the beat.

"And out moving on this play is a New Jersey skater," the announcer's voice rocked the arena. "Gerry Murphy and Belzak mixing it up in the pack."

From the bench, Lottie watched Gerry jab Belzak, who doubled over in angered pain. The fans cheered. "Look how the fans love Gerry," Ruby said.

"And are rip-roaring mad at Roughie and Belzak," Lottie countered.

Lights beat down on the skaters from the top of the arena, making them shimmer. It transformed them from the petty pests Lottie met in the locker room into radiant, larger-than-life icons of battle. Roughie and Belzak towered over the other skaters as the fans' hated visitors. The visiting stars cheated and tormented the home team skaters, all while Gerry remained a heroine of hope.

Lottie noticed Rebecca across the infield, sitting on the other team's bench. Her captain nudged her and pointed to the track.

"Look, they're letting Rebecca in."

Lottie and Ruby watched nervously while Rebecca skated onto the track. She wheeled into the pack of whizzing athletes. With every clumsy move, she withdrew more and more. The whistle sounded and the pack began to whir like a washing machine, with skaters crossing in front of one another at breakneck speeds. One skater hit another and launched her backwards. Two other skaters just missed crashing into one another by a split second. Rebecca lingered sheepishly in the back of the pack.

"It's her first professional jam!" Ruby said.

A jammer escaped the front of the gyrating pack, and in two minutes the jam ended with the sound of the overhead horn.

"No score on the play," the announcer said.

Rebecca returned to the benches, holding her side and grimacing.

"She looked good," Ruby said.

"She looks hurt," Lottie said. "I wonder if someone elbowed her?"

The women completed their period after twelve minutes, then the guys took over the bout action. Lottie's teammates plopped onto the benches, puffing and perspiring. One took a towel to pat her face while another pushed wild auburn hair back into place. Belzak pushed her breasts out and pulled down the V-neck of her jersey.

No one discussed game tactics until two minutes before the women's next period. "Huddle!" Roughie called loudly, motioning to everyone with her arms. "Come in close."

Lottie, hands clasped to her chest, knelt at her captain's skates and looked up. Most of the experienced gals stayed on the bench, hunched around the captain.

Roughie ducked her head low inside the huddle. "Okay. One." She held one hand out, with stubby fingers extended. She used her other hand's fingers to pull on her small finger. "Three." She pulled on her ring finger. "Five." Her hand moved to bend down her middle finger. "Seven," she pulled her forefinger. "Blow-off," she ended, pulling down her thumb. Lottie noticed her captain's pasty fingers. The stubby fingernails were dirty and nibbled-down. Roughie spoke again, using the same hand movements. "One. A white ends up alone, fancy white. Three. A red and a white, monkey-see-monkey-do."

Lottie stared at her blankly.

Roughie rocked slightly while she counted off each number. "Five, a white kill. Seven. A red kill. Blow-off. A red and white break. Get rid of the white at the rear. The white ends up on a late chase. The red tries to throw a jump block, misses with a broadie. White deuce."

Lottie didn't understand a word.

"You ... repeat the period," Roughie said to another player who repeated the plays.

Lottie and Ruby acted as if they knew what it all meant. They nodded their heads like the other players did.

Roughie repeated the whole scenario. This time she rattled the plays off faster, moving one hand in small movements hidden by the huddle from the audience. She moved as if conducting an orchestra and the others nodded rhythmically. "Let's go," she said sharply at the same time the buzzer sounded.

"You two stay here!" Belzak yelled at Lottie and Ruby, pointing to the bench.

The skaters swung back into action, the rolling thunder of skates and shouts hammered their eardrums. The vortex of sound swept Lottie up inside its rolling cyclone. Soon, the whirlwind of mayhem lifted her spirits, and minutes later, it was all over. Halftime.

Chapter 16

DAMN IT! GET IN THE PACK!

Inside the stale locker room, Lottie, Ruby and Rebecca found their seats. Lottie wanted to compare notes with her friends, though she fidgeted with nervous energy. "My knees keep knocking," Lottie said.

"Yeah, my heart's pounding in my chest," Rebecca said.

Cigarettes came out of every skate bag and the dusty locker room billowed with smoke.

"Rebecca, you were great out there," Ruby said.

"I just stayed in the pack. I think someone needed a rest," Rebecca said.

"Did you hurt your rib?" Lottie asked.

Rebecca looked at the floor. "No. I'm okay." Lottie knew she was keeping something back.

"Got a snipe?" one skater asked another. Out came another Lucky Strike.

Lottie looked around the room, watching a wave of brushes appear out of bags as the other players touched up their hair. "Halftime already," she said.

"What'd they say in the huddle?" Ruby asked Rebecca.

"I don't know." Rebecca looked up. "*Red* this, *white* that. They said it so fast. I didn't understand any of it. I guess I left my roller derby dictionary at home."

Ruby sat upright. "They didn't teach us anything about that in training."

"It's some sort of secret code." Rebecca crouched over when Roughie came rolling into the room.

"What's wrong?" Lottie stroked her forearm.

"One of my teammates said that Roughie had it in for me," Rebecca said in a hush.

"What d'ya mean?"

"I guess she thinks I'm cruisin' for a bruisin'."

"Should ya maybe tell someone?" Lottie pulled her eye brows down. "I don't like seeing you all shriveled up like this. Snap out of it."

"I didn't do anything," Rebecca said. "I mean, I don't think I did anything wrong. Maybe she *does* have it in for me." Rebecca scrambled through her bag. "I'm not saying a word," she said, and pulled out a book which she fitfully pretended to read.

"Don't say that." Lottie felt sadness overwhelm her; the camaraderie she had dreamed of wasn't present on this team.

Roughie kicked her locker door. Lottie wondered what fueled the star's anger. The older skater pulled a flask out of her locker, pushed it to her lips and guzzled. Lottie's stomach hardened at the sight and she turned away. Ever since her dad's drinking had started, she resolved never to touch booze.

"Listen, you kike!" Belzak hollered from across the room. She adjusted those big gold earrings. "You new kids just keep out of the way. You don't know how to sell!"

The other skaters laughed. Lottie responded with a small head bow in Belzak's direction, and felt her face flush red beneath sweaty, choppy hair. The hum from the audience droned monotonously inside the musty room, driving Lottie nuts. Her legs tightened up. She felt stiff and panicky. The fifteen-minute halftime flew by in an instant.

"Second half. Let's go, gals," Patty called.

Lottie's nerves rattled.

No one moved. Patty stuck her head through the door again. "All right, second half! Let's go. Otherwise, you won't get paid tonight." It took Patty two more calls before all the skaters traipsed out the door. Backstage, they gathered with the men, forming two groups of teams before entering the packed arena.

Rolling into the infield, Lottie felt a slap on her behind. She turned and caught a narrow-eyed look from Vinnie Christner, one of the guy skaters. He ogled Lottie's chest and licked his lips. The gawking startled Lottie. "What you want?" Lottie frowned.

Vinnie winked.

She looked closely at him. He had sat rows away at the training center. On television, his looks seemed handsome. But up close, Lottie saw a pockmarked face, slanted forehead, brownish teeth and greasy hair. She guessed that these quirky looks didn't translate through the airwaves.

"What's knittin', kitten?" His voice oozed with lust.

She felt his eyes on her, roaming over her body. "Hi." She edged backwards, smelling his bad breath.

"How's tricks?" He stared at her flat chest, and then scratched his crotch.

"Okay." Her breathing cinched. Since his appearance was unexpected, Vinnie Christner's comments about the gals to Charlie Samuels back at the training center took a second to come back to her memory. She felt creepy. She looked down and skated toward the infield benches.

"What's with him?" Ruby asked.

"I don't know," Lottie said.

"I heard some of the guys try to sleep with the new girls. If you do that, then the other gals will hate you." Ruby laughed. "He's sure no Gary Cooper."

"A greaseball for sure," Lottie chuckled. She sat down out of the way—just as the older skaters had ordered. Across the infield, Rebecca sat on one end of the bench. Roughie, Lottie's captain, skated over to Rebecca and pushed her. Lottie and Ruby fixed their eyes on the two while Roughie screamed at Rebecca in a tirade of foul language, pointing toward the center of the bench.

"What's she saying?" Ruby's brows arched.

"She's a visiting coach. What's she doing over there?" Lottie asked.

"None of Rebecca's teammates seem to notice!"

Rebecca scooted down the bench to the center, pulling her arms around her chest.

The women took to the track first in the second half, and the cyclone of excitement spun to life again. Lottie, Ruby and Rebecca warmed the infield benches. The rhythmic drubbing of skates against the track engulfed Lottie in a kaleidoscope of noise. She drank in every sound. When not watching the track action, she started taking mental notes on the audience, cameras and crew.

She watched Oscar Wentworth barking orders to underlings, the men on his crew scampering off one at a time. Three men worked each of the big cameras. Sound booms hung near the telescopic lenses, extending into the audience and over the track. The crowd's enthusiasm grew louder. Thundering skates quaked the track.

Lottie caught a glimpse of a skater wheeling directly toward the bench. She felt lightheaded in a sudden panic. The fans shouted and yelled. The oncoming skater flailed her arms wildly, headed right for Ruby.

"Look out!" Lottie leaned back with raised hands.

The fans' shouts turned into deafening roars. Seeing the color of the uniform, Lottie recognized the out-of-control skater was a teammate, not a skater from the other team. Lottie's muscles tensed, ready to run. The teammate rammed into an unsuspecting Ruby. It was Belzak!

"What the ... ouch!" Ruby screamed, falling backward off the bench. She expelled every ounce of air out of her lungs. Belzak fell directly on top of the girl's chest. Lottie watched while Ruby struggled to gain her breath. Belzak's skate struck Ruby in the mouth. The roar of the fans shook the rafters and they laughed, delighted at the sight.

Ruby's face turned pallid. She took big gasps of air into her lungs, coughing. Then her face saddened. Belzak gave her a half-second glare. Then she skated back to the track, ranting at the supposed skater who shoved her.

Lottie rolled over to help her teammate off the floor. She felt deflated as she lowered to caress Ruby. "Here. I don't think that was an accident." She hoisted Ruby up onto her skates. Out of the corner of her eye, Lottie caught Belzak smirk sinfully back at them.

"What happened?" Ruby's voice seeped with surprise. Blood trickled from a split lip.

"I've got a hankie in my purse." Lottie scrabbled under the bench and offered it to Ruby.

"Thanks," said Ruby, sitting down and dabbing her mouth. "It's not a bad cut."

"New kid! Get out there," Roughie shouted.

Lottie looked up to see the red shirt captain pointing to the roving throng of pack skaters. She froze.

"Get out there, kid!"

Lottie couldn't move.

"Damn it. Get in the pack!" Roughie stomped one skate on the floor. The loud noise snapped Lottie out of her shock. "What are you waiting for?"

Lottie staggered without thought through the infield to the track. "I'm ready. Okay," she teetered. The wind from the storm of activity brushed Lottie's face. Feeling like a little fool, just as she had on the first day of training, she gathered her wits and fought the banks until her tomboy steps got her to the guardrail. It felt like an entire world of eyes was examining her every move, criticizing her impish body.

"Come on, Lottie!" Ruby called out from the bench. "Do it for Elsie Mae!"

One deep breath, and Lottie fell in alongside the moving pack of pounding skaters. Her wheels squeaked and rolled her closer to the others. She thought well of herself. Suddenly, she tripped over another player's outreaching stride. She flew head over heels and landed square on her butt. *Thud.*

The crowd erupted with laugher. Getting to her feet, she waited at the guardrail while the drone of skates echoed around the arena and back again. Her shaking hand let go of the guardrail. She spotted the referee looking at her scornfully.

"Am I slowing the game down?" she called to him.

He sounded his whistle and pointed right at her. "Get going."

Old television memories meshed with the action. Nothing resembled those images from home; everything felt foreign. She plodded her way into the pack, negotiating space with nine others. The next play started with the whistle's shriek.

"And the whistle sounds. This play has started," the announcer yelled.

Voices and cheers from the crowd turned into a cascading racket. Everything blurred together inside Lottie's mind. Arms and elbows flew all around her. She caught a glimpse of Ruby on the infield, holding one hand to her mouth. Lottie felt herself jostled back and forth, hit hard again and again, she fought just to stay upright. The skaters near her talked almost casually. She couldn't understand their words. A hand slapped her helmet down over one eyelid. Another hand tugged her hair. She felt an elbow jab, then a jolting bump. More unseen elbows and arms threw her this way and that.

"Oh!" Lottie fell flat on her face, body in a tangled wreck. The crowd roared with delight.

Ruby squirmed in her seat.

In that moment, Lottie remembered the humiliation after the marble contest, and when the boys had traumatized her in the park when she was six. She felt like a zero. The audience delighted in her mistakes. She got up and skated with spastic movements to catch up with the pack of skaters, just as the racing jammers approached from behind. Someone slammed her between the shoulder blades with a bone-jarring block.

Down Lottie went again with a *crash*, and the other team scored one point over her collapsed body. One of the other team's players skated by, smirking and yelling, "Gotcha!"

The fans applauded and cheered.

Esther raced to the television set, brows drawn close. She hoped Lottie would be one of this week's players. "Television

Tim Patten

time, kids," she said, with the customary bowls of freshly-made popcorn tucked in her arms. She wiggled the antennas. When the picture solidified, she smiled widely. "Kids! Hon! Hon! Come in here! Lottie might be playing!"

Murray grumbled from behind his newspaper.

"Look!" Esther exclaimed to the two girls, pointing at the screen. "Is that Lottie?"

Rhoda held her head in both hands. "Uh-huh!"

"Yes, it is. Look!" Betty leaned forward with one hand on her knee.

Esther let out a slow breath. She sat down on the couch with her popcorn bowl while the girls huddled around the television. Esther raised an eyebrow and smiled. Everyone gave the screen their rapt attention.

"Hon, come here," Esther called out again.

Murray shook the newspaper loudly and turned the page, buried in the day's news.

Esther fiddled with a kernel of popcorn and stared at the screen. A list of players' names scrolled past as the announcer called them out. She edged forward on the couch. "Roughie Barclay, Eve Belzak, Bobbie Beal, Ruby Johnson." The announcer paused. "And Lottie Zimmerman."

"It's her!" Betty cheered.

Esther became misty-eyed.

A corner of the newspaper lowered. Murray peered with one eye at the television from his spot at the kitchen table, then returned to reading.

"Oh, *my*!" Esther yelled when one of the skaters flew over the rail and landed in the crowd.

Rhoda smiled. "I hope Lottie's team wins."

Lottie skated in two more plays. Things weren't going well. She got slammed against the wooden railing. Someone grabbed her hair and tossed her into the infield. She rejoined the pack with aching feet and ankles. She was dumped onto her butt five more times. With each fall, her legs wobbled more and more.

Lottie felt like she'd been staggering on stilts. She had all but lost control over her calf muscles. She was jittering along the track one more time when someone bump-blocked her. Another skater leapt high into the air, jutted her hip out, and body-checked Lottie. That blow threw her onto the track with a *smack*, hard enough to be heard by the audience.

When she staggered back to the dressing area, Patty was at the entrance, "Here you go, honey." She handed her a white envelope. "Listen, Oscar wants his group to look good, so tomorrow I'll take you three to the five-and-dime."

Lottie found money inside the envelope. It was her first pay! "What ya mean, 'five-and-dime'?"

"You can't wear those clothes you came in with," Patty said. The bluntness of the words made Lottie grimace.

"Lottie, I can't believe it." Ruby held out the few dollars from her envelope. "We're getting paid for what we love!"

"And tomorrow we'll get to go shopping," Rebecca said. "You can get rid of those combat boots!"

"I know." A smile spread across Lottie's face. "This is just peachy."

"Better put that paltry rookie bread away. It ain't nothin' to brag about," Belzak warned.

Lottie tucked her money away and joined Ruby and Rebecca in the small corner of the locker room.

"Girls, come over here. I need to talk to you." Patty motioned to a secluded area near a bathroom stall. The girls surrounded her. "You'll learn this in time, but I think you should hear it right away before something happens."

"There's something funny about some of the men who come to roller derby games. They get ideas in their heads about us women."

"What kinds of ideas?" Rebecca searched for lint on her jersey.

"They think we're loose. You know, free with our bodies off the track." Patty looked deep into each of the girls' eyes.

"I just want you to know, some of the girls are accosted by men waiting in cars after games."

"Oh, God." Rebecca's voice quivered.

"Don't worry. It's mostly a bunch of men boasting. Ain't no problem as long as you stay together. Got it? Don't leave the locker rooms alone."

"I understand. We'll stick to one another like glue," Lottie said.

"Good. Now get dressed. You all did just fine."

Just fine? Rebecca's legs wobbled back to her dressing area, and her friends gathered around just as weak and wobbly.

"Something else we never learned in training," Ruby said.

"What did Roughie say to you before the game started?" Lottie asked Rebecca.

"I guess the ends of the benches are reserved for the big stars. You know, closer to the audience, camera shots and all. New kids sit only in the center."

"Everyone hit the showers," Patty called out. "No one gets out without a shower. Oscar doesn't want his fans around smelly skaters, you know."

"That's right!" Belzak said to the new skaters. "The new kids shower first."

Lottie gazed at her friends, all three bewildered by more unwritten rules. They did as they were commanded but knew something was up. With the other skaters going back to their own business, the girls huddled together, getting ready for the showers.

"If you don't like it here, you can always run back to Momma and Dada," Belzak called out from the other side of the locker room.

"My ears are still ringing from all the noise," Ruby said under her breath as she bent over to unlace her skates.

"How'd I do?" Lottie asked. "Patty said we were fine."

No one answered right away. Rebecca undressed.

"Patty might have been being nice to us. You were …" Ruby cleared her throat. "Fine," she finally said. "At least you skated. I didn't skate at all."

"If Mom saw me tonight, she musta pitied me for how I crawled around on the track on my hands and knees. What a crumb."

"I wonder if they'll keep us," Rebecca whispered.

"Say, Rebecca, will you help me write a letter to my mom?" Lottie asked. "You know, penmanship and all. I want to send her a little cash, and I worry about Rhoda and Betty."

Rebecca brightened up. "Of course. We can work on it when we get to the quarters."

Lottie smiled. "I'm no good at writing that kind of stuff."

"Don't worry 'bout that now. I can help you." Rebecca pulled her trunks off. "We can work on penmanship once a day. I'll help you write the first letter." She packed a few items into her bag. "Say, why don't you read the sports page to get your reading up to snuff?"

"I might do that."

"Don't forget to leave your uniform," Patty announced from the doorway. She looked down at the checklist on her clipboard. "Tomorrow I want everyone back here by two o'clock." She searched the room.

Lottie widened her eyes. "Ah, jeez, we have to do it all again tomorrow."

"Oh my gosh, yeah." Rebecca hunched over.

Hope seemed to glow on Ruby's face. "Maybe they'll use me tomorrow."

"I'm already nervous." Nerves fidgeted inside Lottie. She'd do a whole lot better the next day. Maybe. Her legs had turned to rubber and hornets swirled in her stomach.

"We have all night to worry," said Ruby, chuckling.

"Let's not get cranked. We can work on that first letter home," Rebecca said.

"Good idea." Lottie had pushed the jumpy feeling aside, but she still worried about the next day's game. She wrapped a towel around herself and headed for the showers.

Chapter 17

WHO DO YOU THINK YOU ARE?

Rebecca slammed her book shut. *Thump*! Working in the derby meant living in murky locker rooms and hotels. "After four months, this is *certainly* not what I expected."

Lottie was startled at Rebecca's outburst.

"That's for sure," the usually cheerful Ruby agreed.

"Oh, sure, when someone's hurt or needs a rest, they put us in the pack. But mostly we just warm the benches for everyone else."

"What's wrong? You've been acting strange this past week," Lottie said to Rebecca.

"Strange? What do you mean strange?"

"Distant, irritable."

"Oh, it's *nothing*."

"Girl, what you reading now?" Ruby asked Rebecca as she pulled up and tightened her flyaway ponytail.

Rebecca returned the book to her bag. "Just a Hemingway novel, *The Old Man and the Sea*."

"Sounds fancy."

"Sure nothing's wrong?" Lottie lowered the sports page she'd been studying.

"I'm okay," Rebecca said with a sigh. "Really, just fine."

"Okay, guys. Ready to hear a rumor?" Ruby asked.

Rebecca sat up and Lottie put both elbows on her knees. "Sure," she said.

"I'm ready," Rebecca agreed, curiosity pushing the grumpiness aside for the moment.

"Did you know that Vinnie's been gone for the last two weeks?"

"No," Lottie said. "Disappeared? I wouldn't bother looking for him. He isn't my cup 'a tea."

"What do you mean gone?" Rebecca asked. She pulled unruly strands of red hair into place.

"They say he killed his wife. Shot her right in the head! And then hid from the cops," Ruby intimated.

"*Murder?*" Lottie whispered, incredulous.

"That's what they're saying." Ruby's eyes were wide and serious.

"Grummy creep. I bet he just wants another girl."

"Can't trust any of 'em," Rebecca muttered. She settled back in her seat and crossed her arms. "If things had been a little different, that could have been one of us."

"They say the police have been secreting to the games every night looking for him. They want to question him about the night his wife died."

"I wonder if he did it." Lottie felt her blood rush thinking he had made a move on her, maybe if she hadn't overhead what he really thought of gals in the derby ... maybe she would have fallen for it.

"And guess what else I heard?" Ruby nudged Lottie with an elbow as she took a quick look around the room.

"God, what else?"

Rebecca and Lottie edged a bit closer to Ruby. "I heard Oscar's closing the unit," she whispered, serious as death.

Lottie sat up and adjusted her posture. "No! What did you say?"

"The story is that Oscar's closing the derby."

Lottie's breathing stopped. Terror swept through her. The shock would have made tears burst from her eyes if she hadn't been frozen to the core. These ups and down were so hard on them all. "If I lose this job, I'll never get another! You know how bad I did in school!"

"I know, but they're saying the derby's going to close. I'm sick about it too," Ruby put a hand on her belly as if she were going to throw up.

Rebecca's eyebrows knitted together. "The crowds sure have been getting smaller."

"But ..." Lottie's heart was racing. "Not shut us down, right? It can't be." She remembered the last time she had spoken to her dad. "My dad was right. Maybe this job isn't going to go anywhere."

"And Oscar ain't smiled in a long time," Ruby said.

"We *can't* close." Lottie couldn't think straight. "I can't go back home ... I couldn't stand that. What would I ... I guess I could work back at Mason's? But we're learning so much here."

"I sure don't want to go home, either," Ruby said.

"Can't be ... what kind of job ... I mean ... how else could I get into sports?" Lottie's stomach looped wildly.

"I don't know." Ruby softly shook her head.

Lottie sat up straight. "Guys. Let's hope it's a bad rumor." She put on a forced grin. "I'm concentrating on staying on my skates and learning. One day, I'll be one of the best out there."

"Empress, I'm sure you will." Rebecca exhaled.

"Sure. I'll be okay." Lottie ran an old comb through her hair. "I'm the Little Lunatic, remember? I can take it." She didn't quite believe her own half-hearted bravado.

"Lottie, you think one day you'll beat Belzak?" Ruby asked, delivering a punch to an imaginary foe.

"One day, I'll take her." Lottie nodded at the crisscross of the skate laces, and looked up and around at the eccentric roller derby skaters. Suddenly, fear got the better of her again. Her fingers trembled. It wasn't time for her to leave her team, the smoky locker room, the arenas or the noise of the crowds. Not just yet.

"Belzak's a tough cookie. Maybe the toughest," Rebecca remarked.

Belzak, holding court in the corner, raised her voice loud enough for Lottie and the others to hear. "He knew how to treat a lady. And you know that there's no one more of a lady than me!" Belzak stood, bent her spine back and eyed Lottie. "If Hitler had got to her parents, she wouldn't be here."

Lottie felt Belzak's hateful words burn inside. In that instant, she wondered if it wouldn't be better if the derby did close. Her lungs constricted. If she could only get away from people like Belzak. Lottie swallowed her pride and ignored the cutting words. She couldn't imagine anything else in the world for her but the derby, she would have to take this verbal punching ... for now.

Roughie twisted her mouth in disgust at Rebecca. "She can take the darkie and *that* little red-headed bookworm witch with her." She threw her head back and took a swig from her flask.

"Let's be ladies." Quiet Gerry Murphy gently glowered at Belzak and Roughie.

"Who the hell are you, the committee for decency?" Roughie slurred.

"I'm just saying ..." Gerry held a palm up. "Let's be ladies." A long ash crashed from the end of her cigarette.

Lottie, Rebecca and Ruby sat quietly, heads held low, hoping the discussion would end. Several seconds ticked by without another biting remark. The older skaters went back to their tasks. Gerry inhaled more smoke and Belzak toyed with her hair and earrings. Roughie guzzled at intervals, muttering.

"Rebecca," Lottie said, taking a long look at Roughie.

"What is it?"

"I just had a thought." Lottie took another quick glance at Roughie, then back at Rebecca. "Roughie might be jealous of you."

"Don't be ridiculous," Rebecca said.

"I see what you mean," Ruby said. "She's kind of, ya know, *funny*-looking."

Lottie moved closer to Rebecca. "All she can do is skate for the visiting teams, like me. You know, be a bad guy."

"So?"

"She's been on the visiting team all her skating career. You, well, you're pretty and sober. All-American type freckled face, just out of high school and cute ginger hair.

And they put ya on the home team already! See what I mean?" Lottie said.

"You're a shy one all right, but you're pretty, that's for sure," Ruby said.

"You're both crazy." Rebecca shrugged as if she were throwing the idea aside, but she took a quick look at Roughie. "I can take care of myself."

"Then do it!" Lottie said.

"Let's go! Red shirts warm up," Patty called into the locker room.

After a moment of waiting, Ruby stood up. "Ready to warm the benches?"

"And fall on our butts, don't forget," Lottie laughed, inhaling the heavy smoke and musk-drenched air. She heard the warm-up buzzer sound. Patty called again for the teams. Belzak handed Patty, as she did every game, the same stuffed animal that the announcer presented to Belzak at the announcer's table—so she could pretend some guy in the audience had actually gone out of his way to give it to her.

"What a phony," Lottie said while she and Ruby traipsed out of the locker area with their teammates. Rebecca joined them. "See ya after the game, Rebecca," Lottie called, as she left with the visiting team.

After warm ups, the arena vibrated with the sound of hard wheels beating the track. Belzak removed her helmet and bashed one of the smallest home team skaters over the head. The little skater rubbed her head and Gerry came to her side to protect her. The small crowd, loud and excited, screamed at Belzak as they cheered for the home team, hoping for another victory.

"Look, they're letting Rebecca on the track again!" Ruby leaned over to Lottie as the two sat on the bench. "She's gonna play!"

Lottie tracked Rebecca while she rolled around a few laps within the whirling rhythm of skaters.

"Come on, Rebecca," Ruby mouthed in a silent cheer.

"I'm proud of her." Lottie's heart expanded with every move Rebecca made. "I wish I skated as well as her."

Roller Babes

"Get up at the front of the pack, I said!" Lottie could hear Roughie yell at Rebecca. Rebecca fought to catch up. "I said, up front!"

Suddenly, she stumbled and fell. Her outstretched legs tripped another skater on the way down.

"Ouch," Ruby cried. "That was bad. I hope she didn't break something."

Roughie Barclay skated out to Rebecca while the pack was making their way to the other side of the track. No sooner had she arrived than she jumped high into the air. From her vantage point at the side of the track, Lottie could just hear Roughie grunt in mid-air, "No-good new kid." Then Roughie's stout body landed with a *crash* on one of Rebecca's legs. Rebecca howled in pain.

Lottie stiffened and gasped.

"Rebecca's hurt. The audience didn't even see it!" Ruby said.

The fans were conditioned to respond to conflicts between a few established skaters, like Gerry Murphy and Roughie Barclay. And these always happened in the thick of the action, not when some skater took a spill. Conflicts like these could go on without being noticed. Rebecca sat in pain while all eyes besides Lottie's and Ruby's went elsewhere.

"Get up, please get up," Lottie whispered.

Belzak absorbed the audience's attention by ranting at the other end of the track. She pointed at no one in the seats and screamed meaningless provocations. She shaped her breasts with both hands and kept shouting. Several groups of people stood and yelled insults back at Belzak.

Lottie didn't miss this vulgar display, but her eyes didn't move off of poor Rebecca. Rebecca grimaced in misery. Roughie picked herself up from the track and kicked the new kid in the ankle. With pain outlined on her face, Rebecca gathered her composure. She trembled and fidgeted with her jersey.

"This ain't good." Lottie shook her head fighting the urge to skate over there and help.

"Poor Rebecca. I hope she'll be able to get out of the way." Ruby leaned forward.

Something changed. Rebecca jutted out her upper lip, and the rest of her body straightened up. Her face glared with a devilish sort of spite that Lottie had never seen before.

"What's she doing?" Ruby asked.

Rebecca struggled to her feet and pointed a rigid finger at the older skater. With her mouth open wide, she exploded. "I've had enough of you!"

"Oh, my God!" Ruby almost laughed.

"Who do you think you are?" Roughie shouted back at Rebecca. Her rough face, blotchy white, twisted with hate.

Instead of cowering, Rebecca stood her ground. "Who do you think *you* are?" Her face matched the color of her fiery-red hair. Her braid swayed back and forth in a flurry.

"Oh, God!" Lottie stood slowly to her feet.

Roughie threw a long, repulsed stare at Rebecca.

"Nasty cuss. Leave me alone!" Rebecca's face coarsened. She looked powerful in a way that Lottie had never seen. "I'm not taking orders from you!" Rebecca yelled.

"Screw you."

"Take a flying leap!" Rebecca's face was fierce.

Roughie dismissed the youngster with the flip of a finger and skated away.

"Look, she backed down," Lottie chuckled.

Ruby stood and yelled, "Hurray for you, Rebecca!"

"I can't believe it."

Rebecca rolled into the infield. She placed both hands on her thighs, and kept her body weight off the aching ankle. Lottie wanted to go to her friend's side, but she couldn't; she skated for the other team. It wouldn't look right to the fans.

The drumming noises of the skaters continued to hypnotize the crowd and the game spun into its climactic end. The fans stood with hands clapping high above their heads.

Lottie and the skaters left the track to undress and assemble for showers in the locker rooms.

For the third time that week, Roughie threw a tantrum. Her disdain for everybody and everything showed on her homely face. Hate seeped out of her body as she roller-rammed into the locker room before anyone else could get there. Lottie knew she'd be nursing that flask in some corner, seething. "She's going to have it in for someone tonight!"

Chapter 18

BRA AND PANTIES SCURRY

Bam! "Damn kids!" Roughie slammed her locker again. *Bam!* She slapped a towel on the floor and broke open her flask. She kicked her skates off while gulping. "I told you to stay outta my way! And get up front!" Roughie wiped her mouth with one hand and then reached down for her skates, slamming them against the wall with a loud *whack*. "Damn it!" she yelled, forcing Lottie and rest of the skaters to stop and stare. She beat the wall with her skates repeatedly, gouging the plaster into a cloud of dust.

"Pipe down, you old bag," Rebecca said.

Lottie's heart jumped. Everyone in the locker room stood quiet.

"*What* did you say?"

"You heard me," Rebecca's nostrils flared as she jerked her uniform off.

"Don't have a fit, Roughie. They don't know any better," Gerry interjected.

"Shut up Gerry, you witch." Roughie hissed. "You think you're so damn smart." Her eyes strained with years of resentment toward the pretty Gerry Murphy. "I've played second place to you year after year. Selling your ass every game. I'm sick of it!"

"I don't see why you get so mad." Gerry lit a cigarette.

"Why don't you two cram it?" Belzak yelled, tossing her jersey to the floor.

"The new kids don't listen. They're just in the way, and that damn play didn't work." Roughie slammed a locker door shut. "I was supposed to score that point!"

"Oh brother!" Rebecca slung her skating tights onto the floor. Lottie nudged Ruby, nodding toward Rebecca.

"Settle down. It's just a game," Gerry sighed.

"Just a game?" Roughie challenged.

"Sure, we've been doing this for years."

"That's the whole damn point. I'm sick and tired ... same old shit from you! I hate you." Roughie tossed a balled up sock at Gerry, knocking the cigarette from her lips.

"What the hell?" Not far from Gerry, Rebecca stopped massaging her aching ankles to watch this new turn of events: Gerry swearing!?

"And you damn new kids! Why don't you all get the hell out of here?" Roughie swung around and bore down on Rebecca. She looked like she wanted to pull Rebecca's hair out.

"Hold on, Roughie." Gerry moved between them. Roughie threw a fist that just missed her.

Gerry was impassive. "Leave the kid alone."

Rebecca jutted her chin out at the older skater. "You don't scare me!"

Lottie's stomach felt empty as Roughie swirled around, half-staggering. She looked ready to kill.

"You've been in a bad mood for the past three years," Gerry scowled.

"Who the hell are you? Some sort of Sister of the Righteous, here?" Spittle flew from Roughie's mouth. She whirled to her locker, grabbed the flask and took a quick guzzle. She closed the lid and tossed it back into her locker with a bang.

"No," Gerry planted her legs wide. "Not at all."

Roughie leaned forward. "You're the same as the other dirty scoundrels who sneak into the toilet to read dirty books and tell filthy stories, and then come back out and try to spoil everyone else's night."

"You tell her!" Belzak added. "You were always a better skater than that blonde!"

Gerry rocked her head in frustrated unbelief. "You crazy old ..."

Roughie leaned toward Gerry. "You remind me of that no-good husband I left years ago."

"He left *you* is more like it," Gerry raised her voice. "None of us would have left our four-year-old kid at home to go off with the derby."

Lottie tensed and Roughie jabbed a thumb to her chest. "This game needs *me*."

"You think you're bigger than you really are," Rebecca said in a trembling voice. "You're nobody!"

"What the hell do you know? You're just a pissant barely out of diapers!" She lunged at Rebecca, grabbing a handful of red locks. She tugged Rebecca's face to an inch from her own. "Listen here and listen good! I'm bigger than you'll ever be."

"The hell!" Rebecca grabbed Roughie's hair and twisted.

In a feverish thrust, Roughie pushed the younger girl backwards and tumbled down on her. Rebecca tipped over her seat in her bra and panties, trying to claw Roughie's hands away. Still holding a handful of Roughie's hair, she yanked and snarled. "You're just a bully, you bitch!"

"Stop it, you two!" Gerry commanded.

Roughie blinked at the spit that came from Rebecca's words. She flinched and backed away.

"Oh, no." Lottie was amazed that this was Rebecca. *Where did the quiet bookworm go?*

Roughie's eyes narrowed. Her knobby fingers widened like claws, ready to pounce. Gerry stepped between them and gripped Roughie's wrist. "That's enough, Roughie. Leave her alone."

"Don't interfere!" Roughie raised a fist. "You think you're better than me and all of us! Just because you've been dating the referee for two years!"

Someone moaned.

"That has nothing to do with this," Gerry said.

"You don't have anything on me, on the track or off." Roughie pulled from Gerry's grasp and jammed the blonde's arm aside.

"You left your kid with an abusive husband. Or at least you *say* he was abusive. How's that for starters? I've never done that." Gerry frowned. "No one in here would have done that."

A slap of silence hit the room.

"What kind of mother would do that, Roughie?"

"Zip it," Roughie's face flared red. She gave Gerry a good shove, sending her reeling backward over a bench.

"Hands off, you old drunk!" Rebecca shouted when Roughie grabbed Gerry by the neck. Then she fled the room. Lottie noticed Rebecca's flight from the locker room, wearing only bra and panties.

"Where's Rebecca going?" Ruby asked.

Lottie guessed Rebecca had gone to look for Patty. "Maybe she's going to get help. But she ain't got much on for clothes!"

Roughie and Gerry tussled. A chair crashed against the wall. Roughie pulled a clump of Gerry's hair out by the roots. "Damn you!"

Roughie drew back a closed fist for one big punch, just as the door swung open. Patty and Oscar Wentworth burst in through the door. Lottie saw them take in the spectacle. Roughie straightened and gave Gerry one small push, then retreated, sauntering in a snit back to her dressing area.

"Okay!" Oscar bellowed. "Settle down."

The locker room mayhem subsided.

Oscar waited. "Settle," he repeated with his arms extended. "I have some news."

"Did Rebecca come back?" Ruby looked around.

Lottie saw the panty-clad Rebecca slip inside the room and return to her seat. "She's over there, putting her clothes on."

Roughie stopped her tantrum and directed glassy eyes at the boss.

"First, some bad news," Oscar said.

Lottie gulped. She sat unmoving.

"We've been having trouble filling the seats."

Knots bunched inside Lottie's gut.

"This could be it," Ruby said in a low voice. "No more work."

"No, it can't be."

Oscar paused. "So we decided to close one of our units."

Lottie turned white. "God, no," she wheezed.

Other skaters gasped, and Lottie heard someone crying. Lottie guessed she'd be sent home with her tail between her legs. She could practically hear her father sneering at her. She'd be back home in no time, just like he had said. Back to work in a diner and to try to find some guy to marry her.

"We're having trouble with the crowds. They're too small," Oscar said, motioning out to the door to the arena.

"I am not going back home." Lottie's legs quaked with the idea. "I can't go back to work at Mason's diner. It'll kill me."

"I don't want to go back, either," Ruby said. "This is my dream."

"We're closing Unit B," Oscar announced.

Silence.

"Unit B?" Lottie repeated.

"That's the one in Chicago for the Midwest area," Oscar said.

"That means ..." Lottie's mind swam in all directions.

"*This* unit will remain intact," Oscar said.

Lottie's thoughts surfaced from the depths of the ocean. She could feel her heart banging and she tried to calm herself with a lungful of heavy locker room air.

"But we have immediate plans," Oscar continued. "We need to change things up, and get the show up to snuff."

"I'm in. Count me in," Belzak gabbled. She put both hands on her knees and leaned forward.

"That's good. We're going to need all of you," Oscar said.

Blood returned to Lottie's face.

"We're staying open," Ruby said with a deep exhalation. "I won't have to be a house maid."

"Tomorrow, we start a two-year tour of different cities around the country," said Oscar, lifting two fingers in the air. "We're gonna barnstorm. We'll take the game to Wichita, Tupelo, Peoria, Chicago, West Chester, Amarillo, and every town in between."

"Sounds like we'll be all over the place." Ruby cocked one eyebrow.

"We're going to zigzag up, down and across the country, and even hit Billings, Montana. Barnstorming 'til we get this thing right," Oscar spoke with conviction.

"Oh, my God." Lottie's tightened muscles loosened with relief.

"A national tour," Ruby said.

"This tour starts with Wichita, Kansas," Oscar said proudly. "Then we head for Tupelo, Mississippi. And we leave tomorrow."

"*Tomorrow?*" someone questioned.

"We have trains and buses scheduled to take the entire troupe. We'll stay six to ten weeks, maybe more in every city. We'll skate at armories, arenas and outdoor stadiums. Any place that'll take us. You'll stay at hotels and quarters."

Lottie had never been outside her hometown, except for Trenton. Now she'd be embarking on a tour of the country. To her, it sounded like a worldwide excursion; it filled her with wild energy.

"You'll all have to work harder," Oscar said. "Now, about the attendance. It's been in a nosedive for the past six months, so we're going to do something about that."

"What do we need to do?" Gerry rubbed her head while the other skaters looked around the room with bewilderment. Gerry quietly found a new cigarette and popped it between her lips.

Roughie sat back, the earlier altercation forgotten.

"We need to go on a budget. Since we've closed down Unit B for a while, some of those skaters might want to join us. We'll provide travel, meals and board." He stopped, then clapped his hands together once. "But we can't pay a full salary till the crowds come back. You'll get half your regular pay."

"Only half," Ruby said. "That's enough for me."

"Each of you will need to decide if you're going to stay or quit. And you'll need to decide tonight."

A low murmur ran through the room.

"Don't worry, I've been running this thing for over fifteen years now. I know what we're going to do. We need more *color*, like the grudge between Roughie and Gerry. The fans eat it up." His eyes sparkled as he scanned the room, catching each woman's eyes one by one. "We need more of that." He stopped and almost frowned, adding, "We need it on the track, but not *off!*"

Lottie remembered the story Buddy told her about his wife Gloria who fought each game to increase the size of the crowd.

"We understand," Belzak said. "You want more color."

"We can do that." Roughie threw her head back and downed the last of her liquor.

"We'll advertise on a big billboard before we hit each town. It'll read: *Gerry And Roughie Are Back*." His smile belied an ingenious plot and one of his hands streaked through the air as if presenting the message in huge letters.

"Brilliant," Belzak said, sucking up.

"I'm going to need each of you to pitch in."

"Sure, all of us need a job. My family remembers when we were lucky to sell a potato on the streets to get our next meal. I'm with you, Oscar," Belzak said in a sweet voice.

"Once derby, always derby," Gerry said.

"I definitely want to go," Ruby whispered to Lottie under her breath.

"Even if there's less pay?" Lottie asked.

"Sure."

"We'll tighten up the race!" Oscar clenched both hands together. "So, during this tour, we're going to improve. We'll get better. And then hopefully head straight back for the big time again: New York City."

Lottie's blood pounded in her ears at the thought.

"Don't know how I'll afford my booze, but I'm all for that, boss," Roughie slurred from the back of the room.

"All right, then. Thanks, everyone. Patty will help those who decide to leave us here. If you stay, she'll have all your instructions for tomorrow's train ride out of Trenton. I'll see those who stay on the other train." Oscar eyed the room. When he was satisfied that the message had stuck, he left.

Lottie guessed Oscar needed to deliver the same speech to the guys' locker room. She turned to Ruby, still wide-eyed. "Well?"

"I'm staying," Ruby said at once, brimming and bouncing with renewed enthusiasm.

"Me, too." Lottie looked at Rebecca, who'd packed her skates and finally gotten some clothes on.

Turning to Lottie with a heartfelt smile, Rebecca said, "I'm leaving."

"What?" Lottie's mouth widened and her emotions drained. She sat next to Rebecca, who looked away. "What are you going to do? Where will you go? Home?"

"You can't." Ruby's voice trailed off.

Rebecca looked far down the room, as if searching for an old memory. She slouched a little and heaved a shallow sigh. "I'm going to do something."

"What? I don't understand," Lottie said, attention fully on Rebecca. "How can you think of leaving? You just squared off with Roughie! It was great ... and ... well, you can't live with your dad."

Rebecca's eyes brightened. She filled her bag in slow languid movements. "I don't know. I just know I'm going to get off this merry-go-round. I'm through with the whole thing."

"What *thing*?" Lottie put an open hand on her chest.

"*This*. I'm almost eighteen now," Rebecca said.

"You want to become something, don't ya?" Lottie wanted to ignite her friend's dream again, to remind her of the loneliness they'd felt as children.

Rebecca straightened and looked into Lottie's eyes. "Lottie, this was the best thing that ever happened to me. I owe it all to you." Rebecca paused and then her voice became stronger. "I know I can do whatever I want now. I did what you said. I said *no*. And then I went and told someone."

It brought a smile to Lottie's face. She caught sight of the glimmer in Rebecca's eye. She'd said *no* to Roughie's bullying, and then she'd gone and told Oscar and Patty and that had worked now, it would work anywhere. "I'm proud of you, Rebecca."

Rebecca smiled. "I never thought I could do it 'til you encouraged me." Rebecca's eyes puffed up. "I feel so good about myself."

"Yes."

"And now I can move on."

"Stay." Lottie lowered her voice. "Don't forget: Empresses Rebecca and Lottie."

"Empresses of the World." Rebecca put a hand on Lottie's wrist.

"Yeah," Lottie said, remembering how young and naive they once were.

"Oh, Lottie." Rebecca's voice became weak. "I've been thinking about leaving for weeks." She looked directly into Lottie's eyes, and slowly shook her head without taking her eyes from Lottie's. "I don't need to take over the world here, in the derby. I just need to take over *my* world."

"We can have lots of fun, though." Lottie rubbed the top of her hand.

"No. I'm tired of being a misfit."

"I hear that," Ruby chimed in.

"We're *all* misfits. You *can't* just give up."

"I'm not giving up. I'm moving on." Rebecca grasped Lottie's hand lovingly. "I have a new dream now. I want to become a schoolteacher."

"What?"

"You know, a teacher, in the old neighborhood."

"If you can teach Lottie, you can teach anyone," Ruby beamed.

"Thank you, Ruby."

"I'm even reading the newspaper," Lottie said with a hiccup of sweet and sad emotions.

A bunch of books clumped together in Rebecca's skate bag. "I'll never forget about you. I know it might be a while until I see you again, if you're going on the road for two years." She paused. "I've got to do this, though. Besides, maybe I'll meet a nice fella and settle down." She reached inside her bag and pulled out the Hemingway novel, *The Old Man and the Sea*. She handed it to Lottie. "Promise me you'll read this?"

Lottie took into the intense glimmer in Rebecca's eyes. "I think I understand. And I know I'm happy for you, so truly happy. Of course I'll read it." She placed both hands on the top of the book, letting her fingertips run along the dust cover that protected the binding beneath. Rebecca gave a full smile with an unbroken gaze.

"I'll be watching you from the television set at home," Rebecca said. "Little Lunatic." Her eyes sparkled as if the whole world had finally opened up.

"Thanks so much for helping me learn to write letters home and encouraging me to read," Lottie said.

"I loved every minute of it."

"You'll be a great teacher." Lottie looked at the floor a moment, knowing she wasn't just saying that.

"Don't worry about me." Rebecca looked at Lottie eye-to-eye. "Look, I made it this far. But this isn't for me anymore." Rebecca grabbed her bags and things. "I've changed. Lots of things have changed."

"Bye, Rebecca." Ruby gave Rebecca a peck on the cheek.

Rebecca wrapped her arms around Lottie. Warmth rushed over Lottie as they embraced for a long moment. But then she was out the door and away.

Chapter 19

ALL ABOARD

More waiting. Doing nothing but tapping fingers, Lottie felt her heart twang in anticipation of her first real train ride. On the edge of Trenton, reading the newspaper was impossible; it was time to travel.

"The Baltimore Bullets lost their twenty-ninth basketball game last Saturday." She pulled her brows together.

"I imagine they have no one in their audiences, either." Ruby tugged her ponytail tight.

A familiar face came around the corner. "Buddy!" Lottie almost gushed.

"You didn't think I'd let you go without saying good luck, did you?"

"I didn't know. But thanks!"

"This is Dorothy." Buddy took his hat off and stood aside for a tall brunette woman to shake Lottie's hand.

"Hi, Lottie. I've heard a lot about you. This guy can't stop talking about the next big television star."

Lottie looked puzzled.

"That's you, honey," Dorothy laughed.

"I'm hardly a star. Besides, Rebecca quit the other day. I miss her, and Elsie Mae." Lottie felt a flush of heat.

"Sure. I understand kid. But you'll meet more friends," Buddy reassured her.

"I guess so."

"I wanted to say a couple things to you. First, I wanted you to meet my Dorothy. She sells the training center skates, wheels and equipment, and I guess she sold herself on me, too." Buddy blushed.

"I'm so happy." Dorothy held his hand.

"You're going to find someone, too. Look at me, at my age. It can happen at the oddest time in your life," Buddy said.

"Well ... I never think about that." Lottie cleared her throat.

"I don't have to tell you that the derby life is hard, especially on the road. The women can be mean-spirited and envious. I just want you to see some friendly faces before you go, to think about when things get tough."

Lottie remembered the brawling in the locker room and how Rebecca had walked away from it all.

"You stay with it. Roller derby's been good to me. I think it'll be good to you, too."

"Hi, Buddy," Patty waved. "It's good to see you again. You've done a great job with this lunatic. Time for us to get on the train."

Buddy eased back. "Patty, you be sure to take care of my protégé here."

Patty saluted.

"Goodbye Buddy and Dorothy. Thanks for everything!" Lottie hugged them both, then stepped onto the train. They stood by the track as the other passengers piled into the car. Lottie waved to them as the train finally left the station, off on a real adventure. First stop, Kansas City.

The shout hurt Lottie's ears. "All aboard! Kansas City to Wichita, train five-two-seven, leaving on track number one in two minutes."

A shiver ran up Lottie's spine at hearing the conductor calling the trip. "Can you believe it? We're in Kansas already. And we're on our way to Wichita!" She rubbed the golden light fixture swaying above her head, enjoying the elegant shape of the metal.

Ruby sighed. "A long way from home."

The roller derby was on its way to another town after watching a crew of twelve men hand-carry the pieces of the massive roller track, four or five men to each pizza-wedge-shaped section. They had lugged them up a ramp and into one of the freight cars. Once a part of the track had been safely secured in its shipping area, the men rested and wiped sweat from their brows while a second group of workers wrestled the next section of track onto the train.

Behind Lottie, the train's rail car sparkled with finely decorated Art Deco-style cherry wood trim surrounding the windows and reaching all the way up to the ceiling. Small white lights pointed down onto the narrow walkway between the seats. Chock-full of anticipation, Lottie dreamed about what roller-road mysteries lay ahead. This was glamour and excitement. This was spirit lifting.

She eyed the golden lamps that hung along the sides of each seating area. They dangled like Egyptian artifacts alongside the big windows. She wished Elsie Mae and Rebecca could be here to share this and joke around. The train car felt exotic and luxurious; she felt it might just be possible to feel at home with derby Unit A.

"Guess who's getting on the train?" Ruby squinted.

"Who?" Lottie watched new passengers load onto the train car and into the seats in front of her.

"Vinnie."

"A creep! You're kidding. His name makes my skin crawl."

"He must be leaving with us to get away from the police."

"He's back on the team?"

"I guess so. He's a slug. I'm sure he offed his wife." Ruby shook her head.

Lottie looked through the window, peering at an almost empty Kansas City loading area. "I'll steer clear of him like the plague."

"All aboard!" The transom doors opened to Lottie's railroad passenger car. The conductor entered, dressed in a dark brown suit and circular cap. "KC to Wichita! Tickets, please!" He leaned over, reaching out toward one passenger. He checked a ticket and punched the end with his silver ticket punch. He worked a few seats ahead of Lottie and Ruby. Patty sat nearby, keeping a chaperone's eye over her two "new" girls.

Patty searched through her purse. "Let me see where our tickets are."

"Tickets, please."

Patty stuck her ticket packet out, reaching over Lottie and Ruby.

"How many?" The conductor said, eyeing the group. The train wheels slowed to a quiet roll, making Lottie's stomach lurch.

"Three, me and the two here. And I think one more's on the way."

The *clickety-clack-bump* of the train wheels began in slow thuds, along with the *snip-snip* of the conductor's device. Lottie's stomach whirred with excitement. The huge train wheels started a leisurely forward spool causing the passengers' heads to jog rhythmically.

A delicate-looking girl approached behind the conductor. Lottie eyed the girl's stylish wardrobe: a fitted wool suit with extended shoulder pads flattering a tiny waist.

"Hi! My name's Carol." She stood no taller than Lottie, slight and demure. The girl's white-blonde hair surrounded a soft round face.

"Is that a tattoo on your cheek?" Lottie squinted.

"It's a horse. Ain't it boss? I have two others: one on my ankle and one on my tit."

Lottie was taken aback. "Oh my!"

"I've never seen tattoos on a girl before." Ruby's eyes studied Carol, her tattoo, and her chest.

"My dad was in the navy and he came back with three anchors and ships. Then I fell in love with riding the horses whenever I went to camp." A flush raced across Carol's face. "It feels so good to ride. Kind of like sex."

"I'm afraid the sex I've had wasn't fun at all," Ruby leaned back deep in thought.

"I think they look pretty on a woman. Not like the tattooed lady in a carnival show and all," Lottie said while admiring Carol's girlish features. Even Carol's vigorous gum-chewing was fascinating.

Carol posed. "Small and retiring." She twisted an arm like a man. "But tough as shit!" she boomed in a spunky voice, then popped her gum.

"Hi," Lottie smiled, also leaning back in the train's plush seating.

"Okay, who do you have to sleep with to get a good seat on this train?" Carol slapped her thigh and giggled.

Ruby and Lottie laughed. "You'll fit right in here with the other derby gals," Lottie said.

"Carol Anderson?" Patty asked with a smile.

"That's me!" Carol held her head high and smacked her gum. Her self-confidence made Lottie feel like a young, shy girl again.

"Good. We've been expecting you. I didn't know you'd made it." Patty raised another ticket in the air for the conductor. "Why don't you sit here, across from Ruby?" Patty waved a hand to the open seat.

"I got dibs on this seat." Carol slapped the empty area close to Ruby.

"It's the only place left on the train, unless you want to sit in the bathroom," Ruby smiled.

"Girls, Carol will be joining us on the tour. She's one of the new home team skaters," Patty said.

Ruby leaned close to Carols face. "Hi, Carol Anderson. I'm Ruby Johnson, and this is Lottie Zimmerman."

"Conductor, she's the last ticket." Patty pointed toward Carol, who just placed a bag in an overhead compartment.

The conductor punched the ticket and gave it back to Patty, then moved on. "Tickets to Wichita," he announced, working his way down the length of the coach. Lottie thought he had years of practice because he didn't bump against any of the seats on either side of the aisle. She grinned in amusement at his circular hat. It reminded her of storybooks from school. She let the conductor leave her thoughts, and turned to Carol. "I like how ya do your makeup."

"Oh, this takes me two minutes to throw on."

"I don't wear any."

"You should," Carol said. "You're a big television star, you know."

"Naw." Lottie waved her hand in dismissal. She doubted any makeup would help a face like hers. How could makeup help get rid this Bob Hope nose and skinny face?

"Where you from?" Ruby asked.

"Kansas City." The train lurched, Carol lost her balance. She leaned against Ruby and almost fell into her lap. Ruby's dark face meshed with Carol's pale hair, and Ruby grabbed Carol's waist to keep them both from smashing into each other. "Oops, there." Ruby held Carol and inhaled slowly.

"Thanks for catching me," Carol said. "I was in Unit B, but they shut it down last week. Boy, did that throw a monkey wrench into everyone's lives."

"We're from New York," Ruby mumbled into strings of soft hair.

"Wow, ain't that exciting? New York! Amazing." Carol settled into her seat and shoved her handbag underneath after extracting a pack of cigarettes. "You know, I'll miss so many of the skaters in my unit."

"How many skaters stayed on?" Ruby asked.

"You've got nice dimples when you smile," Carol remarked before answering. "I think only me and two guys. They got on here in KC. My best friend couldn't make it. She asked if she could bring along her seven-year-old son. I guess they said no. So she decided to stay home with him instead. Can you believe that crap?" Carol pulled a cigarette out of the package and placed it between pink lips.

"What about her husband?" Lottie asked.

"He said he didn't want to babysit the kid while she went gallivanting around the country." When she spoke, the cigarette bounced dramatically up and down. Carol softened her voice and leaned in toward Ruby. Her eyes darted from Lottie's to Patty's and back to Ruby's. "Ain't that something? She told me that story because I get along with most everyone."

"Men. I guess they like making them, but don't like taking care of the kids," Ruby frowned. "It's disgusting and funny at the same time. I wouldn't call taking care of your own kid *babysitting*."

"You said it," Carol said. "First men flip over you, then they turn into bad news." The three laughed. Everything felt natural and easy between them.

The carpeted steel floor shuddered under Lottie's feet, making her toes tickle. The train noises soon overwhelmed the coach like the lullaby of a rainstorm.

"Girls, I'm going to the bar car for a drink with the other skaters. Stay put now." Patty winked as she stood.

Carol eyed Patty as she left, then leaned forward and put a hand in the air, calling attention to Ruby and Lottie. "Hold on."

Lottie turned to see Patty exit the doors at the end of the car.

"Okay, okay. The boss lady's gone." Carol twitched her eyebrows up and down. "Want to hear something shocking?"

"Shoot." Ruby said with eager expectation.

"Listen to this." Carol pulled in close. "The captain and the top jammer of the white shirt team in my unit were married, see?" Carol's eyes danced. "And one of the blockers and another jammer were also married. Two couples, and all four of them skated on the teams. Well, both men, like chicken livers were cheating with the other's wife!"

Lottie giggled when she noticed Carol's eyes bug out at the same time she popped her gum. "What a story."

"Ain't that the wildest thing you've ever heard?"

"A derby doozy," Ruby said, licking her plum lips.

Lottie lowered her head and rubbed a hand against her heart. The gossip made her think. She leaned back and her face went blank.

"What's wrong?" Carol laughed. "This is the derby; everyone talks about everyone else. I don't know why."

Carol cast a quick sideways glance toward the aisles. "They just do."

Ruby's leg touched Carol's to prompt her on. "I want to hear more."

"Me, too." Lottie hesitated as her thoughts traveled back to the training center at the old Armory. "My friends Buddy Wilson and Elsie Mae used to know lots of things—some great stories that might not even be all true." A rush of loss blanketed her mind.

"Yes, Elsie Mae." Ruby leaned her shoulder against Carol's for a slow moment, then returned.

"Where is she now?" Carol asked.

"She's gone now."

Ruby squinted her eyes at Carol. "It was so bad. Gone now ... so what happened to the two couples?" Ruby asked.

"So get this," Carol said. "They got divorced, and married each other's exes. The wives just switched homes." She pointed her fingers in opposite directions with comically crossed arms and shook her head. "And I guess all four of them decided to stay right there in the KC area."

"What a surprise. Living happily ever after." Ruby sighed. "I've seen some funny things in the derby. It's such a topsy-turvy world. I love it."

Lottie found the story mesmerizing, so full of deception and romance. "Yeah. Things aren't at all like they seem in the derby. You know, on television. We can't see what people are really like."

"Well, that's not all. Listen to this." Carol gestured for Lottie and Ruby to lean in close again. "The red shirt captain ..." her voice hushed and she placed one finger to pursed lips while looking to the front and back of the rolling train car. "... divorced his wife of three years. She skated on my team. Then ..." she swished her wrist, "... a few months later, he met this fifteen-year-old *boy*. They fell in love." She nodded her head with one big knowing movement.

"A fifteen-year-old boy?" Lottie winced.

"Yeah, grummy huh? So the captain, he stayed in KC too."

"Didn't anyone know, he was, you know?" Ruby winked.

"He was married for a while, and worked as some sort of police officer who skated part-time, so who would have guessed?"

"What a twist," Lottie said, looking out over the Kansas landscape. "How do you know so much?"

Carol took a long drag off her cigarette holding it in two fingers, studied the bright pink smudge on it and then looked to the ceiling. "Well." She exhaled the smoke, as if thinking of even more licentious tales. "Like I said, people in the derby like to talk. That's only half the story."

"You mean there's more?" Ruby cocked her head.

"Oh yeah. Get this ... when he divorced his wife, she started to hang with one of the other women on the team, and now *they* live together!"

"Is that the word from the bird?" Ruby asked.

"All true-blue."

Lottie and Ruby looked at each other with delicious shock. The three rocked back and forth with the movement of the train as Carol leaned in again. "When I was fifteen, I had bad asthma. Had it all my life." She took one clenched fist and knocked it against her lungs. Then her voice changed and got louder. "My mom said, as a little kid, I was always coming down with croup, whooping cough and asthma attacks, and they'd have to take me to hospitals, emergency rooms and stuff." She chewed and puffed on the cigarette again.

"Holy Toledo," Lottie said.

"You still have the asthma?" Ruby put one hand on Carol's knee. In response Ruby felt the knee push up into her hand gently.

"When I started sports, you know, when I was about sixteen ... skating, it just went away." Carol shrugged her shoulders and dragged on the cigarette. "Derby saved me, hon."

"That's crazy, man," Ruby said.

"Amazing, actually," Carol popped her gum.

"Like a miracle. You're the only girl transferring to our unit?" Lottie asked.

"Guess so. None of the others wanted to leave their homes or families—or, you know, lovers and husbands and all."

"That's too bad," Ruby said. "But hey, welcome! You can be our new friend if you want." Ruby patted Carol's leg and removed her hand.

"I'm a single gal out to discover the world." Carol placed a hand on Ruby's leg. "Friends!"

"Great. Us too. We're off to see the world!" Ruby's eyes held a spark.

"I love the derby," Carol said. "Not just because it cured me of asthma. Even with all the bruises, sprains and pulled muscles, it feels so right for me. I'm so glad I found it."

"I love how the skates feel when I'm speeding around those banks." Lottie leaned forward.

"I've been with it for just about a year now. Still a rookie." Carol pulled her long jacket closer; snuggling in. "My boyfriend sat me down a month ago. He pinned me just over a year ago. I was still in high school when we started to go steady. He loved me." She dragged a long puff on her cigarette.

"Love?" Lottie glanced away.

"You know love, don't you?" Carol's eyes lit up.

"Well ..." Lottie's posture suddenly went limp.

"Tell us more." Ruby eased forward.

"What happened? I mean, are you still seeing him?" Lottie asked.

"He didn't care for how the derby seemed—so, you know, brutal."

"Not ladylike?" Lottie smirked.

"Yes, all the body contact and fighting and all." Carol drew her hand up, resembling a boxer in the middle of a match. "He didn't go too much for the tough-guy thing. So he got frosted and told me I'd have to choose: him or the game."

"What a jerk," Ruby said.

Both of Carol's hands fell to her lap. "Hell, we had lots of arguments." She popped her gum. "He said I paid more attention to skating than him. After a while, I decided that if he was making me choose, he didn't really care what made me happy. And so I decided to stay with the derby."

"You broke up?" Ruby said.

"Yeah. What the devil? We weren't really right together anyway." Carol shrugged. "He told me he wished I'd break a nail on the track." She laughed.

"Now, that's not funny," Ruby said.

"So far, no nails broken. Besides, back then, I was young and confused." Carol rocked her head. "And all he was interested in was cars. I got tired of the beer and his greaser buddies. All they ever talked about was greaseball stuff, like carburetors, manifolds and wheels."

"I can see that," Ruby said. "Seems like guys love to wail in their hotrods."

"When I'd visit his place, there'd be dirty dishes and underwear all over the place." Carol squinted up her nose. "So I broke it off."

"You have guts." Ruby's eyes searched Carol's. "Not many girls would have done that. You gave up marriage?"

"Damn-sure did. I'm ready for a good time with my own life now." Carol's shoulders swayed with the train's lumbering movements.

"Most girls would have stayed and gotten married because he could take care of 'em," Ruby said.

"Hell, I'm going to take care of myself."

"Me, too. Besides, I've never had a boyfriend," Lottie said. "Boys back home let me play ball with them sometimes, but ..." her voice trailed off while she stared out the window a minute. The train lumbered its way toward Wichita with its roll-*clack*-roll. She couldn't imagine what a boyfriend would be like. Would he maybe make her feel lonely? Or maybe buy her a small gift? She had missed out on so much in high school, and now she regretted it.

"Why?" Carol asked.

Lottie could see the hazy reflection of her puffy eyes in the window which was shaded with dust. She let the muscles in her face relax. The last buildings of the town disappeared as the train reached full speed along the open rail ties.

"I guess I never looked like the other girls. You know, pretty. I always felt like one of the boys. Sort of like a tomboy." She dropped her stare down to her lap, picking a piece of lint away from her trousers. "The boys picked on me a lot. I don't know. They always made me feel worthless or queer. They never saw me as a girl, I guess." Heaviness crept its way inside her. "I remember I just wanted to be beautiful or pretty. I prayed for that every night."

"Well, boys aren't everything." Carol took a deep drag on her cigarette. "I loved screwing my boyfriend's brains out, but other than that you're not missing much."

"I dated this handsome basketball player in high school." Ruby's eyes zoomed to the side.

"What was it like? Tell us about him." Carol scooted forward in her seat, eager to get the dirt.

"He was tall and dark, of course." The trembling of the floor from beneath made Ruby's knees wobble and knock together.

Carol's eyes widened. "Sexy?"

"Sure was. I was real gone," Ruby's eyes looked up at the ceiling.

Lottie felt like a failure. "See, why didn't something like that happen to me?" She wished she had had at least one romance in school.

Ruby continued, "We met in biology class when we had to dissect a frog together. Something clicked between us. Real romantic, huh? Anyway, we'd see each other away from school. I'd go to all the ballgames and watch him."

Lottie saw Ruby look to the left in a lingering blink, as if she were trying to bring the memory of her friend back to life after ignoring it for so long. "Sounds dreamy." Lottie scrunched forward.

"Things were boss for months." Ruby nodded. "Anyway, one day he asked me to meet him behind the school after a ballgame. I said yes. About an hour after the game, I saw Louis with five of his friends." Ruby's eyes puffed up with tears. "They started calling me names, like 'nigger puss.' His friends were all white, and Louis was right there with them. That hurt."

Lottie put one hand to her chest. Her jaw tightened. "Don't sound very romantic."

Carol blew a big stream of smoke from her small mouth. "Rattles my cage."

"I guess his teammates pressured him or something. Then it happened."

Lottie noticed the strain on Ruby's face. Ruby wheezed quietly, looking out the window. Her cadence suddenly slowed. "It was so terrible." She sat back in her seat, shocked all over again by the event.

Lottie's feelings soured. "You don't have to tell us."

"No. I never told anyone. But I want to tell you guys." Ruby's eyes watered. "They held me down and …" Tears choked off the rest of her words. "One after another."

It didn't need to be spelled out. Lottie sat in stunned silence and her extremities twitched.

"Good God! Did you tell your parents?" Carol asked, reaching under her seat to find a hankie in her bag. "Here."

"I couldn't. I felt so dirty. I tried to fight them off, and somehow broke this finger." Ruby held out her hand to show a finger, bent a few degrees to the right. "I can't open it all the way." She bent her hand and laughed a little at how her finger wouldn't move very well.

"Your ring finger." Carol rubbed her own finger with one hand.

"How terrible," Lottie said, still dazed. Romance vanished from her mind.

"I'm glad that's all behind us now." Ruby's finger shook.

Lottie realized that Ruby and Carol had each had an unhappy past, but that didn't matter anymore. They were off on a great adventure. Each turn of the steel wheels beneath them brought hope that one more layer of painful memories would fade into forgetfulness.

"I'm just glad to be with the derby now," Ruby sniffed.

Lottie noticed Ruby's eyes taking in Carol. "Me, too," Lottie said with a smile.

"Me, too," Carol gazed at Ruby.

"Come on, girls. Let's eat," Patty said from the doorway. "We'll be in Wichita soon."

"How far is it?" Lottie asked. The roll-*clack*-roll made her hungry.

"About another hour," Patty repeated patiently. "Let's go to the diner car."

"Food—yeah," Lottie said, imagining a hot pastrami sandwich. That helped push away the ugly images that Ruby had just described.

Carol reached over to place a hand on Ruby's knee. "I'm really sorry about your boyfriend ... that that happened to you."

Ruby peered deeply into Carol's eyes. "Thanks. I've changed now, anyway." Ruby glowed.

"Let's drift," Carol said. "I hope they have ice cream with sauerkraut on it."

"Sauerkraut?" Ruby's eyebrows knitted over an exaggerated gagging face.

"Don't crap in your pants. I'm kidding." Carol nudged Ruby. "Remember, I'm just a kid from Kansas," she boomed. They swayed back and forth, rocking with the train's wheels on the way to the dining car.

Chapter 20

WHITES ONLY

After Wichita, traveling deeper south, the troupe climbed off the train at Tupelo Station. Two cramped and dilapidated buses with faded paint and worn-out seats, commandeered from a school district that had hit the skids, transported the troupe to the hotel.

"Lottie, Oscar wants your name to be Lucy Pingleton while we're in the South," Patty said.

"Why?" Lottie asked. "Did I do something wrong?"

"Just do what Oscar says. He knows what he's doing."

"Okay."

The men and women separated into two groups upon arrival at the hotel. Patty escorted her female players to the small registration desk.

"Look at this place! Another shithole!" Belzak said.

Chunks of plaster dangled from the grubby walls in the feeble light of the registration room. Lottie clutched her bags close, looking for signs of vermin.

"Howdy, y'all." The desk clerk looked up from his papers. "I s'pose y'all's the roller skatin' group?"

"Yes, we are." Patty moved closer to the desk.

"We got two of you gals quartered in room fifteen." The clerk shoved the pen aside, resettled his rimmed glasses on the bridge of a pug nose, and said, "Another six in room sixteen, and the last of y'all are in room twenty." Taking his time, he labeled four cards with a handheld rubber date stamp.

"That sounds just fine." Patty placed her purse on the desk.

"Dadgummit," the clerk muttered when he accidently stamped his thumb.

Carol let out a small giggle and put one hand over her mouth when Ruby nudged her. "That's not funny," she whispered.

The clerk raised his hand to push wire eyeglasses up his nose and examine the damage. Lottie noticed plenty of ink smudges on the clerk's thumb where the same mistake must have been committed over and over.

"Everything okay?" Patty asked.

"Sure is." The clerk shook his thumb, adjusting the glasses. He stamped the last card and scooted the pile to the front of the desk. "There y'are, ma'am."

"Thank you." Patty took the sheets of names and read them. "I'll be signing for everyone."

"If y'all let the hot water run for a couple minutes or so, it'll warm up just fine." He eyeballed the group, stopping briefly at Ruby. He stared for a long time and tapped a finger against the desk.

"The rooms. They're a bit down this hall and up one set of stairs," he added.

Patty examined the small hallway as though she could see the stairs. "Yes, I see."

"Oh. Except'n for you." He pointed to Ruby and nudged his glasses up again. "You gots to git on down to the Hotel Medford."

Ruby squirmed. Lottie didn't understand.

"It's a hotel for Negroes. This is *whites only*." He jutted out his chin and added an upward nod. Ruby was silent.

"You can't leave us," Lottie said loud enough for Ruby to hear. She remembered her pained childhood, being singled out as the one who didn't fit in. As an outcast, she recognized the humiliation that lay across Ruby's face.

"Are you sure? Can't she stay with us?" Patty asked.

"We gots rules here in the South," the clerk said matter-of-factly.

"What can we do?" Carol asked under her breath. "I want her with us."

"I like her, too." Lottie smiled then grew quiet. "But I don't know what we can do."

"It's on the south side of town." The clerk seemed pleased that Ruby would be far away.

Some of the skaters raised their eyebrows, pursing their lips as if to say, "I told you so."

"Ugly monkey-face," Belzak sputtered.

"Okay," Patty said emphatically. "You two, Lucy and Carol, you're in room fifteen," she said. "Roughie, you and Belzak and your group will be in room sixteen. Everyone else, you're in room twenty."

"We got management in room twenty-one for you and your cook, ma'am," the clerk said.

Lottie saw Belzak's eyes dance with spite. Belzak leaned in to Roughie and muttered, "Maybe she'll cut out and run home to mammy now!" She turned and looked pointedly in Ruby's direction. "They're all a big problem."

"Oh, brother," Roughie said, loud enough for the others to hear. "I knew she'd be a mistake." Roughie moved toward the stairwell.

"Now git!" the clerk shouted and pointed to the door.

Lottie's blood turned ice cold.

"We can't let this happen," Carol said under her breath to Lottie. Ruby's eyes bagged, her chin drooped and her brightness drained away. "I've never seen her so hurt and hunched over." Lottie remembered how scared Ruby said she had been in grade school when she'd peed herself. "I don't know what to do."

"We're in room sixteen," Belzak bellowed to her clique, starting down the hall. Her shoulders sagged under the weight of the skate bag. "Come on, let's get going. I want to go out and see if I can get a man tonight."

"Go ahead to the room," Lottie said to Carol.

"All right," said Carol reluctantly.

"Let me think." Lottie balled a fist. "I'll be right there," she called to Carol, who looked back on her way to their room. "I've got an idea." Lottie moved close to Ruby, extending the small bag she'd been carrying. "Here, Ruby," she said loudly. "I think this is yours." She glanced around and gave Ruby a wink.

"Oh. Sure. Thanks," Ruby said blankly.

"Lucy, can you be sure to walk down to the Medford and pick Ruby up tomorrow?" Patty asked.

"Of course," Lottie said to Patty, then turned to Ruby. "We can pick you up at your hotel before the game." Lottie winked again. She drew close and whispered. "I got an idea. Wait outside for two minutes." She caught the eye of the hotel clerk and pushed the carrying case into Ruby's outstretched hands. She patted Ruby on the back and whispered, "Give me two minutes. Okay?"

"Okay," Ruby said as she lugged the bags out of the hotel's entrance.

Lottie ran to catch up with Carol. Opening the door, Lottie stared at a dingy room with two beds closely cramped together. An old dresser and a rusty sink sagged in one corner. Plunking down her bags in the center of the room, Carol claimed the bed near the window. "What are you doing?" she asked Lottie, who leaned over Carol's bed to look outside.

"Looking to see if Ruby's waiting." She opened the big window.

"I hope she's okay."

"Look at that sign." Lottie pointed. On a telephone pole hung a white sign with red lettering that read *Proud Home of the Imperial Knights of the Ku Klux Klan.*

"Oh, no," Carol said. "No wonder they covered up your Jewish name."

With bags hanging heavily on both arms, Ruby stood in the street gutter. She moved off the sidewalk to allow the white people free passage of the walkway.

"This is cruddy! She looks so out of place," Carol said.

"Ruby!" Lottie called in a loud whisper, waving a hand out the window.

Ruby looked up with a puffy face.

"Come on," she called. "Quick, tie two sheets together," she said back to Carol.

"Got it." Carol yanked the sheets off the beds and tied them into one long cord.

Ruby latched onto the idea from Lottie's gestures and moved closer to the window.

"Good thing the hotel's only got two floors and wide ledges," Carol said.

Ruby grabbed hold of the extended makeshift rope of sheets. Ruby tossed the two small bags up to Lottie, gazed left and right, and climbed up the sheets. With three easy steps, she entered the room.

"Can you believe this backward town? What louses. This'll be so much better for you if you stay here." Carol's eyes appeared red.

Ruby managed a smile and hug for Carol.

Lottie eyed the two small beds. "There's three of us now."

Lottie clapped Ruby on the back. "There. You can use that bed." She motioned to the one nearest the door where she had left her bags. "I'll sleep on the floor."

"Oh. You don't need to do that for me," Ruby said.

"It's okay. I've slept on the floor before. Think nothing of it." Lottie held her chin high.

"But ..."

Lottie hesitated before speaking. "I know ... we're the only family we have now. We have to take care of each other. You're my derby sister."

"You're so good to me." Ruby looked ready to break into tears. "I wish I was never born this color."

"Don't be silly." Lottie put a hand on Ruby's shoulder. "You're just Ruby Johnson to us."

"We have to be our own family." Carol nodded and popped her gum. "I'll be Mom! Ruby, do you want to be Dad?"

Ruby laughed. "If we get caught, there'll be trouble."

"Leave that up to Lottie and me. We'll protect you."

Ruby's dimples returned. "Thanks, Lucy." She laughed at Lottie's new name. "You too, Carol." She winked and Carol blushed.

"You're family. You belong here. We all belong here," Lottie felt a warm flush across her face.

Tears welled in Ruby's eyes. "Family. Thanks," Ruby whispered. "I didn't want to go to that other hotel. I didn't want to be alone, or separated, because I'm different."

"I don't like it either. I've been different all my life." Lottie choked back a sob.

"Hey. They're just crazy down here in the South, I guess," Carol laughed.

"The South. Yassum," Ruby answered in her best southern accent.

"Why, sugah, dey all just don't know yawl is a big stah." Carol laughed.

"Sho' 'nuff. If dey only knew who ya are. Shore-ly dey'd love ya!" Lottie giggled.

"We'uns all big stahs," Carol carried on. "Dadgummit." She let out a belly laugh that made Ruby and Lottie break into laughter.

"Yeah," Lottie said. "It's all over now. You're with us. Friends." Lottie hugged Ruby, and Carol joined in.

Morning came with a sturdy knock. Patty charged into each of the rooms with the day's orders. "Good morning, girls." She saw Ruby and paused, but said nothing of the broken hotel rule. "I want you to suit up here in the room." Patty passed out the uniforms. "Put your coats on over your uniforms and carry your skate bags the ten blocks to the arena." Patty handed out directions. "We have two shows to do."

Lottie and Carol wound a big scarf over Ruby's face, tucking it tightly around her ears. They marched, clutching Ruby between them, and traipsed through the hotel registration area. Ruby snuggled between the others, hidden behind dark sunglasses and the scarf.

Once on the street, Lottie and her friends laughed all the way to the arena. Each time they saw a sign that read *Whites Only*, they laughed even harder.

An older man on the street stared. "What the hell you nigger-lovers doing here like this?"

Ruby pulled the scarf closer around her face.

"What's the matter, your dick smaller than your brains?" Carol said. "Can't you see we're just friends?"

"T'aint right," he threw a hand in the air and moved on.

Early, ardent fans formed a waiting line at the arena's entrance. Lottie spotted the stage door and the girls found their way to the back, sneaking in without anyone noticing. The smell of piping-hot breakfast filled the air. Lottie, Carol and Ruby sat together at one table and the older skaters sat at the others.

"In today's games, let's start the heat right after the first white shirt point," Belzak's rough voice sounded over the clinking of forks and spoons.

"Let's set two white shirt points on the first two jams. Then Marywell 'til the end of the period," Roughie added.

"Yeah, we did that in Jersey a few years ago, and it went over real good," Gerry said.

"That'll give the reds a reason to start some shit after the first two jams." Belzak laughed.

"Then we can just run the 'hey' period the rest of the night," Gerry said.

"Yeah," chimed in all of the older skaters. "White points, red block out. White goof, rough red points, red zigzag, ending with white out." The established stars chanted like schoolgirls and then ended it with a single-handclap *"Hey!"*

Lottie, who still didn't understand the jargon, glanced at the captains. She caught Belzak's eye. "You new kids will never get anywhere. You've got no showmanship!" Belzak shouted.

"We got to learn to get this color point lingo," Lottie said to her roommates. "I remember Buddy used to say the home team and the visiting team. He never said red or white."

"I don't understand it, either," Carol said.

"You don't know how to sell," Belzak said. Her voice scratched loud enough for everyone to hear. "And you got no tickets!" She pointed at Lottie's chest.

Lottie placed a hand over her flat chest. Instead of always yelling at the new girls, Lottie wondered why the experienced skaters didn't show them how to sell. "Listen close next time. I bet *red* means the visiting team and *white* means the home team."

That night, Lottie and every one of the other skaters noticed that all the Negro fans were directed to the uppermost balcony. The white fans sat in the lower tiers of stands.

"Lucy Pingleton," the announcer called out, introducing Lottie. She had almost forgotten her new name, but she managed to skate her single introductory lap to small bits of applause.

Lottie and Ruby hated the introductions—not only because they were unknowns, but because the single lap seemed to take an hour while the audience waited for the big names to be announced.

"And finally," the announcer said, "for tonight's visiting team, Ruby Johnson."

Ruby skated her lap. Respectful applause filtered down from the auditorium's upper tiers, lighting up Ruby's face. She looked upwards, surveying the balcony, tipping her head back and closing her eyes. When a few polite claps followed from the white sections of the arena, Ruby placed a hand on her chest and she skated forward; tall. Lottie saw Ruby's eyes mist up.

After her introductory lap, Ruby bowed and sat on the bench next to Lottie. She exhaled deeply. "That felt good. Happiness. Now, if I can just get to skate tonight ..."

Chapter 21

OSCAR'S BARNSTORMING

Amarillo, Texas. Lottie browsed a bookstore and picked up *The Last Frontier*. She found the story appealing. It sparked her interest about the history of Scotland and the subsequent evolution of the Roman Empire.

Taking a thrashing each game, Lottie learned! She learned when she read each new book; she learned with each game. She discovered what Oscar meant by *barnstorming*, especially when a game went haywire or the fans started to walk out before the end of play.

In every dressing area, Lottie would quietly ease her lucky hat with the yellow band and flower out of her skate bag. After rubbing two fingers around the brim, she would enter the arena with the teams. They skated an especially eye-opening night in Peoria.

Ruby and Lottie had been promoted to *cigarette* skaters, skaters who worked the pack on infrequent jams. Aside from that, the two were professional bench-warmers: sitting next to one another, comparing notes on the game action, and sharing a little harmless gossip.

Ruby leaned close to Lottie. "Did you hear Eve Belzak slept with the white shirt men's captain last night?"

"No, I heard she slept with the red shirt captain last Friday." Lottie rubbed a sore bump on her knee like it was Belzak and she could massage the angry presence away.

"She gets around," Ruby said.

"Being on the road gets lonely." Lottie's eyes crackled. "You know, um ... sometimes, I ... well, I wonder ..."

Crack! Just then, a loud noise shattered the air and Lottie winced. "What was that?"

Ruby stood, pointing. "Look, Bobbie Beal!"

The sound shot deep into Lottie's soul. "Something wrong?"

Snaps and cracks weren't unusual. Skaters fell every night, but the muffled sound of snapping bones turned Lottie's gut.

"She's hurt," Ruby hissed through clinched teeth.

The audience's cheering died down. Bobbie Beal was on the track, twitching. This was not an act. It was raw nerves triggering the spasms. Her ankle turned out at a right angle. Bile rose in Lottie's throat. "Someone, help!"

Skaters rolled close and stood around her. Each face was stony with fear carved into it. Quiet murmurs could barely be heard from the audience. An eerie calm swept over the entire arena. Lottie cringed at Beal's grimacing pleas for help. "Ow, help me! Might be broke."

Lottie placed one hand over her eyes. The game stopped. An ambulance arrived minutes later. Big men gently rested Beal on a gurney and raced the skater to the emergency room.

By the time Bobbie was taken away, half the audience had walked out. Lottie noticed the pallor on their faces. No one had expected to see hardcore violence during a night of sports entertainment. Neither had Lottie.

In the locker room, a naked Belzak shouted, "You're not much more than a fan. See what can happen if you don't watch yourself out there! Pay attention. And be sure to stay out of my way!"

"Shut up, you old bag," Roughie crowed.

Belzak snorted. "I just don't want to get hurt! I'm sure we won't see *her* back in the game again."

"Just like that," Ruby snapped her fingers. "And we could be sent back home."

"New skaters are always injuring us *real* pros!" Belzak ranted.

Roughie yelled, "That Saunders play could have been turned into a pull-a-way! But a new kid was in the way!"

"You have no color or showmanship. You can't keep the fans' interest!" Roughie lifted her flask.

"Oscar ain't in charge of us."

"No man is in charge ... I am!"

This was when Lottie realized that an injury could send her to the hospital, or worse; back home. She also saw a new power dynamic inside the organization. Belzak and Roughie wielded power like madmen in skirts.

That night, Lottie was besieged with a dark nightmare. Her pigeon appeared, injured again. One little bone was broken. It struggled for life and no one helped. Lottie nestled the bird in her arms. She went to jump or fly away, but her tummy flipped as she fell straight down the side of a high rock bluff. She writhed in terrible pain. Just before Lottie and her friendly bird hit the hard, rocky surface, a naked Belzak screamed into the locker room. Then Lottie crashed. She jumped right up in bed. Stupid, naked Belzak. Lottie thought this was another way the star wielded power: using her naked body to make everyone cower.

Over time, the unit hit Indiana, a bustling, all-American state where no one was rich or poor. Then they railed into Boise, a flatland town where the fans were quiet, but intent upon scrutinizing the derby's wheeled ruckus. Lincoln, Nebraska, was next, where the auditorium was full of college students. Lottie and the troupe were bussed, trained and shuttled from city to city, working ten or twenty live games and then disappearing into the night like a traveling carnival on wheels.

Every month she wrote a letter home and put a few dollars in the envelope, hoping the money would help buy her sisters new socks, dresses or shoes.

Every morning she read the local paper. Scanning the news, Lottie looked up. "Did you hear about the New York Giants? Willie Mays finished first batter for the National League."

Ruby said nothing. Over the past year, Lottie had noticed that the bond between Ruby and Carol had grown closer.

She lowered the paper to her lap as a flush of warmth was followed by a tingling in her chest. She was happy for them, but didn't want to be a third wheel. She remembered how Tommy never paid attention to her while he fawned over Elsie Mae. Could that happen with Carol and Ruby? Always something changing, always something new to learn.

Lottie realized that the early skaters, like Buddy, had developed secret plays and passed them down through generations of skaters using code words. She decided to be patient. At most games, while on the bench, Lottie became engrossed in watching. She'd found herself sinking deeper into the roller-drama and turning into an infield fan, swept away by the excitement of it all. She compared notes and gossip with Ruby.

"Did you hear? Roughie was arrested last night for fighting someone in the bar down the street."

Lottie gave a matter-of-fact smirk. "They say she broke a beer bottle and jabbed it into another girl's eye. Cut her bad."

Lottie watched her peers whirl, sling, block and fight on the track. She recalled a night in West Chester when Oscar said something Lottie had never forgotten: "I bring the crowds in, and it's up to you, the skaters, to make them enjoy and *want* to come back." She recalled his words while watching the relentless whirlwind from the infield and listening to the skaters jabber from within the pack.

Once inside the locker room, Ruby nudged Lottie. "I heard some news from the unreliable grapevine again."

"What?"

"One of the skaters had a lawyer write Oscar and ask for a twenty-five thousand dollar donation to start a pizza shop." Ruby's eyebrows arched. "But that's not all. The letter asked that the money be a gift, with no promise to pay a penny back!"

"Who would do that?"

"I hear it's someone on our team."

Lottie looked around. "Let me guess. Roughie."

"Right!"

"What did Oscar do?"

"I hear he ignored the letter."

"What a charlatan. What would make someone do something like that?"

"I guess she thinks she can hold him hostage or something? After all, she *is* a *big star.*"

"Manipulative."

On the buses and trains, Lottie was able to keep some balance in her life. She finished reading *The Old Man and the Sea*. It was the first serious book she had ever completed. She found her eyes glued to the pages about the ridiculed fisherman's struggle with the mighty fish. She didn't know why she enjoyed the novel about a fight between an old man and a stupid fish, but she was grateful that Rebecca gave the book as a gift. At the end of the story, she felt breathless and exhausted, as if she had experienced the battle herself. It reminded her of her own battle as she struggled every day with her teammates.

Captivated by Oscar's barnstorming, Lottie barreled forward on a nonstop roll. From arenas to gymnasiums to armories, time passed. It was 1954 ... the older skaters still kept her out of their secret world of plays and *color*. That was another method they used to maintain power over others. Resembling a dusty circus, the derby packed up its track and journeyed in the gloomy, early hours of the morning. Every few months, the cavalcade disappeared from one town and, like an ephemeral vision, mysteriously materialized in another.

Lottie played in places like Springfield, Little Rock and Omaha; exciting people with the derby's magic. Each city had a soul and flavor of its own. She loved the new sights, the different food; never really missing home, but she did miss her mom and sisters. Every week, she still wrote a letter home and put a few dollars into the envelope.

It had been nearly a year since her team first set out from New Jersey. Lottie no longer felt like a beginner. She was ready to develop her own color, if the older gals didn't want to help her, include her in the plans; then she would make her own play for audience attention. The few letters from home helped—until another dream came true. Oscar made an announcement.

"The Cuban government has invited us to play in their country for twenty-four games," he said. "This is a great opportunity for the derby. A little warning: it's subtropical and past the hurricane season, so it'll be hot and humid."

"Cuba ... I don't know anything about it." Ruby's brows rose.

"Me neither, except it's south of Florida." Lottie felt a surge of energy and fear at the thought of leaving the United States.

"We'll be staying in a swanky part of town," Oscar said. "You know, they call Cuba the playground for the rich and famous." He paused. "There'll be a few changes to the lineups for the games. Ruby and Belzak, you'll both be skating for the home team."

The skaters' eyebrows arched. Lottie felt her chest expand for Ruby's home team upgrade.

"Gerry and Carol, you two will skate for the visiting team."

"What the hell?" Belzak said. "You know I don't care to skate on the home team. I'm a red shirt."

"You're going to do it and you're going to like it, till we return to the States. Got it?"

"Yes, sir."

Lottie chuckled, seeing Belzak humbled by Oscar. The skaters talked for hours. The excitement of the derby being so popular—and invited to another country—swept everyone's imagination into a swirl. Full of egomania, the skaters bragged about their feats on the track. Lottie just kept skating, bench-warming and planning; doing her best at all times, ready to grab opportunity the second it opened up.

Chapter 22

CUBA

Lottie's knuckles whitened as fingers clutched the chartered airplane's armrest. Her tummy roiled on takeoff, immediately followed by sweat beading on her forehead. It was her first time in the sky. The propellers were buzzing, the little aircraft was shaking. It felt like a heavy metal ball had dropped into the pit of her stomach. Lottie closed her eyes and let the world spin, allowing memories to dispatch the fear like the setting sun. She pictured her old Bronx neighborhood, her family, Rebecca Peterson, Buddy Wilson ... and the whole country of America. Anxiety dissolved out of her mind and soul. Lottie eased back and told herself, *I'm doing this for Elsie Mae.*

"I'm scared." Ruby laid her head on Lottie's forearm.

"What have we done?" Lottie chuckled through a nervous smile.

"Don't crap your pants," Carol laughed.

The alien sensation of flight faded. The passengers grew subdued by hours of vibration and buckling shakes. The trio sat in quiet thought. Danger had become monotony.

Finally, Lottie's belly flip-rolled as the plane suddenly angled down. She peered out the window. It was a dizzying sight that made her feel nauseated. She took a deep breath and held it in for more than a minute. There it was! She was descending into a foreign land. Lottie's imagination became seduced by thousands of brilliant water inlets surrounding the island. Cuba appeared blissful, caressed with sparkling beaches that blended into the lush greenness of the land. Her muscles relaxed as the wheels hit Mother Earth. The little plane rattled, bounced and made firm contact.

"We made it alive!" Carol piped.

Moments later, the group was walking down three small steps to the ground below. The air was hot, scented with airplane fuel and an unfamiliar spice. Lottie's heart quickened when uniformed officials carrying rifles escorted the troupe off the airstrip and into an idling bus.

"*Mejor solo que mal acomomado,*" said one brown-eyed escort with a sparkling smile.

"We must be special guests." Lottie was in awe.

"I heard a rumor last week," Carol whispered.

Ruby leaned close.

"They're saying she's injecting herself with heroin every day!"

"Who?" Lottie's eyes widened.

"Roughie! And that what's-her-name, the one with long black hair on the home team. Both of 'em are addicted."

"Besides the booze? What next?" Ruby shook her head.

"Why don't she get fired?"

"They say that Oscar and Roughie used to, you know." Carol circled two fingers and poked another finger in and out of the hole.

"Uh-*huh.*" Ruby and Lottie nodded.

The rickety bus had been built in the 1940s. It was dented and hack-painted a dull green. They filed down the narrow aisle, looking for seats with relatively clean and intact upholstery. Lottie was unsuccessful in this effort, eventually plopping down on a seat worn down to the steel frame.

The girls were surrounded at all times by Cuban guards. No one in the roller derby spoke Spanish, and none of the men in uniform spoke much English. Lottie felt awkward as the bus journeyed outside Havana and into the small town of Bauta, sandwiched between rolling hills covered with palm trees and lined with stone mansions.

"This ain't nothing compared to Paris," said Belzak. "Not like any of you would know."

Ruby said under her breath, "I'll bet Belzak will have some of the guards in bed in no time."

"Knowing the language or not." Carol and Lottie giggled.

For Lottie, just taking in the scenery was living it up. After driving for half an hour, the bus passed four glamorous, brown stone homes. Each house looked like an antique mansion. They had thick, dirty stone walls, manicured yards, fountains and arch-topped doors. The bus clanked to a stop.

The team exited the bus through a cloud of exhaust. Lottie stared up at a large, eight-unit apartment complex with a wide porch. The guards escorted the guys to one of the apartments while Lottie and the girls were moved into the second story on the other side of the complex. Next to the living room a hallway with five bedroom doors stretched past Greco-Roman figurines adorning marble tables. The walls held big, brightly-colored paintings of the countryside: farmers with happy faces working the land. Large ceiling fans languidly pushed warm air throughout the room.

"Look how big it is!" Patty said as she scanned the spacious setup. "Even a swimming pool!"

"The living room is ten times the size of my house in the Bronx." Lottie gawked at everything, wandering in and out of rooms with vaulted ceilings and arched doorways. "My mom's not going to believe this."

For the moment, the entire group was getting along. There were no nasty comments or conflicts as Lottie and the other women drifted around the apartment. The living room area was in brownstone. Huge windows overlooked green, rolling Cuban mountains in one direction and multicolored neon lights of downtown Havana in the other.

"I feel so rich." Carol swished through the faded opulence of the old building. "Just like a queen."

Some of the girls giggled.

"A queen from Kansas," Ruby smiled. "Are you wearing your ruby slippers?"

"Eat it."

Lottie stood taller. She felt like a real sports star. Just two years ago she had watched the derby from the sidelines, benched on the couch eating popcorn. The action had been far away, beamed to her imagination through a television screen. Now, that life was hers.

"Did you see the bar in the lobby?" Belzak asked. "Looks just like a scene from *Casablanca*."

"Yeah. Look. We even have maids." Ruby pointed to the scheduled cleaning times beside two Spanish names. "One is Juanita and the other is Carmen."

"I s'pose, without the derby, we'd be cleaning homes back in the Bronx," Lottie said.

"I might be fixing car transmissions with my boyfriend!" Carol grinned ecstatically.

"Or worse ..." Ruby touched Carol's shoulder.

"Not as nice as the hotel I stayed at in Europe. You scrubs still ain't seen nothing," Belzak said. "Just because Oscar put you on the home team, don't get a big head," she rasped at Ruby.

"And I'm on the red shirt team," Carol said.

Belzak pointed. "Take a look out the window."

Lottie, Ruby and Carol looked down from the two-story apartment at local Cubans on the streets.

"Look at *him*." Ruby pointed.

Lottie saw a dark man strolling the street, wearing a silk shirt with four pockets. He held his head high, greeting friends, smiling and smoking his cigar. Other Cuban neighbors flocked around him.

"They're savages, the same as you, Ruby," Belzak said. "That's why you're on the home team. You Negroes look more like them than most of us."

"I think he's handsome," Lottie said.

"Sure," Carol chimed in.

"Savages. All of you!" Belzak said. "Listen, I'm even on the home team down here. That's because I have a nice tan. But remember, I'm German. I ain't no colored or no spic!"

"Holy cow."

"And I never let a man tell me what to do on the track!" Belzak continued.

"Come on Ruby, let's find our room."

Ignoring Belzak, skaters paired up to choose beds and bedroom partners. Ruby, Lottie and Carol found a room at the far end of the hall. They loaded their bags onto the beds. "This'll be great for us," Lottie said while helping adjust Carol's bag.

Belzak entered the room. "*I've* got dibs on this room."

Lottie's heart made a dull thud. "What do you mean?"

"This is ours." Carol stood square with her feet planted wide.

"No, you don't!" Belzak screamed.

"You're not assigning rooms." Lottie set her face firm.

"I'm in change! This room's mine! Find another." Belzak jutted a finger toward the other rooms. Even in Cuba, Belzak was intolerable. The three began to look for another room. An altercation was not worth the effort.

"Don't mind her," Ruby mumbled. "I heard she slept with four of the Globetrotters. Remember when we met them in Billings, Montana?"

Belzak's mouth dropped. "And it was good!"

"Oh, brother." Carol touched the tips of her fingers together. "She's just something else!"

"That's not all." Ruby chuckled. "She got caught by a porter in one train bathroom with a pro wrestler on the way to Tulsa!"

"I can only imagine what went on in Wyoming with the Green Bay Packers." Lottie placed another bag on one of the beds as they laughed.

"I own you little bitches," Belzak reminded them.

"Seriously, you ever notice when someone rubs you the wrong way?" Carol frowned.

Ruby paused and said, "Yeah, but it doesn't matter. My pa taught me to stay away from finding trouble with the people you work with."

The sound of Patty's voice changed the mood. "Oh, come here, everybody. Come here!"

"What the hell is it?" Belzak shouted, crossing the hall.

"The bathroom. It's all white."

Lottie's first thought was *Whites Only* again. She and Ruby found their way to the bathroom, leaving Carol in the bedroom.

"And tile everywhere!" Ruby spun in a half circle.

"It's so bright in here, I'll need to wear sunglasses to take a fucking shit," Belzak laughed.

"Huh ... even two toilets!" Ruby said.

"They're not both johns," said Belzak with an open-mouthed laugh.

"What's that one?" Lottie pointed.

"Yeah. Look. See, one is regular, and the other one has no seat. And inside, there's some sort of silver water jet."

"That's right." Patty's finger made a circular motion.

"I don't get it," Lottie said.

"You turn this handle on the side," Belzak said. Patty turned the silver handle. A spray of water shot straight up and landed back in the white basin. "See? The water goes up." Belzak chuckled.

"Like a water fountain!" Lottie had no clue.

Belzak laughed. "Oh, you gals, you're so outta orbit! What squares! This is what the French call a *bidet*."

Ruby arched her brows. "A what?"

"A bidet!" Belzak half-shouted. "Oh, you know, to rinse your ass!"

Lottie noticed the other faces crack into smiles. She covered her mouth with both hands and let a muffled laugh escape.

Belzak winked at Ruby and hollered, "Hey, Carol, come here."

"Look, it's a shower for midgets." Belzak pointed to the bidet.

"Huh. Really?" Carol looked inside the basin and frowned.

"Look close."

Carol bent over. "Look at what?"

"Don't do it," Ruby called out.

Belzak peeled her lips back in a sneer and pulled on the silver handle, sending up a fountain of water. The water splashed Carol in the face. "Stupid ass," guffawed Belzak.

Carol jerked back, clawing at the spray with both hands. Water dripped from her hair. She gasped for air.

"Not funny," Ruby said, coming to Carol's side.

Blood thumped in Lottie's eardrums.

"Trying to protect your girlfriend?" Belzak berated.

"Just not funny," Ruby repeated.

"Piss on you." Belzak marched away.

Everyone left the bathroom. Back in the room, Carol said, "I'm startin' to hate her."

"I told you. You just have to get along." Ruby caressed Carol's back.

Carol smiled. "Well, I'm surprised she can breathe at all in those skintight clothes she wears, with those big tits spilling out." Carol laughed Belzak off for now.

The sun was just cresting the cityscape when the battered bus returned. It transported the troupe to an outdoor field for the evening's game. Two armed military men were aboard, as well. Within minutes, the paved street abruptly changed to a dirt road full of potholes. Large tracts of fertile land sprawled everywhere, divided by great farm estates and dotted with small shacks.

"Farmland," Carol said. "Just like Kansas."

Lottie looked out the window at one thatched roof after another. These weren't like the farms back home at all. Her heart sagged at the sight of raggedly-dressed field workers and hungry-looking children. Some of the small children wore only underwear. She saw a young boy in a field of deep green stalks laboring with an ox hitched to a heavy wooden cart. The hunched, dark-skinned boy wiped his brow with dirty hands.

"Working so hard ..." Lottie's lips pressed together.

"Maybe it's sugar cane," Carol suggested.

"It reminds me of how the Negroes on the southern plantations lived back home," Ruby said. "Slaves. My dad showed me photos and told stories. But this is terrible."

"I guess this isn't like Kansas after all," Carol's voice wobbled.

Lottie's stomach tightened when she saw Ruby's somber face. "They look so poor and hungry."

The bus neared the track which was already set up in an open baseball field. Large stands waited on one side for patrons. On the other side stood the big semi-trailer that had carried the sections of the track.

"It's nothing more than a fucking pasture," Belzak cracked. "Everyone ready for a roll in cow shit?"

"Brother," Ruby muttered, scratching her neck in irritation.

Before going to the infield with her team, Lottie pulled her mother's Betmar Sylvie wool hat out of her canvas bag. She inhaled and touched the delicate flower.

"Why do you do that?" Ruby asked.

"It's my good luck charm."

"Wish me a little luck, too."

Lottie had a sinking feeling as the stands filled up with farming families. Children wore torn scraps of clothes. The men wore weathered straw hats and the mothers looked tired. Lottie straightened when a line of young armed guards arrived to stand between the track and the outdoor benches overflowing with locals.

Music started to play. Lottie's chest tightened when President Bautista's anthem sounded from the cheap loudspeakers. Everyone stood at attention. The military men watched closely. When two farmers didn't stand at attention, armed guards dragged them away.

"Why are they being removed?" Lottie asked, shocked.

"They're peasants," Gerry said. "Most people here have respect for the government. But there's always a couple troublemakers."

"It scares me. Did they do something wrong?" Carol wondered, looked almost as tired as the peasant women.

"They don't care for the rebels here. Watch yourselves!" Gerry demanded.

To Lottie, the people in the stands looked poorer than the kids in her old Bronx neighborhood. When Belzak and

Ruby were introduced, everyone in the stands went wild. They loved them. That was when Lottie realized why Ruby was on the white shirt team with all the other dark-skinned players.

The locals skated with a vengeance as they warmed up. The color contrast couldn't be ignored. Lottie saw hate and division at the root of the team change.

When the game started, the crowd grew angry each time a home teamer was blocked. Each time a white shirt was knocked on their ass, the crowd got more and more furious. Suddenly, fifty or so people stormed toward the track and were forced back into the stands by military security. Sticks and guns were wedged between the farmers and the military guys.

Lottie's body trembled, straining to pick up on the cues from the announcer speaking the local language. Eventually, she caught the exotic sound of the other skater's names. She learned to judge the jam time by the announcer's cadence and volume.

Ten minutes into the first period, Belzak scored a point. The people in the stands went into great cheers, whooping and hollering at the score. A few tossed their tattered hats into the air. Belzak skated like the sweetest white shirt Lottie had ever seen. The fans loved her. She scored one point over Gerry.

"*Punto a Cuba en esa jugada,*" the announcer cried.

With sweat dripping down her face, Belzak stood panting at the rail. Her jersey, soaked with perspiration and humidity, was becoming transparent atop huge breasts. She glowed from the attention.

"What a two-faced ham." Carol pulled at her earlobe.

Gerry came up behind Belzak and swung a clenched fist, hitting her in the back of the head.

The announcer yelled. Hundreds of audience members stood and leaned in, attentive and growling.

"They do this almost every game," Carol said.

"Gerry makes a pretty good red shirt, but ..." Lottie felt ill.

Belzak recoiled and fell to one knee. Ruby skated past the fallen star. Men lunged toward the track as the guards rebuked them. Gerry reached out, grabbed Ruby's jersey, and brought the girl down with a *thud*. The fans spiraled out of control, angered with Gerry and the entire visiting team. People stampeded the track.

"Here they come again!" Lottie squeaked.

The guards couldn't hold them back. Twenty rioters broke through. Guards were flung to the ground and pushed aside. A rush of angry farmers collided with the rails and the side of the track. They used their hands to pound on the wooden banks. *Thump, thump!*

"*Quitenses de la pista, por favor,*" the announcer said.

"It's the real McCoy. They're mad at us." Carol's eyes were as big as saucers.

"What's happening?" Lottie put an open hand on her heart.

"A riot!"

The locals waved closed fists at the skaters, sending a bolt of fear through Lottie. She clutched her purse.

"Move back!" someone yelled out. All of the skaters retreated to the infield, then moved up the track's skating surface. Carol bit her lips and stumbled on the grass infield. A couple of the male skaters helped stand guard on the track as more fans rushed the sides, crushing forward as they went.

"*Por favor vuelvan a sus asientos,*" the announcer said.

Lottie shrieked.

Two of the peasants, legs first, crawled onto the track. Others moved past the guards. One farmer head-locked a guard and flipped him head over heels onto the track. After falling, the guard grabbed the peasant's pant leg and took him down with a crash. They wrestled. Another farmer pushed and shoved yet another guard. Arms and hats waved everywhere, chanting on the fight.

"We got to get outta here!" Lottie said.

"Things are outta control!" Gerry hollered.

A fight between a male skater and a farmer broke out. They tumbled onto the track, thrashing and throwing fists. Lottie heard the sound of the big semi-trailer's engine. She felt hot and breathless and turned to see it back up to the far end of the track. It butted against the track's guardrails, just feet away. *Thump, whump, thud.* Fans trampled up onto the track. "What should we do?" Lottie's breath caught in her chest.

Oscar waved. "Get in!"

"*Por favor vuelvan a sus asientos,*" the announcer said over and over.

Skaters raced forward with skates clunking and clacking. They hopped over the railing and jumped into the back of the empty trailer. The door slammed shut behind the last of them. Inside was blackness. Lottie tasted lumber dust in the darkness.

"Oh, my God," Lottie whispered, her heart racing.

"Safe. I hope," Carol said.

"We're okay now." Ruby hugged Carol.

The trailer jolted as Oscar—or someone—started the engine and drove several yards.

"What the hell happened?" Vinnie asked.

"We started a fucking race riot! I told you they were savages," Belzak said.

"Cut the heat!"

"I should have known better," Gerry said. "We know the heat's part of the game, but down here they're taking it seriously."

"You *should* have known better," Vinnie jutted a finger at Gerry.

"How would I know?"

The semi stopped moving. The back door opened a crack, and Oscar's face appeared. "I guess there's a serious government takeover going on down here."

"What?"

"In America, it's part of the game. Not here. There's political trouble down here." Oscar ran a hand through graying hair. "I'm sorry I didn't warn you." He stopped and looked back toward the fans. "They're starting to go back to their seats."

For another ten minutes, Lottie listened to the announcer plead for the fans to return to their seats.

"Let's go back and continue with the men's period, no heat," Oscar directed.

"All right. We'll cool it," Gerry said.

"Good." Oscar left.

Once the trailer had backed to the rail, the skaters returned. The game continued with the men's period.

"I wish I was back in Kansas right now," Carol said.

"We'll be okay as long as we stop the heat," Gerry said.

The girls returned for the next period. Lottie and Carol were told to skate in the pack. Neither knew what would happen when they rolled off the track and onto the infield.

"Oops!" Lottie's skate wheels dug into the soft grass and stopped abruptly. Her body weight lunged her forward, and she ended up face-first, eating infield dirt and grass along with some of the manure resting there. The fans roared with delight.

I guess this is better than another riot, Lottie thought to herself.

The home team won with the crowd yelling, "*Viva Cristo Rey!*"

With the game over, all of the skaters stayed on the track as the farming families left. Oscar's subsequent game plan required two hours of training that blistered the balls of Lottie's feet. By that point, they were already mangled meat.

Lottie and her friends got a ten dollar raise in their pay envelope. Thankful, Lottie guessed that it would compensate them for the trauma the Cuban jaunt had caused them all.

That night, Lottie dreamed that the bus was passing a wayside vegetable stand on the way to the outdoor game. A smiling young boy in a tank top and ragged shorts waved. His pet pigeon was perched in a cage next to him. After the game, the bus passed the boy's vegetable stand again. This time, it was demolished. The pigeon lay dead inside the cage, brutally bludgeoned.

Chapter 23

AMERICAN SAILORS

Before leaving Cuba, Oscar summoned his loyal troupe to a meeting. "We're going home, and I have some news. It's been two years since we started touring, but we still need to improve our game before we go back to New York."

The skaters groaned and Oscar eyed them, standing tall. "We need to bring the game up. We have to see more people in the seats." A playful grin appeared on his face. "I've decided to move the operation to California. The game needs tightening and more color. We'll be featuring more of the women skaters."

Lottie's heart pounded.

"California ..." Carol covered her mouth with one hand. "Damn!"

Oscar's eyes gleamed. "I have a favor to ask. Try to doll yourselves up." He stood with his legs spread wide. "You know, soften or bleach your hair—and for God's sake, wear nylons, makeup and nail polish. Act like ladies ... off the track, *ha ha.*"

A few of the gals frowned.

"I'm serious. You need to stop looking like tomboys and ruffians off the track; the difference between off and on has to be big."

Lottie swallowed. "I'll never be able," she whispered to Ruby.

"Don't be silly," Ruby said. "You'll be fine."

"I can be pretty," Carol smiled.

"Oscar, we can do that." Belzak crossed her arms. Her gruff voice sounded to Lottie like something that was not ladylike at all. Lottie groaned, knowing she wouldn't make Oscar happy this time. Carol was a cutie and Belzak had tickets. Lottie was plain, skinny and unimportant on the track with scraggly hair turning darker brown now from the dirty blonde she was as kid.

"We'll open up with two teams, the Los Angeles All-Stars and the Bay City Bombers. We'll travel to L.A. where the All-Stars will skate white. In San Francisco, the Bombers will skate white. Your unit managers will have all the details. And guess what? No more two-hour trainings. We'll train two days a week instead of every day. How's that sound?"

Cheers came from the players.

Patty stood next to Oscar, head held high. Oscar widened his hands to silence the chitter-chatter. "Sadly, there's some personnel news today, too. Roughie Barclay will be leaving the derby."

"Oh, no," someone moaned.

Carol leaned into Lottie. "Some said her friend ... what's-her-name ... the one with the long black hair. Well, she overdosed."

"No!" Lottie said.

"She was taken to a hospital somewhere in Bauta, in the Artemisa Province."

Skaters muttered their mixed reactions.

"She's decided to retire and won't be following us to the west coast." Oscar looked at the other skaters. "We'll all miss her. She's contributed tremendously to our game." He lowered his head, paused a moment, and held back a dry grimace.

"Oh, God." Lottie felt numb with surprise.

It was quiet. Oscar lifted his chin. "That means there's room for the new kids to move up and use more color."

Lottie's chest fluttered. She wanted to work harder. She fussed with her blouse as if removing a wrinkle.

"And we're going to be able to pay everyone your regular pay again."

The skaters whooped. Lottie was thrilled, knowing she could send more money home. "And I guess I'll need to buy some ladylike clothes." Lottie swung one leg back and forth.

"One last bit of news. Ken Nydell, our publicist, came up with nicknames. You know, to give each of you some character."

The skaters looked around with palpable tenseness. Lottie sensed that their minds were devising their own nicknames.

Oscar grinned. "Here's some examples of what I mean: Carl 'Moose' Flanagan." The group laughed. "Gerry Murphy, you're 'The Blonde Avenger.'" Another chuckle rumbled through the players. "Elmer 'Elbows' Fredrickson. Annis Kelsy, you're called 'Big Red.' Carol Anderson, your new name is 'The Flashing Bombshell,' and Lottie, you're still 'The Little Lunatic.'"

Ruby and Carol laughed and nudged Lottie in the ribs. Lottie thought of Buddy Wilson and how he'd started that name. It seemed like such a long time since she had first worked out with Buddy and started training.

"Patty and our other unit manager for the guys have a list of nicknames." The unit managers started handing each player a slip of paper. "So, that's it, gang. You have your new character names. And in one week, we'll be in San Francisco."

Everyone applauded.

"We'll see the Golden Gate Bridge!" Carol said.

"I don't know ..." Lottie's eyes squished, her mind raced. *How can I look pretty?*

"Did you say something?" Ruby asked.

"No ... I just don't know." Lottie began to sweat. "Who is The Little Lunatic, anyway?"

Relief flushed over Lottie once she was back on terra firma in the United States. She had been weighing the pros and cons of prospective futures. Right now, the fresh air outside the airplane thrilled her. The people in Cuba lived in another world, one in which Lottie always felt out of place. Everything there was old and ancient; rigid. She never felt at home. What's more, living in the same quarters with some of the other skaters had wracked her nerves. Descending the plane's steps in San Francisco, Lottie and the derby troupe were charmed by the sights and sounds of a west coast fairytale. For the moment, her worries were eased. From the airport to the train station, this modern city seemed as magical to Lottie as if it were inhabited by pixies and elves.

"This is an army and navy town," Ruby said.

Small stones scrunched beneath Lottie's feet. These same stones had carried army heroes returning home from foreign lands, loved ones reuniting in long embraces. She widened her eyes at the hum of activity and quaint cable cars climbing up the steep, narrow streets. Lottie's eyes followed the hilly horizon up and down, gazing out over the enchanted land.

"The weather's so fresh and salty." Ruby inhaled. "It's just like spring in New York."

"Is it this way all year 'round?" Lottie wondered out loud.

"That's what I read in *Life* magazine," Carol said. "Springtime, all the time." She popped a big wad of bubble gum.

"Listen." Lottie put a hand up to her right ear. "You can hear the traffic and foghorns." Lottie and her friends stood still for a moment, taking in the distant foghorns and the clanging of cable cars.

"This is a great city." Patty adjusted her bags. "I've visited San Francisco before. There're some incredible theaters here."

"Nightclubs, too, I bet." Carol made a jump onto the balls of her feet.

"You know, we're old enough to go now," Lottie said.

"Oh, that reminds me of this little club in one of the neighborhoods." Patty rubbed her chin. "It has that authentic San Francisco flair. Everyone new to San Francisco should visit. It's near Coit Tower, in the North

Beach area." She pointed, to see if anyone had recognized the landmarks. "It's two blocks off Broadway and up this narrow alley. It's sorta famous."

"Famous?" Carol asked.

"Tell you what," Patty said. "Let's go this weekend. I'll escort everyone."

"Okay." Lottie shivered, eager to become sophisticated in this worldly city. The derby troupe went through the customary set-up of their temporary homestead by erecting their elaborate track at the Cow Palace.

That Friday, Lottie experienced her first nightclub. The small alley was dark, with individual strands of moonlight working through a growing fog. Lottie walked into a door at the address, unassuming and unattended. She noticed how large the room was, with its old eighteenth-century-style furnishings. The walls, shelving and bar were glimmering, polished mahogany and the bar corners were carved perfectly round. The bar stood on cabriole legs with brass mounts and was topped with naturalistic carvings of fruit and leaves.

The *maitre d'* seated the small group on the second level facing the stage. Lottie gazed across the large room. It was filled with small tables covered in white tablecloths and tiny yellow lights. The entire downstairs was packed with well-mannered patrons.

"Soda for me." Remembering her dad quaffing beer, Lottie wanted to stay away from alcohol.

"Three root beers, and I'll have a martini," Patty said.

A man dressed in a tuxedo swooped onto the stage and sat at a large black piano topped with a bright orange, low and spreading flower arrangement. The audience quieted. The lights dimmed and he played a fanfare while another man announced in a deep voice over the speakers, "Welcome, everyone. Thank you all for coming. Tonight, we have a guest from Hollywood, an old friend of mine who decided to stop in to say hello." The man on stage pounded out a piano drumroll.

Shivers ran up Lottie's arms.

"Just for you, San Francisco, here she is ... that legend of the silver screen, Gloria Swanson!"

The piano kept pounding and a spotlight hit the front door. Everyone turned to look at Gloria Swanson. She stood tall in a glorious turban, bedecked in sparkling jewels, sunglasses, a puffy white fur stole and long leather gloves.

Ruby sighed. "She's so beautiful."

The bright spotlight followed Gloria as she slunk slowly, gracefully, toward the stage. She used grand gestures to greet patrons, bowed and held out one hand ceremoniously for small kisses. Lottie's eyes caught the spotlight bouncing shattered rays off the movie star's twinkling jewelry. The light fragmented through smoky air into shimmering snowflakes of show dust.

When Gloria made it to the stage, she grabbed a microphone. "Thank you, thank you. You all remember that I made my most notorious movie, *Sunset Boulevard*, in 1951."

Gloria's voice was too deep. It was a man's voice! Everyone laughed along with Lottie, who just realized that this was not the real Gloria Swanson, but an impersonator.

"It's a guy!" Carol half-shouted, tickled by the whole thing.

"I played a delusional movie star named Norma Desmond," the man went on, amid chuckles. "Aside William Holden. He played my lesbian lover." The joke threw the audience into a howl.

Gloria Swanson looked out into the audience and pointed at a lady at a front table. "If you ever become a mother, can I have one of the puppies?"

Everyone cackled.

Lottie looked at Patty. "What's the name of this place?"

"Finnochio's," Patty said. "It's the best drag palace in the Bohemian district."

"*Drag*?" Lottie asked, noticing that Ruby and Carol were holding hands. Patty noticed, too. She turned and winked at Lottie.

"Places like here and the derby, they're safe spaces. You know what I mean?" Ruby grinned wide.

"Sure, I do," Lottie said.

"We don't have to keep looking over our shoulders, worrying what people might say or do to us."

Lottie paused, processing all this. "That's good. But, um, you know I'm not, um, that way. I hope I'm not in the way."

"Don't get crazy on us. You're our best friend."

"Thanks," Lottie said, but she felt alone. She thought that what Ruby and Carol shared was like what Tommy and Elsie Mae must have felt. She wished, with a longing hope, that there would be a man in her future. Still, the vibrant show drew her in. She enjoyed the jokes, quick changes and music and dance numbers, all with men impersonating leading women from stage and screen. Their performances sent her into hysterics. Elsie Mae would have loved it.

"My favorite was the big Mae West," Patty laughed as she spoke while the group left through the nightclub doors and started down the narrow city streets. They'd have to walk five blocks to find a taxi back to their quarters near the Cow Palace. "Get in line, boys." Patty attempted a Mae West imitation. "I feel like a million tonight. But I'll take 'em two at a time."

"I loved the Bette Davis part," Lottie said.

"I loved it all!" Ruby enthused as Carol danced by her side.

"Hey, you!" A group of sailors in a car were stopped at a red light. They stared long and hard. They yelled, whistled and honked their horn, stirring Lottie from her momentary happiness. The skaters turned to look.

One of the young sailors yelled, "Lesbians!" The others in the car ogled and howled. "You need a real man!"

A sudden coldness hit Lottie's core, was there always going to be something bad to balance out the fun times? The group turned to see who the sailors were shouting at. Fans normally yelled at Lottie and her teammates when they skated, but she wasn't prepared for this public attack. And fans never used words like 'lesbian.' Her heart pounded in her ears.

"Are they talking about us?" Carol's voice cracked.

At the show, the word lesbian had struck Lottie as comical, an inside joke with a close group of friends. Here on the street, it sounded filthy and hateful.

"Just ignore them," Patty said, as the group kept walking.

"Queers!" The car rolled closer.

"Oh, no." Ruby's face turned ashen.

"Do we need help?" Carol grabbed Ruby's arm and hugged close.

"There must be six of them," Lottie murmured clutching the buttons on her jacket.

"Lesbos!" The sailors flailed their arms. The insults grew louder and more vicious.

Lottie fought the urge to run. She knew she was in danger.

Patty turned and took two steps ahead of her group. "We're in trouble."

Lottie's breath hitched when Patty turned, stopped walking and stood her ground. She waved for the car of drunken sailors to move on. "Get out of here!"

The car roared closer. "Fag!" came a loud catcall. The back car door opened, one man jumped out, and a beer bottle came hurtling near. It crashed to bits at Ruby's feet.

"Look out!" Ruby shouted. She sidestepped the flying beer bottle.

"I'm scared." Lottie's hands trembled. Time stood still.

"Homosexual bitches!" a young man shouted.

"They're comin' after us." Carol pressed close to Ruby.

Lottie sensed the fear in Carol's voice.

"What should we do?" Patty's elbows pressed to her sides, as if to make herself smaller.

"We'll beat your asses!" came the sailors' yells.

Lottie's gut dropped to the sidewalk. She searched the streets. All the stores and shops were closed. "There's no place to run."

Carol whimpered.

"Let's get 'em," one of the men said. Two weaving sailors approached. The car careened, screeching its wheels. It bumped up onto the sidewalk and came to a stop, horn blasting as if the driver were holding it down.

Lottie swallowed. Her mind spiraled into a fog of fear. Another bottle flew through the air, smashing violently near her legs. "God," she whispered.

Carol pushed herself out of the group, ahead of Patty. With her head rigid, she screamed back, "Fuck you!" Carol's face was filled with anguish under the anger.

The night went stone cold.

Veins bulged at Carol's temples. "Get out of here!"

"Freak!" one sailor yelled. He extended his middle finger.

Lottie's chest pounded. She felt a throbbing pulse in her throat. Then she jammed a fist high. "Kiss my ass!!" erupted from her throat, sounding every bit as rough as old Belzak.

The sailors stopped still.

The tendons on Lottie's neck bulged. "HEEEYYYYY! Get outta our way!" Her voice exploded, and her face snarled. She picked up a stone and heaved it in the direction of the car.

Lottie's friends rallied, and followed her lead.

"Lesbians!" another voice yelled. The car engine revved a deep roar, rattling Lottie's grit.

"Don't worry, girls." Carol placed both hands on her hips and stood in a defiant wide stance. Lottie did the same and raised a clenched fist.

The two men on foot scattered back into the car. The car drove away with a screech.

"That'll show 'em to mess with us," Carol said.

Silence. The group walked without a sound.

Lottie's chest felt full. She wondered how the others felt. This must have been what Rebecca felt; pushed as far as could be and finally pushing back no matter the cost.

"Hey, sailors, *don't* come up and see me *any* time," Carol parodied the Mae West impression. She pushed her hair up and put one hand on her hip. "How do ya like that?"

"And!" Lottie copied. "I'll take the army boys from Company B any day." Her rattled nerves turned to giggles. The group laughed.

"There's the taxi stand," Carol pointed.

Chapter 24

NEW TRAINEES?

Dismal attendance had lodged a thorn in Lottie's throat. She could tell the rest of the derby players had been down and out during their three month stay in the City by the Bay. Nose to the grindstone, the skaters worked on plays that probably would have thrilled other audiences. Without Roughie, a new hierarchy of power was being invented. It was taking a while for the fans to warm up to a new roster of leading skaters.

"Have you guys noticed how the captains have stopped talking about the plays before the games?" Ruby said.

"I see them by themselves a lot," Lottie said.

"We're not included much. I thought skaters would move up the ladder after Roughie left," Lottie remarked.

"I bet they're afraid we'll catch on," Carol said, weaving back and forth. "You know, steal their thunder. Controlling, huh?"

Lottie thought for a moment. "Yup, you're right. What should we do?"

"Well ... we know now that it's the plays that get the audiences excited," Ruby said.

"We can't do the plays they do. You see by the crowds, those bits ain't working anymore," Carol said.

"We'll have to come up with our own plays!"

"Something new? That's shit for crap. How?" Carol asked.

Ruby made a slow, determined shake of her head. "We can do it. We'll do it for Elsie Mae and Rebecca!"

Lottie scratched her head while searching through her skate bag. She rubbed the lucky hat with two fingers.

"I can't think of a thing," Ruby said.

Suddenly, Vinnie walked past. "Hey kids, how's tricks?" Vinnie eyed Lottie. "You're getting better. Not bad. Not bad for a chick-a-dee." He winked.

"Go away," Lottie grumbled.

Carol and Ruby turned their backs.

Vinnie gave a crooked smile with his yellow teeth. "I have good news."

Lottie frowned.

Vinnie stuck his chest out and bounced on the balls of his feet. "Buddy Wilson is here tonight."

Lottie slowly turned her head. A feeling of warmth hovered around as if his name was magic. "Buddy? Really?"

"That's so crazy," Ruby whispered.

"Sure, he's here with a few local gals who want to learn to skate. They'll be coming by. We thought you might help train 'em."

Lottie widened her eyes. "Me? *Train* 'em? It'd be great to have new blood in the group."

"Do it, Lottie." Ruby nodded.

"That's right, honey." Vinnie licked his lips. "They'll be here in about an hour, and we decided to pick you to help train them."

"Want to help me, Ruby?"

"The blisters on my feet are killing me. Not tonight," Ruby said.

"I'll stay with Ruby." Carol looked into Ruby's eyes.

"Well ..." Lottie's spirits soared. "Sure. I'll be ready. I'd love to help."

"There're two of them." Vinnie studied Lottie's face, then his gaze lowered down the length of her body. "After you shower, instead of going back to the quarters, come on back to the track. I'll be here to let them in."

"Okay," Lottie said, and hurried through the nightly routine.

"We're going for dinner," said Ruby.

"I'll have to miss it tonight," said Lottie. "I'm excited about seeing Buddy. I'll make it to dinner next time."

Everyone else left. Lottie's feet echoed on the wooden floor, for some reason it felt ominously wrong. She squinted.

All but a few lights had been turned off. Soon, she was at the track's side. Lottie waited patiently. She couldn't wait to see Buddy again. She wanted to tell him about Cuba. She ran training drills through her mind, hoping Buddy would train right next to her.

The sound of shoes echoed in circles. "Buddy, are you here?" Lottie called. "Buddy?"

There was no answer—then a voice. "Say, hon. How's tricks?"

"Oh, hi." Lottie jumped and forced a tense grin.

Vinnie had appeared out of nowhere. Lottie looked past him and searched the area. "Is Buddy here?"

Vinnie looked around. "Not here yet."

"Is he with the new skaters?"

Vinnie smirked. "Maybe they're in the back."

"Huh ... in the back?" Lottie's gaze bounced from corner to corner of the dark arena.

Vinnie teetered slightly and scratched at his crotch with one hand. "Being new, they might not know where to meet us."

Lottie frowned. "Oh, um, let me go look."

Vinnie bowed and swung an arm, like a butler admitting her into a mansion.

Lottie turned toward a backstage corridor, but sensed a nagging alarm in her gut. Maybe they were late—or maybe something worse.

"Here, let me go with you." Vinnie grabbed hold of her arm. "We don't want anything to happen to you, too, do we?"

Lottie's toes curled and she swallowed uncomfortably. She leaned away as a whisper tugged inside, and they walked alongside the seating area.

"Maybe back there?" Vinnie pointed.

Lottie's skin tingled, her eyes widened. She was looking down a lonely corridor, peering into the dank darkness. It was empty. With each step, she felt squashed bubble gum and popcorn on the cement. The place gave her the creeps. Suddenly, Vinnie's grip tightened and her legs were moved faster by his pushing force; four steps deeper inside the cave.

Vinnie's breathing came faster, stiffening the hairs on the back of Lottie's neck. Vinnie stared at her abdomen. A pang of anxiety went off inside her like a fire alarm. "I don't see anyone."

"They might be right up there." Vinnie pointed up the corridor with a mischievous grin. Lottie cringed as his face muscles tightened like he was grinding his teeth together. He pushed her forward.

"Buddy, where are you?" she called in a loud voice.

"Up here." Vinnie jerked her by the arm deeper into the depths.

"Hey, up where? Don't touch me." She tried to control her shaky voice.

After three steps, Vinnie grabbed both her shoulders and faced her.

"Wait!" Lottie stopped.

He wrapped one hand around her waist. "Come on, toots." He pressed closer.

Lottie could smell alcohol on his breath. "You stink."

He pulled her arm and waist, then drew her close to his pockmarked face. His eyes glazed over.

Lottie let out an awkward, muffled sound. "No ... wait." Feeling tricked by him, she felt fear shoot through her mind and body.

Vinnie used the other hand to push her hair back and rub her cheek. "I've been watching you."

His breath nauseated Lottie. "What do you mean? Leave me alone." She shuddered and grappled for words. Lottie was worried that any words might anger him.

"Babe, you know what I mean." Vinnie grinned and moved his greasy face inches from hers.

"No, I ... I don't know." She evaded his gaze. White-hot repulsion traveled up her spine.

Vinnie pressed his body against Lottie, letting his hips gyrate slowly. "You know you want me."

"So, there's no Buddy or skaters?" Her stomach turned to a putrid soup. "Me—want *you*?" She refused to look and her palms pushed his chest away, attempting to get a fresh breath.

"Feisty, huh?" He backed her against the wall. She was pinned ... trapped. His hands gripped her more forcefully.

"Quit!"

"Now, now. No need to worry. I can make you feel better." He moved his face closer to hers, then opened his mouth.

"No! You're disgusting." She turned her face to one side.

Vinnie frowned and grabbed her cheeks with one hand. His grip tightened; lips spread wide into an open position. "You been sending me signals, honey."

Vomit churned inside Lottie's stomach. "I didn't mean ... just leave me alone."

"Not 'til I'm finished."

"I'm warning you."

"Come to daddy, sweetie." He laughed and pushed his hips forward, touching his crotch against her.

Lottie's brain spun. Her dad had a drinking problem, but he was no sleaze or rapist. Vinnie's remark struck a nerve. Her jaw tightened. In one supercharged move, she pulled a clenched fist backward and hit him in the jaw. "HEEEYYYYY. Get outta my way!" her voice exploded.

Vinnie flew a foot toward the ceiling, and fell to the ground.

"You make me sick!" Lottie spat on the floor.

Before she could move or run, Vinnie threw himself at Lottie with a vengeance. "Strong, huh?" His breathing was fast and loud. He wanted to make her pay. "I like that in a gal," he snarled. "It's a turn on."

Lottie's breath froze.

"Come here, bitch," Vinnie wretched.

Lottie closed her eyes. The worst was about to happen.

"Lottie! Where are you?" a voice called out.

Vinnie stopped. He darted his eyes to the left where the voice had come from. Sweat beaded on his brow.

"Lottie?" the voice called out again.

After a blank, jittery instant, Lottie yelled out, "Here! Here!" Her eyes stayed fixed on Vinnie. A wave of ugly wrinkles and furrows etched themselves onto his face.

"What're you doing back here in the dark?" Ruby appeared.

Vinnie let go, and pulled back a step.

Ruby squinted. Her expression immediately changed to anger.

"Ruby!" Lottie gasped. "Oh, God," she wheezed.

Vinnie looked at Ruby with narrowed eye slits. Ruby stiffened. "Keep your crummy mitts to yourself!"

Vinnie drew his head back and looked at Lottie. "I see, you're one of them!" He spit in her hair.

Lottie flinched.

"I said, mitts off!" Ruby's voice boomed down the hall.

Vinnie's eyes reflected the moonlight from an overhead window. They scanned the room like searchlights. "Some of the other guys thought so. Now I know." One hand wiped his wet brow, and he flicked the sweat into Lottie's face. Smelly drips spattered her cheek.

"So what if she is? You get the hell away! Just back off!" Ruby's shouts bashed against Lottie's ears, it was practically a bellow.

Vinnie's spine straightened. He sniffed, and took two steps back. "No skin off my fucking ass."

"It will be, if you bring your *fucking* ass near either of us again!" Ruby's shouts made Vinnie's eyes register alarm. He glared at Lottie.

"Horse's ass!" He turned, retreating into darkened halls.

Lottie's body went limp; tears slid unbidden and unnoticed, they were from fear and the sudden relief.

"All men rape!" Ruby's brows furrowed. She looked at Lottie.

Lottie quivered. Her muscles weakened. She stumbled back a step and sighed. "I hope not *all*. Thank you."

"Don't mention it." Ruby hugged Lottie a moment, but she kept one eye directed over Lottie's shoulder. Lottie sensed Ruby's warm body buzzing with adrenaline. She felt safe.

"Come on, let me walk you back to the quarters."

They both turned and Ruby held out a sturdy hand to her best friend. They ambled slowly away. Lottie held Ruby's hand, and her heart felt full. For the first time in her life, she wanted a stiff drink to help sort through these overwhelming emotions.

Chapter 25

DISCOVERING COLOR

Lottie skated through many games, improving with each Cow Palace event. She continued to feel disappointed over attendance. The small groups of fans who trickled in, combined with twice-a-week trainings, made for weeks of unrewarding exhaustion.

As Lottie's team wheeled into the arena each night, she saw more wood in the stands. "The well's running dry," she said to Ruby.

"But you know Oscar. He'll squeeze every dime out of this city before hitting the road. Besides, two weeks ago he started to film for television." Ruby tilted her head from side to side, as if weighing choices.

"He must be spending a fortune. I'd like to stay here longer." Lottie felt a quiver in her stomach.

"You don't think he'll shut down, do you?" Carol crossed and uncrossed her arms with restless energy.

"I hope not. But look at the small audiences," Ruby said.

"Hey, I have an idea. Let's go on down to a show tomorrow after breakfast," Patty suggested. "The Fox Theater."

"The theater? Another 'swishy' show?" Ruby winked.

"Even better! Patty's eyes widened. "The Fox downtown is grand, the best in the world. I think the latest Gene Autry picture is showing, or *Rebel Without a Cause*."

"I'll go," Lottie said.

"James Dean is sexy. No need to twist my arm." Ruby laughed.

"Sexy, huh? Where Ruby goes, I go," Carol giggled.

"Anything's better than looking at drab wallpaper and empty Cow Palace seats." Ruby eased one hip out to the side.

Lottie sensed that another discovery lay ahead. Smack dab in the center of downtown, on Market Street, the Fox Theater glimmered with luscious red carpet and gold-topped banisters. Lottie's heart thrummed as she entered this imperial palace framed with magnificent columns. The grandeur was fit for gods. Her eyes sparkled. It was a sight that only San Francisco could offer.

Feeling like Hollywood stars, Patty, Ruby, Carol and Lottie sauntered under the theater's gilded ceiling.

"Let's sit up in the balcony." Carol pointed up the curve of the ascending staircase.

Ruby tilted her head back and dropped her jaw.

"I love the view from there," Patty said.

"We wouldn't want to mix with the riffraff," Lottie said in an English accent.

They sashayed up the steps chortling. Nearing the top, Carol turned and laughed at herself. "Welcome to my palace. Now sit the crap down!"

They laughed, shared popcorn and hunkered down in the plush seats, ogling the ornate paintings and sculptures that decorated the walls and ceiling. Far below, the gigantic movie screen was framed in velvet drapes. A pipe organ carved of wood stood at center stage, poised to spring to life. Lottie inhaled the richness of the curtains and the smell of the wooden stage mixed with fresh theater dust and warm popcorn.

"I can't wait!" Carol crossed her legs.

A newsreel short flickered to an end. "What's this?" someone whispered.

"It's a Three Stooges flick," Patty said, as Victorian hanging lights dimmed overhead.

"I saw them on television at home," Lottie said.

"They're like Laurel and Hardy," Patty said. "Or Abbot and Costello."

"Everyone knows the Three Stooges," Carol said.

"Ssshh!" someone hushed from behind.

Lottie noticed that Carol had once again seated herself close to Ruby. Carol's face was beaming, but all her attention seemed rapt upon the stage. The organ burst into sound and the thick velvet curtains parted. A shiver washed through Lottie. She was transported. Giggling at the men on the screen, she was soon laughing so hard that she couldn't catch her breath.

"It's funny!" Ruby whispered.

Up on the screen, an angry Moe stretched out his arm, clenching his fist. Curly hit Moe's fist with his own closed one. Moe's arm swung in a big circle, only to land on Curly's head with a loud *boink*. The crowd chuckled. Lottie put one hand to her mouth to stifle her noisy laughter.

Curly recoiled, and his head bounced back and forth as if on a spring. The entire audience tittered as Curly grimaced and slapped his own face. Lottie sat mesmerized as an idea clicked inside of her brain. Meanwhile, Moe took charge of the other two, his face scrunched with anger. He commanded them loudly, so when *he* goofed up by hitting his finger with a hammer, the audience laughed even more.

Lottie and the audience loved him. The slapstick *shtick* tickled her belly with fun. Lottie got a kick out of hearing Moe use her line, "Outta my way." Her eyes brightened when Moe topped off those famous words by saying, "You knuckleheads!" Lottie roared with laughter.

"I like Larry's hair," Carol whispered. "And how it looks like they're hurting each other."

Lottie was happy but quiet—thinking. Inside her mind, strings of loose ends suddenly connected. "It's giving me an idea."

"*Hu-hum,*" Ruby grunted from the back of her throat.

"You want to hit my finger with a hammer?" Carol chuckled.

"Ssshh!" someone hushed them.

On screen, the infuriated Moe furrowed his brow, narrowed his eyes, and drew his hand back, ready to throw a knuckle sandwich at Larry. Just when it seemed like Moe was going to make contact, the wild-haired Larry ducked. Moe reeled forward with his mouth open and accidentally slammed into Curly with a *klonk*. Curly recoiled. "Ouch!" He shaped his mouth into a large O, and fell square on his butt.

The audience roared as Lottie's chest drummed. She bottled up her breath, staying calm yet sitting on an ocean of an idea.

Curly sat up, looking like a big clown. He raised one hand and rubbed his head as if wondering what had just happened. His face beamed a *what-did-you-do-that-for?* expression at the camera.

Lottie was no longer watching the action. "I've got it!"

"What?" Ruby whispered.

"Damn it, what?" Carol said, irritated to be drawn away from the film.

"Shhhh," someone scolded again.

"Slapstick. I think this'll work!" Lottie threw a popcorn kernel into the air.

"What are you talking about?" Carol frowned.

"That's it!" Lottie's eyes gleamed as she watched Moe's funny face after he realized he'd just clobbered Curly. "Look, look, look!" She pointed at the screen.

"Have you gone loony tunes?" Ruby hissed. "What the heck are you talkin' about?"

"Slapstick. *Color!*" Lottie snapped a finger in the air.

"Quiet," someone hushed again with noticeable annoyance this time.

Lottie nudged Ruby and whispered. "See? Color!" Lottie exclaimed with a nod of her head, pointing at the screen. She had a grin that couldn't be contained. Her brain spun: wondering, inventing. She couldn't wait to put this new color into action!

Excitement was uncontained at the following evening's backstage prep time. The locker room looked as dank and dingy as any Lottie had ever seen it, but tonight, bits of light tinkled their rays onto the dirty plasterboards, giving her an extra jolt. Lottie heard the sound of skate wheels echoing down a long corridor and Ruby and Carol appeared. Lottie motioned them closer. "This is gonna sound crazy." Her brain tied the ideas together like a puzzle.

"Uh-hum, so what else is new?" Ruby asked.

"Let's try something, okay? It might not work, but we gotta try something." Lottie leaned toward Carol and Ruby.

"I'm in." Ruby moved closer. "I gotta hear this."

"Me, too," Carol said.

Lottie whispered and created the scene with her hands, drawing imaginary set-ups in the air. She noticed Ruby opening her eyes wider, while Carol nodded and laughed. After their talk, the three entered the sparsely-filled arena. Lottie wondered how the other skaters might react to this scheme.

Late in the roller game, on cue, Carol broke away from the pack, saying, "Outta my way, knuckleheads!" She sprinted on the jam for the Bay City Bombers.

Lottie nervously observed the audience. She snickered at her idea. Carol skated on the home team, the Bombers, while she and Ruby skated on the visiting team, the Los Angeles All-Stars.

"The Flashing Bombshell, Carol Anderson, is now out on the jam for the Bay City Bombers," the announcer said in his dramatic voice.

Lottie tingled all over.

The fans were, as yet, unmoved.

Ruby sped away from the pack, following Carol's sleek style.

"And out moving quickly on this play is Ruby Johnson from Los Angeles, chasing the Flashing Bombshell," the announcer declared.

The two pushed one another and flew around the big track. Taking a long time to reach the rear of the pack, Ruby taunted the Bombshell with jabs followed by elbows.

"Johnson's pounding on our Flashing Bombshell!" the announcer cried. His voice could be felt in the vibration of the floorboards.

Lottie caught glimpses of the fans starting to pay closer attention. "They're sitting up," she said to herself. A smile appeared on her lips.

Ruby lifted her hands into the air and bashed her friend on the back. Carol's spine wrenched upright.

A small moan came from the crowd. People leaned in.

"Looks like an illegal block," the announcer yelped, as Carol shuddered from the perceived attack, clomping on her skates to regain control. "I guess the referees didn't catch that."

Ruby hit Carol again.

Lottie was breathless.

The crowd called out with boos and catcalls at what looked like a bone-splitting punch.

Lottie pushed herself to the rail; the pack had left her in the defending position against the oncoming Carol. She set herself up with her legs wide and her shoulders outstretched. Lottie looked, for the moment, big and tough. She furrowed her brow and narrowed her eyes, just as she'd seen Moe do. Carol approached. Lottie's heart raced and she let go a digging elbow smash, seeming to hit the pretty Bomber girl in the abdomen. "Take this, you chowderhead," Lottie yelled as loud as she could.

A small *oooh* came from the crowd when they saw the play-acted pain on Carol's face. The announcer spiked up his volume. "The Flashing Bombshell, beaten back by the Little Lunatic."

A rush of energy raced through Lottie. "It's really working!"

Ruby wheeled up behind the Bomber and rammed Carol from behind. "Let's do it, Moe!" she hollered, waving a hand at Lottie.

The Bombshell staggered, careening forward out of control. She rolled right into the defending Lottie. Lottie's brow was sweating. She wound her arm in a big circle.

Exaggerating another big elbow block, she rocked the Bomber backwards. "Take that, goon!"

Carol's head flew back, recoiling in mock pain, and the crowd responded with terrified cries. Carol wobbled on the tips of her wheels.

Someone yelled out, "Stop her!"

"The Little Lunatic and Johnson are taking care of our Bomber out there!" the announcer yelled. "It looks as if the two Los Angeles skaters are doubling up on the defenseless Bomber."

"I can't see," Carol yelled when she bounced forward. "I can't see." She reeled backward after taking another pantomimed elbow block from Lottie.

"Why, I oughta!" yelled Lottie with a strong arm bash.

"I've got my eyes closed!" Carol's face took on a look of anguish for the audience.

The fans were mesmerized, their eyes fixed. Lottie heard shrieks. She kept her game face on, frowning and gritting her teeth. The fans hated her.

"There're just five seconds left. It appears there will *not* be a score on this play." The announcer's voice was tense and genuine, he had no idea this was set, figuring it was a locker room dust up that carried over to the game.

With three seconds remaining, Carol careened toward Lottie one more time. Lottie took a deep breath and lifted her elbow. She held it high, ready to deliver a terrible arm smash to the smaller Carol. She threw her entire body into the Bomber. The crowd braced, waiting for a devastating blast.

"HEEEYYYYY, get outta my way, you knucklehead!" Lottie screamed.

With a lightning-fast reaction, little Carol sidestepped the walloping arm block. Ruby rolled directly behind Carol, toward Lottie.

The fans cheered and clapped.

"The Blond Bombshell has sidestepped the Little Lunatic!" the announcer bellowed.

Lottie caught Ruby's eye at the last minute, too late to stop her momentum. Ruby was in the way!

"No!" Ruby shouted, arms flailing.

Lottie flinched, pulling her block away at the last second. *Bam!* She slammed into Ruby, who crashed into a heap on the track. The fans cheered. The two bad guys had just smashed into each other! At the same instant, Carol slid by Lottie for a point.

"And there's one Bomber point by the Flashing Bombshell," the announcer cheered as loud as the fans.

The buzzer sounded and the small crowd roared. Belzak's brow furrowed. Ruby sat on the track with one hand rubbing her head, pouting. Lottie staggered above her, then suddenly stumbled and fell on top of her own teammate.

"Looks like The Little Lunatic has some trouble staying on her skates."

The fans guffawed and the announcer gave a small chuckle. Lottie tried to get up, looking embarrassed. *Clump, clump!* Her feet slipped again and again. Then both skates went out from under her. She crashed to the track again. Her butt hit with a resounding *thud*. Her head snapped back and her mouth opened to yell, "Ouch!"

"The Little Lunatic's got quite a problem out there."

The crowd responded, laughing and jeering.

Then it came time for Ruby's antics. Trying to help her teammate off the track, she pulled Lottie up by her hands, but pulled too hard. She fell backwards with Lottie toppling on top of her in a precarious position. Lottie's face landed right between Ruby's outstretched legs. With her face stuck in Ruby's crotch, Lottie lifted her head and wobbled it left and right, as if trying to shake cobwebs out of her brain.

The crowd guffawed.

"Go home!" someone yelled, prompting more laughter.

Belzak skated close, her mouth open. She attempted to kick at Lottie. "Stop it! What's going on?"

Lottie reached a hand upward for help. Belzak grabbed and Lottie pulled her hard, crashing her headfirst onto the track with a *thwump*. Belzak rolled onto her butt and spat at Lottie.

The fans cheered.

Roller Babes

In one last move, Ruby stood, hovering over Lottie, and tried to help her up. Instead, she accidentally tugged the red jersey up over Lottie's head. "Lift your arms," Ruby said in a quiet voice.

Lottie put both arms in the air, and Ruby pulled the jersey almost off, blinding Lottie.

"*Look out!*" the announcer yelled.

The sparse crowd soared into hysterics at the sight of Lottie's exposed bra. Lottie scampered around trying to pull the jersey back down. Then she stumbled and fell onto the track again. The audience went berserk; they'd never seen anything so scandalous or exciting.

Lottie staggered foolishly and tripped over herself, pretending she couldn't see. She clamored on her skates, as if unaware that her white underwear was shining under the arena lights in full view. The crowd zinged into a state of ecstatic delight.

Minutes later, the game rumbled to a tumultuous end.

"Thank you for coming to tonight's American Roller Derby League game. Tell your friends, and come back again."

Lottie skated backstage, pulling herself back together.

"Now *that* was color!" Patty congratulated Lottie at the locker room door. She handed Lottie two letters.

"Thanks," Lottie said, between heavy breaths.

"What do you call it?" Patty asked, marking a check on her paper.

"A ping-pong with a red goof," Lottie said after thinking for a second.

"That was the best time of my life," Carol beamed.

"Well, keep it up. They loved it," Patty said. Lottie took the two letters. "Good job, girls," Patty said, congratulating Carol and Ruby. Then she added, "Oscar's given each of you a small increase in pay."

Gerry smiled at Lottie.

Lottie caught the resentful stare from Belzak.

"Sure, Patty, thank you so much," Lottie said, with satisfaction written on a perspiring face. She now understood how her pay was directly related to how the fans reacted to her skating.

"So, I suppose we're to accept your kind now, because you made the audience laugh?" Belzak clenched her teeth.

"We invented a play, that's all." Lottie sat and massaged fresh knots and bumps from where she had fallen.

"Your people run the world's money and banks, but you don't run *derby*!" Belzak yelled.

"I'm not trying to."

"Your kind don't belong in a derby uniform!" Belzak took a step closer, pointing at Lottie and Ruby with her veins bulging. "Especially you and you!"

Lottie's heart ached. She looked away, they should have been teammates, helping each other and then the whole derby would have been stronger. Soon, though, her brows lifted. Perched inside her locker were the letters. She angled her body to one side and eyeballed them. Lottie tore into the first, a letter from home. It had recent news. Mom's letters always warmed Lottie's insides. She studied the second letter. She knew it wasn't money. It wasn't payday yet.

Then she realized. "It's a fan letter!" she gulped. There was a figure drawn on the front near her name. She pushed herself into a remote corner of the dressing area and opened the envelope.

The letter was scrawled in pencil, apparently written in haste, judging by how the words strayed beyond the ruled lines. The left-hand side of the paper appeared smudged with fingerprints. Who could be the source of this communication?

Lottie Zimmerman,

You're the best skater out there. I know this may sound frank, coming from a young man about your age, but I just couldn't take my eyes off you. I am a private in the Army stationed at the Presidio, and have been coming to every game for a week. I just wanted you to know that I'm a big fan of yours, and you look very pretty out there.

Lottie stopped reading. Her pulse rose and her face felt like a furnace. No man ever had told her she looked pretty. *He couldn't take his eyes off me.* She returned to the letter.

This may sound crazy, but I'd like to meet you. I will be at the next game, if you're interested.

Your fan and friend,

Harold Grays

"Whatcha readin', Moe?" Ruby asked. "You look shocked."

Lottie tossed the second letter inside her skate bag.

"What's the letter say?" Carol asked.

"Oh. That was just a letter from home. You know how I get homesick sometimes. Say, I hear Oscar's been broadcasting the Cow Palace games in New York and the Bronx."

Ruby pushed her skate bag in front of her, dropping her skates inside. "That's really good news. Think it's true?"

"Mom said so." Lottie's little finger trembled. She held that finger with her other hand to cover her nervousness. "Mom said Dad might even be turning into a fan. It makes me miss home."

"I miss the old home, too."

"Hey, a bunch of us're going dancing. Let's go shake a leg," Lottie changed the subject.

"Umm. Maybe. Let me ask Carol," Ruby said. "By the way, I really loved that play you came up with."

"Thanks. Let's do more, like Patty said."

"I'm with ya, Moe."

After Ruby and Carol left, the hurt girl inside Lottie returned. Her breath quickened. Boys had taunted her all her life. Could the letter be real? *What if the fan letter was no more than a cruel joke?*

Chapter 26

FAN MAIL

Lottie felt her fingers quiver as she concealed herself backstage, unnoticed. She had received another letter. Apprehension tugged at her gut. She pulled the letter from the envelope; a sense of joy spread inside at seeing Harold's manly handwriting.

The scrawling made her feel at home, as though she'd found a long-lost friend in an otherwise foreign land. With no real roots in San Francisco, Lottie felt the letters easing the lonely edge of homesickness. Just as she had the last five letters, Lottie read this one over and over, imagining what Harold looked like. "I wonder if he's taller than me? Is he strong? I hope with dark hair and blue eyes," she quietly mouthed to herself.

She pulled the letter close to her chest, feeling her heart race. She glanced left and right to ensure privacy before reading it once more.

Lottie Zimmerman,

I wanted to tell you this in all my other letters, but didn't have the guts to do it. So I'm finally asking now. I will be at the backstage door right after tonight's game, and I'd really like to meet you.

I've enjoyed watching you on the track so much; I'd like to talk and get to know you better. In case you're interested, I'll be waiting outside the rear door tonight.

I should stand out from others because I am six feet tall, and I will be wearing a dark blue suit, white shirt, and black tie. I wear a derby-style hat that I'll wave in the air when I see you. I will wait until ten o'clock.

If you don't show up, I'll understand, but I do hope you will be there.

Harold Grays

"Meet *me!*" Her heart went *thud.* Lottie's mind churned in circles. *What do I do? Can I get out of this? What do I wear or say?* The fan letters others got had never asked this type of favor, or at least no one had admitted it.

Is this a crazed fan or a real friend? She thought a moment. Heart pounding. All of her sensations were heightened, and she felt as if she were about to burst. *Don't be a louse. Give it a try.* She motioned with her head to Ruby. "Come here, will you?"

"Sure." Ruby dropped her jersey into a nearby box and hurried over to Lottie. "What is it? I see you got more letters."

Blood rushed through Lottie's body, pulsating out of control. She'd never been in this situation before, and the attack from Vinnie came whirling into her imagination. She turned to Ruby. "Can I count on a little help? You know, some support?"

"Sure. What is it, hon?" Ruby put a hand on the top of Lottie's shoulder.

"It's a little embarrassing. Can you walk with me through the gate tonight?" Lottie's heart thrummed like a schoolgirl's.

"Of course. I'll be leaving in about ten minutes." Ruby searched through her skate bag for a hairbrush.

"Oh, thanks."

"Why? What's this about?" Ruby crossed her arms.

"Nothin' special. Just a personal thing."

"Personal? I want in. My ass don't suck milk. What's going on?" Carol moved close.

"That spark in your eye, how come you're blushing?" Ruby smirked.

"Well," Lottie paused. "I just want you to be with me. I might see someone. A friend."

"A man friend?" Carol asked.

"Like who? Who do you know in San Francisco?" Ruby challenged.

"If it's who I'm thinking about, I might go to dinner with him." Lottie looked away.

Ruby's eye's widened. She nudged Lottie's shoulder gently. "You have a date? You've met a guy. You're not a very good fibber, you know."

"I *told* you," Carol said.

Lottie scrunched a foot into the floor. She looked down.

"Oh! This is really terrific!" Carol said, jumping up and down. "What's he like? Do tell."

Lottie welled up with excitement. "I don't know yet," she said after a hard swallow. "He's in the army. He's a fan, I guess. He comes to the games." She stopped.

"That's *all* you know? You've never seen him yet?" Ruby asked.

"I've been getting his letters. He says he enjoys my skating." Lottie made a small shrug with her shoulders, suddenly feeling silly about the whole thing.

"What if he's like James Dean?" Carol asked.

"I've been imagining what he looks like." Lottie cocked her head up. "Sounds crazy, huh?"

"This could be trouble, girl," Carol hooted, placing one hand over her mouth. "Remember that fan who sent Patty the sexy underpants?"

"I know." The air in Lottie's chest deflated. "That was just sorta like a joke. But this is different. He's been writing me, and wants to meet me. And I've never, you know, had a date." Lottie looked away.

"Been writing you a lot, and you been keeping it from us? How is he different?" Carol asked.

"I don't know. I have a feeling."

"Finally, your first date!" Ruby did a small dance. "How exciting!"

"I guess it's about time, huh?"

"Sure is."

"Oh. Dating is simple. All you have to do is just be yourself," Carol said. "And don't give in too easy!"

"And it's about time you got out, hon," Ruby said.

"What harm can come from it?" Carol asked in an encouraging tone.

"Don't worry, kid. I'll walk you out. Just give me a look if you want me to scram. Otherwise, I'll stick around to help get rid of the crud." Ruby went back to dressing.

"I'll hand you my skate bag if it looks good." Lottie lifted her bag up in a gesture.

"Good idea. Both of us will go with you," Ruby offered, tapping Carol's hand. "We'll be your moral support. And stand ready to clobber him, just in case he's a scum."

"You guys are the best!" Lottie hurried through her dressing, taking extra time to fix her hair. Since Oscar wanted the girls to look good, she'd learned a few things about hair and makeup. She didn't think any of it helped much. She still felt like the pill from the stickball games.

Carol spent several moments watching Lottie bungle attempts at brushing her hair. Then she grabbed her shoulders and took over. "Here, hon." Carol took the brush. "This'll make you look, well ... like a movie star. I know how to do this. I think I know what men go for."

"I'll never look like a movie star." Lottie lowered her chin.

Ruby edged forward, placed a finger under Lottie's chin and raised it. "Head up, girlfriend."

Carol groomed, forming shiny bangs out of Lottie's chaotic tangles. "That's better," she said, exhaling. She took a step back to look before moving in again to add a few touch-ups. She inspected Lottie like a prize hog, one eyebrow arched in serious contemplation.

"What's wrong? I look pretty bad?" Lottie asked nervously. Her insides shriveled.

"Let me see." Carol pulled a silk scarf from her bag. She held it next to Lottie's cheek. "Wear this. I think it'll look nice … I'm sure of it."

"If you think so." Lottie took the pink scarf and unfolded it with a gleam in her eye. She tied it over her hair and pulled the two ends under her chin, making a knot. "There, any better?" She frowned.

"*Uh-huh,*" Ruby said, with conviction.

"It's getting there, but let's see what else we can do." Carol tugged the scarf back another inch to reveal the luster of Lottie's styled light brown hair. She framed Lottie's face to accentuate her eyes and high cheekbones. She cocked her head left, then right. "Who *is* this girl?" She looked Lottie up and down.

"Give her some color," Ruby chuckled.

Lottie was uncertain. "I'm afraid to look." She'd learned to pretty herself up for Oscar, at least somewhat. She had grown up without cosmetics and accessories back in high school. Any of that would have been an unimaginable extravagance that her dad wouldn't have allowed, certainly never would have paid for.

"Now, let's brighten your lips." Carol pruned and catered like the cosmetics saleslady at Bergdorf's as she handed Lottie a tube of pale red lipstick, almost a pink.

Lottie smoothed the firm gloss over her puckered lips, trying hard not to color outside the lines.

"It matches the scarf." Carol released an appreciative sigh.

Ruby stood in front of Lottie and balanced her curls so the left side matched the right. Then she winked, whistling softly.

"Let me help." Carol grabbed her own blush and added contour to Lottie's cheeks. "You're a real belle now!"

"Naw!" Lottie said with an embarrassed laugh. "I'll never be nice looking."

"Oh, I wouldn't be so sure. *And now,* for one more girlie secret, watch this!" She affected the tone and cadence of the derby announcer.

"What are you doing?" Lottie asked.

Carol cinched the blouse behind Lottie's back and tightened it around her waist.

"Just tightening things up a bit." Carol's pupils enlarged, and a little color entered her cheeks.

Ruby made a little giggle. "*Tickets,* as Belzak says."

"A very classy chassis, indeed," Carol spoke through chuckles.

"Tickets?" Lottie mumbled and turned to look in the mirror. She stared for a moment. As if seeing herself for the first time in years, her eyes soaked in the alien image. "I'm another person. That's not me."

"Uh-huh," Ruby skimmed her fingertips along her jawline.

"Oh, that's you all right." Carol pushed the small of Lottie's back, straightening her shoulders and pushing out her breasts. "See?"

Lottie extended a shaking hand toward the mirror, as if to touch her reflection. "It can't be. Can it?"

"Oh, it is, girlfriend!" Ruby said.

Lottie put two fingers up to her lips and caught her breath. "I'm pretty," she whispered.

"You know, you've blossomed." Ruby took in her look with an appetite. "You *sure* aren't that goofy girl that I met at the Armory years ago anymore."

"Truly," Carol reassured Lottie. "You're attractive, and I'm sure your friend will be amazed now that you're out of that gunny sack of a uniform."

"You think so?" While Lottie loved the derby, she could see that the bulky jersey wasn't much help to her figure. In fact, she hadn't known she even *had* a figure until this moment.

"You're quite the *femme fatale*! And don't ever forget it." Ruby's almond eyes pouted and she looked as if she were ready to cry.

"*Femme fatale*? Really, guys ..." Lottie's heartbeat quickened. She couldn't keep her voice from quivering as she gazed into the mirror. Her knees wanted to buckle.

Perhaps, in the past months, she had simply been too busy to linger in front of mirrors. Where before she'd had a Bob Hope nose dominating her string bean face, large, bright eyes now sparkled atop elegant cheekbones. The awkward tomboy features had faded and filled up into feline curves. Dirty dishwater blonde locks had turned into a sweet light brown. Lottie had developed a muscled, smooth, athletic frame. "This is all I've ever wanted my entire life ... just to look nice." A tear glistened in one eye.

"A knockout!" Ruby said.

A lump grew in Lottie's throat. *So many years of feeling ugly and rejected.*

"You're what they call a late bloomer," Carol said. "Now don't cry, or we'll have to redo your makeup!"

Lottie felt the blood rush to her face as she squelched the waterworks. "I'm glad you guys are here. It's so unbelievable. Like I'm ... I'm ... oh, God, now I'm really nervous."

"We're more than happy to help, hon," Ruby said.

Skate bags in hand, the three girls walked to the exit. With each step, Lottie's stomach tied itself into a denser knot. Outside the door, it took but an instant for Lottie to find the tall man in the Gregory-Peck blue suit. Deep pockets, wide shoulders, high collar and a sharp black tie: this could only be one guy.

"Hi, Lottie." He waved his derby hat high in the air while extending a bouquet of yellow flowers.

Lottie's breath tightened. She waved back; all apprehension disappeared. It melted into a deep and complex pool of emotions. She and Ruby walked over to him without saying a word. Lottie eyed his strong jaw and white teeth. Her first thought was that the man looked like he spent most of his time happy. "Harold?" she asked, once she'd gotten closer.

"Lottie. I'm glad you came." Harold's eyes lingered on her, apparently not noticing Ruby. "You're a knockout."

Lottie's heart when *thud*. His eyes shone bright blue, a dreamy blue. She caught her breath and tugged on Ruby's coat. "This is my friend, Ruby," she said.

"Oh, yes, ma'am. Hi. I saw you skate tonight." He glanced quickly at Ruby, then returned his attention to Lottie. "The crowds have been getting bigger."

"You think they're coming to see someone running around in her bra?" Ruby smiled playfully.

"I don't know about that." Harold shrugged, as if he didn't know what to say. "I just know the matches are really exciting. But not half as exciting as this." He stared at Lottie.

Lottie's heart beat faster, as if it were about to take wings. "Yes, so, you're stationed here at the Presidio?" Lottie's insides fluttered as she stammered through the awkward introductions.

"It's a ten-minute walk from the barracks." Harold scuffed one of his feet. "It can be a little lonely being an army guy so far from home."

"Where you from?" Ruby asked, helping Lottie out.

"The Bronx, in New York."

"Really?" Lottie responded in astonished relief. "Me, too!" She felt amazed at how such a small statement could stir a fire deep in the pit of her stomach.

"Isn't that something? Say, you wouldn't want to grab a bite, would you?"

"Um." Lottie took a quick look at Ruby, who nodded slightly. Lottie handed her skate bag to Ruby. The signal. "Why not? I'm starved."

"I can imagine, after all that work on the track tonight. Let's eat!"

Ruby grabbed the bag and called out to Carol. "Hey, Carol. Wait for me. You two have a bopping good time." Carol and Ruby left, walking close to one another. They grinned and made furtive glances at the couple as they departed, but Lottie was too preoccupied to notice.

"We will. And thank you, Carol and Ruby," Lottie said, not noticing that she was many steps away from her friends. Suddenly, Lottie was alone with a man, walking into the darkening evening air.

Harold held out an arm for Lottie to clasp. A thrill zapped through her. She'd never walked arm and arm with a man before. The night's possibilities unfolded like a limitless horizon. It was like hearing a favorite song for the first time.

The two found a cozy Chinese place, the Fortune King, a few blocks from the Cow Palace. Bill Haley and His Comets' *Rock Around the Clock* was playing quietly.

Harold said, "It reminds me of home."

Lottie grinned. "Yes, I see that."

"Hey, do you remember? Well, I mean, I used to go almost every weekend to Patio's Paradise Theater with my friend, Jimmy, to watch the movies. Do you remember that theater?"

"Sure. I went there, too."

"I remember this really scary movie, *The Undying Monster*." His eyes roamed to the left as he recalled his childhood.

"I went with my friend Rebecca to see that one."

"That was the movie where my friend Jimmy ate too much popcorn." A smile drew around his white teeth. "We were in the balcony and he threw up, bending over the railing and hitting the audience below." He laughed, gently tapping the table with a big hand. "Ha ha … maybe not something to say just before we eat, sorry."

"I was there that night! Me and Rebecca! I remember everyone talking about the boy who threw up on the audience." She laughed. "That was you and your friend?"

He nodded. A small silence stretched out. Then Harold almost blurted out, "I miss the elevated trains and little shops." He smiled. "There're similar things here, but it's not the same."

"Me, too." Images of her old neighborhood sailed in and out of her mind. "But I've fallen in love with San Francisco."

"I like it more than the other American cities I've been to. I'm getting used to it."

"You know, you're easy to talk to," Lottie said.

"You, too," he said.

Lottie and Harold talked about their families. He had a younger brother, she had two younger sisters, and both had parents still around. "We're all a family in the derby now; they're good people."

"You know, I had been thinking of writing you for … weeks, really. But I was afraid …" Harold eyes slid to the left, then back to her.

"Afraid? What about?" Lottie playfully shoved his upper arm.

"Well, you know, you being in such a rough sport and all."

Lottie looked at him inquisitively.

"Well, the other guys said you might be a tomboy and mean or only like other girls."

Lottie laughed. "I don't see anything wrong with one girl liking another, but I like men."

Harold laughed. "Glad to hear it!"

Lottie looked at the table. "I've just never dated anyone before. I'm usually competing in some sport with or against men. I guess I never had time to get around to it; always working my way up … 'til now." She unconsciously parted her lips. It was a welcome change to talk to a man who wasn't trying to elbow her off a track or beat her at stickball.

"Never dated, huh? So you must be single?"

"Now you sound like my mother," Lottie chuckled.

"Oh, I don't want to be your mother." He laughed and paused for a moment, holding strong eye contact. "Maybe a friend."

Lottie's heart banged. "That's a nice thing to say."

"What do you want in your life?"

"I don't even know what there is. I guess that's one reason I was attracted to the derby." Lottie stopped and stared off.

"Well, there's a whole world out there." Harold gestured at the scene beyond the window, sweeping his hand from one side of the table to the other. "And it's just waiting for you."

"That sounds wonderful." Lottie felt his gaze on her lips.

"Who knows what lies ahead for you?" he asked.

Lottie and Harold ordered two unfamiliar dishes from the menu. Both feeling adventurous. Minutes later, they gobbled their way through a plate of savory noodles and a small golden duck. They laughed at the expression on the duck's face—the head was still attached to the body. Harold pointed out that it looked kind of like the skater from Lottie's team.

"Belzak?" Lottie trilled.

"Is she the one who's very aggressive and kind of ... vulgar?" Harold searched for the polite word.

"Yes, the one and only! You know, I think I do see the resemblance."

Lottie wished the evening would go on all night. "It's getting late," she finally said. "I need to get back."

The pair left the restaurant. Soon, Harold leaned his shoulder near, letting his arm brush hers. Lottie felt tongue-tied as they eased through the streets. Foghorns moaned in the distance and a chilly blanket of fog feathered the area. Lottie felt safe. Every once in a while, her knees weakened as expectant euphoria tickled her gut.

"I really enjoy your company," Harold said. "I'd love to meet up with you again."

"I'd like that." Lottie's heart climbed. *If this is what being with a man feels like, it is amazing!* She had no idea how to control these new feelings. Far too soon, she found herself at the quarters, where Harold shook her hand. It wasn't a parting scene like one in a Hollywood movie, but she wasn't sure how these things went in real life. She watched as his tall silhouette disappeared from view before she headed in.

"Is that you, Lottie?" Ruby's voice came in a whisper.

"Yes." She squinted, feeling her way through the quarters and over to her friend's bed. She stuck her head under the covers and Ruby did the same so the two could speak in private.

"Well? Tell me. He's so handsome. What's he like?"

"So sweet!" Lottie smiled in the dark and gushed. "I'm so confused about it all."

"He didn't try anything, did he?"

"He wouldn't take his eyes off me. It made me feel special."

"You liked him. I can tell."

"Oh, I guess."

"Come on. I'm dying to know. You look absolutely gay!"

"I feel gay for the first time! Well, he's great. His eyes are the color of the water I see in pictures of Hawaii."

"Oh, my God!"

"He's so gorgeous. He seems kind and thoughtful. And strong!"

"I think this'll be good for you, Lottie."

"He said he liked the color of my lips."

"Maybe he wanted to kiss you."

"I doubt it."

"Of course he did!" Ruby nudged Lottie with a friendly bump. "That's what men want when they keep looking at a girl's lips."

"He was interested in everything I said, and he remembered it all, too! It feels like I've known him for years."

"Sounds like it could be love, hon!"

Lottie laughed, withdrawing from the blanket. She picked up a pillow and smashed Ruby over the head.

Suddenly, a third pillow came down on both of them. Lottie and Ruby could hear Carol's girlish chuckle.

"Lottie's got a boyfriend!"

"Oh my gosh. What do I do now?" Lottie flopped onto her bed; totally thrilled with the world.

Chapter 27

HAROLD'S BOWLING BALLS

Fresh letters from Harold poured in for Lottie over the following two weeks. Soon, she eagerly accepted another date with him. The couple visited a bowling alley on upper Haight Street where they laughed over the funny shoes given to them by the sign-in clerk.

Harold's shoes came with a surprise: a small hole in the big toe of the right shoe. Lottie felt impressed when he didn't complain or ask for another pair. He pushed his finger through the hole before putting them on. "Look." He laughed and wiggled his finger at Lottie. "Peek-a-boo."

"You're funny." A tune played from the snack counter. "Listen. What's that song playing on the jukebox?"

"That's *Hound Dog* by Elvis Presley."

"Elvis? Well, I'll be. My friend Ruby told me years ago he'd be big. I like that tune."

"So do I." Harold bobbed along to the music. "His latest song is called *Heartbreak Hotel.*"

She turned her attention to the sound of rolling balls vibrating beneath the floorboards. When a ball popped up, it made a gentle clacking noise as it rolled into the ball-return gullet. She watched how the other bowlers held their balls and heaved them down the laneways.

Lottie grabbed a heavy bowling ball from the rack, surprised at its weight. "Prepare to lose!"

"Let me help you." Harold pushed his holey shoe on without tying his laces, and scrambled over to Lottie. Standing in front of her, he reached out to help her hold onto the ball in her hand. "It looks heavy."

"No, I can do this myself." She pushed her fingers inside the holes and smiled with a roughish grin. Her breath stuck in her throat. His hands lingered so close to hers that she involuntarily shuddered from the anticipation of touching his fingers.

"No, no." He chuckled and placed both hands around the ball and tugged lightly. "Let me help you." His eyes locked onto her lips.

"I've ... um ... got it." Lottie felt the electricity arc. She noticed Harold's trembling hands.

"Here." He offered to take the ball from her.

She'd never been so close to a man before, so close that she could inhale his smell, which was mixed with the scent of aftershave. With each breath, her heart throbbed.

"Here, what?" Lottie was helpless.

"Let me."

What is he doing? Lottie didn't need help with some old bowling ball. Harold edged closer, and energy sparked through Lottie, making her feel like a rope pulled tight.

"Here." They both touched the marble smoothness and Harold's hands hesitated.

"Here, what?" she whispered again.

"I got it." He fumbled with the ball, then tightened his grasp.

"Got what?" Lottie lost her coordination. She stumbled a few steps.

"The ball," he said.

An awkward tussle started. He attempted to catch her when she fell back two feet. She held one arm out. She realized that Harold was trying to be a gentleman, like the men in the movies. She wanted to let him take the lead, but didn't know how. She felt like they'd engaged in a dance to which she didn't know the steps. Who should lead? She tried to release her hand from the bowling ball. "My finger's stuck." Lottie's confusion boiled over.

Ain't That a Shame by Pat Boone played in the background. The moment was confusion, with every intention missing its mark. Energy shot between them. Lottie loved being so close. It filled her with zigzagging thrills, but things had spun out of control.

"I'm sorry."

"Sorry?" Shaking, Lottie reverted to her old familiar line and blurted, "HEEEYYYYY. Let go!" She tugged back and forth. The weight of the ball moved left and right. Off balance, Harold stepped on a loose shoelace. He stretched out the other leg. The maneuver came to a sharp halt once the lace tightened. The ball tipped left and Harold toppled over, taking Lottie and the ball with him.

"Oh, no," Lottie whispered, mid-tumble. The ball hit the wooden planking with a deadening *thud*, and the two sprawled out on the alley. Lottie laughed out loud with embarrassment.

"Wow, we must be putting on quite a show!"

They laughed until Harold's face slackened. His hand caught a strand of her hair. He pulled her head forward and kissed her. In a jolt, Lottie's mind fogged over. She could maintain only a singular attention to the moment. Passion scurried through her entire body. She stopped breathing as the rest of the world disappeared in the distance.

"Um, sorry," Harold apologized, and he darted his eyes away.

Lottie's eyes cleared. The music changed, and *Mr. Sandman* by the Chordettes wisped sweetly through the wood-dusty air. Time stopped and a daydream sensation enveloped her.

"You have something special. You're a real woman." Harold smiled softly.

Lottie's mind stirred with blurred emotions, but her body was absorbing every word like a dry sponge. Finally—the words she had longed to hear for so many years. "It's like you can read my mind," she whispered.

Harold stuttered. "I always wondered," he said, helping her up. "You know, what it's like to skate on that track."

Lottie loved how awkward he looked. His vulnerable face made her love him more. "Oh. It's nothing," she said, disappointed that the intimate moment had been replaced with shoptalk.

"No, really—what's it feel like?" he asked quietly.

"Feel like?"

"Well, to be a professional skater." His eyes never left hers.

Lottie caught the spirit of his request. "Your feet get to rolling on those wheels, as if you're flying faster and faster," she began slowly. "You're like a bird, like you can soar and be free for the first time. You feel in control, speeding up and down the banks. It's like being on a roller coaster; and your stomach flips while you're barreling down the steep hills." The joy she felt while skating overtook her; the happiness she'd felt with Harold moments before returned. She looked deep into his blue eyes and added, "It's the most wonderful feeling I've ever felt."

The two looked intently at one another.

"Until right now," she added. Vibrations radiated between them. Her heart was full. She moved close and placed her lips on his.

"Wow." He exhaled from the kiss.

Lottie was feeling everything with a new intensity: his embrace, his loyalty and a sense of being treasured. She wished these feelings would last forever.

That night, the pigeon appeared again in her dream for the first time in months. It was covered in iridescent feathers splashed amongst the bright white feathers. Its brilliance filled the skies, and the bird carried her heart to new, unvisited places.

Chapter 28

IS THIS PARADISE?

Lottie and Harold dated as often as possible over the next six weeks. He could always be seen around the games, and the skaters started to talk. Lottie could barely think about the derby because her brain was obsessed with Harold. She forgot about what the other skaters said and did. She ached for the sincerity of Harold's smile. She ignored the dank locker rooms, cheap hotels, cramped quarters and crowded lunchrooms. She dwelled instead on dinners with blue-eyed Harold. Even Belzak drifted to the back of her mind.

These romantic feelings bubbled up from deep within. When she was a young girl, a boyfriend had been the most foreign of concepts to Lottie. She had no orientation. She needed a role model. She racked her brain to think of someone to ask, settling on two skaters she knew who appeared to be deeply in love.

"Hello again, Alfred," Gertrude said as she and Alfred stood in the cafeteria-style line. Oscar had made an advertising deal with the cafeteria next to the skaters' quarters. In exchange for free lunch for his troupe, the cafeteria's name was painted onto the penalty boxes, so game patrons and the television cameras would see it.

"Hi, Gertrude. How are you today?" Alfred asked with a polite bow. Lottie listened in.

"Just fine, as usual," she said.

"Would you mind if I carried your tray to the table?" Alfred opened a palm and swept it to one side.

"What a gentleman. I love our meals together."

"It's one of my favorite times with the derby." Alfred gently put the trays on the table. The two sat across from each other. "Let me hold your chair," he said. When Gertrude said, "Yes," Alfred pulled the chair out.

"What're you listening to?" Ruby asked, moving food off her tray. Ruby, Carol and Lottie were seated one table away from Alfred and Gertrude.

"Them. I've been watching them for some time." Lottie's eyes blinked.

"They've been together for a while," Ruby said. "Not married yet."

"What about those two?" Carol pointed her fork toward a pair of married skaters. "Tony and Margery. Margery is seven months pregnant." Carol took the gum out of her mouth with two fingers and stuck it to her plate. "She's gonna have to leave the outfit soon."

"That's why Margery never falls on her butt anymore." Ruby forked a hunk of lettuce into her mouth. "She lowers herself against the track and rail, then pulls faces at the audience and cameras." Ruby poured a paper cup of gravy over her chicken. "I think Oscar thinks his audiences are not ready for a pregnant sports figure. Especially if she's on the home team."

"*America*'s not ready," Carol said.

"That's why she wears the baggy jersey. And did you notice that the announcers never mention she's expecting?" Ruby pointed out.

"I wonder why she doesn't go home to have the kid," Lottie said.

"I hear Tony plays around with the guys on the side." Carol wagged her eyebrows. "You know what I mean?"

"Sex?" Ruby asked. "Bi-coastal?"

"*No!*" Lottie said.

"Yup. So she stays with the unit so she can keep an eyeball on him." Carol poked her fork at the couple.

Carol leaned close. "Besides, I hear the kid ain't Tony's!"

"Nooo!" Ruby hissed.

"That's why Tony ended up in the ER with a kitchen knife wound." Carol winked.

Lottie's attention went back to her favorite lovers. "I like Alfred and Gertrude." She sighed. "They talk so nice to one another."

"Everyone likes Alfred and Gertrude." Ruby sipped a spoonful of soup.

"Alfred looks so neat with his short hair. Not trendy like some of the other guys."

"You mean not like those two," Carol said with another discreet gesture at the married couple. "You know, the so-called dashing brunette and the speedy what's-his-name. Yuck."

"He's speedy, all right. So fast he's bedding down some local gal after the games. His wife caught him playing backseat bingo with some fan last night," Ruby said with a scowl.

"And I hear them argue about it day and night. She's pretty cranked," Carol said. "And the story is that he's a pill-popper." She took a pea off her plate and tossed it into her mouth, gulping it down without chewing.

"Stop, now," Lottie said.

Ruby frowned. "I heard he likes to use ropes and force. You know, rough stuff, and his wife don't, so he looks elsewhere."

Lottie stroked her throat and grimaced.

"Cut the gas before they hear us," Carol warned.

Lottie turned her head, sat upright, and listened to her favorite derby couple. They were more interesting than Ruby's gossip.

"We've got a trip coming up," Gertrude said. "I heard it's a flight. Hawaii."

Lottie stopped eating. "Hawaii?" she whispered with her mouth dropping. Her belly squirmed. She thought of Harold's blue eyes. "We can't go now. Is that true?" A sting burned inside her. *Leave Harold, now?* How could she do that? Things were going swell.

Ruby looked at Lottie. "This is the first I've heard of a trip to Hawaii."

"Crazy-assed rumor, maybe?" Carol sliced some unidentified type of meat.

"But I don't want to leave Harold. I'm just getting to know him." She felt every muscle in her face sag. Her brain went empty.

"I know." Ruby tapped Lottie on one hand.

"Don't be heartbroken, Lottie," Carol said.

"Shhh, listen." Lottie leaned forward a bit.

"Oh, Hawaii. I heard that, too," Alfred was trying not to talk while chewing.

"That's going to be glorious. Imagine the volcanoes, hula dancers and leis. We'll all be on a flight out of San Francisco together."

"We have ten days of games in Oahu," Alfred said.

"Only ten days," Lottie whispered, tapping Ruby's arm.

"You can go without Harold for that long, can't you?" Ruby smiled.

"Hell, yes," Carol added.

"I guess." Lottie hunched her shoulders and tried to brush away the emptiness.

"After all, you do it when we're down at the L.A. games."

"Hawaii's different. We've only been to Los Angeles twice, just for a weekend. And Hawaii is so far away. Harold won't be able to drive." Her ears picked up the conversation again.

"The weather's perfect. You know, it's called *paradise*." Alfred's eyes glowed directly at hers. The two appeared connected with joy.

"Paradise." Ruby's eyes glistened.

Carol leaned her head on Ruby's shoulder.

Lottie's gaze drooped. Lovesickness traveled from her gut to her chest.

"It's the home of the most famous beach in the world," Gertrude said.

"Waikiki?" Alfred asked.

"Yes, people worldwide say there's no other beach like it." Gertrude smiled.

"I'm looking forward to the trip. Especially with you." He held her hand between his fingers.

"It must be true," Carol said.

"God, I'll miss Harold."

"We can walk on the beach after the games," Gertrude swooned.

"I'd love that, Gerty." Alfred returned to eating.

Lottie got all goose-bumpy inside when she heard Alfred use a pet name for Gertrude. It gave the lovebirds one more bond that separated them from the rest of the derby couples.

Lottie, Ruby and Carol stopped talking for a moment, and Lottie's thoughts of Harold swam in circles. Her gut ached and she sighed again. "It won't be paradise without Harold. I hope Harold and I are as good a fit as Gertrude and Alfred."

"Oh, you are," Ruby reassured her.

The Oahu Civic Auditorium hosted the derby, and the population took to the high-speed game instantly. Derby became an overnight success throughout the islands.

On the first night, Alfred snapped his ankle when he leapt over the entire pack of fallen skaters. He'd done this maneuver successfully in other games, but this time he landed awkwardly. His ankle wrenched and cracked! Then, the very next play, Gertrude broke her leg when skaters crashed into the infield benches. It was a madhouse, with medics carrying the two off on stretchers to rush them to the hospital.

Outside the games, Lottie spent time on the beach. The ocean waves rolled back and forth, massaging the white sand on Waikiki. The sounds of the waves buffeted Lottie's ears, drowning her in imagined solitude. She felt left out of the larger group experience. She had skated in front of sold-out Oahu crowds and lived with the troupe, but still, she ached with loneliness.

The water retreated, sloshing back out to the blue ocean. Small bubbles glistened with every slush. Balmy air mixed with a bouquet of freshly-cut grass over local flora which filled her nostrils with an exotic blend. The lush aroma of the tropics ignited unexpressed romantic passion inside Lottie. She sauntered slowly down the shoreline, enjoying the glorious radiance and sun-bleached sands. Her toes were decorated with sand clumps with each step.

"Did you hear the news about Alfred and Gertrude?" Ruby's voice came up behind Lottie unexpectedly. Ruby was wearing a big purple hat that kept the sun off her face.

"Yes, I heard that Alfred proposed to Gertrude in the emergency room," Lottie said with a far-off look. She gazed at a nearby palm tree, its green branches gently swaying in the breeze. Her eyes searched the waters in a private reverie.

Ruby flapped the rim of her hat. "Yeah, and they're both hobbling around on crutches with casts on their right legs."

"Sounds romantic." Lottie was still half-daydreaming. "I heard she was in pain, and he proposed anyway."

"That musta been a sight." Ruby sighed. "Real gone. So much in love."

"They invited the emergency room doctor to the wedding," Lottie said. "Are you going?"

"Oh, sure, it will be when we get back to the mainland. Everyone in the derby'll be there."

"It's making me think." Memories stirred within Lottie as another wave broke underfoot sucking their feet into the sand. The waters washed back out to the endless ocean.

She turned to stare at Diamond Head, the extinct volcanic crater nearby. She had read a brochure about the Hawaiian goddess of fire, Pele, who lived inside the volcano. Red-hot lava had once showered the island from deep inside its secret geological heart, but now the volcano stood in a permanent sleep. She felt in awe of Pele which morphed over into a universal loneliness joining Lottie with the world, yet still separating the skater from her solider.

"Be careful; thinking is dangerous." Ruby squinted up at the sun.

"Well, when I see Alfred and Gertrude, you know, how they live and work in the derby ..." Lottie clutched one hand to her chest. "It makes me wonder about Harold," Lottie said. "I mean, *Harold and me*."

"Do you think he'd ever work in the derby?"

"Naw, that'll never happen. He's military. I write and he writes back, but it's not the same as what Gertrude and Alfred have."

"I think of that with Carol. What would we do if one of us got injured or had to leave?" Ruby lowered her head.

"That's what I mean. What would we do? The derby's all I know. I don't know what else I could do to make a living."

Another wave lapped ashore. The suds oozed and twinkled into the sands.

"You really love him, huh?"

"So much. I'm torn." Lottie felt trade winds brush against her body. "Lately, I've thought of leaving the derby to try and settle down with him."

"You can't do that," Ruby said. "If you quit now, you'll regret it. You can't leave your family. You've worked so hard."

Lottie's mind wandered for a long moment. "It's just impossible." Water bubbled up onto the sand, almost touching her feet.

Ruby nudged Lottie's elbow. Up the beach a few yards two tanned bodies caught Lottie's eyes. She stared at a man with wide shoulders, broad chest, slim waist and muscular legs dressed in black swimming trunks. His big arms wrapped around his girl, who was adorned with a beautiful movie-star hairdo.

"He's handsome," Ruby said.

"Yes. I don't judge looks, but with Harold, I'm interested." Lottie stared at the man as the ocean's waves bathed the sand.

"What do you mean?"

"See, I wonder what Harold's like." Lottie felt her face turn all sorts of colors.

"You mean, what's he like in swimming trunks?" Ruby giggled.

"I know ... but, well, yes, I've been thinking of that. He's so muscular."

Ruby laughed. "You've got it bad, girlfriend."

Lottie approached the scantily clad lovers. The girl on the beach turned toward Lottie and Ruby. They instantly recognized the gaudy jewelry and compact body.

Lottie felt her heart skip a beat. She stood still and held Ruby. It was the face she wanted to forget. "It's her!"

Belzak was sprawled in the sand, enveloped in the man's arms. Her bathing suit strap fell off her shoulder, revealing a tan line. Belzak ignored her fellow skaters, soaking up the summer sun with her young stud. She knocked her bag over with a leg, and ole Bessie fell onto the sand. It lay half-buried next to a red scarf and a couple of tampons.

"Oh brother, Belzak!" Ruby exhaled. "Come on." Ruby tugged at Lottie's arm. They picked up their pace.

"This'll sound like I've snapped or something, but sometimes I think, maybe ten years from now, I'll end up like that," Lottie said. "It's my worst nightmare."

"Like *Belzak*?"

"Yeah. A man in every town, desperate and lonely. Using any man that can walk." Lottie frowned.

"That's not you, Lottie. You never were that way. And you'll never *be* like that."

Lottie exhaled a long sigh. "I guess you're right. But I see how it can happen."

"Derby can do some funny things to a person, but you'll never be like Belzak. She's a tramp! Besides, I just heard she stole the tall referee away from Gerry!"

"After Gerry and him had been together for two years?"

"Right," Ruby said.

"I can't imagine how Gerry feels."

"Terrible—and now take a look at Belzak!"

Hawaii's lushness stayed inside Lottie's heart. Soon, their stint was over, and she and the derby gang were back on the plane, headed to the mainland.

Lottie's heart thumped when the plane thundered down onto San Francisco's Airport's runway. She couldn't wait to disembark and get inside the terminal, where blue-eyed Harold was waiting to greet his roller star. How would life be, with her traveling and Harold waiting? Somehow, it didn't seem right.

The following Saturday was Alfred and Gertrude's wedding at Grace Cathedral. Everyone from the derby was chrome-plated: decked out in their best. Oscar used the marriage as a publicity stunt, so San Francisco's Knob Hill was teeming with reporters, gossip columnists, local celebrities and derby players.

Everyone was respectful. The setting made Lottie lose track of time, and her mind wandered. Taking slow, even breaths, she imagined that it was she and Harold at the altar. His hands moved in slow motion. He comforted her as the vows were read. She dreamed of his warm embrace, and their departure inside a long, white limousine to a house with a white picket fence. She laughed to herself when Alfred and Gertrude left the scene in a rented yellow cab. The newlyweds were gone, and Lottie was ready to return to the banked track where Oscar had planned a big announcement.

Chapter 29

BLOOD TURNED TO ICE

Another roller battle had just been resolved. Lottie and the rest of the players looked on as Oscar used his long arms to motion everyone near. He had arranged a meeting for after the fans had cleared from the arena. Slowly, he widened his stance, ready to make his announcement. Lottie looked at Ruby. "Well, Sherlock, have you heard about this one already?"

"Not a word from the bird, I swear."

"Another great game, and a happy audience, gang!"

Lottie nudged Ruby. "What happened to that nose for news?"

"You bopped my nose two weeks ago, remember? Since then, my rumor-meter has lost its magic." Ruby smiled.

Oscar continued. "And there's good news! I called you all here because I have an announcement." He waved his arms.

Everyone pressed in. Lottie wheeled closer, holding Ruby's arm. "Sorry I slugged you."

Ruby rubbed her nose. "Once was enough, honey."

"Listen up everyone. I'm impressed with how your plays are working. Still, we need new color, new personalities." The players nodded as Oscar lifted his chin. "We've expanded the number of television stations." Oscar's voice swelled with a promoter's pride. "And with the increased attendance, we'll be visiting more cities."

The skaters clapped.

"Good," Carol said.

Lottie took a deep breath.

Oscar continued. "Keep up the good work, gang. We need *more* grudge action. What Lottie, Ruby and Carol are doing is bringing the crowds in. I like what I see. And so does the rest of America." Oscar paused.

Lottie's arm hairs tingled.

"Hear that, Lottie?" Ruby pulled her ponytail tight.

Oscar scanned every eye in the room before continuing. "And soon, we're going to take the unit back to New York City!"

"Oh, my!" Ruby teetered back.

"Freaking fiddle-sticks, the *Big* Apple!" Carol enthused.

"New York!" several skaters yelled in unison.

Right then, a hole bored its way into Lottie's chest. Her eyes glazed over. That would mean leaving Harold.

"But we love it here," someone said.

"Don't worry. We'll be shooting more television shows from Madison Square Garden. And we *will* come back to this lovely city, bigger and better than ever! Tomorrow, we have over 14,000 tickets sold, all to see you."

Lottie couldn't hear Oscar's words. They fell upon deaf ears as her thoughts whirled around. Harold. What should she do? Should she break up with him? The idea of separating again hurt. It was a pain she didn't want to experience again.

"Okay, gang. Let's get ready for tomorrow's game. Have a good night."

Skaters grabbed their belongings and left for the dressing areas. Quiet blanketed the big building.

As if sensing Lottie's dilemma, Ruby tapped her hand before going backstage. "I'll see you in a minute or two. I know you've got things to think about."

Ruby and the others left. Lottie was alone with her thoughts, in total quiet.

"Lottie?" a sweet, girlish voice said.

"Yes?" Lottie raised her head. Belzak stood nearby with a friendly look on her face.

"What's shakin'?" she said still in that girlie voice.

"Nothing much." Lottie didn't meet her gaze.

"Can I talk to you a minute? It's a little personal." Belzak smiled like an old friend.

"Sure. I'm all ears." Something squirrely wormed inside Lottie's gut.

"I have something to tell you." Belzak sat next to Lottie, wearing a loving grin.

"What is it?" Lottie's brows arched.

"I hope we can still be friends."

"Well ... we're on the same team, aren't we?"

"Yes, we are." Belzak's smile widened. "I slept with Harold last week."

Lottie was uncomprehending. Her heart froze.

Belzak's face flattened. The words sliced deep. An ache radiated inside Lottie's chest. She knew that Harold would never do that. Her gut sickened, and she began to shiver. "I don't ... what do you mean?"

"I've seen him at the games. Surely, you noticed how he looks at *me*." Belzak pushed her chest out.

"He'd never ... I didn't ..." Lottie stammered for words. "Weren't you dating one of the referees?"

Belzak cocked her head. She stood up and leaned over Lottie with her fully loaded bra. "That doesn't stop a real woman. I have my ways with all men."

Lottie's heart was breaking. She wiped her nose. "You're *not* a real woman."

"More woman than any man can handle." Belzak shoved her chin toward Lottie and rolled up her sleeves.

A spiked heel stabbed into Lottie's heart. "But I don't get it. Why would you?" Her feelings had dropped so far that she couldn't see a way out. There was no solution. Trying to tolerate Belzak was impossible. The stabs of the skater's words plunged deep. Her last remembered moment of happiness with Harold brought a new trembling inside her chest.

"Listen, honey." Belzak tightened her jaw, and her voice deepened, "I just gave him what you wouldn't. You're not much of a woman. You don't know how to keep a man."

Tears filled Lottie's eyes. "You didn't. That's impossible."

"Independent derby women are tough. You're soft."

"But ... that's not ..." Lottie's speech hitched.

"You'll never be better than me. You're half the woman I am!" Belzak scowled.

Lottie stalled, motionless and nauseated. "You're making my head spin."

"Listen sister, you've been spinning since you got here."

Lottie straightened her back and balled one hand into a fist. "I'm not your sister."

"Hell, no. Look how you dress. You're skid row."

"Ease up on me!"

"No need to get angry. I'm just telling you I got your lover."

"That hurts, Belzak. Why don't you lay off me?

"Why would I do that?"

"Did you complain to Oscar that me and our new plays would injure you?"

"Hell, no!"

"What did I ever do to you? Have I done something wrong?" And then, *wham*—Lottie had it. Her eyes narrowed. "I'm wise to your racket."

"Wise? I don't have a racket. Don't make me sick." Belzak's mouth opened wide in faked innocence.

Lottie wagged a finger under Belzak's nose and ground her teeth together. "I'm getting too good for you! You're losing control!"

Belzak took a step back and eyed Lottie up and down. "I don't *need* to control anything, you oddball. I have the control. It's mine."

"I'm no oddball." Lottie caressed her chin. "You know, if you got paid for sex, you'd make a fortune."

"And you'd be penniless." Belzak snarled her nose.

"Better that than be a whore." Lottie jutted her jaw toward Belzak.

"You're jealous 'cause I slept with your man."

"You're lying. I don't believe you, Harold would never." Lottie felt more knives cut into her chest, but she pushed back on them.

"You wish!"

"Go away." Lottie's heart turned cold. She wished it were all a bad dream. *It's over.* She relaxed, relieved that Belzak's poisonous grip had loosened.

Then, in a sudden rush, Belzak sprang back in Lottie's direction. "And another thing. You forget I'm the *top* red shirt, you hear?" Belzak grabbed Lottie's skate bag and wrenched it open.

Lottie flinched. "What're you doing?"

"I know it's in here." Belzak's hands rifled through the canvas bag.

"What?"

"You have that stupid thing." Belzak spied what she wanted, and pulled out Lottie's mother's heirloom. The hat! "What the hell is this?" she shook it in Lottie's face.

"It's nothing." Lottie reached two hands out, attempting to grab it.

Belzak jerked the hat out of Lottie's reach. "You're lying, you sick bitch!"

"Really, it's nothing. Something from my family." Lottie's face felt puffy. Her heart softened.

"You touch this thing every game." Belzak shook the hat in Lottie's face again.

"Please, give it back."

"It's some Hebrew hocus-pocus *superstition*." Belzak slammed the hat to the dusty floor, and the yellow flower fell off the velvety rim. "You're just a no-good kid. A fan. You'll never be a star!"

Belzak was stabbing Lottie in places she never knew she had. "Stop," she pleaded.

"Ha, ha, look at you." The hatpin came loose and went flying.

"Don't!" Lottie got on her knees and scurried, making a grab for the precious gift. "Leave it alone. It's personal."

"Personal. Ha!" Belzak spat.

"Really ... please." Lottie gently picked up the flower.

"Look at you beg. You're pathetic. I wouldn't give you a drink of my piss if you were dying of thirst."

"It's special to me." Lottie knee-walked two feet and picked up the hatpin.

"I suppose we're trying to be special?" Belzak curled her lip.

Lottie eased the hatpin back into her treasured family gift. After a glance at Belzak, Lottie lovingly placed the hat and pin back into their hiding place. "It's just a good luck charm. Something from my mother."

"You're an ugly, impoverished immigrant from a dirty old country," Belzak spat.

Lottie's head hung with the stinging words.

"A no-good gypsy, same as the rest of us. And you'll never keep Harold," Belzak shouted.

Lottie stood up, her back to Belzak. Her heart swelled and contracted. She couldn't contain herself. Her insides hardened.

"You ain't nothing, kid." Belzak jabbed a finger in Lottie's back ribs. "Hear me?"

Lottie pulled her shoulders back, stood tall, and turned to face Belzak. She looked directly into the eyes of her teammate. "You've been tryin' to push me down ever since I started." Lottie leaned toward her, now face-to-face.

Belzak held her ground. "Push you down? Oh, please. You're nothing. Back off, tomboy!"

"You're envious, aren't you? You're jealous. From Day ONE!"

"To hell with you and your hat, you dirty Jew!"

"I love the derby as much as anyone, but I hope I never become a bitter old bag like you."

"Blow it out your stinkin' wazoo," Belzak shouted. "You're not gettin' rid of me!"

"You're one smelly piece of rat filth."

"You don't want to screw with me ... or ole Bessie!" Belzak turned away.

Grotesque images of dead bodies clutched at Lottie's brain as sweat beaded on her forehead. "Don't try anything, or I'll squash you."

"Ha. Squash me. Like it's a lead pipe cinch. Is that the best you can do? What a laugh." Belzak tapped her big bag. "Careful, or someone's gonna end up in the intensive care unit!" Belzak frowned and trampled backstage.

Lottie watched her go.

Belzak shot one last glaring look at Lottie.

Lottie's blood turned to ice. Her sweat chilled and her insides felt like tar being steam-rolled. She crossed her arms around her belly and rocked slightly, thinking of an escape. Her mind searched for freedom. Then something more dangerous came to mind.

Chapter 30

TELEGRAM

The next day's game was a tremendous hit. The fans cheered until they were hoarse. Lottie had been unable to eat all day, worrying about how she'd tell Harold that the derby was leaving San Francisco. After the game, her chest felt as tight as a drum as she scurried to meet him behind the Cow Palace. Waiting in the darkness, Lottie pulled her breath in, then slowly released it. Her eyes ping-ponged toward the service road, then over to the stage door and back. Finally, her breath caught. It was Harold! He eased his hat off in a slow, uneven movement.

Lottie waved and forced an enthusiastic "Hi!" She smoothed her hair and walked slowly, but she was concerned; something appeared to be different.

Harold smiled and lowered his head. Shadows from the streetlights cast strange angles on his face, hiding his eyes. "I have a bit of news."

"Good news?" She knit her brows.

"Well, not really."

Lottie's stomach corkscrewed and her chest burned. She crossed her arms in front of her bosom. "I know. You're seeing another woman."

He pulled his head back. "No, no, honey. You're the only gal for me. You have to know that."

Lottie's muscles tightened. "Are you sure?"

"There's no one else."

"But Belzak said she slept with you." Lottie placed a trembling finger to her lips, searching Harold's eyes. She hadn't thought that Belzak's admission had much chance of being true, but seeing the look on Harold's face had ushered that horror straight back into her heart.

He frowned and cocked his head. "I'd never do that!"

"But she said ..." Lottie took a step closer and clenched a fist.

Harold's eyes bore deep. He was not looking away. "She's like some old used mattress. You're the only one for me."

Lottie squared her head and shot him a glance. "Why would she say that?"

"I don't know ... she's probably jealous. You and I have so much to look forward to. Our futures are as bright as a shiny new penny."

It all made sense, it was what she figured but then that look on his face just now caused all those doubts to jump back. Lottie's heartbeat slowed down. Her body grew tranquil, and her worry seemed silly now. Belzak was hardly someone Harold would consider, right? Lottie knew that Harold was being honest. She exhaled, and her chest eased. "Thank God. I was so worried."

Harold adjusted his weight. "So, are you ready for some news? It's good news, actually. Well, much better than that."

Lottie shifted on one foot and back again, wobbling with nervous energy. "Okay."

"We're being shipped out."

Lottie felt like she had been slugged in the gut. This was the last thing she'd expected! "Shipped out?" she asked, repeating his words. Her mind was a sea of chaos and she wanted something to latch onto. "Where are you going?"

Harold removed his hat and held the brim at his waist. "It's a military secret. I can't say."

"A secret. But, well ... when? When are you going?"

"This Friday."

"Friday!" The word came out sounding choked. "So soon. Can't you stay?"

"I have to go. Orders from the top. I'm saying goodbye tonight."

"Tonight?" Lottie's heart was a shipwreck. What had she come here to say? Thoughts of the New York separation were swallowed up by a far greater sadness.

His jaw was motionless as she met his blue eyes searching deeply into hers. "Tonight," Harold's soft voice burrowed into Lottie's heart.

"You're leaving right away, so soon? So this means goodbye?" She dropped her head.

He paused. "Yes, I'm afraid this is goodbye *for now*. But this isn't the end of us."

Lottie stared at the ground. Her legs wobbled. "What do you mean, *not the end*?"

He placed one finger under her chin to lift her head. "I mean just that. This isn't the end of us. We've got our whole lives ahead of us."

Lottie's heart began to hum. "I hope so. I want that so badly."

"Listen, I have something." He reached a hand out to hold one of hers.

"What is it?"

"I went down to Union Square today." He tucked the other hand into his pocket.

Lottie's heart beat faster.

He pulled out a red velvet box. "A small gift," he said, thumbing it open.

Lottie's eyes widened.

He ushered the box near her chest. Inside rested a silver necklace with a thumbnail-sized heart pendant.

Lottie's eyes sparkled. "Ohhhh."

"For you."

Lottie's heart raced. She blinked as slivers of light reflected from the moon above. It was what she had longed for without even knowing it: a gift from a boy. "Oh, my, Harold."

"I know it's not much. It's my promise that I'll be true to you and return."

"Oh, it's wonderful! I love it." For a second, her mind forgot everything. Her heart was bursting; a subconscious dream had just been fulfilled. And gloriously unexpected.

"Here, let me. Turn around." He pulled the chain out of the box and draped it around Lottie's neck. "Just something to remember me by."

Lottie's stomach fluttered as she turned around and pulled her long hair over one shoulder, exposing her neck. Her skin prickled at the touch of his hands. "It'll always remind me of you. My army man," Lottie whispered.

"There." He locked the clasp and turned her to face him.

"I'll cherish it," Lottie beamed, caressing the precious gift in her fingers.

Harold cleared his throat. "That makes me feel good. I'm sure I won't be gone long."

"I'll wait for you." Lottie choked on her words. She hooked a hand into his belt loop, still stroking the pendant. Her breath quickened, and tears welled up in her eyes. "Do you know when you'll be back?"

Harold pulled her close. "I'm not sure, honey; the brass won't say anything."

He's being strong, Lottie thought. It made her love him even more. "We can stay in touch through letters. I'll be here, waiting for you to return." She inhaled deeply, trying to capture his scent in a way that she could always remember it.

"Of course I'll write you," he said.

Lottie tugged at the belt loop just as he grabbed her in his arms. He pressed his lips to hers, and lingered.

Pulling back, she blinked, remembering. "In a few weeks or so, we're going to New York. Madison Square Garden. You can send letters to me here, and I'll make sure they get forwarded."

"That's exciting. My Little Lunatic, skating star. Sure. I'll send letters here."

"Good." Lottie's breathing eased.

He nodded with the gravitas only a soldier could possess and sent a shiver squiggling up Lottie's spine. "I have to go now."

"I know."

"Goodbye."

And then he turned and walked away. Each stride melted him further into the darkness. The single light above the building's backstage door cast eerie shadows against him and the old blacktop service road. The night was quiet. She listened to his footsteps until they became silent in the distance. His figure darkened. He made one last turn, waved with a soldier's salute, and disappeared.

Hollowness filled Lottie. He was gone. She worried how long he'd be away and that her derby job would keep them apart forever. She'd never considered that *his* job would be the one to separate them. She rubbed the heart-shaped jewel, and it sent a surge of warmth through her heart.

Several agonizing days passed before the first letter arrived, and four others quickly followed. Lottie guessed that there had been a delay along the military channels. Her intoxication welled up with each love note. She answered Harold's letters, keeping him informed about the derby and her day-to-day life. She ended every letter with X's and lipstick prints in her signature color of dark reddish pink, the first shade she ever wore.

Lottie had little privacy in the locker rooms. Belzak was always around.

"Ooooh, another letter from *him*?" Belzak made a kissy face.

Lottie ignored her. "It's none of your business."

"He doesn't love you, you know." Belzak pushed a finger into Lottie's arm. "And *no more stealing the show ... see?*"

Life managed to move along at a drowsy pace. Lottie found safety backstage after every game.

It was a Friday. The game had ended and she was finishing another letter. Lottie lip-printed it carefully so as to leave no smudges. She enjoyed the sounds of the locker room fuss: clothes getting ruffled, cigarettes being lit over muffled conversations mingling with a mass of voices. She hummed along to The Four Knights' tune *I Get So Lonely* as it drifted from the loudspeakers outside the room.

Lottie's fingers were caressing Harold's gift when the sound of footsteps click-clacked into her corner of the locker room. Lottie knew it would be Patty. Never unhappy to see the older woman, Lottie turned to see her standing with her shoulders slumped forward. Lottie clutched the necklace tighter, her lips parting. Everyone turned to look as Patty eased toward Lottie with a paper nestled in her trembling fingers.

"What is it?" Lottie asked.

"Another letter?" Ruby asked from the next shelf over.

Patty sniffed, and pulled a hankie to her nose.

The locker room went silent.

Lottie's eyes traveled back and forth between Patty's reddened eyes and the letter. "What? What is it?"

Patty held the letter out. "It's from the government." A soft, squealing moan leaked from between Patty's lips. She quickly stifled it, and looked away from Lottie.

"Government?" Lottie said under her breath. She tugged Harold's necklace and grabbed the envelope. She looked up at Patty, and before looking back down, searched her damp eyes for a hint or warning. Then she examined the official lettering: typed, not handwritten. Lottie swallowed.

To Lottie Zimmerman STOP We sincerely regret to inform you that Private First Class Harold Grays was SEVERELY INJURED AND PASSED AWAY in A MISSION-related ACCIDENT on March 12 STOP

Lottie's nose dripped. She mumbled, uncomprehending, "... severely injured and passed ..."

Carol gasped. "Lottie ... no!"

Ruby placed one hand on Lottie's shoulder and grabbed Carol close. "Not Harold?" Ruby hushed.

Lottie read more.

His commanding officer Major Donald Watson and the entire platoon send their most sincere condolences STOP

Lottie's body convulsed once; acid stung her tongue. "An accident."

"I'm so sorry, Lottie." Patty's voice lowered. She moved close. The room was thick with the smell of bodies and cosmetics.

Lottie's arms and legs shuddered. "This can't be, it has to be a sick joke." She slowly melted down onto the floor, leaning against a locker door.

"I'm afraid that is an official telegram," Patty whispered.

"But …" The words went fuzzy on the paper, then a primal howl came from deep inside Lottie. "*Noooo!*"

"Oh, God." Carol sat down on the dirty floor to hold Lottie's shaking shoulders.

"Now, now, honey," Patty whispered, powerless.

"Oh my … no." Ruby's lips trembled.

Lottie lapsed into a thousand-yard stare. As her friends looked on, silent tears welled in her eyes. Her chest convulsed; body shaking sobs started to take form.

Patty placed a hand on her back. "Honey."

"No, no, no. It can't be; it can't be." Lottie rocked.

"I know, sweetie. I know," Patty eased down, sitting next to Lottie.

"Dead … lousy world." Lottie lowered her head onto Patty's shoulder. Her mouth trembled. Soft moans escaped from inside her throat. An invisible knife was gutting her, and she just had to sit there while it sliced and yanked.

"Poor little baby." Patty lowered herself all the way to the floor and rocked Lottie back and forth.

After a minute, Lottie straightened. She felt tears staining her eyes and cheeks. "This isn't right."

"No, it isn't. Life can be cruel." Patty's words were hard to hear.

"But why?" Lottie gasped.

"I don't know. Years ago, I had Oscar's and my baby … a little boy … Charles," Patty words stuck in her throat.

Lottie's gut squeezed in another deep sob.

"He died three weeks after birth … it's not fair." Tears traveled down Patty's cheeks.

Lottie pushed back from Patty. "But why is it so hard?"

"I don't know. Sometimes it just is."

Lottie paused, motionless. She dropped her hands and looked around. "I need to be alone." She moved awkwardly from the floor and out of the locker room, tears running down her face. She wandered through darkened hallways, out the back door and all the way back to her quarters.

"What's wrong with her?" Belzak asked, back in the locker room.

No one answered.

Numb to the world, Lottie found derby a much easier burden than her grief. She mechanically managed to work her new plays: the ping-pong with a red goof and subway. They came off brilliantly. She threw her aching soul into her skating. Audiences tossed mean calls onto her deaf ears. Off the track, she drifted aimlessly, like a ghost. She neglected her life, ignoring Ruby and Carol, and talked to no one.

After a month, Oscar Wentworth called his troupe together for another announcement. Lottie stood with the crowd, going through the motions and paying little attention.

"Three days from now, we leave for New York. The Panthers will be red shirts, New York Chiefs are white shirts."

Smiles appeared on every face but Lottie's. The words didn't land. They were meaningless.

"We have three more days here." Lottie could tell Oscar had caught the empty look on her face, and she didn't care. "Then we leave for the Big Apple, New York's Madison Square Garden! And raises for everyone!"

Lottie wrote home, pouring raw feelings out to her mother on the other side of the country. "I love you all so much," she added to the end of the letter. "I can't wait to see you, and I miss you more than anything else in the world right now."

These days, Lottie's dreams were dark pits. She was aware of them upon waking, but there was nothing to remember. There were no birds to comfort or guide her. Sleep offered no rest from sadness.

Chapter 31

ROLLER BABES

The derby whizzed like a whirling tornado into the Big Apple. The sight of Lottie's old stomping grounds warmed her damaged soul. The telegram lingered in her thoughts, drowning out what would have been good news on any other day: the beloved New York Yankees had just defeated the Milwaukee Braves, but the victory didn't register in the dull din of Lottie's mind.

The pigeon visited Lottie's dreams; it strained to reach the heavens. Its wings trembled and fluttered spasmodically. Its eyes blinked, and its neck stretched forward. Lottie's emotions were awakened when a cyclone wrenched at the little pigeon. Shattered debris and broken twigs engulfed the white bird in a black/brown blur. Soon, its wings were stuck, full of branches and dirt. A windy gale ripped the pigeon's wings and feathers into bits. The torn body spun into a black vortex, out of sight. She woke with a start and renewed grief, remembering what she had once had.

The old gray structure adjacent to Madison Square Garden had been converted into the derby family's makeshift kitchen. Scanning the group and taking a mental note, Lottie noticed the skaters clattering, eating and laughing. She felt disconnected from it all.

"Okay, gals, today we need three of you for promos." Patty marched into the big room. "The boss has picked the people, so listen up."

Lottie watched while Belzak and the other skaters babbled about this promotional event. Who might be chosen? What did it matter to her?

Oscar called the first day in New York 'Promotion Day.'

Everyone listened with genuine excitement, and Lottie felt a spark respond to the excited spirits of the other skaters. Some of the high-energy exuberance was rubbing off.

"Things need to be just right so the word about roller derby can spread," Patty said. "Today's going to be a make-or-break day. This game's the big one." She unfolded a sheet of paper.

Lottie gazed at the paper. She still had her derby life. Her thoughts slowly bubbled to life, and began to take their place in the expectation and excitement. It felt like she'd been out in the cold. At the sight of Patty's proud stance, Lottie's muscles stiffened. She wanted to get back to work.

"Okay. Bobbie Elgin, Gerry Murphy are white shirts, and Lottie Zimmerman, you're the red."

Startled because she had never been spotlighted like this and was totally unprepared; Lottie's heart when *thud*. *Not me, not now!*

"I want all three of you at the arena's front entrance at noon today." Patty lowered the paper to her side and looked through the group, eyeing the three chosen skaters. Lottie's brows arched.

Ruby turned to Lottie. "They picked you!"

"Don't crap your pants, Lottie!" Carol giggled, giving Lottie an encouraging slap on the back.

Patty glanced at Lottie. "Suit up, Little Lunatic, and don't wear your tights. Instead, just wear the trunks."

"Okay," Lottie said, eager to do as she was told, but at the same time terrified that her shortcomings would be on display to the world.

"What do you think?" Ruby asked.

"It's a chance, right?" Lottie knew if she blew it, Oscar would never ask this of her again.

"I know. Good luck." Ruby hugged her friend.

"We'll tighten your trunks and jersey, and take things in here and there." Patty gestured with an invisible needle and thread. "I'll be there with my sewing kit."

"You'll look sexy," Ruby said.

"A roller derby vixen," Carol giggled.

Those words sent uncertainty through Lottie's mind. "You mean *sexy*? Photos and newspapers?" Lottie stared off, her lip trembling.

"Of course. You have what it takes!"

Patty continued, "First, the entire group will skate from Times Square at 8th and 47th Avenue. We're rolling about fifteen blocks, to 8th and 31st Avenue. That's the ticket entrance at Madison Square Garden. Wave and smile. Draw attention. Invite people to follow. Just don't be boring."

The skater's grinned, absorbed with interest and ready to take on the challenge.

"When everyone's at the ticket area, a press conference will begin. Everyone but the three names I just called, please go to the dressing rooms. The three promo skaters, you'll be interviewed."

Lottie felt hornets spinning inside her belly.

"There'll be five local reporters. They'll take photos and ask questions, so put your game faces on!"

Lottie's heart shrank. Her family might read the newspaper and see the photos. "What if I look awful and sound like a pill? What'll I say?"

"Don't worry so much. Be yourself." Ruby elbowed her playfully.

Belzak glared; Lottie ignored her. A few other chilly looks shot in Lottie's direction as the other skaters chit-chatted like hens over birdseed. Lottie bucked herself up; she wanted Oscar to be pleased. She rehearsed in her mind, trying to imagine important and confident things to say to a reporter. *I wonder how I'll sound?* Her thoughts were broken to bits by Patty's booming voice.

"All right. If there're no questions, I'll meet you three at the ticket area. Noon." Patty marched out, taking one final inspection of the room.

Rolling, waving and smiling, the entire league of players put on their best faces, attracting attention. Heads turned at every roll bump along the designated route. Finally, they arrived at the Madison Square Garden ticketing area. The crowds gawked and pointed. Pedestrians followed the skaters just to see what the roller-commotion was all about. Lottie, Bobbie and Gerry lingered as all of the other skaters disappeared inside the massive building.

Lottie's knees knocked.

"Look this way, please," a tall reporter said. Flashbulbs popped in Lottie's face, blinding her. She blinked, feeling overheated as her face reddened.

Positioned in a semicircle around the women on wheels were twelve men in suits with cameras. They had big notepads and hats with press passes stuck into the bands.

"I didn't know there'd be this many reporters." Lottie's hands were clammy.

Behind the reporters stood fifty onlookers. They eased from side to side, surrounding the press like bees in search of sweet nectar. Some narrowed their eyes. Others rubbernecked. Lottie felt their eyes staring at her bare legs. She felt naked and cold.

"Can you stand with your back to us?" One reporter pulled a wet cigar out of his mouth. He motioned to Lottie as he held his camera.

"Who, me?" Lottie shrugged. Her mouth was dry.

"Sure, babe," he smiled through a nod.

Lottie's muscles quivered. She slowly turned, extending one leg in front of her. She was embarrassed to expose her legs. Her stomach squirmed.

"More legs, honey," the man said.

Shocked by his forwardness, Lottie straightened her back and bent forward. Her butt pushed out and her leg muscles bulged.

"That's it, doll face." Crackles came from the burning bulbs. Pop after pop, each flash sent a chill down Lottie's spine. This was a new egghead feeling being the center of reporter's attention.

Gerry placed one hand on a curvy hip. A camera flash popped. Then Bobbie put on a beaming smile. Soon Lottie and the other two women were mugging for cameras. They twisted left and right, tossing their hair. People standing nearby edged closer.

"So, why would a gal want to do this kind of sport, anyway?" one reporter asked Lottie, his pencil poised between thin piano-player fingers.

Lottie felt tongue-tied. She opened her mouth, but no words came out. Her heart pounded, and she licked her lips. Gerry jumped in. "I enjoy the competition." The reporter scribbled madly. "It gives me a chance to do what the men do." As Gerry Murphy talked, Lottie backed up a foot, listening with a sinking heart. She was a failure.

"But isn't it rough? Aren't you afraid of getting hurt?" another reporter asked.

"Oh, sure, it's rough. Last year in Chattanooga, my skate got caught in the kick rail. I broke my ankle." Gerry pointed down her extended leg. "I was on crutches for nine weeks." Reporters surrounded her. They took pictures and jotted on small notepads.

Lottie swallowed hard. "Listen here, pipsqueak! It's rough, all right." She stopped awkwardly, her own voice frightening her. She raised her brows. "Hey, guys, we're not playing tiddlywinks out there, ya know?"

The reporters laughed at Lottie's quip. "But why such a rough sport?" one asked.

Lottie gulped. It was too late, the Lunatic persona needed to show up for the good of the whole derby. "Why not? We're just as good as the guy creeps. We try to keep our tempers from flaring."

"That's right, we don't want to get mad!" Gerry added with a contrasting purring voice.

A sense of calm washed over Lottie. "We wouldn't want to start a fight!" she wrinkled her chin. Reporters swung their torsos toward her. She winked. "We'd louse up the game and *lose*."

"What do you mean, *no fighting ... keep your tempers?*" All ears focused on Lottie.

Lottie took a few easy breaths. "This isn't the roller vanities. We're competitors. Things ... happen."

"Is there hostility among the gals?" A reporter moved closer to Lottie.

"Oh, sure, on and off the track! Not like the men."

Pop! Flash bulbs exploded.

"So you have *grudges*?" A reporter scratched his pencil under his chin.

"Grudges, spite ... hell, sometimes in the heat of the bullring." Lottie held her hands loosely behind her back, arched her spine and watched their eyes ogle her breasts. "Listen, fellas, I get so angry if someone else messes up my game plan. Well, ya wouldn't know. But then I look down, and there's a clump of hair in my hand." She gestured with one fist cocked high, elbow bent.

People moved to stand in the ticket line. Every reporter moved further from Gerry and Bobbie. They hovered around Lottie like johns at a whorehouse. Lottie stood in the center of the throng, her muscles relaxed and her eyes searching the men up and down. Their pencils moved furiously across their notepads.

"What makes you pull out someone's hair?"

"Women aren't pills. What would *you* do when the other team starts to cheat?!" Lottie chewed on her gum. "And the referee ain't able to see 'em cheat most times. That really cranks me!" The reporters scribbled. More onlookers congregated around the scene.

"Women cheat in this sport?" someone hollered.

"Sure!" Lottie smiled, chewing her gum with exaggerated smacking, just as she'd seen Carol chew. "Everyone wants to win, and we women have chips on our shoulders. So don't cross me!"

"We heard that. Why are women so violent?"

Lottie noticed Patty appear beyond the reporters, among the crowd. Patty winked and gave a thumbs up. Lottie pulled her shoulders back and followed Patty's body gesture by pulling her shirtsleeves up. She angled her arm and balled her fingers into a fist. She put it under the reporter's chin, as if giving him an uppercut. "You wouldn't know," Lottie knitted her brows, "because you ain't a professional athlete!"

Mumbles and commotion coiled around her. The reporter pulled back.

"Hey, don't be a wet smack!" The Little Lunatic withdrew and spun. "We lay tracks competing every day. I gotta stay on my guard and beat the other gals." She pirouetted and reached out a friendly palm to rock the reporter's shoulder. He relaxed and scribbled notes.

Flashbulbs popped. Patty nodded. Lottie was hyperaware of her actions and everything around her.

"Some say it's fixed. You know, *fake*," a reporter shouted.

There was silence.

Lottie crossed her arms and pushed out her chin. Gerry rolled in front, thumb thumping her chest. "If someone knew the outcome, I'm the captain … and I'm sure I would know! In all my years of skating, no one's said anything to me."

Then Bobbie rolled forward. "It's real, and I've got the broken nose to prove it." Bobbie laughed as she showed her crooked-nosed profile.

People chuckled.

"Why don't ya put some skates on and see for yourself?" Lottie challenged. "I can get the lead out!"

The reporter raised a hand to try to ease Lottie back. "What did you say your name was again?" he asked.

"Lottie Zimmerman, or The Little Lunatic. Whatever fits ya best. You interested?" Lottie drew her face close, and nudged a finger into the reporter's shoulder. The reporter teetered, his face reddening. He plastered on a wry smile and wrote down The Little Lunatic's words.

Onlookers laughed. "This is the best sports interview I've had in over ten years!" His brows arched and he tipped his hat to the three skaters.

"Are you married?" another reporter asked.

"No, but I'm looking," Lottie answered coyly. She fluffed her hair, puckered her lips and posed. Another bulb flashed, catching the glamour-magazine pose perfectly.

More reporters and bystanders laughed. Lottie's warm sensations were expanding. She fiddled with her heart pendant and beamed.

A reporter with round black glasses spoke. "A recent report said that the roller derby is contributing to the masculinization of women in America. It said that women are being plucked from home and put into the nitty-gritty world of work and sports. What do you say to that, Miss Zimmerman?"

Everyone went quiet, waiting to see what The Little Lunatic would say.

For a brief moment, Lottie's mind whirled back to her painful past: Mom, Dad, Elsie Mae and Harold. That past was nothing to be nostalgic about. She forced those thoughts aside, and took a deep breath. "Now, what makes you boys so insecure that you think I'd take your job away? So you think I'm a tomboy, or something? I've always been popular, but I just haven't found the right man. But if I did, I'd sure cook for *him*."

The reporters stumbled and lowered their heads, writing with huge grins.

"Besides," she cocked her hip and bent over, showing cleavage and long legs. "Does this look masculine?"

Flashbulbs popped. "No, ma'am!" the reporter's finger pushed back the rim of his glasses.

"But do you like men?" another reporter asked.

Lottie came a step closer. "Yeah, I'm no slack wet smack! But I haven't had a date in a while. I'm a professional woman, you know?" Lottie used her eyes to focus on his feet and then slowly searched up his legs to his waist, where her eyes lingered, as if she could see him naked. Her search continued up his torso and to his eyes, then stopped. She put a finger under his hat and mischievously tipped it backward. It was her best Mae West imitation to date.

Roller Babes

The reporter pulled out a handkerchief and dabbed beads of sweat from his brow. He readjusted his hat and swallowed. His swollen Adam's apple plunged up and down in the process.

"Where did you grow up? And how old are you?"

She laughed. "I grew up right here in the Bronx, and I played stickball with the fellas in the streets. I was the best hitter." The reporters scribbled. "But I'm not telling ya my age; that wouldn't be ladylike, would it?"

"How fast can you gals get going out there?"

"We put the pedal to the metal! Come in tonight and see." Lottie put one hand on her hip. She motioned a finger in the direction of the ticketing booth. "We haul ass!"

"I've been clocked at thirty miles an hour," Gerry chimed in.

"I can skate faster than all of 'em," Bobbie said.

"Say, roller babes, can we get a group shot?"

The three skaters came together, Gerry and Bobbie flanking Lottie. The trio placed their hands on their hips and kicked, first to the left and then to the right. They resembled Radio City Music Hall's Rockettes—but on wheels with muscular legs and confident, challenging expressions. Each beamed their pearly whites, and flashbulbs popped over and over.

"That's great. Just great!"

"Say, Lunatic, what do you think'll happen to the future of roller derby?"

She popped her gum. "That's easy, fellas. There's gonna be an all-women's roller derby."

"Wow," someone said under his breath. "Unbelievable!"

"Rugged and outrageous," a reporter gasped.

"Hey, how about dinner after the game?" one reporter asked.

"Whatcha say I race ya around the track first, and then we go to dinner if you can keep up?"

"Well, uh," the reporter stammered.

"Wanna see a real athlete? Get a ticket. Times have changed, and you ain't seen nothing till you've seen me in the derby!"

Cameras angled and flashbulbs popped. People lined up for tickets. Gerry smiled at Lottie. The reporters and bystanders buzzed, and the skaters began to skate away. Lottie hoped it had been a job well done. Patty walked a few yards behind, with one hand anchored at her hip.

Chapter 32

THE PROMOTIONAL GAME

Rolling nervously backstage, Lottie noticed her adrenaline had spiked to new heights. Her shenanigans had been a homerun! She removed her skates and donned her tights, covering up the legs just flaunted.

The other players were already suited up, and soon, the locker room chatter lulled. The captains murmured amongst themselves. Tonight was just the promotional game, so Lottie expected the audience to be middling, as the official grand opening had been scheduled for tomorrow.

"One, three, five. One: a red and a white break. I'll break late, and get rid of the red. Then I'll fall back with the pack. Fancy white," Belzak called the period.

Lottie didn't hear her name mentioned. She wasn't surprised. It was revenge, since she'd been chosen to help promote the game. She slouched and thumbed the heart-shaped pendant.

"Three. A red goof-up. Five. Subway, no score," Belzak rattled on.

Lottie dropped her head and closed her eyes. Her mind replayed the photo session over again, remembering the looks on the reporter's faces. She smiled to herself. She took a deep breath, planning how she'd work the pack tonight. She'd do it better than she'd ever done before. She followed the others to the arena to complete the usual team warm ups.

"Look, Lottie! Someone's trying to get your attention!" Ruby pointed out into the audience.

Peering out into the crowd, Lottie saw her mom, dad and two sisters. "Hi!" she yelled, waving ecstatically. Her heart beat in her throat. Her sisters caught her eye and waved like mad. "Look! My family!" Lottie shouted. "My kid sisters, Rhoda and Betty. They've grown so much! I hardly recognize them."

Suddenly, the buzzer sounded. The crowd roared as the referee's whistle beckoned the women skaters to the starting line. The announcer's voice rattled the overhead speakers, and the rolling thunder of wheels against the wooden track blasted off. Lottie skated with a confidence won from experience and purpose.

"What's this play?" Carol asked anyone around.

"Whip," Belzak hollered, tapping Lottie's back to signal the move.

"Ruby, whip!" Lottie yelled in immediate response to the signal. Ruby broke from the front of the pack, followed by Lottie and Belzak. Lottie planned the moves, inhaling as she reached back and connected herself to Ruby and Belzak. Her brow was already thick with sweat as she lunged and cracked the whip. The force flung Belzak reeling: directly down the straightaway at lightning speed.

"Johnson and The Little Lunatic giving Eve Belzak a double whip," the announcer called.

The fans booed.

Lottie and Ruby caught their breath as both skaters rejoined the pack. Carol shoulder-nudged Ruby, jostling her into the whirling group of skaters.

Belzak screeched around the track. Way out front, tits high, arms pumping, she brayed taunts at the audience. At the rear of the pack, Belzak scored.

"Two points: Panthers," came the announcement, followed by boos and groans from the fans.

Lottie wiped her brow and noticed Belzak waving her arms as the fans gave the thumbs down.

The game thundered on until the final play was a pullaway. The whistle sounded. Lottie pushed the other skaters aside and broke out of the pack. Behind her was Belzak. Speeding into the corner, Lottie pushed hard and reached back. She flung another whip. Belzak careened down the track to more audience protest. Gerry was right on her heels.

"On this jam, Eve Belzak, followed by the Blonde Avenger, Gerry Murphy," the announcer blared.

The fans cheered Gerry on.

Lottie rejoined the pack.

"Get back in here," Carol said to Lottie.

"Whites up front," Bobbie Elgin called. Lottie slowed. The home team formed a wall, interlocking elbows. In an arm blast, Belzak was blocked hard by Gerry. Belzak crashed into the rail.

"Belzak is blocked hard by the Blonde Avenger." The announcer's voice rose with excitement.

The fans rejoiced.

"Pick up that red," a skater yelled. One of the white shirts sped up. She raced after the fallen Belzak. Catching up, the Panther pulled Belzak upright, and soon, both were consumed by the rolling pack. Lottie patted Belzak's back, giving a thumbs up.

"Thirty seconds left in this final women's period, and the Blonde Avenger is in scoring position," the announcer bellowed.

The crowd was tense.

"Reds, go! Pull away!" Belzak ordered with one hand signaling high and pointing forward.

Lottie's heart jumped. "Let us out!" She edged her skates left and right, then broke through the Chiefs' wall, pushing skaters high and skittering them apart.

Carol yelped as she slammed into a railing.

Lottie looked back for her teammates and mouthed, "Come on!" Ruby followed behind Lottie.

The fans started to clap and stomp in time to their own excited chant.

Lottie crouched and strode at a feverish pace, with all of her Panther teammates in tow. The entire red shirt team whooshed up and down the banks, whirring in synchronicity. Lottie glanced up to see her family leaning in, Betty biting her lip. Lottie's heart soared as her team rolled out a race of rhythm and speed.

The audience booed.

"It's a Panther break away, led by the Little Lunatic," the announcer's voice accelerated.

"Let's go!" hollered Gerry. The white shirts gathered into a line. They pushed with pulsing arms and legs, pumping and zooming forward like an arrow. When they were just five feet from the running red shirts, the fans cheered. Both lines of skaters looked like speeding bolts. Each skater was crouched over, striding like a freight train ... the distance slowly lessened. Cacophonic sounds rolled out from the track like musical mayhem.

"Fifteen seconds left in this play and New York is on the chase," the announcer called.

Lottie puffed. Sweat rolled down her face.

The fans whooped and stomped their feet.

Gerry yelled, "Whip!" She reached out to her Chief skaters. Grabbing hold, she received a whip from Carol that shot her wheeling toward the Panther runaway.

"Our Flashing Bombshell whips her teammate, The Blonde Avenger, moving up to the Panthers. Only ten seconds left in the jam time," the announcer rattled.

The fans shrieked.

"She's just feet from the last Panther."

Gerry pushed hard. She rolled down and inside, speeding past all but one Panther.

Loud *oohs* came showering down. The fans were enthralled.

"The Blonde Avenger passes four Panthers! Only one Panther left: the Little Lunatic."

"Go, go, go!" the crowd chanted.

Gerry pushed with long power strides as Lottie raced away.

"Two seconds remaining," the announcer called as the audience cheered madly.

With one incredible side-stride, Gerry rushed past Lottie. "Five points for the New York City Chiefs on the play!" the announcer yelled just as the buzzer sounded.

The fans broke into an uproar.

"It's a grand slam!"

Lottie sucked in a ragged breath. The horn sounded. It was the end of their skating period, and her muscles relaxed. She hoped her family was happy watching her in action. Tonight, she was an expert at managing the pack formations.

The New York City Chiefs had triumphed. The skater's walk-rolled back up the steep track as the men rolled on the final period. The gals exited through rail openings, making their way to the walkway leading to the locker rooms as waves of audience thunder ebbed and flowed around them.

Thatches of well-mannered fans waited to catch a glimpse of their favorites and ask for autographs. Lottie maintained a simple smile. Most of the fans adored the home team skaters, but Lottie couldn't wait for her personal hometown rooting section that was waiting behind the throngs. Lottie scooted through an opening in the track's railings. She fanned herself and pretended to faint as she clump-walked toward her family. Her eyes sparkled when Betty and Rhoda ran down to meet her.

"Lunatic! Little Lunatic!" the two girls shouted, waving.

Lottie smiled wide. "Hi, girls. Hiya, sweet pea." She remembered living with these precious sisters, their secrets and sharing. Her eyes prickled as she patted Rhoda on the head. She did a double-take, realizing she didn't need to reach down any more to do so.

"Hi, Lottie!" Mom said.

Lottie felt lightness in her chest. She raised her chin, exposing her neck. "Mom, Dad! It is so good to see you!" Lottie stretched her arms out wide.

"Lottie, I'm so proud." Esther embraced her daughter.

Lottie's words hitched. "Mom. I missed you."

"You did it," Mom said in a way that made Lottie's heart surge. They separated, and Lottie stood back to study her dad. He seemed different ... softer. His hair had grayed on the sides, and his eyes were clear. Lottie stood with arms akimbo, grinning full on.

Murray stepped up to her. "You look good, honey."

Lottie's lips parted as she noticed he no longer held a clenched jaw and furrowed brow. "So do you Dad. Thanks, it's nothing." She suddenly felt like a child again, and looked down at her feet.

"No, it's really good." Lottie's Dad reached, grabbing Lottie around the shoulders. "That's my girl, come here."

Lottie's heart melted. She had waited all her life for this embrace. "Daddy," her voice wiggled.

Murray pushed her back, eyes roaming her face as his voice cracked. "I'm proud of you, Lottie." He wrapped his arms around her again. "I'm so very proud of my little girl."

Lottie's nerves tingled with satisfaction. She felt her eyes water with pure happiness. She was safer than she had ever been on the old rooftop where she, Rebecca and Elsie Mae had played as teenagers. Dad's embrace was rock-solid. Her eyes went blurry, and the old anger faded. All of her youthful anxiety wilted. "Dad, what happened to you?"

"I'm sorry about those younger years. I musta acted like a tin. I got a new job, just … straightened myself out." His smile stretched wide.

"Oh God! That's so boss!" Lottie's heart pounded in her throat.

"Working hard drove me to drink, but no more."

Lottie stepped back. She beamed, and slugged his shoulder. "What about those Yankees?"

"Beat the Braves with a homerun in the 8th!"

"Just like me and stickball in '52," Lottie laughed.

"Yes indeed! Honey, you really showed me! You're a wonderful daughter, better than I could have asked for."

"Oh, Dad." She felt whole.

Dad frowned, and waggled a finger back and forth. "You've done something great. My little girl, grown up. So strong." Then he just laughed. It was the warmest moment of Lottie's life. Her eyes misted through her own giggles. "My girl, it's hard to believe it's you," he grinned squeezing her biceps.

Lottie shrugged. "It's me. I learned to be strong from you. And just a little stubborn."

"Don't that beat all?" He grabbed her in his arms for another big hug.

"Oh, Lottie," Esther whimpered.

Lottie looked over her dad's shoulder at her mother's happy face. Mom's trembling fingers wiped away a tear. "I'm so glad to be here to see all this!"

Mom patted Lottie on the back. "Oh, honey. I'm so proud of you, too. We're all proud of you." Her eyes sparkled like bright stars.

"Yeah!" Rhoda jumped on her toes. She presented the newspaper's sports page. "Look!"

Lottie's mouth dropped. It was the sports page of *The New York Times*, featuring a photo of Lottie skating around the Garden in skimpy shorts. *Super Athlete hits New York City,* read the headline. She gave a quick yelp and glanced at Mom and Dad.

"I was wrong. Women can play professional sports!" Dad said.

"You're a star!" Rhoda pressed her palms to cheeks.

"Well ... I'll be." Lottie held the newspaper and drifted off on a cloud for a moment. "Well!" She exhaled. "You're both so big now," Lottie said, turning to her sisters.

"You're an athlete!" Betty's eyes sparkled.

"You look like a movie star. You're the berries," Rhoda said, awestruck.

"Oh, sweeties." Lottie hugged her two younger sisters.

"You're both much prettier than me. You just wait 'til you're my age. You'll knock 'em dead!" Lottie put both hands on Rhoda's shoulders.

"Really? You think so, Lottie?" Rhoda asked.

"Really!" Lottie kissed Rhoda and Betty. "When you're adults, you'll both be oh-so-irresistible."

"We watch you every week on television," Dad said.

"You all look so wonderful." Lottie made an awkward grin. She scooped Rhoda and Betty up in her arms again and gave them another big hug. "I've missed you so much."

"Hey, Lottie. Remember me?" came a shout.

Lottie and her family turned toward the voice. It was Buddy and Dorothy Wilson! "Oh, my God! I can't believe it," Lottie yelped. "Buddy!"

"What did I tell ya, kid?" Buddy said, extending a hand. "This is one hell of a skater!" Buddy said to Lottie's family.

Instead of shaking hands, Lottie opened her arms and wrapped them around Buddy.

"And such a beauty!" Buddy laughed. "You're home now," Buddy whispered in her ear while he wiggled his fingers. "Little Lunatic."

"Great teamwork," Dorothy said.

"Thanks, Dorothy, and thank you so much, Buddy!" Lottie smiled at her mentor. "Dad, Buddy was my coach at the Armory. Remember when you signed?"

"I sure do." Murray shook Buddy's hand. "You taught her to do all that?"

"Oh, no, she picked most of that up on her own." Buddy dismissed the notion. "I had a feeling about her all along."

"Well, thanks to you, I'm a happy father," Murray said.

"*He* named me Little Lunatic!" Lottie laughed pointing at him.

"I see you're making friends?" Buddy said.

"Yes, and then some. The derby's my other family."

Just then, there was some commotion a few yards away. Two little girls were scampering in Lottie's direction. "Can I get an autograph? Can I? Can I?" One girl held out a program and bounced like she had to pee.

"Me too, me too, you're my hero!" the other one said in a whispery voice.

"Why, of course you can!" Lottie moved close and took the program. She grabbed the pen and inscribed her name across the front.

"You're so fast!" The girl's eyes twinkled.

"Thank you, honey. What's your name?"

"Ellen."

"Well, Ellen, how old are you, and what do you want to be when you grow up?" Lottie asked.

"I'm three, and my sister is two. I want to be an athlete," she said, "just like you, but maybe with the winning Yankees!"

Lottie rubbed her shoulder. "You can do whatever you want." Lottie paused. "Are your parents here?"

The little one pointed. "Over there."

Lottie looked up, and there stood Rebecca Peterson, with one hand trembling on her chest. "Hi, Empress," she said, coming closer.

"Rebecca!" Lottie's brows arched high and breath caught in her throat. It was four years since they parted!

"Meet my husband, Jack." Rebecca smiled. A tall man smiled as his shoulder pressed against Rebecca's. He held his hand out.

"Hi, Jack." Lottie's heart chugged. "Married?!" Lottie beamed as she shook Jack's hand. Then she angled in front of Rebecca and gave her a big hug. "Congratulations."

Rebecca said, "I'm a special education teacher now. I'm helping others who need a little push." The two relaxed. "I want them to fit in. The way I needed a little help years ago."

"That's wonderful. It's perfect, and I'm so very happy for you." Lottie hugged Rebecca again. "Exactly something you'd be so good at. You look great!" She looked down at the girls. "And your daughters are darling."

"Thank you." Rebecca smiled a proud mother's smile. "You've done very well for yourself, too."

"Honest, I couldn't have done it without your help," Lottie said. "I read *The Old Man and The Sea* three or four times, and other books too—all because of you."

"I guess I was a teacher back then, too."

"Yes. Listen, girls." She kneeled to look squarely into both little girls' eyes. "No matter what you want to do, you can do it. But can you promise me something?"

"Sure, I promise," one nodded.

"Be a team player. And most importantly, don't hurt anybody with what you do or say. Okay?"

The two girls looked starry-eyed. "Okay," they chimed.

"Now come here and give me a hug."

The three hugged.

"Understand what I mean?" Lottie asked.

"Sure!" the tallest girl said. She turned and looked at her mother.

"Oh, and go to bed early, and eat your fruits and vegetables." Lottie laughed, trying to remember all the standard advice.

"That's what my mom says," the smallest girl said, rolling her eyes.

Lottie winked. "She's right, you know."

"Thanks, Lottie," Rebecca said. "For everything." A tear ran down her cheek. "And I mean *everything*!"

Lottie stood to grasp one of Rebecca's hands and whispered, "Did you notice that my family is here tonight? Isn't that just keen?"

"That's great for you." She brushed a tear out of her eye. "Here's our address in case you want to write." Rebecca handed Lottie a slip of paper. "We have to go now. School and homework to think about."

"Of course." Lottie gave one last gentle rub to Rebecca's hand, and the young family descended out of the massive arena.

Chapter 33

GAME FACE

Lottie's exploits and Oscar's publicity machine saw her face plastered on posters all around the city. There were scoops for *The New York Times* on backstage preparations, and a daily skate along Central Park's 5th Avenue. The publicity predicted a grand opening at Madison Square Garden and a bustling success. Oscar's genius for promotion had captured the city's appetite for something new and exotic.

The photo of Lottie skating around the Garden in skimpy shorts and bare legs generated another type of buzz. Lottie and her legs had been the main feature of the news story.

The next day, it was almost time for gameplay when Lottie walked into the back of the Garden sports center. "Hey, Lottie," a backstage worker called.

"Hi," she said.

"Everyone's talking about you. It's all over New York City."

"What do you mean?"

"At my barbershop and on the subway; everyone has their face buried in the sports pages. They're reading all about you."

"Oh, that?" Lottie smiled.

"I'm telling you, it's going to be a sellout tonight. My barber thinks he's in love with you."

"Oh, gosh. Thanks for the support. Tonight, I'm going to skate like I've never skated before—like a rotten egg."

"I'll be watching from backstage." He winked.

Lottie was in the locker room two hours before the big game. She heard the chitter-chatter of throngs of fans who were lined up way early for the game, stretched out for three city blocks. Her gut buzzed with energy. Ticket-sellers were selling as fast as they could. Once the normal seats sold out, they sold standing-room-only passes.

Hornets were spiraling out of control in Lottie's gut. Backstage, she took a peek at the empty arena. It was hustling with last-minute activity and a television crew was adjusting its equipment and lights. Workers were completing red, white and blue bunting and banners. She returned to the locker room and waited.

"I'm mad as hell!" Belzak crashed her skates into a locker. The sound shattered Lottie's eardrums. Patty sighed audibly. "Stay clear of me," Belzak insisted.

"Calm down, everyone. It's a full house, but you're all ready," Patty coached. "Years of barnstorming have paid off. Every one of you is at the top of your game." Patty's words calmed Lottie.

"Stay out of my way out there when the heat begins!" Belzak yelled.

Patty folded her arms across her chest. One set of fingers tapped her forearm. "Say, we heard that a troubled fourteen-year-old fan wanted to commit suicide and came to the game last night, instead." Patty looked directly at Belzak.

"So? What about it?" Belzak said. "What's it got to do with an old heifer like you?"

"The game inspired him. He regained his will to live. Ain't that something?" Patty's brows lifted.

Belzak rifled through a big bag. "So what?"

"So he waited outside the rear gate to meet skaters. You, Belzak, picked him up, got him drunk, and had sex with him. Isn't that right?" Patty frowned.

Carol's eyes narrowed. "No."

"I fucked him. I *saved* him," Belzak shouted. "You would've done the same!"

"Not me," Gerry said.

"*Uh-hum,*" Ruby mocked.

Lottie couldn't believe the sewer sludge that was spewing out of Belzak's mouth.

"Figures," someone muttered.

"Belzak, you need some help." Patty shook her head.

"You're just jealous!" Belzak grimaced.

"He's *fourteen*!" Patty yelled. "Don't you realize how that reflects on the derby? On all of us?"

"The best fourteen-year-old ass I've ever had! You'll never catch a fourteen-year-old, you old fart."

Tossing things inside her locker, Lottie felt twitchy. "Ruby, you ready to give the audience the best red shirt game of their lives?"

"Of course." Ruby crossed her arms glancing over a shoulder at the mess that was Belzak.

"Hell, yes. Count me in." Carol pressed her lips together.

"Let me see, here." Lottie pulled out her bag and searched through the contents. She didn't know what she was looking for until she laid her razor-sharp eyes on it: the eight-inch-long hatpin stuck in her lucky hat. It looked dangerous and downright evil. She inconspicuously pulled the long silver pin out of the hat and bag, grasping it like a weapon. She felt a lovely, burning desire: revenge.

"What you going to do with that?" Ruby whispered.

"I don't know yet. But it'll come to me."

"Okay, everyone, let's hurry up!" Belzak yelled. "I have a date tonight!" She taunted against the disapproving stares.

Lottie glanced left and right, then slipped the silver hatpin inside the cleavage of her bra.

"It looks like we're gonna have one heck of a game tonight," Carol said with bright eyes.

"Sure does," Lottie replied. She reached one hand into her bag and rubbed the brim of the lucky hat with the same two-fingered motion that was her ritual. The hornet's nest spun nonstop in her stomach. She found a quiet place amid the smell of socks, away from the nervous chatter. Time to prepare her game face. She exhaled deeply, circle/stretched her head and caressed the heart stone on her necklace. Then she closed her eyes.

In her mind's eye, the pigeon was falling from the heavens in a death-spiral. Wings tight, eyes closed, the bird plummeted headfirst like a lightning bolt. It nosedived to earth faster than the speed of light. In that moment, Lottie heard the bullies from the schoolyard. The boys were throwing her to the ground, then holding her down. The memory was as fresh as the day it happened. She lay helpless on the ground, gagging for breath. She begged them to leave her alone.

Her fear turned to anger. Teeth clenched, she breathed hot air in measured breaths. Her back straightened. She felt a taut wound waiting to be let go. Her knuckles tightened. "No. *NO!*" she shouted to herself. Lottie's pulse pounded. "*Assholes!*" she screamed in silence. She inhaled, took a wide stance and faced the bullies. A fire burned within her, visible in her eyes to the bullies, whose brows arched in surprised at being faced down. Their mouths dropped open. Lottie attacked, lunging toward the leader, screaming and clawing. *"I hate you! Get outta my way!"*

Lottie rewrote her own history in her imagination, laughing as the kids fled. "*Cowards ... chicken livers!*" The pigeon's nosedive straightened. The bird's white wings spread open and captured the winds, fluttering to safety. Light bounced off snowy white feathers. The feathered body glided smoothly into the clear horizon, unhurt.

Lottie's breath evened out. The scene faded away; her mind emerged from the trance. She heard the faint click of a locker being shut. Her muscles relaxed as a sense of calm washed over her. With her eyes open, Lottie noticed that the flipping in her stomach had settled. She gritted her teeth, and her veins pumped with anticipation. Without a glance in the mirror or a word spoken, she rolled out of the locker room. Lottie was ready for battle.

Chapter 34

ROLLER HYSTERIA

Roaring thunder rocked the arena, pulsating from floor to ceiling as the roller-warriors entered to rapturous applause. The fans rushed the track, lining up and clamoring close to Lottie and the other skaters. Wide-eyed, they were hoping to catch a glimpse of someone they'd seen on television or read about in the papers. Lottie basked in the spectators' reverence for the New York team. Her face was emotionless, yet her stomach was in knots. The players rolled and clacked onto the track. Lottie clump-walked across the banks. *Oops!* Suddenly, the hatpin fell out of her bra. It tumbled down the inside of her jersey and landed on the infield. A few New York fans caught a glimpse, and frowned. Lottie scooped the object up and shoved it back into her bra.

Belzak performed her usual display. The announcer called her trackside with a gift from a fan. It was a box of candy she had bought herself. Lottie's insides rolled.

"Ladies and gentlemen, welcome to the American Roller Derby League. Before we start tonight's game, I'd like to introduce, sitting right here in the front row, popular stars of the silver screen, Pat O'Brien and Mickey Rooney."

The packed audience clapped. Cameramen adjusted their levers and lenses.

"Next to them, Bette Davis, of stage and screen!"

More applause. An oversized camera zoomed in close to those famous eyes.

The skaters came to the starting line. Lottie crowded behind the lineup. Her entire body surged, raring to go.

"Are the referees ready?" The announcer paused to heighten the anticipation. "Are the trainer and doctor ready?" He waited. Cheers erupted. Lottie focused, body and mind sharp as the tip of the hatpin. "Well then, hold on to your hats, because here comes the derby!" His voice shot across the auditorium.

The horn buzzed, the referee's whistle shrilled.

Twenty athletic legs banged and pounded. The arena floor reverberated loud enough to shake the rafters.

"Go, New York, *GO!*" the crowd chanted.

Lottie sucked in air and jostled left, then right, with precision. The skate noise droned louder, radiating from the track and vibrating into the atmosphere. It thumped inside Lottie's head. A rocking chant, a roller-rhythm, penetrated Lottie, releasing age-old aggressions.

Lottie hip bumped an opponent aside. "Red deuce!" she yelled, ready to out-skate and out-block the best of the best. She heaved left with a jab. The bone-crunching marathon was on! She broke away from the pack in muscular strides.

"And already out of the pack," the announcer called. "The Little Lunatic for the Panthers is on the jam! For those new to the rules, a skater must start a play by leaving the pack, round the entire field within two minutes, and then re-approach the pack from the rear. For every opposing skater passed, the passing skater's team is awarded one point."

Orbiting the track, Lottie glanced at the eager faces. A feeling of uneasiness hovered in the air as she crouched, whirring nearer to the rear of the pack.

"Now, with the Panther skater approaching, Bobbie Elgin and the Blonde Avenger are setting up a double block to defend for New York," the announcer called out.

The audience leaned in.

Lottie eased, then approached. She sped up, attempting to bust through the double block, but rode out a backlash. She was bumped backward. She lowered her head, pedaled her skates, and sped up again. The blockers braced to heave her backwards. Lottie inhaled and raised her arms high, as if grasping a machete. She plowed downwards.

"The Little Lunatic, on the offense one more time!"

The audience was quiet.

Lottie curled her face and busted through, tossing apart Bobbie and Gerry. The blockers were sent spinning into the railing.

"Two points, Panthers!"

The fans moaned while the trackside cameras zoomed in to follow Lottie. She glanced at Gerry, catching her smile. Belzak scowled. The pack organized, and the next play was underway. The teams rotated.

"Ping-pong with a red goof!" Lottie hollered.

"Let's go. A red and a white. No score," Belzak demanded.

"Ping-pong with a red goof," Lottie countered in a calm voice.

"Stay on script, bitch!" Belzak pulled her elbow pad down and gave Lottie a boney jab to the ribs.

Lottie winced. It hurt, but it hadn't drawn the audience's attention. "Let's go! Ping-pong with a red goof," Lottie called.

"Pipe down!" Belzak said.

The skaters' eyes lit up; two jammers rocketed away from the pack. "I'm outta here," Carol announced.

"Here I go, Moe," Ruby followed.

"Two jammers are out on this play," the announcer called.

The sprinters raced around the track, jostling for position.

"And now, in the lead for New York is the Flashing Bombshell, Carol Anderson."

The fans cheered.

Belzak's brows furrowed. Lottie shoulder-slammed a New York blocker, and positioned herself in defense. The cameras followed.

Ruby hunkered down in pursuit. Ruby was on Carol's tail. Both skaters synchronized their paces—leg to leg, stride for stride, whirling forward. Nearing scoring position, Ruby lunged forward with a bash, starting the familiar pantomime. Carol arched forward with the seemingly jaw-rattling blow.

Angry fans moaned.

Lottie widened her stance. She slammed Carol, appearing to clatter her bridgework. Carol feigned pain and gulped for air. She grimaced, holding one arm in mock agony.

The fans nearest the track widened their eyes.

Ruby smashed Carol forward again.

"That's it, Ruby. Come on!" Lottie gritted her teeth and waved. She swung a wide leg block and bounced Carol back again, arching the skater's back.

Restless sounds bubbled up from the audience.

Carol staggered.

"Take that!" Ruby knocked Carol headfirst.

The fans *ooohed*, feeling the pain.

"Help me!" Carol screamed.

"Things don't look good for the Flashing Bombshell," the announcer intoned. "Ruby and The Little Lunatic are pulverizing her with a gridlock prison."

Belzak attempted to help Lottie, but blockers in the pack held her back. Her own teammates bounced her forward. "Let me back there!" Belzak's arms flailed.

The crowd cheered.

"Ten seconds. Nine. Eight." The announcer raised the tension.

Ruby pushed Carol careening forward, and Lottie threw a Chicago-Bears-style body slam. Then Carol jumped aside. Lottie just missed the girl by an inch, and nailed Ruby instead. Ruby fell to the track with a deafening *thud*.

The fans screamed.

Ruby's apparent condition warranted the doctor's attention. Ruby seemed pissed off at the Flashing Bombshell *and* her teammate, The Little Lunatic.

The fans' yelling echoed like fireworks in Lottie's ears. She skittered to the rail and grabbed it. Breathing deep, she came to a stop and shook her head *no*, as if to say she was sorry to Ruby.

"The Little Lunatic takes out her own Panther skater! Ruby Johnson is down!"

The fans howled at the red goof.

Lottie angled a stiff jaw toward the audience and camera while Ruby sat on the track, rubbing her head in a daze. An ocean of laughter poured forth.

"Why, I oughta murder ya, Curley," Lottie said to Ruby.

Belzak rolled past Lottie, jabbing a knuckle into sore ribs. "Cut it out. You're drawing too much attention!"

Lottie heard a call from the audience. "Lunatic, go home!"

"Not until I take all your money!" Lottie furrowed her brow and threw her fist toward the audience. Then her eyes popped open. Her own momentum had thrown her off balance. Her brows arched; her legs flipped into the air. She hit the track ass-first with a *crash!*

The fans cheered, belly-laughed and guffawed.

Lottie outstretched her legs, frowned and raised her palms up at her sides.

The fans roared and waved.

"Go back to where you came from!" screamed a furious lady in the front row, baby in her arms.

"Oh, shut up!" Lottie stuck her tongue out at the mother. She wobbled to her skates and stood.

The entire arena rocked at full-tilt, applauding and stamping their feet. Trackside, the angered lady tossed her baby into the air at Lottie! Lottie caught the infant, completely shocked. She exhaled, and eased it back to the cursing mother.

The fans screamed.

One by one, the other skaters rallied behind Lottie—all except Belzak, who yelled out, "No score. Red ends up alone. Kill play!"

The shrill sound of the referee's whistle knit the pack together. "Next play, let's go," he said, motioning the skaters faster. The pack spun, skates pounded and the wooden Masonite reverberated. The arena rocked out a rhythm of volcanic fury. The referee sounded the whistle again.

Lottie mugged and jagged. Skaters rotated. The New York captain slipped out from the pack and sped away on the next play.

"And a New Yorker, Gerry Murphy, is out on this play. The two-minute jam time has begun," the announcer blared.

Fans rallied and cheered.

Lottie dug in, muscles rippling as she took off right behind the New York skater.

The fans booed.

"And now, the Little Lunatic, shaken loose from the pack, is on a late chase right behind Gerry Murphy." The announcer's voice picked up a wave of enthusiasm.

Halfway around the track, Lottie scrunched up her face and pulled out the shiny hatpin from her bra. She narrowed her eyes and glanced at the audience. The hatpin glistened under the bright lights. A woman lifted her hands to her mouth and cried out, "No!"

Lottie glared, pulling her hand back in a wind-up movement. People shrieked. Lottie aimed at the New York target. *Oooh*s erupted. Lottie looked like she was going to ram the sharp device into Gerry's buttocks.

The crowd blared and wailed.

Lottie's adrenaline jolted, eyes on fire. She swung, seeming to stick the pin where the sun don't shine.

Thwump! Gerry fell into a crumple.

"Oh! Gerry Murphy is put down!"

Lottie snarled and hid the pin, tucking it back in her cleavage.

"She has something in her jersey!" someone cried out.

Speeding fast, The Little Lunatic jumped and sidestepped the New York blocker. Lottie stood tall, nodding with satisfaction. She had scored one point and cut the jam off.

Gerry teetered up to her skates, rubbing her butt.

"Oh, no," the audience responded.

"One Panther point," boomed the announcer. "Scored by The Little Lunatic over the Blonde Avenger!"

Lottie caught Murphy's edge-eyed squint as it squeaked into a wink.

The fans rasped sounds of disappointment.

"Hey. Who the *hell* told you to score?" Belzak yelled.

Lottie ignored Belzak. She was full of the competitive moment and her face focused with power. *"Ad-lib!"* she commanded the others.

The game tightened, glued together by an unstoppable rhythm of red shirt violence. Passions rippled like molten, red-hot hell on wheels. Lottie drove deeper into her powers. Then New York scored, keeping the score tight—only one point from the other team. The audience was wild, sucked in for the finish like they were the ones out there throwing elbows and skating for the win.

"Just five minutes left in this game," came the announcer's harried voice.

Lottie heard the fans pounding their feet. Bloodlust rose into the atmosphere. The whistle trilled. Sweat gathered under Lottie's arms as Carol broke again.

The fans cheered.

Carol hunched down in a speed-swept style as Lottie raised her chin.

"And out in a flash again is the Flashing Bombshell!"

Suddenly, Lottie signaled with a hand in the air, and pushed hard. She felt the sheen of sweat on her cheeks as she screamed out of the pack, right behind Carol.

The fans jeered as Lottie caught up with her friend.

Then Lottie's mouth turned down, her teeth bared, and out came the hatpin! Lottie was about to lay into Carol!

The audience shrieked bloody murder.

"The Little Lunatic is on the attack!"

Lottie swung her arm upwards. She set upon the little New Yorker, with one hairpin-swinging motion. "Here you go," Lottie called. Her arm jabbed downwards like a knife ready to kill. *Pow!* Carol flew into the air, holding her seemingly-injured upper butt.

The fans retaliated with despising screams. "Stop her! You cheat!"

Carol's legs flew out from under her. She crashed to the track, sprawled flat, and rolled slightly, rubbing a damaged backside.

"Another New York skater has been put down *hard!*"

The fans booed Lottie, who, with an evil-eyed glare, again hid the hatpin in her jersey.

The referee's whistle sounded a warning. The doctor came to tend to Carol. He hovered over the Flashing Bombshell.

The crowd's empathy poured out to the wounded warrior.

Lottie smiled to herself, knowing they hated her, just as she had planned.

"Throw her out of the game!" someone shouted.

Breathing easily, with jet-propelled maneuvers, Lottie scored two more points.

"Two more points by the Little Lunatic!"

The crowd hastened to its feet, booing.

"How can she cheat and then score?" someone hollered.

"That wasn't supposed to be your point!" Belzak scowled. Her eyes glared.

"I hate you," one fan yelled at Lottie.

"You doink! Go back to the funny-farm!" someone screamed.

"You're full of bull," the baby-thrower screamed.

"Go back to the looney-bin, you damn lunatic!" another irate fan yelled.

"Stop it! Now!" Belzak's veins were popping at each temple, and deep lines furrowed her forehead.

One woman sneered, "Throw The Little Lunatic out. Throw The Little Lunatic out!" Jeering voices rattled the building.

The referee called Lottie off the track with a short whistle blast. The game came to a momentary halt.

The fans cheered. "She has a weapon!" they began to scream.

Lottie turned her back and secretly pulled the hatpin from her bra and slipped it inside her hair.

The fans booed, then hushed.

The referee patted Lottie down. He patted her breasts and searched her jersey. He found nothing.

"Are you blind?" hollered outraged fans.

Out of frustration, the referee blew a whistle trill and fined Lottie twenty-five dollars.

"A fine for insubordination on The Little Lunatic."

The fans cried out their approval.

Lottie jutted out her jaw and mouthed exaggerated cusswords at the official, all for the fans' benefit.

"Two minutes left in tonight's game!" The announcer was electrifying the audience. "Your New York City Chiefs are tied with the Panthers!"

Lottie eyed every skater on the track. She had made a mental map of every location, and she felt good. Now the final plan could unfold.

Resting at the rail, chest heaving, Lottie pulled both sleeves up to her shoulders. Then she adjusted her underwear like a man adjusting his crotch. She threw her shoulders back, sniffed, and rejoined the whirling pack.

The fans booed.

"The pack is back together, ready for the FINAL play of the night!" The announcer raised his voice.

The cyclone of skating reverberated at an ear-splitting volume. The thundering and pounding buffeted Lottie's ears. The whistle shrilled. The audience was almost exhausted with the excitement, they were covered in sweat and screaming so loud voices were cracking.

"Out of my way!" Belzak pushed Lottie as she huffed and puffed. Lottie and the other players jogged, bumped and jumbled against one another as Belzak broke from the speeding pack. Her arms flew around like windmill blades.

"Belzak out for the Panthers!" exclaimed the announcer.

The hypnotized fans needed a New York skater out, and this play would determine the win. People leaned in and yelled with all their might.

The teams charged, locked in mortal combat. In a shot, little Carol flew out of the pack after an atomic whip. The fans, shouting and waving #1 signs, jumped to their feet as Carol sped like a bullet along the straightaway.

"And now, out of the pack," the announcer yelled, "comes our own little Carol Anderson, New York's Flashing Bombshell."

The fans jumped up and down.

In the midst of the whirlwind, Lottie fixated on her target. She gulped down a lungful of air, pushed her skates forward, and with superhuman lunges, broke away on the jam!

As Carol blasted down the straightaway and screeched around the corner, she closed the space between herself and Belzak. She glanced back to see Lottie.

The fans screamed, waving Carol, their hero, on.

The announcer's voice shook the house. "I can't believe it, ladies and gentlemen. It's The Little Lunatic on the jam *again*! *Never* in the history of the sport has anyone, man or woman, jammed this many times in one game!"

The fans moaned, "*Arugh!*" They fumed as if witnessing a serial killer on the loose. The game spiraled into a flurry of angst.

"Just one minute left in the game!"

Live television cameras captured the roller-battle. Zooming lenses whirled through the air to match the speed of the skating swarm.

Belzak held the lead, just one small step ahead of Carol. Belzak looked back to see Lottie gaining ground. She was taking hunkering strides. "Get out of here. This is my play!" Belzak waved her teammate off.

The fans rooted for their New York hero. They sighed and hoped for the best.

Lottie followed Carol. Gasping for air, heart pounding, legs burning, Lottie focused her attention on her mark without losing a stroke.

Someone screamed, "Stop the Lunatic!" A young fan's face scrunched with ghastly fright. To the audience's horror, out came the hatpin.

The announcer's booming voice penetrated the arena. "The Little Lunatic's ready to destroy Anderson!"

Belzak was in the lead, with Carol just inches behind as Lottie wielded the gleaming dagger in her hand.

The arena spun into full-tilt terror. Emotions in the arena fast-tracked, with every eye and ear focused. Fans screamed for the referee to stop the action! Save their hero!

Lottie readied her lethal assault on Carol as skates clumped and banged. Women shrilled in terror. Lottie pulled the hatpin high over her head like a slaying knife. She yelled, "Duck!" to Carol.

No one breathed. Lottie's heartbeat quickened as she lunged, the pin aimed directly at Carol. Lottie felt sweat under her armpit when she swung her arm. The audience raised their hands to their faces. Suddenly, Carol ducked low on her skates, teetering, almost falling. *Whoosh!* Lottie missed Carol and stabbed Belzak.

The audience exhaled in excruciating moans.

The pin jammed Belzak's backside, penetrating her uniform and skin. Lottie's brows ballooned into hoops.

Belzak screamed, "You bitch!" The crowd roared. Then Belzak tripped and crashed wildly. Lottie shook her head in an exaggerated *NO*. The audience howled, clapping and stomping.

"And the Lunatic clobbers her own teammate! Anderson, the Blond Bombshell, now in the lead!" the announcer stressed.

Lottie hid the hatpin. Her mind boiled over, focused and raw. Belzak glared and shouted obscenities. She sat up and bounced atop her tender ass.

The announcer's raw voice cracked. "Three seconds left in this game!"

The audience was on its feet. Belzak gasped for fresh air. Little Carol sped, rolled and scooted past Belzak; she made one sidestep jump and ducked, teetering uneasily. Then she scored the final winning point. Deafening cheers erupted from the audience.

"The Flashing Bombshell scores!" The hoarse announcer's voice hit an eardrum-piercing pitch. "And the New York City Chiefs win!"

The house shuddered with delirium. The buzzer sounded the end of the game, again and again. "New York wins, just in the nick of time!"

Lottie's heart pounded. She wiped her brow and turned to help Belzak off the track. Belzak jumbled to her skates, seething at Lottie. The audience hooted and jeered. Belzak gritted her teeth and lunged.

The audience gasped in shock.

"Look out! Look out! Belzak's after her own teammate!" the announcer shouted.

Belzak flew through the air, fists flailing. She sucked air, clawing at Lottie's hair and scratching at her face. Lottie bobbed and weaved. Then Belzak grabbed the necklace from Lottie's neck, snapping it off with one hard pull.

"Belzak, breaking something from The Little Lunatic's neck?" said the announcer incredulously.

The sound made Lottie wince. She stopped, and her gut sank into oblivion. "*No!*" she cried.

Belzak's chest heaved. She examined the glistening jewel. "Something from old Harold, huh?"

"Yes, please, no." Lottie reached with an open hand.

"You and this are pieces of shit!" Belzak tossed it into the air and let it fall back into her hand.

"Please," Lottie whimpered. Belzak heaved the chain into the audience.

"Belzak seems to have thrown something off the track," the announcer's voice cracked.

Lottie's spirits dropped. The gift represented all she loved about life.

"What do you think of that?" Belzak spat.

Lottie's gut hardened and her teeth clenched. A volcano erupted inside her chest. First Harold, and now his gift … gone forever.

"You're nothing!" Belzak screamed.

Blood coursed through Lottie's body. She panted in and out through her nose, and knew what she had to do. Her inner fires burned like a furnace. Uncontrollably, she snarled, "HEEEYYYYY! Get outta my way!"

Belzak's brow's lifted.

Lottie pulled back and delivered two roundhouse punches, just like a man: no girlie clawing, just direct connections to the face. *Smack, smack*, hitting Belzak's jaw, rattling her hair into flying strands. Sweat flew off under the punches given so close the first few rows knew there was nothing fake about that.

Loud gasps came from the audience.

"The Little Lunatic, fighting mad!" yelled the announcer.

Belzak scratched Lottie's face, drawing blood from her cheek.

"Damn you!" Lottie cursed as she threw another blow. *Whack*.

Fans applauded.

Belzak's head bobbed back, hair askew and lips cranked toward the ceiling. Then her head rubber-banded back to take the next knuckle-smack in the jaw. *Pow!* Her movie-star hair unraveled.

Fans cheered.

"Look out!" the announcer shouted.

Lottie wound up an uppercut punch and connected with a superhuman knockout directly into Belzak's jaw. *Thwak!*

The audience was hysterical.

"Incredible!" the strained announcer's voice shouted.

Belzak flew a foot into the air, landed on the track, and bounced. *Flump!*

"Fans! I've never seen—"

Chaos engulfed the entire building.

Deep lines were wrinkling Belzak's forehead. She cried out, "I'll get you!" and straggled toward Lottie, only to meet knuckles. *Smack!*

The audience moaned, "*Oh!*" as Belzak teetered in slow motion and fell, head tilted back and mouth wide open. She slumped unconscious, and hit the track with a loud *plop*.

The house came down in one glorious, rocking crescendo.

"Belzak—is—*out!*" the delirious announcer rasped.

"That's it, Lottie!" Ruby yelled.

Carol and the other skaters cheered along with the fans.

"What a night at the derby! What a night! Action every minute!" The big speakers quivered from the announcer's excitement. The audience pounded their feet and clapped out a frenetic rhythm.

Belzak stood up groggily and rolled into the infield benches. She reached under her infield seat, grabbing something from her purse. Ol' Bessie rested in her hand.

"No!" yelled Ruby.

Lottie was sweating profusely.

Belzak's eyes glazed over. She rolled, wobbled and stood on the track's high bank, pointing the pistol directly at Lottie's chest. Belzak's hand shook. "I'm gonna send you to hell!"

"What's this?" the announcer gasped.

A hush fell upon the audience. Someone screamed.

"No." Lottie's face turned white. She stared at the end of the gun barrel. All showmanship had ended.

"Someone stop her," the announcer pleaded.

Lottie's heart stammered. Her mind flashed back to JC, when he had used a gun to threaten Buddy—only this time, she was the one staring down the barrel of the weapon. She held her breath.

"Now you die!" Belzak screamed, sliding her finger onto the trigger.

Carol moaned, "Oh God, no."

The barrel shook, and Lottie stared down her own mortality. Her life's history flashed before her. Time stopped. Death clung to the horror-filled air.

Lottie squeezed her eyes tight.

Suddenly, Ruby came flying out of nowhere. Rustling sounds shook across the audience.

Just when Lottie thought her life was over, her eyes opened once more. Ruby's body rocketed through the air and slammed Belzak with a flying hip check. Belzak's back was sent careening out of control. The gun arm flailed.

The audience sighed with a loud, cathartic "*Ohhhhh.*"

Belzak's hand pointed toward the ceiling. The trigger pulled, and a shot rang out; the cannon sound echoing back from the rafters.

Everyone jumped. Carol *yip*ped, hunched her shoulders and plugged her fingers into her ears.

The bullet scorched toward one of the top lights of the arena. It shattered the bulb in a puff of smoke. The noise clanged in Lottie's ears.

Ruby landed squarely on her feet.

Lottie exhaled.

"Yes!" Carol cried.

The gun flew out of Belzak's grasp and skittered into the infield. Belzak teetered, her arms whirling. Her left skate rose into the air. She balanced on one skate and wheeled uncontrollably down the banks, crashing into Vinnie Christner. Her skate wheels crushed his groin.

"Not the nuts," Carol groaned.

"You old whore!" Vinnie shrieked in pain.

Lottie clasped a hand over her mouth.

Slowly, the audience's gasps turned into hysterical laughter. A great fog of tension lifted from the entire building. A blizzard of electricity connected everyone who had witnessed the wild action.

Rolling and bending, Carol picked up Ol' Bessie with two fingers, and delicately dropped it into her bra. She shook her boobs, letting the dark gun settle against pale, large breasts.

The audience's collective voice soared with laughter.

Carol winked at Lottie, who returned a friendly smile. The blood returned to Lottie's face. Her shoulders sank, then a tear came to the edge of one eye. Gerry Murphy skated over to Lottie, and Ruby raised each of their hands into the air. *Champions!*

"The best game in roller derby's history. Good going!"

The fans cheered and applauded.

Belzak got to her knees, breathing heavily. Then she wavered and collapsed again. No one came to her aid.

She rose on all fours, extending her right hand, searching for Ol' Bessie. Her right earlobe was bleeding; Lottie had ripped the earring out. A puddle of blood formed on the arena floor. Belzak made several attempts to rise, only to sink back down, exhausted.

"What an unbelievable night!" the announcer said. "Plenty of good seats available for the next big game! See you there!"

Belzak turned over and sat on the cement floor as she unlaced her skates. Ruby rolled next to Lottie. All three—Carol, Ruby and Patty—slung their arms around Lottie and leaned in close. The audience, arms in the air, swayed back and forth.

Lottie watched Belzak struggle, cross-eyed, her face ghostly white. "I hate you all!"

The doctor, frozen in place, finally walked over to Belzak. He assisted her off the track. Vinnie left the arena, bent over in pain, holding his injured groin. The throngs sent out catcalls and laughter.

Soon, the fans stampeded the track, and the whole place pulsed with relieved adoration. The skaters left the track. New groupies clamored toward Lottie and her best friends. Lottie's adrenaline finally slowed. The adoration of her fans surprised her. She'd become such a bad guy that the fans actually loved her. *The best red shirt game in history*, she thought.

Euphoric but exhausted skaters rolled into the locker room. Everyone thanked and congratulated Lottie, Carol and Ruby, who let out a huge collective breath. Once inside, Lottie felt relaxed and fulfilled. Her heart slowed, and a big smile appeared across her face. She grabbed Ruby and hugged her. "Thank you, friend!" Tears welled up. "You're amazing."

"No, Lottie, you're amazing. I thought I'd crap my pants." Carol chuckled and pressed her hands to her stomach.

There was shaky laughter, and suddenly, every eye in the room opened wide. People leaned or turned away. The chatter hushed when Belzak staggered in. No one said a thing.

"What's the matter with all of you *bitches*?!" Belzak balled her fists.

Lottie flopped back in her chair, watching Belzak wobble and almost fall. Carol's eyes rolled heavenward.

Again, no one came to Belzak's aid. She pulled herself up and screamed. "I quit!"

The legendary thirty-eight-year-old limply tore at her clothes with awkward movements. Her movie-star hair had tumbled, flattened and unkempt. She reminded Lottie of a small, fumbling misfit.

No one consoled Belzak. They watched her storm out of the locker room for the last time, going God knew where.

Chapter 35

THE TRENTON RETURN

In 1958, televisions were blazing with the rough-and-tumble exploits of The Little Lunatic and her fellow derby skaters. The sport had grabbed viewers' imaginations, and the shows had blossomed into a walloping smash hit across America. Millions watched, transfixed in their living rooms. People stood in front of appliance shop windows, peering at rows of television sets, all of which beamed the roller mayhem. America thrilled to The Little Lunatic's sizzling world of roughneck shenanigans. The heyday of roller derby had become an inspiration for everyone.

Ruby leaned back, stretched her legs out, and pulled the newspaper close to her face with a yawn. "I love the smell here." She inhaled the moldy odor of old socks. Stale smoke eddied through the dusty room as she rested, waiting to be called to the track. "*Um-hem.* The jock aroma of Trenton again," she sighed whimsically.

Holding a cup of coffee, Lottie walked to her dressing space. "He's a one-eyed, one-horned, flying, purple ..." She was humming *The Purple People Eater* by Sheb Wooley. "Reminds me of when we started, years ago."

"In two weeks, we move on. Don't crap your pants." Carol chuckled, puffing on a cigarette as she sipped from a cup filled with iced Coca-Cola.

"I hear we'll be going up to Boston," Gerry said to Lottie from across the dressing area.

"One of my favorite towns. Big crowds."

"Did you hear? Vinnie was fired," Gerry said.

"No. What happened?" Lottie asked.

"They say he's been visiting massage parlors," Gerry said. "You know, the kind with the added service."

Ruby laughed. "Sex?"

"Right, Miss Obvious," Gerry tapped her shoulder. "He claimed all those massage visits on Oscar's insurance, saying he'd hurt his back in a game."

"*No!*" Ruby said.

"No wonder you hear Oscar has insurance headaches," Gerry said. "So Oscar fired him." She snapped her fingers. "Just like that."

"That sounds like Vinnie. Thinking with his you-know-what again." Ruby pointed a finger between her legs and smiled.

"His dick," Carol laughed.

The skaters burst into laughter.

The door swung open, revealing two new girls. Everyone turned to look at them.

"Come on in, gals." Patty happily waved them in. "The new skaters are here," she announced. "This is Leslie Patrick and Shirley Hernandez."

Lottie noted the new kids' faces, flushed with excitement and naiveté. Shirley Hernandez's brunette hair stood tousled and messy. Leslie Patrick's platinum blonde hair was pulled back into a tight ponytail. Both carried Lottie's mind back to many years ago, when she, Rebecca and Ruby had stood at that very door.

"*Hola*," Shirley said in her native language. "Hello," she repeated in English.

"It's The Little Lunatic." Leslie's jaw dropped. The young girl plopped her bag onto the floor and managed a trembling handshake.

"Hi." Lottie gave them a welcoming wave.

"I been watchin' you for years," Leslie said. Her quiet voice caressed Lottie's heart. "Can I get your autograph?" She pulled out a program yearbook featuring a photo of Lottie on the cover.

"Sure. What's your name again?"

"Leslie Patrick."

"*To Leslie Patrick. Welcome to the derby ... your new family.*" Lottie wrote like a pro, and with a glad heart.

"I'll cherish this," Leslie said big-eyed, hugging the program to her chest. "The papers say you're one of the most famous people in America—a household name."

"And because of you, the games' ratings *sobrepujar*." Shirley paused. "As good as," she smiled, "those of football and baseball. And, they say, arenas around the world are sold out for the derby."

"Welcome," Ruby said.

Shirley mumbled, "*Las primeras mujeres negras para patinar* derby!"

"Now, now." Lottie sipped her coffee and whimsically swirled it back and forth. She felt warm. She paused and leaned closer to Shirley. "Be careful of what old Oscar Wentworth puts out for promotions. I'm just a skater like the rest of you guys."

Ruby smiled.

"But the papers are saying," Leslie rolled her eyes toward the ceiling, remembering the phrase, "that your athletic gift will set millions of women free, giving women a new history to look forward to."

"We're all part of that history." Lottie waved her hand and stretched out her legs. "And now you're part of it, too."

"It's because of you and Ruby that I'm here. You know, looking up to you on television." Shirley's eyes puffed, reddened and shed a single tear.

"Here, let's see if your uniforms fit, girls." Patty handed the new skaters a uniform each. "Shirley, you'll be skating on Lottie's team, and you," Patty turned to the blonde with the ponytail, "Leslie, you'll be skating on Gerry Murphy's team."

"Oh, God," both gushed, their faces red.

"Tonight, we'll be working the first and second parts of a Saunders play in the first period," Lottie said. "Then, in the second period, we'll work a monkey-see-monkey-do and end with a white pull-away."

"Huh?" Leslie cocked her head.

"*Lo sentimos, no me-*" Shirley looked on with a blank face. "We don't …"

Lottie blinked and smiled. "I know, I know." She patted Leslie's shoulder. "Now that you're in the pro league, you'll learn to entertain the audience. You know, learn the plays."

"It's more than skating." Carol popped her gum with a smile. "Don't worry, we'll take you under our wings." She made a gesture with a crooked arm, tucking an imaginary person beneath it. "We'll have a blast. Don't crap your pants!" Carol hooted, and threw herself forward into a rickety folding chair. Suddenly, she and her paper cup both hit the floor. Her blonde hair absorbed most of the spilled cola, and when she lifted her head, wet, coke-stained locks slapped against her cheeks.

Everyone laughed.

Ruby chuckled, "In six months, you'll know all the moves, and really be able to blast through them. The fans will love you." She slapped Carol's hand and tossed her friend a towel to mop up her Coca-Cola-plastered hair.

"Thanks," Carol said.

"You gotta turn yourself into the Flashing Bombshell tonight, remember?" Ruby joked.

Carol sighed. "I know."

"I want to say *gracias*. Thanks for the *ayuda*, I mean, *help*," Shirley said. Her words gratefully tugged at Lottie's heart.

"Sure, we're gonna help you." Lottie raised her cup of coffee. "Ruby and Carol will explain the plays once you uniform up. During the game, keep an eye out for us; you can learn in no time, but you might have to sit on the benches for a while."

"Anything you say." Shirley nodded her head.

"When you're ready to learn the Saunders play, let me know." Ruby pulled the newspaper away.

"We can take you through the moves back here, first." Carol patted her hair with the towel and pointed to the cracked cement area between the worn benches.

"At halftime, I'll draw the plays out on this napkin." Lottie lifted the napkin wrapped around her coffee cup and patted it out onto the bench. She stopped. "Say! I got it!" Lottie snapped her fingers.

Ruby sagged the newspaper's edge, peering. "Uh oh. I know that voice."

"Yup. An idea," Lottie said.

"What do you say, the second half, we skate ad-lib legit!"

"Legit?" Ruby's eyebrows rose. "You know it can't be real."

"Well, all ad-lib, you know, all-out."

"No one has injuries," Gerry looked around the room. "So we're fit enough."

"You mean full-on?" Carol asked.

"That's what I mean."

"I think it'll be lots of fun. We may invent a new play in the process." Ruby dropped her paper onto her lap.

"We're gonna have a good time tonight," Carol said.

"Yeah!" Everyone agreed.

"I'll do my best, Lunatic, I mean, Lottie," Leslie said. "You're a big star. I appreciate it."

"We're all a team here. We're all stars." Lottie put a hand on Leslie's shoulder. "We're gonna get along peachy!"

The evening's game soared into a whirly-gig of speed, body contact and mayhem. Once the rolling havoc had ended, Lottie was leaving the building when a fan approached her and said, "I read your article in *The New York Times*."

"Oh, that. And do you go to the games, too?" Lottie asked, stopping to acknowledge him. After meeting many fans over the years, she spoke with confidence. Fans usually wanted to know why she hated an opponent, or why she had beat the tar out of another player. Sometimes they asked what made her so mad that she cracked an opponent's head. Lottie had skated so many games, she'd get them confused, forgetting an incident from long ago. Still, she was charmed by the moments that impressed her fans.

"Well ..." he stuttered.

This time, she found herself looking deep into the man's eyes. Something unknown—a mystery—captured her attention.

"Let's just say that I've been keeping up with your career." A hint of a smile widened across his chiseled Irish face and firm jaw.

"I'm flattered." Lottie's mind tried to place the man's eyes. His face, edged cheekbones and gleaming eyes appealed to her.

"Actually, to be candid, I'm not a fan," he said.

She raised an eyebrow.

"I mean, I did read about you. You were on the cover of *Time Magazine*. You know, the Athlete of the Year story."

Lottie tugged her coat together. "Just doin' what I love."

The man looked deep into her eyes. "You've made history. Sports history has been changed forever because of you."

Lottie looked sideways. "You're not some sort of goof, are you?"

"Heavens, no."

Lottie's face cocked left. "What's your name again?" She felt his eyes pierce deeply. Suddenly, she realized they were the same blue as forgotten Harold's eyes. Electricity zinged between the two of them, ready to ignite her with a move, a word or a phrase.

"My name's David."

She scratched her head. "You sure I don't know you?" His aftershave wafted toward her, making her thoughts reel.

"I'm David. David Cunningham," he said, looking as if he were inspecting a precious diamond.

"What brings you to the roller derby?" she asked.

"I'm one of the advertisers. We sell." He stopped in an awkward pause. "Well, none of that's important. But I do go to some of the games at the Garden. And I did see that you're the Most Valuable Player in pro sports."

"You *are* keeping up." *Eyes like the ocean of Hawaii.* She lost herself. For a moment, she wanted to believe that he, David, could live up to the dreams she had once cherished with Harold. All of that seemed like a lifetime ago now.

"Sure. The articles said you're the highest-paid female athlete of the century."

Lottie's face warmed. "You know how reporters can get carried away."

"This is going to sound silly, but ..."

As he talked, a memory of Harold sitting in the red faux-leather booth at the Fortune King in San Francisco washed over Lottie. Her eyes watered. She could see his eyes and wide shoulders, and hear his voice so clearly. She worried that she was mixing the two men up in her head. "What is it?"

David said, "Many people think sports isn't a place for women."

"If I've heard that once, I've heard it a thousand times," Lottie groaned jovially, tugging her thoughts back to the present moment.

"Your efforts in sports ..." he paused. "Your fight against society's norms will inspire the stories of many young girls who have yet to be told that they can be whatever they want."

Lottie swallowed, her lips parting. "I appreciate that. It means a lot to me, knowing how out of place I felt as a young girl." Lottie felt humbled. "One day, there'll be an all-women's league."

"I read that you made that statement."

"We're gonna start the league soon," Lottie said, with a hint of pride, pulling her neck high.

"That'll be great for girls. And the fans will love it. Besides, if anyone can do it, you can." He took a step closer, and she felt the chemistry between them increase, zapping in static bursts.

"Truthfully, I never thought so," Lottie said, glancing down at an old piece of pink bubblegum stuck to the sidewalk.

"Trust me."

"It's funny. I just met you, but I *do* trust you." She had lost herself in his small movements. Her heart fluttered.

"I'm confident. You have so much more to do in this life." He was beaming and his cheeks glowed.

He wasn't Harold, after all. This was someone different. Not better or worse, just different. She pushed that memory into her past. Rippling with nervous energy, she examined David's face. "I hope you're right. I do want to do more."

"I'm sure you will. And, even with all you've accomplished so far, you're still a mystery."

It seemed he knew too much about her—and yet it didn't frighten her at all. She looked at him quizzically, and a curl of heat unfurled in her stomach. *Where did this guy come from?* "What do you mean?" she finally asked.

"Well," he explained, "I've read about you in the papers and magazines, and I've been to games." An affable, sexy smile crept across his face, exposing his bright teeth. "But," he continued, "I know so little about you."

"Oh." She felt hot and her eyes drew back up to his. Instead of feeling stalked, she felt engulfed and nurtured. Lottie found his knowledge of her sport appealing. Self-confidence oozed from him, and she sensed that he had never suffered from shyness or feelings of inadequacy, as she had in her younger years. Her old, natural shyness kicked into high gear.

"I have a feeling about you. You have something special," he said.

Lottie had heard that before, and the flutter in her stomach grew stronger. "You're startin' to get under my skin," Lottie admitted, her bosom pounding.

"I hope that's in a good way?" he asked with a laugh. "Would you like to stay in touch?"

His scent whispered in the air, filling Lottie's nostrils. Her heart felt as though it were flying, and she felt like she'd been waiting for this man for a long time. "What are the things you like to do?"

He put a hand under his chin, as if to ponder. "Well, I like going to the movies, dancing and eating out." He thought for another moment. "Late-night drives." He looked away. "Puttering around the house, mostly. And don't forget bowling." He laughed. Pale blue eyes danced as he slowly swept them over her.

His thoughts of normality and just 'puttering around the house' touched Lottie deeply. Her belly felt empty. She calmed the excitement bursting inside, and took two deep breaths.

"Let's stay in touch," he said.

Lottie cocked her head to the side and smiled. "Oh, well, sure. You're on! Here's my number." His smile brought peace to her competitive soul, and his expression made her breathless. He turned wide shoulders to her, but quickly turned back. He reached deep into his pocket. "I almost forgot something. I think this is yours."

"What is it?"

He held a silver necklace, which she immediately recognized. "I had the broken chain repaired." He held it out of the box, and the thumb-sized heart pendant swung in the air, everything fully intact.

"But—" Lottie's chest tightened. Surprise swept through her, and joy pounded in her chest. "Where'd you get this?" she gasped.

"I told you." He held the necklace out. "I go to the games at the Garden."

Lottie extended a trembling hand. She inhaled and touched it gently as a loving memory gently settled in her brain. "You mean, you were there?"

"Yup." He smiled proudly. "She tossed it right at me. I caught it, and I've kept it all this time. I hoped that one day I'd meet you in person. Can I put it on?"

Mist came to Lottie's eyes. "Of course." She turned, pulling her hair up and feeling David's hands clasp the chain. Her neck shivered with prickly bumps. "Unbelievable. I don't know what to say." She turned and clasped the heart in her hand, caressing it with her forefinger and thumb. She felt warm from being so close to David. She was safe. *God, what a sensation.*

He placed both hands around her, and paused. Caught up in the moment, Lottie leaned forward and kissed him on the cheek.

Chapter 36

THE GIFT

A year of locker room living and frenzied derby madness had passed. The smell of beer, cigarettes and sweat fused together and wafted through another arena's cavernous backstage area, sparking memories of Lottie's career. The many years of games whirled through her mind as she settled herself backstage. Mumbling from the crowd just outside stopped her from dwelling on the past. Ruby and Carol were standing by her side.

"You've been seeing David for a long time. Is it going good?" Ruby asked.

"Good?" Lottie asked with a nervous laugh. She pulled her thoughts away from the arena's activities. "It's great. I really like him. Gosh, we've been seeing each other for a year." She felt a flush of delightful bliss.

"Carol and I are happy for you two." Ruby rubbed the kinks out of Lottie's shoulder.

"We go everywhere together. You know, dancing, dinner and the movies. Last week, we saw Joanne Woodward in *The Three Faces of Eve.*"

"What about bowling?"

"He loves to bowl!"

Ruby smiled. "We knew things must've been swell, 'cause you bebop out of the arena after every game."

"You can't fool us," Carol said. "*We* think it's *love.*"

"Nah." Lottie looked away and waved a hand in mock defiance. Inside, she felt a thrill, a sense of security and purpose.

Carol laughed. "You know, you're not a very good fibber. Never have been."

"Well, the other night, we went dancing." Lottie went into a dreamlike trance as she spoke. "I could feel the heat from his body, his heart beating, and his breath. I looked up, saw his face, and, well, it was just wonderful." She felt her pulse quicken. "Ain't that silly?"

"U*h huh*," sounded from the back of Ruby's throat. "Love, honey. Are you ready for the big night?" she asked, changing the subject.

"Sure." Lottie knocked her knees together in anticipation of the trophy ceremony. Her mind replayed her skating history like a slideshow, with images of home, Buddy's marathon days, lost friends, old and new lovers, and the tumultuous battles on and off the track. "We practiced the whole trophy exchange this afternoon."

"Then you're ready," Ruby said.

The ruckus in the arena swelled. "And now, for the first time in history …" The announcer's voice echoed through the sold-out stands and into the backstage area, interrupting the skaters' chitchat.

Lottie stiffened. She exhaled measured breaths and waited for him to announce her name. She was ready for her cue to roll to the front of the stage area and accept her award.

"Don't crap your pants," Carol chuckled.

"This is it." Lottie heaved an audible sigh and wiped her sweaty palms on her uniform.

"Go get 'em!" Ruby said.

Lottie stood up.

"The American Roller Derby League is proud to present," the announcer blasted to the thousands of fans, "a special lady who has been voted to receive this year's prestigious award. Lottie Zimmerman, The Little Lunatic, our Roller Derby Queen of 1959!" The announcer's voice rocketed; the arena filled with ecstatic cries.

"Congratulations!" Ruby yelped over the applause, patting Lottie on the back.

"You deserve it!" Carol exclaimed.

As Lottie entered the bright arena and moved to where her award waited, she saw signs that read, 'We love The

Little Lunatic,' 'Need a hatpin?' and 'I'm running away to join the roller derby!'

Genuinely humbled, Lottie felt an overwhelming sense of amazement. "I don't believe it." She waved to the thunderous crowd. Her long-ago decision to start skating had grown to touch so many people. She recalled how it had seemed like an impossible idea when she had hatched it in her mind in front of that old television set. Yet it had ended up being the right decision. She prepared to accept the award, bowing to the crowd.

"Lottie Zimmerman is the first roller derby queen from the visiting team," the announcer beamed. "Playing the villain, but stealing all of our hearts."

Lottie's hand reached out and grasped the big award. She completed several more nods and bows while the band finished its rendition of *That's My Baby*.

The announcer said, "And, tonight, we have a surprise."

A hush descended over the audience.

"Are you surprised?"

Lottie's face went blank. She hadn't rehearsed this part. Her nerves tingled.

"We have a special guest," the announcer said, cueing someone.

Lottie swallowed deeply and eyed the stage wings. The audience applauded.

"Come on out!"

A tuxedoed and elegantly-groomed David entered under the bright lights. Lottie's heart flipped. She lowered the award down to her side.

"David Cunningham!" the announcer presented. "Advertising executive from *Sports Illustrated*. Lottie, I know you didn't expect this, but David has something he wants to say."

"Okay," Lottie whispered in a wobbly voice.

David knelt before Lottie, a move that hushed the entire audience. He adjusted himself on one knee. "Hi, Lottie," he said; the mics gave a slight feedback buzz ensuring the whole audience was leaning forward in anticipation.

Lottie's breathing halted as she heard the slight tremor in his voice. Her heart raced. "Hi," she squeaked back. Low chuckles rippled through the throng.

David lowered his head, cleared his throat, and looked up into Lottie's eyes. "We've been seeing each other for a year."

"Yeah," she whispered, tugging on a strand of hair. Suddenly, nothing existed except David and his words. The audience disappeared into the back of her mind.

"I hope you know how I feel about you. And please don't feel you have to rush into this." He reached one nervous hand into the upper pocket of his black tux. Small flecks of perspiration beaded on his forehead.

The crowd leaned in to catch every detail.

"Oh, no!" Lottie half-stepped back.

"Yes." He held her wrist with one hand, keeping her from falling backward, and gazed more deeply into her eyes.

"I'm here to ask the roller derby queen if she'll be *my* queen." He pulled something out of his pocket. His hands shook as he positioned the object in the palm of his hand.

It was a blue velvet box. Her breath went taut. It couldn't be what she thought. Everything whirled inside. The audience clapped, but Lottie said nothing. The impatient audience grew louder, until they were yelling out shouts of approval.

Tears trickled from the corners of Lottie's eyes. She couldn't believe her ears. She'd never seen this vulnerable expression on David's face. It melted her heart. "Right here? Now?"

"Here and now." He pulled her close. "I'd like to begin a new life with you. I'm on my knee to ask for your hand in marriage. Will you be my wife?"

Lottie touched one hand to her mouth.

David thumbed open the box and a diamond sparkled under the arena's lights. "Will you marry me? I promise to support you and your derby dreams for as long as you wish." The ring sparkled like a million stars in a dark sky as it quivered in David's shaking hand.

"Marry?" Lottie's voice hitched.

He pulled the ring out and slipped it onto her finger. Startled, Lottie stared at the ring ... and the face she loved so much. "God," she said with a gasp. Her breathing increased. Words escaped her, anticipation whirled, and the crowd murmured with pleasure.

David swallowed.

Lottie's heart pounded, and then her thoughts abruptly stopped. She looked into David's eyes. A lump caught in her throat. "I've waited so long for this," she finally whispered in a quiver.

"All you need to do is say yes."

Lottie felt her insides fall back into place. All was right in the world. Joy spiked through her nerves. "Yes. Of course. Yes!" she said in a breathless voice.

David stood up, and Lottie turned her hand from side to side, gazing at the ring and then back at David.

The audience sounded a long "*Ahhhh*," followed by more cheering. David held her arm.

"Ladies and gentlemen," the announcer said. "It looks like The Little Lunatic, our own Lottie Zimmerman, has just accepted David Cunningham's hand in marriage."

The crowd stood, applauding and yelling. Lottie blinked, realizing the audience was watching her as if each member were giving her a warm hug. That same warmth entered and spread throughout her body. She'd become more than a television sports star; she had become a part of each fan's life. Now, they were sharing this intimacy with her.

Standing tall, David reached an arm around her and Lottie melted into his bold embrace. Then he moved his mouth close to her ear and whispered, "Let me hold you forever."

She closed her eyes. "This is the most important moment in my life." Years of pent-up exhilaration burst from deep within.

"I'll see to it that you have many more wondrous moments," he said.

In that very instant, the taunts of the youths from the Bronx disappeared forever. Vindictive behavior from other skaters shifted to some distant part of her past. All of those thoughts and memories were washed away, and replaced by complete and utter contentment.

The wedding took place several months later, in Lottie's favorite paradise: Hawaii. Lulled by the ocean's relentless, calming waves and warm, sweeping trade winds, Lottie and David fell under the hypnotic spell of love and marriage.

Lottie's mom and dad, Rhoda, Betty and even Buddy and Dorothy Wilson all enjoyed first-class flights to the tropical isle. Lottie lodged Rebecca Peterson and her family, along with everyone else, in the five-star Halekulani Hotel on Waikiki's beach. Even Oscar Wentworth and Gerry Murphy honored the event with their presence. Ruby and Carol were Lottie's maids of honor. They held hands during the ceremony. In addition, Carol played chauffeur, entertaining and shuttling everyone to and from the airport and hotel.

After the festivities, Lottie's parents found a gift box when they returned to their room. Esther opened it, and inside rested the cream and yellow lucky hat and a note.

Dear Mom,

I can't thank you enough for this wonderful gift of love that you gave to me some eight years ago.

I have kept it with me always as a special gift, like my own personal guardian angel from you. It has watched over my every move, and has never failed to bring me luck and strength.

With my marriage to David, I now have my own lucky wedding hat and hatpin. I am returning this one with great love. I hope it continues to bless the two of you forever.

Lottie

Lottie and David awoke early in their new home, and enjoyed the birds trilling, bacon sizzling and coffee perking. The sun poured through the kitchen window ... a pigeon appeared there on the sill, joining them for breakfast.

EPILOGUE

From 1935's desperate beginning, Roller Derby was invented. It grew, flourished and continues to this very day. The game and the players have evolved along with tremendous social change. Skaters from all around our amazing planet have found self-esteem through teamwork and athleticism on skates. Derby has been a trailblazer for women's roles in our society, and has always embraced diversity of gender, color, culture and orientation. Today, thousands of leagues and teams are in operation. There are women's, men's, and coed teams and leagues dotting our world's cities. Every skater, including myself, stands on the shoulders of the early risk-takers and innovators of this wonderful world of roller derby.

The best is yet to come.

Tim Patten

Made in the USA
Lexington, KY
18 March 2016